FEAR STREET

THE BEGINNING

KT-479-728

FEAR STREET

THE BEGINNING

The New Girl; The Surprise Party;
The Overnight; Missing

R.L. STINE

SIMON PULSE

NEW YORK   LONDON   TORONTO   SYDNEY   NEW DELHI

This book is a work of fiction. Any references to historical events, real people, or real places are used fictitiously. Other names, characters, places, and events are products of the author's imagination, and any resemblance to actual events or places or persons, living or dead, is entirely coincidental.

SIMON PULSE
An imprint of Simon & Schuster Children's Publishing Division
1230 Avenue of the Americas, New York, New York 10020
This Simon Pulse paperback edition September 2020
The New Girl, The Surprise Party, and *The Overnight* copyright © 1989
by Parachute Press, Inc.
Missing copyright © 1990 by Parachute Press, Inc.
Cover illustration copyright © 2020 by Matt Griffin
All rights reserved, including the right of reproduction in whole or in part in any form.
SIMON PULSE and colophon are registered trademarks of Simon & Schuster, Inc.
FEAR STREET is a registered trademark of Parachute Press, Inc.
For information about special discounts for bulk purchases, please contact
Simon & Schuster Special Sales at 1-866-506-1949 or business@simonandschuster.com.
The Simon & Schuster Speakers Bureau can bring authors to your live event.
For more information or to book an event contact the Simon & Schuster Speakers Bureau
at 1-866-248-3049 or visit our website at www.simonspeakers.com.
Cover designed by Sarah Creech
Interior designed by Mike Rosamilia
The text of this book was set in Goudy Oldstyle Std.
Printed and bound by CPI Group (UK) Ltd, Croydon, CR0 4YY
4 6 8 10 9 7 5 3
Library of Congress Control Number 2020935508
ISBN 978-1-5344-7784-1 (pbk)
ISBN 978-1-4391-1605-0 (*The New Girl* eBook)
ISBN 978-1-5344-8291-3 (*The Surprise Party* eBook)
ISBN 978-1-5344-8301-9 (*The Overnight* eBook)
ISBN 978-1-5344-8292-0 (*Missing* eBook)
These titles were previously published individually.

CONTENTS

THE NEW GIRL

PROLOGUE

Bye, Anna.

Good-bye.

Look at her down there, all crumpled. Her dress all crumpled.

She wouldn't like that. She was always so neat.

She wouldn't like the blood, so dark and messy.

You were always so perfect, Anna. You were always so bright and shiny, as if you were sparkly new every day.

"My Diamond," Mom always said.

And who was I, then?

Who was I while you were Little Miss Perfect?

Well, you're perfect now. You're perfectly dead, ha ha.

I shouldn't laugh. But it was so easy.

I never dreamed it would be so easy. Oh, I dreamed about it a lot. I dreamed it and wished it, and, oh, did I feel guilty.

But I never knew it would be easy.

One push.

One push, and down you go.

Look at you down there, all crumpled. So perfectly crumpled.

And now the front door is opening. They are returning. And I am starting to cry.

It is a horrible tragedy, after all.

A horrible tragic accident.

I must cry for you now. And I must run and tell them.

"Anna's dead, Mom! Come quickly! It's all too horrible—but Anna's dead!"

CHAPTER 1

When Cory Brooks saw the new girl for the first time, he was standing on his head in the lunchroom.

Actually, he was standing on his head and one hand while balancing a full lunch tray in his free hand, his black Converse hightops reaching straight up to where his head would normally be.

A few seconds earlier David Metcalf, Cory's best friend and fellow daredevil from the Shadyside High gymnastics team, had suggested that Cory couldn't perform this feat.

"That's too easy, man," Cory had said, shaking his head. Cory never passed up an opportunity to prove David wrong. He hesitated for only a second, running his hand back through his curly black hair and looking across the large, crowded room to make sure no teachers were watching. Then he flipped over in midair, landed, and balanced on his head and hand, without even tilting the loaded tray.

And now David was applauding and whistling his approval from a nearby table, along with several other laughing, cheering spectators. "Now do it no hands!" David called.

"Yeah, do it!" Arnie Tobin, another gymnastics team pal, urged.

"Do it with no head!" another joker yelled. Everyone laughed.

Cory, meanwhile, was beginning to feel a little uncomfortable. The blood was rushing to his head. He felt a little dizzy, and the top of his head began to ache from pressing against the hard tile floor.

"I dare you to eat your lunch like that!" David called, always challenging Cory on to greater glories.

"What's for dessert? Upside-down cake?" a girl yelled from near the windows. Several kids groaned and hissed their disapproval of this bad joke.

"Cory—lookin' good!" someone shouted.

"What is going on?" called an alarmed voice, the voice of a teacher.

The jokes, the loud voices, the cheers and laughter all seemed to fade when the new girl floated into Cory's view. She was so pale, so blond, so light, so beautiful, at first he thought he was imagining her. All the blood rushing to his head must be causing him to see things!

She was walking against the far wall, heading quickly to the double doorways. Cory caught only a glimpse of her, upside down. She stopped to stare at him. He saw pale blue eyes. His eyes connected with hers. Did she know he was staring back at her? Was she smiling or frowning? It was impossible to tell from his position. Then she shook her blond head, as if purposefully breaking the connection, and vanished from his view.

Those eyes.

Who is she? Cory thought. She's incredible!

Thinking about the new girl, he forgot to concentrate on the delicate balance that was keeping him upright. The tray fell first. Then Cory fell, his face sliding messily into his food, his chest hitting the floor hard, his long legs sprawling behind him.

The room erupted in laughter and sarcastic applause.

"Do it again!" Arnie Tobin's voice boomed. Arnie could outshout any crowd.

David hurried over to help Cory up. "Any more bright ideas?" Cory groaned, pulling spaghetti and tomato sauce out of his hair.

"Next time just get a sandwich," David said, laughing. He had carrot-colored hair, and freckles almost as orange, and he had a whooping, high-pitched laugh that could make dogs perk up their ears for miles around.

Cory used the front of his T-shirt to wipe spaghetti sauce from his face. When he looked up, Mrs. MacReedy, the lunchroom monitor, was in front of him. She didn't say anything. She just shook her head.

"Sorry about that," Cory said, feeling more than a little foolish.

"About what?" Mrs. MacReedy asked, keeping a straight face.

Cory laughed. Thank goodness Mrs. MacReedy had a good sense of humor!

"It was all Arnie's idea," David told her, pointing back to the table where Arnie was busily shoving pretzel sticks into his mouth three at a time.

"I don't think Arnie's ever had an idea," Mrs. MacReedy said, still straight-faced. Then she gave Cory a quick wink and walked away.

Still dripping with noodles and tomato sauce, Cory bent down to pick up the tray, "Hey, David, who was that girl?"

"What girl?"

"The blond girl. The one who walked out while—"

"Who?" David seemed confused. He picked up Cory's scattered silverware and tossed it onto the tray. "A new girl?"

Cory groaned. "Didn't you see her?"

"No. I was watching you making a total dork of yourself."

"Me? It was your idea!"

"It wasn't my idea to do a face dive into a plate of spaghetti."

"She's blond and she was wearing a pale blue dress."

"Who?"

"The girl I saw."

"You saw a girl wearing a *dress* to school?"

"You don't believe me, huh?" Cory looked to the doorway as if she might still be there. But then his stomach growled, and he remembered he'd just ruined his lunch. "Hey, David, you got any money? I'm starving."

"Don't look at me, man," David said, grinning and backing away.

"Come on. You owe me." Cory put the tray down on an empty table and started to come after him.

"No way, man."

"Where's your lunch? We'll split it." Cory changed direction and headed toward David's table.

"My lunch? Forget it. I haven't—"

Cory took the apple off David's tray, then grabbed a handful of pretzel sticks from Arnie's.

"Hey—I need those!" Arnie protested, making a futile swipe to get them back.

"Be a pal," Cory said through a mouthful of apple. "We've got practice after school, right? If I don't eat, I'll be too weak to climb onto the balance beam."

"Break my heart," Arnie said as he broke off the pretzels in Cory's hand and shoved the halves quickly into his own mouth. "Maybe the rest of us will stand a chance."

Cory detected more than a little resentment from Arnie. He felt bad about that, but what could he do? He couldn't help it if he was a more talented gymnast than his teammates. He had been on the varsity gymnastics team since his freshman year at Shadyside. And Coach Welner really thought he had a chance of making the all-state championships the following spring.

It's a good thing Coach Welner didn't see me fall into my lunch, Cory thought. He finished off the last of Arnie's pretzel sticks and slurped up the last few drops of David's chocolate milk, then crushed the cardboard container in his hand.

"A well-balanced lunch," he said, hiccuping.

Arnie was busy showing David a new way to slap someone five. He had a serious look on his normally grinning face, and he was slapping David's hand again and again, trying to get it just right. "Not like that, jerk," he kept saying.

Cory couldn't figure out who was the jerk. "Later," he told them, tossing the crushed milk carton into a trash basket halfway across the room. They didn't look up.

He headed toward the double doors, ignoring some kids who were laughing about his stained shirt and the congealed tomato sauce in his hair. "Hey, Cory—think fast!" Someone threw a milk carton at him. It bounced off a table and hit the floor.

He didn't turn around. He was thinking about the girl in the blue dress again. He had seen her for only a few seconds, upside down. But he knew she was the most beautiful girl he had ever seen.

Hauntingly beautiful.

The phrase popped into his head.

He realized he was looking for her as he headed down the hall to his locker.

Where is she? Who is she? I didn't imagine her—did I?

"Hey, Cory—you swim in your lunch?"

He didn't turn around to see who that was. He realized he must look pretty bad. Suddenly he hoped he wouldn't run into the girl now. He didn't want her to see him with tomato sauce in his hair and all over his shirt.

He stood in front of his locker, trying to decide what to do. Was there time to head down to the showers? He looked at his watch. No. The bell for fifth period would ring in less than two minutes. Maybe he could cut English. No. Mr. Hestin was explaining the term paper assignment today.

Lisa Blume walked up and began turning the combination lock to open her locker. She pulled the lock open, then looked at him. "You look great."

"Thanks." He looked down at his shirt. "This remind you of when we were little kids?"

"No. You were neater then." She laughed.

Cory and Lisa had lived next door to each other in the North Hills section of town for their entire lives. They had played together since they were toddlers. Their two families were so close, they were like one big family.

Living so close together, Cory and Lisa had managed to stay friends even through those years when boys only play with boys and girls only play with girls. Now, as teenagers, they knew each other so well, they were so comfortable with each other, their friendship seemed a natural part of life.

Lisa had long black hair that tumbled in curls down to her shoulders, and dark lipsticked lips that curled into a half smile whenever she said something funny, which was often. A lot of kids said she looked like Cher. Lisa pretended not to be flattered by the comparison, but she was secretly pleased.

Now she stared at Cory in front of their lockers. "I was standing on my head in the lunchroom," he told her as if that fully explained his appearance.

"Not again," she said. She bent down to pick up some books from the floor of the locker. "Who were you showing off for this time?"

Her question annoyed him. "I didn't say I was showing off. I just said I was standing on my head."

"David dared you to. Right?"

"How'd you know?"

"Lucky guess." She stood up, her arms filled with texts and notebooks. "You can't go into class like that. You smell like a pizza."

"What can I do?"

"Here. You can borrow a T-shirt." She bent down again to rummage in the cluttered locker.

"A girl's shirt? I can't wear a girl's shirt!" He grabbed the sleeve of her sweater and started to pull her up.

She pulled out of his grasp. "It's not a girl's shirt. It's from the Gap. It's for girls or boys. You know. It's just a shirt." She pulled the black-and-white-striped T-shirt out and tossed it up to him. "But wash your hair before you put it on."

The warning bell rang. Locker doors slammed. The hall grew quiet as kids disappeared into their fifth-period classes.

"Get real. How can I wash my hair?"

She pointed to the water fountain across the hall. He smiled at her gratefully. "You're smart, Lisa. I always said you were smart."

"That's a real compliment coming from a guy who puts his head in his spaghetti," she said, her mouth sliding into that familiar, wry half smile.

"Hold the water on for me," he said, walking quickly to the low white fountain. He looked down the hall to make sure no one was watching. The hall was nearly deserted.

"No way, Cory. I don't want to be late." She followed him anyway. "And I certainly don't want to be seen with you."

"You're a pal, Lisa."

He didn't see her frown. She hated that word. She hated to be a pal. She sighed and turned the water knob. Then she stood there hoping that no one would come by as he plunged his head into the fountain and frantically struggled to scrub the dried sauce from his tangled curls.

The bell rang. She let go of the fountain. "Cory, I've got to go."

He stood up, water pouring down his face. "Good thing the water in this fountain never gets cold," he said. He pulled off the stained T-shirt and dried his hair with it.

"Cory—really. I don't want to be late." She tossed the clean T-shirt at him and, struggling to hold on to her armload of books, ran to class.

The striped shirt fell onto the floor in front of Cory's sneakers. Still rubbing his hair dry with the dirty shirt, he bent over to pick it up.

When he stood up, he saw her again.

First he saw her blue dress. Then he saw her blond hair.

She was halfway down the hall, hurrying to class.

There was something strange about the way she moved. Her feet didn't make a sound as she ran. She was so light she seemed to be floating a few inches above the ground.

"Hey, wait—" he called to her.

She heard him. She stopped and turned her head, her blond hair swirling behind her. Once again her blue eyes connected with his. What was that in her eyes? Was it fear?

Her lips moved. She was saying something to him, but he couldn't hear her.

"Please don't."

Is that what she had said?

No.

That wasn't it. That couldn't be it. Cory was a terrible lip reader.

"Please don't?"

No.

What had she really said? Why did she look so frightened?

"Please, wait—" he called.

But she vanished into a classroom.

CHAPTER 2

Cory slammed the gym locker shut and angrily pounded his fist against it.

"Hey, what's the matter with you, man?" David asked, still in his practice sweats.

"I stink!" Cory shouted. "I looked like a newbie on the bars today."

"So what else is new?" David said with a shrug. "At least you didn't sprain your ankle." He rubbed the ankle, which was swollen nearly to the size of a softball.

"Later," Cory muttered disgustedly. He tossed his wet towel over David's head and angrily shoved his way out through the locker room door. He'd just had the worst practice of the year, maybe of his life. And he knew why.

It was the new girl.

Cory had been looking for her for three days. He hadn't seen her since that brief moment in the hall before fifth period on Monday. But he hadn't been able to get her out of his mind ever since. She was just so beautiful!

He had even dreamed about her that first night.

In the dream he was eating lunch in school. She seemed to float across the lunchroom. She came up to his table, her blue eyes shimmering like the ocean in sunlight. She leaned down and her hair fell over his face, soft and fragrant.

She started to kiss his face, his cheek, his forehead, his other cheek, soft kisses, so soft he couldn't feel them.

He wanted to feel her kisses. He tried to feel them. But he couldn't feel a thing.

He reached up to touch her face. His hand seemed to go right through her.

And he woke up.

The dream stayed with him. It should have been a nice dream, an exciting dream. But it wasn't. There was something eerily cold about the dream. Why couldn't he feel her kisses or touch her face?

For the next three days he had looked for her in the lunchroom and in the halls between classes. He had even waited by the front doors after school, hoping to get a glimpse of her. But she had never appeared. And none of the guys Cory had asked knew who she was or even remembered seeing her.

Now, as he trudged through the empty corridor, he tried to think about why his timing had been so off during gymnastics practice, but her face kept floating into his mind. And once again he imagined her floating across the hall.

"Are you real?" Cory asked aloud, his voice echoing off the tile walls.

"Yeah, I'm real. But what are you?" a girl's voice replied, nearly startling him out of his high-tops.

"Huh?" He spun around to find Lisa behind him, a questioning look on her face.

"Talking to yourself these days?"

He could feel his face reddening. "What are *you* doing here? It's after five o'clock."

"It's my school, too, you know. I can stay as long as I like. You jocks think you own the place."

He shrugged. He wasn't in the mood to joke around with her.

"I was working on the *Spectator*. We were pasting it up today."

Lisa was assistant editor of the Shadyside High School paper. "I suppose you were doing flip-flops in the gym?"

"It's not flip-flops," he said grumpily. "We have a match against
Mattewan Friday night.'"

"Good luck," she said, punching his shoulder. "They're pretty
good, right?"

"They're not that good."

They walked down the hall, their footsteps echoing loudly. At
their lockers they stopped to pull out jackets and bookbags.

"You going home?" Lisa asked. "Want company?"

"Sure," he said, although he really didn't.

They walked out the back doorway and stepped down into the
teachers' parking lot. Beyond the parking lot stood the football
stadium, a concrete oval with long wooden bleachers on two sides.
And behind the stadium stood Shadyside Park, a wide, grassy park
dotted with ancient oaks and sycamores and sassafras trees, sloping
gradually down to the banks of the Conononka River, actually a
narrow, meandering stream.

The nearness of the park made it an afternoon hangout for
just about everyone who didn't have an after-school job. It was
great for meeting friends, relaxing, enjoying after-school picnics or
impromptu parties, studying, making out, playing endless games of
Frisbee, taking an afternoon siesta, or just staring at squirrels or the
slow-flowing river.

But not tonight. The wind was cold and gusty, and it swirled
tangles of brown leaves in fast circles over the parking lot. Zip-
ping their down jackets against the unexpected cold, Cory and Lisa
looked up to a sky that was heavy and dark, a November sky, a
snow sky.

"Let's go the front way," he said. They headed around toward
the front of the school. She leaned against him as they walked. He
figured she was trying to keep warm.

"Guess it's really winter," she said.

They turned up Park Drive and headed toward North Hills, a walk they had made together thousands of times. Tonight seemed different to him somehow. He guessed he was just in a bad mood.

They were silent for a long time, leaning up the hill, the gusting wind first behind them, then blowing hard in their faces. Then they both spoke at once.

He: "Have you seen a girl with blond hair and—"

She: "Are you doing anything this weekend? Saturday night?"

They both stopped talking at the same time, then started again at the same time.

She shoved him. "You go first."

He shoved her back, but not as hard. "No. You."

A car horn honked at them. Probably someone from school. A dark blue Honda Accord sped by. It was too dark to see who was inside.

"I asked if you were doing anything Saturday night," she said, leaning against him again.

"No. I don't think so."

"I'm not either," she told him. Her voice sounded funny, a little tense. He decided it was just because of the wind.

"Have you seen a girl with blond hair and big blue eyes?" he asked.

"What?"

"A very pretty girl, but strange-looking. Kinda old-fashioned. Very pale."

She let go of his arm. He didn't see the disappointed look on her face. "You mean Anna?" she asked.

He stopped walking and turned to face her, his expression suddenly excited. The streetlights flickered on. It looked as if he were lighting up because of her answer. "Anna? Is that her name? You know her?"

"She's a new girl. Very pale. Blond. Has her hair just brushed straight back with a barrette in front? Wears dresses all the time?"

"Yeah. That's her. Anna. What's her last name?"

"I don't know," Lisa snapped, then regretted revealing how annoyed she was. "Corwin, I think. Anna Corwin. She's in my third-period physics class."

"Wow," he said, still not moving, the trees casting shadows across his face as they bent in the wind. "You know her. What's she like?"

"No, Cory, I don't know her. I told you. She's a new girl. I don't know her at all. She never says a word in class. Sits in the back row, as pale as a ghost. She's absent a lot. Why are *you* so hot to know her?"

"What else do you know?" Cory asked, ignoring her question. "Come on."

"That's it," Lisa said impatiently. She started walking on ahead of him, taking long strides.

He ran to catch up. "I thought I made her up," he said.

"No. She's real," Lisa replied. "She doesn't look real. But she's real. You in love with her or something? Oh. I know. David and you made a bet to see which one could get a date with her first." She shoved him again, nearly knocking him off the sidewalk. "I'm right, aren't I? You two always pick on the new girls."

Again he didn't seem to hear her. "Don't you know anything else about her? Whose homeroom is she in? Where does she live?"

"Oh. Yeah. I did hear that. She transferred here from Melrose. Her family moved into a house on Fear Street."

"Fear Street?" Cory stopped short, suddenly chilled.

Fear Street, a narrow street that wound past the town ceme-tery and through the thick woods on the south edge of town, had a special meaning for everyone in Shadyside. The street was cursed, people said.

The blackened shell of a burned-out mansion—Simon Fear's old mansion—stood high on the first block of Fear Street, overlooking the cemetery, casting eerie shadows that stretched to the dark, tangled woods. Terrifying howls, half-human, half-animal, hideous cries of pain, were said to float out from the mansion late at night.

People in Shadyside grew up hearing the stories about Fear Street—about people who wandered into the woods there and disappeared forever; about strange creatures that supposedly roamed the Fear Street woods; about mysterious fires that couldn't be put out, and bizarre accidents that couldn't be explained; about vengeful spirits that haunted the old houses and prowled through the trees; about unsolved murders and unexplained mysteries.

When Cory and Lisa were kids, their friends liked to dare one another to go for a walk on Fear Street at night. It was a challenge few kids were willing to accept. And those who did never stayed on Fear Street for long! Now, even though Cory was older, the words *Fear Street* still brought a chill.

"I think Anna belongs on Fear Street," Lisa said, giving Cory her half smile. "She could haunt one of those old houses as good as any ghost."

"I think she's the most beautiful girl I've ever seen," he said, as if he felt he had to defend her against all attacks.

"So do you have a bet with David or what?" she asked.

"No," he snapped, lost in thought.

They reached their houses, dark shingled ranch houses, almost identical, set back far from the street behind tall hedges of evergreens, on wide manicured lawns, as were most of the houses in North Kills, the nicest section of town.

"About Saturday night—" she tried again.

"Yeah. Right. See you tomorrow," he said, and began jogging up the long, paved drive to his house.

Anna. Anna Corwin. The name repeated in his mind. What a nice, old-fashioned name.

+ + +

"That's right, Operator. The family's name is Corwin. It's a new number. On Fear Street."

"I'm looking for it, sir," the Information operator said. There was a long silence.

Why am I so nervous just calling Information? Cory asked himself.

He had thought about Anna all through dinner. Now, up in his room, he had decided to get her phone number. I know I'm going to be too nervous to call her, he thought. I just want to get the number. In case I want to call her someday.

There was a long silence. He sat leaning over the desk in his room, pencil poised over the yellow pad he kept near the phone.

"Yes, here's the number. It's a new listing." The operator read him the number, and he scribbled it down.

"And what's the address on Fear Street, Operator?"

"We're not supposed to give that out, sir."

"Come on. I promise I won't tell anybody." Cory laughed.

Surprisingly, the operator laughed too. "I guess it's okay. It's my last night, anyway. It's Four Forty-four Fear Street."

"Thanks a lot, Operator. You're a nice person."

"You're nice too," she said, and quickly clicked off.

Cory stood over his desk and stared at Anna's phone number on the yellow pad. Should he call it?

If he called her, what would he say?

Call her, Cory. Go ahead. Don't be such a chicken. She's only a girl, after all. Sure, she's the most beautiful girl you've ever seen. But she's only a girl.

He picked up the receiver. His hand was cold and clammy even though it was quite hot in his room. He stared at the number on the yellow pad until it blurred before his eyes.

No. I can't call her. What would I say? I'd just stammer around and sound like a jerk. She already thinks I'm a jerk after seeing me standing on my head in the lunchroom.

He put down the phone receiver.

No. I can't. I just can't.

Sure. Why not?

He picked up the receiver.

This is stupid. I'm going to make an idiot of myself.

He punched her phone number.

Put the phone down, Cory. Don't be a jerk.

It rang once. Twice.

Maybe she won't even remember who I am.

It rang again. Again.

Nobody home, I guess. Whew!

He let it ring four more times. He was just about to hang up when he heard a click at the other end, and a young man's voice answered, "Yeah?"

"Oh. Hello." For some reason he wasn't expecting anyone but Anna to answer. His mouth was suddenly so dry, he wondered if he could speak.

"Yeah?"

"Is Anna there?"

"What?"

Who was this guy? Why did he sound so annoyed? Maybe Cory had woken him up.

"I'm sorry. Is this the Corwin house?" Cory asked.

"Yeah, it is," the young man rasped in his ear.

"Could I speak to Anna please?"

There was a very long silence.

"Sorry. This is the Corwins. But there's no Anna here."

The phone clicked off.

CHAPTER 3

When Cory arrived at school the next morning, Anna Corwin was the first person he saw.

It was raining hard, a freezing rain driven by gusty winds. He ran into the building through the side door, his letter jacket pulled up over his head. His wet sneakers slid across the floor, and he nearly collided with her.

"Oh." He grabbed the wall and stopped. He pulled down his jacket and stared at her. Her locker was the first one next to the door. She was pulling books off the top shelf and didn't seem to notice that he had nearly run into her.

She wore a white sweater over a gray skirt. Her hair was tied back behind her head with a white ribbon.

She's so pale, he thought. It's like I can almost see through her skin.

Suddenly the young man's raspy voice on the phone came back to him. *This is the Corwins. But there's no Anna here.*

Well, here she was.

What was that guy trying to prove? Why had he lied to Cory?

Maybe it was a jealous boyfriend, Cory thought. Or maybe Cory had dialed the wrong number, and the guy was just pulling a mean joke.

"Hi," he said, swinging his bookbag down off his shoulder. A stream of water poured from it, onto his already soaked sneakers.

She turned, surprised that someone was talking to her. Her eyes, those amazing eyes, looked into his, then quickly looked down. "Hello," she said. Then she cleared her throat nervously.

"You're new," he said.

Brilliant line, Cory. Wow, that's a real winner. You say two words to her and she already knows what a dork you are!

"Yes," she said. She cleared her throat again. Her voice was little more than a whisper. But she seemed pleased that he was talking to her.

"Your name is Anna, right? I'm Cory Brooks."

That's a little better, Cory. Just calm down, man. You're doing okay.

He reached out to shake hands. He had to touch her, to know for sure that she was real. But his hand was dripping wet. They both stared at it. He quickly brought it back to his side.

"Nice to meet you," she said, turning back to search for something in her locker.

"You moved onto Fear Street, right?" It was almost time for the bell to ring, but he didn't want to leave her. It had taken so long to find her.

She cleared her throat. "Yes."

"You must be pretty brave. Have you heard all the scary stories about Fear Street? About the ghosts and things—"

"Ghosts?" Her eyes grew wide and her face filled with such sudden fright, he was immediately sorry he had said that. She seemed to grow even more pale. "What kind of stories?"

"Just stories," he said quickly. "Not all of them are true, I don't think."

Nice going, Cory. Was that the only thing you could think of to say? How feeble can you get?"

"Oh," she said softly. The fear didn't leave her eyes.

She's so pretty, he thought. Everything about her is so soft, so light.

His dream about her came back to him. It made him feel a little embarrassed.

"Hey, Cory—lookin' good!" some guy called to him.

He turned to see who it was. It was just Arnie, giving him the okay sign from down the hall.

"Later, Arnie!" he called. He watched Arnie go into the wood shop, then turned back to Anna.

"I—uh—I called your house last night. I—I just wanted to say hi. Uh . . . a guy answered and said you didn't live there. Did I have the wrong phone number, or—"

"No," she whispered, closing her locker and locking it.

Then she turned without looking back at him and ran down the hall, disappearing into the crowd of kids heading to homeroom.

"Good mat routine," Coach Welner said, giving Cory a hearty slap on the back. Cory, still breathing hard, grinned back at the coach. He knew he had done a good routine, but it was always nice to hear it from the coach. Mr. Welner, a stern, powerful-looking man with a body builder's physique even though he was in his late fifties, was sparing with his compliments. So when he said something nice, it meant something.

Behind them the match against Mattewan, the first match of the season, continued. Cory looked to the bench for David, wondering if his friend had witnessed his near-perfect routine. Then he remembered that David had sprained his ankle at the last practice. David was somewhere up in the bleachers feeling sorry for himself and being miserable.

"Now, don't press too hard on the rings," Coach Welner warned. "You've been pushing yourself, trying to go too fast up there, and it's been throwing you off your rhythm."

"Yeah," Cory said, still trying to catch his breath.

"You feel nervous?" the coach asked, staring at Cory as if trying to see the nervousness in his eyes.

"No. Not really. Just excited."

"Good. That's what we want." Mr. Welner seemed very pleased. "Just remember—don't push it. Easy does it." He turned away from Cory and let out a loud groan. "Get up, Tobin. You can rest later!"

Arnie had just done the backflip to finish his mat routine and had landed flat on his backside. The twenty or thirty spectators in the bleachers were laughing their heads off. Arnie's face turned bright scarlet as he pulled himself up and slumped off the mat.

Coach Welner closed his eyes and shook his head disgustedly. Arnie's slip wasn't going to help the Shadyside team score. And the floor routine was the best part of Arnie's program. He was a complete klutz on the rings, and his parallel bar work was uneven to say the least.

The Mattewan guys were smaller compared to Cory and his teammates. But that gave them an advantage. They were light and strong and agile.

A guy like Arnie should be playing tackle on the football team, Cory thought. Whatever made him want to be a gymnast?

Whatever made Arnie decide to do anything? He was one of the flakiest guys Cory had ever known. He just grinned his way through life, seemingly without ever having a serious thought cross through his mind.

"Okay, Brooks." Coach Werner's voice broke into Cory's thoughts. "Go show 'em how it's done."

Cory took a deep breath and headed to the rings. For some reason they always looked so much higher at a real competition than in practice.

He shut the world out as he started his routine. He didn't need his brain. The moves were all locked in his muscles. After practicing these moves thousands and thousands of times, he was like a machine, a smoothly running machine.

Okay. Up. And over.

Very smooth, Cory. Now faster. Get ready. Here comes the hard part. Up, up . . .

And he saw Anna sitting in the bleachers.

Was it really Anna?

No. It couldn't be—could it?

. . . And over. And again. Stop. Reverse . . .

No. It was another blond girl.

The eyes. Those were her eyes.

Yes. It was Anna. What a surprise! She was staring up at him with those blue eyes.

She's watching me, he thought. She came to watch me.

He stared back at her. And he slipped. And dropped hard to the floor.

He didn't feel any pain. He was just confused. He didn't really fall, did he? He didn't really blow the whole routine just because a certain girl had caused him to lose his concentration?

"I'm falling for her!" he said aloud, laughing as he slowly climbed to his feet.

"What's so funny, Brooks?" Coach Welner was shouting.

"I'm falling for her," Cory repeated to himself. It was the second time he had fallen because of her, the second time he had embarrassed himself in front of a lot of people.

Was that true love, or what?

"What's so funny, Brooks?" Coach Welner looked concerned. "Are you hysterical or something? You didn't hit your head, did you?"

"I'm okay," Cory said, kicking the edge of a mat. "I just slipped, that's all."

"There'll be other matches," Coach Welner said. He suddenly

looked very tired. "This one's a comedy act. Go shower, Brooks. Then go home and forget about today."

"Right, Coach." Cory looked up to the bleachers.

He remembered just where she was sitting—in the center of the third row.

But she wasn't there now. He stared at an empty space in the row.

His heart sank. Had she been there in the first place? He hadn't imagined her, had he? Was he cracking up because of this girl?

No. Of course not.

"I have to talk with her," he told himself. "I have to call her again."

CHAPTER 4

Cory stared at the calendar hanging over his desk. Saturday night. Saturday night, and I'm sitting up here alone in my room, Walkman blasting in my ears, staring at my desk, not even hearing the music, thinking about Anna Corwin.

A guy could get pretty depressed, he told himself. He tore off the Walkman headphones and tossed them onto the desk.

Anna. Anna. Anna.

It's spelled the same both ways.

Brilliant, Cory. Just brilliant. Your mind really is turning to cheese, isn't it!

He knew he had to stop thinking about her. But how could he? She kept floating into his thoughts no matter what he did. He had liked other girls before—but never like this!

He leaned over and grabbed the phone. "I'll ask her to a movie or something," he told himself. "If I can just get to know her a little, maybe I won't be so crazy, so obsessed."

Those eyes. That whisper of a voice, as faint as the wind.

No. Stop. I can't call her on a Saturday night.

You can't call a girl on a Saturday night.

She's probably out.

I'll try her anyway, he decided. She seemed so pleased when I talked to her at her locker.

No, I can't call her. She'll be insulted. She'll think I'm calling on a Saturday night because I know she wouldn't be out with somebody.

I'll call David instead. Maybe he and I can go down to the mall and check out the action.

No, David can't go anywhere. He's hobbling around with crutches because of his ankle.

Call her, Cory. She'll be thrilled to hear from you.

Oh, sure. Thrilled. The klutz who always falls on his face when she looks at him.

He put down the receiver. Not tonight. No way.

I know. I'll catch her at her locker on Monday, maybe ask her to the basketball game next Friday.

He felt a lot better. He had a plan.

Now what should I do? The clock on his desk said eight twenty. His parents had a hot Scrabble game going downstairs with Lisa's parents. Cory decided maybe he'd wander next door and see if Lisa was doing anything.

"Lisa home?" he called into the den, pulling on a sweatshirt.

"Yes, she is," Mrs. Blume called. "Why don't you go over and keep her company? She was kinda down in the dumps because she didn't have a date tonight."

"Okay," Cory said, grabbing a bag of potato chips and a box of chocolate chip cookies off the kitchen shelf to take with him. There was never anything to eat at the Blumes' house. That was probably the real reason Lisa was depressed. She was probably starving, he figured.

I can talk to her about Anna, Cory told himself. He was eager to discuss Anna with someone. Whenever he brought up the subject with David or Arnie, they just teased him and made bad jokes.

"How'd the match with Mattewan go?" Mr. Blume called.

"Don't ask him that," Cory heard his mom say.

"Don't ask me that," Cory repeated.

"He fell on his keester," Cory's dad said in a whisper loud enough to be heard across the street. They all laughed.

"Thanks, Dad," Cory said. "Thanks a bunch."

Holding the cookies and potato chips in one arm, he pulled open the back door and stepped out into a frosty night. A sliver of a moon was partially hidden by thin wisps of clouds. That moon is so pale, he thought. It's the same color as Anna's hair.

Uh-oh, Cory. You'd better watch it, man. You're starting to see her everywhere—even in the moon! You're getting weird, man. Too weird. You've got to cool it.

He had to knock three times before Lisa opened the back door. She was wearing cut-off jeans and an enormous old white shirt that must have been her dad's. "Oh, hi," she said, sighing. "It's only you."

"Who'd you think?"

"I thought it was a burglar. You know, someone exciting." She backed up so that he could walk in. She smiled. "I'm only kidding. I'm glad you came over."

He held up the food packages.

"Now I'm really glad," she said, grabbing them both out of his hands. "I'm starving!"

He followed her into the den and sat down on the brown leather couch against the wall. She poured the potato chips into a big ceramic bowl and sat down next to him. "Another fabulous Saturday night."

"What were you doing?" he asked, grabbing a handful of chips and dropping them down into his mouth one by one from above. They tasted better that way, he thought.

"Nothing. I rented a movie, but I haven't started it yet. Want to watch it with me?"

"I don't know. What is it?"

She walked over to the counter under the TV and held up a

videotape box. "A Star Trek movie?" He gave her a double thumbs-down. "I'm not into Star Trek."

"Neither am I," she said, sighing again. "I got to the video store late. Everything was gone."

She slumped back down onto the couch, closer to him this time. They both reached out for more potato chips at the same time. Her hand grabbed his. She quickly let go. He didn't notice that she looked embarrassed.

"So how are things, Cory?" she asked, turning to face him. Their knees touched.

"Not great," he said, shrugging.

She put her hand on his arm. He could feel the warmth through his sweatshirt. "Poor baby. What's your problem?"

"Oh, I don't know. Nothing really. Everything."

She tsk-tsked. They didn't say anything for a while.

She moved her hand up to his hair and began to finger his curls. "I heard about the gymnastics match," she said softly.

"I blew it," he muttered, shaking his head. "I just blew it."

She leaned against him, still rolling her finger lightly in his hair. "Don't be so tough on yourself, Cory. It's only the first competition." She shoved the potato chip bowl aside and scooted even closer to him.

"Anna Corwin was there," he said. "I saw her watching me, and I was so surprised, I guess I lost my concentration."

"What?"

"I said Anna Corwin was there. I saw those blue eyes staring at me and—"

"Creep."

"What?"

"Nothing. I didn't say anything." She pulled away from him and jumped to her feet. He looked up, bewildered. Why did she look so angry?

"Have you ever talked with Anna?" he asked.

She stood over him and crossed her arms in front of her. "Cory, I think you should go home."

"Huh? I just got here."

"No. Really. Go home. Okay?"

"But why?"

"I—I'm just not in the mood for company. Okay? I'll see you in school Monday. I just don't feel like talking tonight."

He got up slowly, still confused. "Okay. Sorry you're not feeling well. Should I leave the chips and cookies?"

She glared at him. She picked up the box of cookies. For a second he thought she was going to fling it at him. But she put it in his hand. "Take the cookies. I'll finish the chips. What the heck? Might as well get fat. Why not?"

"Glad I could cheer you up," he said, trying to get her to smile. She didn't.

A few seconds later he was back outside, heading over the frosty hard grass to his house. A few seconds after that he was back in his room, sitting on his bed, trying to figure out what to do for the rest of the night.

What was Lisa's problem? he wondered. It wasn't like her to be so moody. She wasn't depressed just because she didn't have a date. Something else had to be bothering her. But what?

He glanced at his desk clock: nine twenty-five. His eye fell on the yellow pad beside the phone. He walked over to the desk and stared down at Anna's phone number.

Without stopping to think about it, without giving himself time to get nervous, time to talk himself out of it, he punched her number.

It rang once, twice, the sound seeming very far away even though it was just on the other side of town.

After the third ring he heard a click. Someone picked it up. A soft female voice said, "Corwins. Hello?"

"Hello, Anna?"

There was a long pause. Cory listened to the static on the line.

"Who?" the woman's voice repeated.

"May I speak to Anna please?"

"Ohhh!" The woman let out a loud gasp.

More silence. Then Cory heard a loud screech in the background. What was that awful sound? It sounded like a girl screaming.

Yes. Must be the TV, he told himself.

It had to be the TV.

"Why do you call here asking for Anna?" the woman demanded angrily.

"Well, I just—"

Again Cory heard the girl shrieking in the background. *"Let me talk! It's for me! I know it's for me!"*

The woman ignored the girl's cries. "Why do you call to torture me like this?" she asked Cory, her voice trembling.

"Well, is Anna there?" Cory asked.

"No, no, no!" the woman insisted. "You *know* Anna isn't here! You *know* she isn't! Stop. Please—stop!"

He heard the beginning of another scream. Then the phone clicked off.

CHAPTER 5

Cory listened to the hum of the dial tone for a while as he waited for his heart to stop pounding. He played the conversation with the woman over and over again in his mind until the words became a blur. And over the blur he heard the screams, the girl's screams of protest in the background.

Let me talk. It's for me! I know it's for me!

What was going on there?

Cory's mind whirred with crazy, frightening thoughts. What were they doing to Anna? Why wouldn't they let her come to the phone? Why did they keep insisting she wasn't there?

Fear Street. Was it claiming another victim?

Was Anna being held prisoner in her own house? Were they torturing her?

"You've seen too many bad movies," he told himself. "You're being ridiculous."

Then what was the explanation?

"I'll go over there," he said aloud. The idea just popped into his mind. It seemed simple enough. He glanced at the desk clock. It was just a little after ten, still early.

He examined himself in the mirror on his closet door, straightened the sleeves on his sweatshirt, pushed his dark curly hair back from his forehead with his hands, and headed out of his room and down the stairs toward the den.

He stopped halfway down the stairs.

Hold on a minute. Do I really want to go to Fear Street—by myself? What if something horrible really is happening in that house? What if those screams were real?

The big local news story of a few weeks before suddenly flashed into his mind. A family of three had been found murdered in the Fear Street woods. No one was reported missing. No one came forward to identify them.

Just another Fear Street unsolved murder. . . .

Cory decided to call David and ask him to come along. David was sure to be sitting home, staring at his ankle, bored out of his mind. He needed a little excitement.

To Cory's surprise David thought the idea was a little strange. "Let me get this straight, Brooks," he said after Cory had explained their mission. "You want to drive over to Fear Street and break in on someone's horror movie to find a girl who isn't there in the first place."

"Right," Cory said.

"Okay. Sounds good to me," David replied. "Pick me up in ten minutes."

"Make it five," Cory said, and hung up before David could change his mind.

Good old David, Cory thought. I can always count on him to be as stupid as I am!

The Scrabble game was still going strong downstairs in the den. The board was nearly filled, and all four adults sat staring at it in silence, concentrating on finding a usable open space.

"I'm going out for a short while," he told his dad. "Which car can I take?"

"Kind of late, isn't it?" his mother asked without looking up from the board. She had a letter square in her hand, a blank, which she was rolling over and over between her fingers.

"It's only ten."

"Take the Taurus," his father said. "Don't take your mother's car."

"Where are you going?" his mother insisted.

"Just over to David's." It was partly true.

"Are you going to make a word, or what?" Mrs. Blume asked Cory's mom with that impatient tone everyone gets near the end of an endless Scrabble game.

"How's David doing?" Mr. Brooks asked.

"Bad," Cory told him. "He's on crutches. He's pretty depressed."

"Poor guy," Mrs. Blume muttered, staring at her letters.

"I pass," Mrs. Brooks said, sighing unhappily.

Cory grabbed the keys off the front counter and headed out to the car. David lived about six blocks away in the northern corner of North Hills, almost to the river. It was a two-minute drive.

Cory knocked on the front door and waited. It took a long time for David to get to the door. "Sorry, man. I can't go with you" was his greeting.

"What do you mean?"

"I mean I can't go. My mom won't let me." He looked embarrassed.

"Hi, Cory," David's mother called from behind David in the hallway. "I really don't want David to go out tonight. He's got to stay off the ankle. Besides, he's getting a cold. You understand."

"Sure, Mrs. Metcalf," Cory said, unable to hide his disappointment. "A cold." He grinned at David. "We wouldn't want Mama's angel to catch a nasty cold, would we?"

David rolled his eyes and shrugged. "Give me a break."

"I'll call you later and let you know what happened on Fear Street," Cory said. "If you don't hear from me, send out the marines or the National Guard."

"Have you seen *Poltergeist?*" David asked. "If you go in that house, you might be sucked right into the TV screen!"

Cory didn't laugh. "You think this is all a big joke, don't you!"

David gave him an exaggerated, wide grin. "I think it's a riot."

"Well . . ." Cory turned and stomped down the flagstone walk back toward his car. "You're probably right."

Cory drove south on Park Drive and headed toward Fear Street. It was a cold and raw night. Thick clouds of fog drifted rapidly down from the hills. He turned up the heater and pushed on the radio. He needed some loud music to keep up his spirits.

"It's a Q-ROCK Beatles Blast!" the disc jockey screamed enthusiastically. "Twenty-four hours of Beatles hits in alphabetical order!"

Cory laughed. Why would anyone want to listen to music in alphabetical order?

He wished David were there to share the laugh. He wished David were there period. He really didn't like the idea of roaming around Fear Street on a cold, foggy night on his own. "Oh, well, I won't get out of the car," he told himself. "I'll just drive past the house and see what's going on."

The fog grew thicker as he passed Canyon Road and entered the valley. It was always misty at night down in this part of town, even in the summer. The car headlights seemed to hit the swirling mist and bounce back onto the windshield. He tried the brights, but they were worse.

An oncoming car swerved to miss him. Other drivers couldn't see either, Cory realized, a thought that didn't make him feel any more confident. "This is a mistake," he told himself.

But the fog lightened as he turned down Mill Road. A small Toyota, jammed with a least six teenagers, honked as it sped past him. They were probably coming from the deserted mill at the end of the road, a favorite makeout spot for Shadyside kids.

The dream about Anna in which she was kissing his face flashed into his mind. He turned the radio up. Q-ROCK was up to the L's. They were playing "Love Me Do."

Tapping his hands against the wheel to the music, recreating the sexy dream in his mind, he nearly missed the turn onto Fear Street. He realized where he was and hit the brake hard, making a skidding turn across the wet pavement.

It seemed to grow darker as soon as he turned onto the narrow, curving street. Tall maples and oaks lined both sides, their bare creaking branches nearly forming an archway over the road, tangled limbs blocking much of the pale gray light from the streetlamps.

He couldn't see it in the dark, but he knew that he was passing Simon Fear's burned-out mansion. He sped up and turned up the heater. The houses, rambling old Victorians for the most part, were set far back from the road behind unkempt hedges or overlooking lawns still thick with swirling brown leaves.

"How am I ever going to find which house is hers?" Cory asked himself, wiping the inside of the windshield clear with his sweatshirt sleeve. He squinted out through the smeared glass, trying unsuccessfully to see a street number.

"What was her number?" he asked himself, beginning to panic. Had he driven all this way without even knowing her house number? No. It was 444. He remembered.

He pulled the car over to the side of the road and shifted into park. He turned off the headlights and waited for his eyes to adjust to the darkness. He could actually see a little better with the lights off.

He turned off the engine, opened the door, and slid out of the car. If he was going to find her house, he'd have to do it on foot. The numbers were on the front doors of the houses. There was no way he could read them from the car.

He shivered. The sweatshirt didn't offer much protection from the damp cold. He took a deep breath. The air smelled sour; decaying leaves most likely.

An animal howled nearby, a long, mournful wail.

"It doesn't sound like a dog," he told himself, looking in the direction of the sound but seeing nothing. "Could it be a wolf?"

The animal howled again. It sounded a little closer.

Cory suddenly remembered being on Fear Street before. He was a kid, nine or ten. His friend Ben had dared him to walk in the woods. Somehow he had gotten the courage to try. But he had walked for only a few minutes when something grabbed his shoulder.

Maybe it had been a tree branch. Maybe not. He had run screaming down the street. He had never been so scared in his life.

"Stop thinking about it," he said aloud.

His sneakers crunched over the gravel that lined the side of the road. He came to a metal mailbox tilting at an angle toward the street. Squinting in the darkness, he tried to read the faded name on its side. But it was too dark, and the letters were all peeled away.

The animal howled again. This time it sounded farther away. The wind suddenly stopped. The only sound now was the crunching of his sneakers. He passed a large weather-beaten house, its window shutters peeling and hanging at crazy angles. For some reason a rusting ship's anchor rested in the very center of the patchy lawn. An old station wagon, its rear bumper missing, two of its windows covered with cardboard, stood in the drive.

"Nice night for a stroll," Cory told himself. He started humming "Love Me Do" to himself. Then he started singing it. Why not? There was no one around to hear him. Fear Street was deserted. Nothing moved except the scrabbling brown leaves driven by the shifting wind.

One house was brightly lit. A porch light cast bright golden beams over the lawn, and all of the downstairs and second-floor rooms seemed to be lighted. Was that Anna's house?

No. The sign on the porch said 442.

The wind picked up again, sending a chill down Cory's back.

He shoved his hands into his jeans pockets to try to warm them. He had a sudden hunch and turned back to see if the car was okay. He couldn't see it. The street had curved too far.

Should he go back?

No. He'd come this far. The next house had to be Anna's.

If she lived there.

He began walking faster. The pavement beneath his sneakers was wet and slippery, and he slipped a couple of times but quickly regained his balance.

A ragged, low hedge bordered the yard of the next house. Was this the Corwin house? Cory couldn't find a mailbox. Oh. There it was. Down on the street. It had fallen off its pole.

He picked up the mailbox. There was a number on its side: 444. This was it. He dropped it back to the street and wiped his wet hands on his jeans.

The house was completely dark and silent. No sign of life. No car in the driveway. Cory peered over the low hedge to the front porch. A screen door hung open, banging against the side of the house when the wind blew. An overturned lawn chair was beside it.

Cory stepped to the edge of the drive. What now? Go up to the house and knock on the door? There doesn't seem to be anyone home.

He looked at the overgrown shrubs, the thick covering of unraked leaves, and tangles of waist-high grass and weeds. It didn't look as if anyone had lived there for years!

It's got to be the wrong house, he thought.

Then he heard something. Something moving across the gravel. A footstep.

He listened. The wind picked up. He couldn't hear anything. It must have been leaves. Or an animal of some sort.

He decided to walk back to the car. There was no point standing out in the cold staring at a deserted old house.

He heard another footstep, then another.

Someone was behind him.

Someone was following him, coming up fast.

Cory picked up his pace, started to jog, hoping to leave the sounds behind, hoping it was just leaves, just a dog, just a lonely field cat.

But the footsteps came faster. Someone was chasing him. Someone was right behind him.

He started to turn around when a hand grabbed his shoulder.

CHAPTER 6

Cory cried out and spun out of the man's grasp.

The man looked more startled than Cory. "Sorry. Didn't mean to scare you."

Cory stared at him, gasping for breath, his muscles tensed for a fight. Or for a fast escape.

He was a tall, powerful-looking man, wearing a faded gray slicker and a battered old tennis hat. He had a day's stubble of gray beard, and he smelled of stale cigarette smoke. "No need to be frightened," he said. He had a high-pitched voice for someone so big.

"Why—why'd you—" Cory was still too out of breath to talk. He backed up another few steps, relaxing a little but still eyeing the man warily.

"I saw you stop your car," the man said, pointing back in the direction of Cory's car. "I live down the street. I was walking Voltaire. That's my dog. I thought maybe you were lost or in trouble. So I came after you."

"Where's your dog?" Cory asked suspiciously.

The man frowned, seemingly annoyed by Cory's mistrust. "Voltaire doesn't like strangers," he said slowly. "He's very protective of his turf. I put him back in the house before I came to see if you needed help."

Cory was beginning to breathe normally again. But he knew he couldn't relax his guard. There was something strange about this neighbor, not just his appearance, but in his menacing stare, the way he kept looking Cory up and down, his face tight, expressionless.

"Car break down?" the man asked.

"No," Cory said.

"Then what are you doing out here? You lost?"

"Not exactly. I was looking for the Corwins."

"You found them," the man said, gesturing with his head toward the dark house. "You know them?"

"Well . . . not really."

"They're strange people. I wouldn't go up there uninvited, I don't think." The man scratched at his stubble.

"What do you mean?" Cory shivered. He'd never felt so chilled in his life.

"Just that."

"Oh."

They stood staring at each other for a long moment.

"They keep to themselves mostly," the man said. He put his hands in his slicker pockets and turned back toward the street. "If you're not lost or anything, guess I'll head back."

"Yes. I mean, no. I'm fine. Thanks," Cory said uncertainly. He looked up to the Corwin house. A light flickered on in an upstairs window.

So. Someone was home after all.

"They're pretty strange folks," the man repeated, walking quickly now. He turned around. "Of course, everyone's pretty strange on Fear Street." He chuckled as if he had just made a really good joke, and slipped off into the darkness.

Cory waited to make sure the man was really gone. Then he turned and headed slowly toward the car. He stopped and looked back to the house. The light was still on in the second-floor room.

Should he go up and knock on the door?

He'd come this far. Why not be brave? Why not just do it? Act now—think later. Why did he always have to go back and forth, think things out so carefully before he acted?

Besides, he'd have something good to tell David about later.

He imagined how his friend would make fun of him if he told him he just stood at the end of the drive and stared at the house. He'd probably hear about it for weeks. The jokes would never stop.

Okay, Cory. Go for it.

He began jogging up the Corwins' driveway. He jogged partly to get warm, partly because he knew he'd never go through with it if he didn't do it quickly.

A gymnast learns he has to be aggressive, he told himself. He has to grab on to the rings and push himself where his body normally wouldn't go. As a gymnast, Cory was quick and sure.

But this wasn't gymnastics. This was life.

He jumped up onto the front porch, dodged past the overturned chair, slid on some long carpenter nails that were scattered over the porch floor, and nearly crashed right into the front door.

He steadied himself, leaning against the shingled front of the house, located the doorbell and, without hesitating, without giving himself a chance to back down, pushed it hard.

He didn't hear it ring inside the house. He pushed it again.

He straightened his sweatshirt and pushed back his hair with one hand.

The bell didn't make a sound. It must be broken.

He knocked, lightly at first, then harder.

Silence.

He cleared his throat, practiced a smile.

He knocked again.

This time he heard footsteps, someone hurrying down a stairway.

The door opened a crack. No light poured out. The house was dark inside. An eye stared out at Cory. The door opened a little wider. Two eyes stared suspiciously out.

The porch light flickered on, casting a pale yellow glow on the porch and front lawn.

A young man stood in the doorway. He had a very round face with puffy, round cheeks. His blue eyes were small and watery and set close to his bulby, round nose. Despite the fact that he appeared to be quite young, in his early twenties most likely, his blond hair was thinning, revealing a lot of forehead. It was tossed messily over his head. A rhinestone earring sparkled in one ear.

He stared at Cory for a long time without saying anything. Cory stared back uncomfortably. Finally he said, "Hi. I'm Cory Brooks. Is Anna home?"

The young man's watery eyes grew wide. His mouth twitched once in surprise. "Anna? What do you know about Anna?" His voice was raspy, as if he had a bad sore throat.

"I—uh—I go to Shadyside too."

"Shadyside? What's Shadyside?" the young man said, and then coughed for a long time, holding tightly on to the front door, a wheezing smoker's cough.

"It's the high school," Cory said when the young man finally stopped coughing. "I met Anna in school this week and—"

"That's impossible," the man interrupted, hitting the door frame with his fist. He glared at Cory. His eyes seemed to glow red in the porch light.

"No, really. I—"

"You didn't meet Anna in school. Anna isn't in school."

"Yes, she is," Cory insisted. "She—"

"You the one who called?"

"Well, yes. I—"

"Anna is dead," the young man rasped. "Don't come here again. Anna is DEAD!"

CHAPTER 7

He didn't remember driving home.

He remembered staring into the young man's watery eyes. He remembered the long, awkward silence, the pain on the young man's face.

He remembered the words. They repeated in his head over and over, like a record stuck in the same groove. *Anna is dead. Anna is dead. . . .*

He remembered uttering some kind of apology. "Sorry." That was it. That was all he could say. "Sorry." How stupid. How meaningless.

But what else could he say?

Then he remembered the scowl on the young man's puffy face, the shadows closing over him as the front door slammed shut. And Cory remembered running to his car, running to safety with the words following him. *Anna is dead. Anna is dead.*

He couldn't run fast enough to leave the words behind.

He remembered the chill wet air on his face, the crunch of dry brown leaves beneath his sneakers, the sharp twig that cut his ankle as he ran.

Stay away from Fear Street, he told himself.

What were you doing on Fear Street so late at night?

The stories are all true, and now you are one of them.

He remembered how his hand trembled as he tried to get the key into the ignition. And he remembered his panic when the car wouldn't start.

Then the motor had kicked over and he had sped away, his hands gripping the wheel as if it were a lifesaver in a storm-tossed ocean.

But he didn't remember the drive home. It was a blur of swirling yellow headlights and black roads. And he didn't remember sneaking back into the house, or silently tiptoeing up the stairs to his room, or getting undressed and climbing into bed.

He just remembered the young man's narrow, watery eyes. The pain in those eyes, pain mixed with hatred. And the words.

Anna is dead. Anna is DEAD!

He didn't fall asleep until after four in the morning. And then it was a light sleep, a fitful sleep filled with floating faces he didn't recognize and tilting car headlights that sometimes seemed to be heading right at him and sometimes seemed to shine right through him.

On Monday morning he skipped breakfast and hurried to school to look for Anna. He got there early, twenty minutes before the first bell would ring. He waited by her locker. There were a few other kids down the hall. They seemed to be yawning at each other, leaning against their lockers as if they would fall over if they didn't.

He tried opening Anna's locker, but the combination lock wouldn't budge. He sat cross-legged on the floor and waited. After a while the corridor became noisy and crowded as kids arrived. Some of them said hi to Cory as they walked past.

"What are you doin' down there, Brooks?" Arnie asked as he lumbered through the door.

"Just sitting," Cory told him.

The answer seemed to be enough for Arnie. He swung his bookbag at Cory, trying to knock him over. Cory dodged away. Arnie laughed and stomped down the hall.

Where is Anna?

Anna is dead.

Anna is a ghost.

But there are no such things as ghosts.

Her locker was real. He spun the dial and pulled at the lock again. The bell rang.

He climbed to his feet. He felt as if he weighed four hundred pounds. He hadn't been able to sleep for two nights in a row. The hallway was emptying quickly. Kids were hurrying to their homerooms. He had to hurry too. He had already been late twice this term, and he didn't want to get a detention.

But where was Anna?

She wasn't coming today.

Of course she wasn't coming today. Anna was dead.

But he had seen her with his own eyes. He had talked to her.

He made it to homeroom just as the bell rang. The rest of the morning was a struggle to keep his eyes open. Luckily, none of his teachers called on him in any of his classes. In fact, no one seemed to notice he was there.

Maybe I'm becoming a ghost, too, he told himself.

He looked for Anna in the hallway between classes, but he didn't see her. Just before lunch he ran into Lisa as they were depositing their bookbags in their lockers.

"Was Anna Corwin in physics this morning?" he asked her eagerly.

"Good morning to you too," Lisa said sarcastically.

"Oh. Sorry. Good morning, Lisa. Was Anna Corwin in physics this morning?"

She angrily slammed her locker shut. "No."

"Oh." Cory tossed his bookbag into his locker. He didn't see the annoyed look on Lisa's face. "Then I guess she was absent."

"You're a real Sherlock Holmes," Lisa said, shaking her head.

She jammed the lock shut and started to walk away. But then she changed her mind and came back to the locker. "What's your problem, anyway?"

"Problem?" How did Lisa know he had a problem?

"Why are you acting so weird?"

"I'm not acting weird. I just—" He started to make some excuse, but then he decided to tell her. He had to tell someone. And she was his oldest friend, after all.

As they walked down to the lunchroom, he told her about the rest of his Saturday night.

He told her how he drove to Fear Street, how he knocked on the door, how the strange-looking young man told him Anna was dead.

Lisa listened to the story in silence, her face drawn in a tight frown of disapproval. But when Cory finished talking, the anger disappeared, replaced by concern. "Something's wrong here," she said softly, following him into the lunch line.

"A *lot* is wrong here!" Cory exclaimed. "I just can't stop thinking about—"

"I think you got the wrong house," she interrupted. She smiled, pleased with her idea.

"What are you talking about?"

"That's it. You got the wrong house. You woke this guy up. So he decided to play a mean joke on you." Lisa watched for Cory's face to brighten, waited for him to realize that her theory was a good one.

But his only reaction was a weary sigh. "Get real," he muttered gloomily. "I didn't have the wrong house."

"You don't know for sure," she insisted, although she could see this theory wasn't going to go over. "What did you think you were doing, anyway?" she asked, poking him in the ribs the way she'd been doing it since they were kids. "Why are you driving to this girl's house in the middle of the night? Why are you looking for her all day? Why are you so obsessed with Anna Corwin? There are other girls in the world, you know."

He didn't say anything. He seemed to be staring right past her.

"Cory—did you hear a word I said?"

"Yeah, sure," he answered quickly, still not looking at her. "You said the guy in the doorway was playing a mean joke on me."

Anna is dead. Some joke!

"Bye, Cory." She gave him an exaggerated handshake and started to leave.

"What about lunch?" he called after her.

"I'm not hungry anymore. Hey—you want to walk home after school?"

"Can't," he called to her. "Monday's the day I work in the office." A lot of kids did clerical work after school in the office. The pay wasn't too bad, and the work was easy, mostly copying and filing.

He watched her make her way through the crowded lunchroom to the double doorways that led to the hall. Why had she accused him of acting weird? She'd been acting pretty weird herself, he decided. So temperamental. Always so angry at him. Why? What had he done to her?

Suddenly an idea formed in his head.

The office.

Of course. Why hadn't he thought of it before?

The office.

After school in the office he would be able to answer all his questions.

He got out of the lunch line and started toward the door. He decided to go outside and get some air, maybe walk a bit. He wasn't feeling hungry either.

Cory's fingers were black. They always were after he used the copy machine. And the ink stayed on for days.

He finished copying the announcement about the faculty blood drive. He had one other copy to run off before his office chores were finished.

Moving more quietly and sneakily than he really needed to, he made his way to the door of the inner office and peered in. The room was empty. He had overheard that Mr. Sewall, the principal, had left early with a toothache. And one of the secretaries was out sick. That left only Miss Markins, who was busily typing away in the outer reception area.

The coast was clear. And would probably stay clear.

He slipped into the inner office and pulled the door nearly shut. His hand went for the light switch, but then he realized it might be a bad idea. Miss Markins was sure to notice it.

He crept over to the principal's desk in the center of the small office. Framed photographs of Mr. Sewall's two sons seemed to stare at him disapprovingly. Cory walked silently around the desk to get to the object of his search.

Against the back wall were the gray filing cabinets. They contained the permanent records of every student at Shadyside.

These were the sacred permanent records, the secret files that could make you a success in the world—or destroy your life forever.

At least, that's what most Shadyside High students were led to believe.

"I'm sorry—but this will have to go on your permanent record." If a teacher or Mr. Sewall ever said that to you, you knew you were doomed forever. Whatever it was, whatever crime you had committed, whatever error you had made would follow you for the rest of your life. There it would be, in your *permanent* record.

Cory ran his hand over the first row of file drawers, quickly scanning the little identification cards on the front. Just being in the same room with the permanent records made him nervous. The fact that he had no business in there and that he'd have to do some fast explaining if he was caught made him so nervous, he could barely read the ID cards.

He stopped his search for a second, held his breath, and listened. Miss Markins was still typing away. Whew. He allowed himself to breathe once again.

"I can't believe I'm doing this. What am I doing in here?" he asked himself, stooping low and pulling out a long file drawer on the bottom row.

He knew the answer to that question. He was going to take a look at Anna Corwin's permanent record. He was going to find out the truth about her. He was going to find out everything he could about her.

His fingers sifted quickly through the files. He knew this wasn't right. He knew it was crazy behavior. He knew he never did things like this. At least, before Anna he never did things like this.

Footsteps.

He took a deep breath.

He listened for her typing, but it had stopped.

He dived under Mr. Sewall's desk just as she entered the room.

"Safe!" he told himself. Or was he? Had she heard him in there?

He almost cried out. He had left the file drawer open. If she saw it, she'd know he'd been in there.

She stood behind the desk. Her legs were three inches from his face. For a second he imagined reaching out and grabbing her knees just to see how loud she'd scream. Just for a laugh.

A last laugh before they took him away. Suspended him forever. Put it all on his permanent record.

He held his breath. It seemed as if he'd been holding it ever since he sneaked into this office. She was leaning over the desk, writing something. Leaving a note for Mr. Sewall, most likely.

I can't believe I'm sitting here under Mr. Sewall's desk, he told himself silently. But Anna's face flashed into his mind again. And he heard the words of the strange young man at the doorway of her house. And he remembered why he was there.

Miss Markins finished her note and walked out of the office without noticing the open file drawer. As soon as he heard her resume her typing, Cory darted out from under the desk and returned to the file drawer, moving his hands quickly through the C's.

What would Anna's file tell him? What truths would it reveal about this beautiful girl who had so completely taken over his thoughts?

Corn . . . Cornerman . . . His hands moved quickly, pushing the files back. At last! Cornwall . . . Corwood . . . Corwyth . . .

Wait a minute.

He went back through the last five or six. Then he moved forward nine or ten more.

He hadn't missed any. And none of them were filed out of order. The files went from Cornwall to Corwood.

There was no file for anyone named Anna Corwin!

CHAPTER 8

"Timberrr! Look at that guy go down!" Annie's voice boomed over the cheers of the crowd.

"He's too tall!" David cried. "He's seven feet tall, and he's just a freshman!"

"He's still growing!" Arnie added.

They looked over at Cory, who was staring straight across the gymnasium.

"Hey, Brooks—Earth calling Brooks!" David shouted right in his ear. But Cory didn't respond.

The Shadyside cheerleaders did a quick routine during the time-out. Then the basketball game resumed. It wasn't much of a game. Westerville, with its seven-foot freshman center, was running the Shadyside Cougars off the floor.

"They have only one play—toss it to the big guy," David observed.

"I'd like to toss it to that cheerleader on the end!"

Arnie shouted, loud enough for half the auditorium to hear.

David and Arnie both waited for Cory to add his opinion. But he didn't say anything. He looked at them as if seeing them for the first time. "Good game, huh?" he said, forcing a smile.

"What game are you watching?" Arnie snapped. "We're losing by twenty points."

The weak, forced smile faded from Cory's face. He turned and started surveying the auditorium again.

"You're a lot of laughs these days, Brooks," Arnie said, reaching across David to punch Cory as hard as he could on the shoulder. "Aw, I'm goin' down to get a Coke." He pushed his way down the aisle and disappeared around the side of the bleachers.

"You feeling okay?" David asked. He had to ask it twice before Cory heard him.

"Yeah. Fine."

"Well, how come you missed practice this afternoon?"

"I don't know. Just forgot, I guess."

"Welner was furious. That's the second practice you missed this week, Cory. And the Friday practice is the most important—especially since we have a meet tomorrow."

"I know," Cory said, sounding annoyed. "Give me some slack, David. You're not my mother."

"Hey—" David looked really hurt. "I'm your teammate, aren't I? I'm your friend, aren't I?"

"So?"

"So—you tell me. What's your problem, Brooks?"

"Oh, nothing. Just—"

The crowd roared. All around them people jumped to their feet. Something had obviously gone Shadyside's way. But David and Cory had missed it. The cheerleaders came back on the floor. The bleachers were shaking under the deafening noise. Cory looked to the scoreboard. The Cougars were only behind by fifteen now. That must explain the excitement.

"It's that blond girl, isn't it?" David said when it became quiet enough to talk.

"I guess." Cory shrugged. He didn't really want to get into any big discussion with David. He felt bad. He really had forgotten about gymnastics practice. How was that possible? Was he really losing his mind over this girl?

"You going out with her?" David asked.

"I haven't seen her," Cory said, looking across the basketball floor.

"What?"

"You heard me. I haven't seen her all week. I looked for her every day, but she hasn't been in school."

"And that's why you're acting like a zombie?"

"Get off my case, Metcalf," Cory scowled.

"You're screwing up your gymnastics rating because of a girl you don't know that you haven't seen? Well, that makes sense to me."

Cory didn't say anything. Then he suddenly blurted out, "I don't even know if she exists!"

He regretted saying it immediately. It didn't make any sense, and he knew it. And now he had given David even more of an opportunity to put him down and give him a hard time.

But to Cory's surprise, David reacted with real concern. "What do you mean, Brooks? You told me you saw her—more than once. You told me you talked to her. You told me she's in Lisa's physics class. You told me all this stuff about her because that's all you talk about these days. So what do you mean, she doesn't exist?"

"I work after school in the office on Mondays. You know. So Monday afternoon I went into the permanent files and looked her up. There was no file for her!"

David looked shocked, but not for the reason Cory imagined. "You—you can get into the files?" he cried. "Great! What does mine say about me?"

"I didn't—"

"I'll give you ten bucks to look at my file. Better than that, I'll pay you back the ten bucks I owe you!"

"No deal," Cory said disgustedly. "You don't understand. I went to her house last week, and this guy said—"

The crowd groaned. Loud boos echoed off the tile walls. Cory's eye caught the scoreboard. Shadyside was losing by twenty-two.

Arnie pushed his way back into the row and plopped down beside David. "That guy's too tall," he said. He had spilled Coke down the front of his sweatshirt. "They've gotta raise the baskets!"

"Or lower the floor!" David said, and they both began to howl.

Cory stood up. "Guess I'm going," he told them. "This is a drag."

"You're a drag," Arnie said, grinning.

"She's a transfer student, isn't she?" David said, pulling Cory back down to the bench.

"Yeah."

"Well, maybe her file hasn't been sent over from her other school yet."

David was smart. Maybe he was right. But Cory didn't really believe it. It was November already. How long did it take to transfer files?

"Is he talking about that weird blond girl again?" Arnie boomed, leaning over David to shout right in Cory's face. "What have you been doin' to her?" he leered. "Must be pretty good or you wouldn't be missing practice so much." Arnie laughed as if he had just said the funniest thing ever spoken.

Cory just shook his head wearily. He realized he must seem pretty weird to his two friends. He seemed pretty weird to himself.

He'd never been haunted by someone this way before. He'd never had anything that he couldn't shut out of his mind, that he couldn't force himself to stop thinking about. He had always been in control of his thoughts. And now . . . now . . .

Was he out of control?

"See you guys later," he said, and quickly headed the other way down the row so they couldn't pull him back. The crowd groaned, then groaned again. The small contingent of Westerville fans across the floor was cheering wildly.

It looked like a bad night for the Cougars. A bad night for everyone, Cory thought. He had searched the bleachers row by row for Anna. But she wasn't there.

He climbed into his car, shivering against the chill. After three tries he got it started. He drove around aimlessly for a while, heading down Park Drive, then across Hawthorne to Mill Road. The streets were empty. Most houses were already dark. He turned on the radio, but no one was playing any music he liked, so he clicked it off.

He realized he was very tired. He hadn't slept well all week. He spun the car around and headed for home.

He was asleep when the ringing phone woke him. He squinted at his alarm clock. It was one thirty in the morning.

His hand knocked the receiver off the phone. He fumbled around until he grabbed it up. "Hello?"

"Stay away from Anna."

"What?" The voice on the other end was a hoarse whisper, so quiet he could barely make out the words.

"Stay away from Anna," the strange voice whispered slowly and distinctly, each word filled with menace. "She's dead. She's a dead girl. Stay away from her—or you'll be next!"

CHAPTER 9

Cory suddenly felt very cold. He climbed out of bed and walked in darkness over to his bedroom window. He checked to make sure the window was closed. Then he reached down and felt the radiator. Heat was coming up full blast. He stood there for a long while trying to get rid of the chill, staring out at the silent stillness of his backyard lit only by a pale half moon.

The voice on the phone still whispered in his ears. Cory reached up and pulled his black curls hard, trying to make the harsh whispers disappear, trying to make the threatening words stop repeating in his mind. It didn't work.

Realizing his chill came from the inside, Cory stepped away from the radiator and, tripping over a pair of sneakers he had left in the center of the room, made his way back to bed.

Someone had threatened his life. Someone knew where he lived. Someone knew how to reach him.

Someone knew him and knew he was interested in Anna.

Someone wanted to make sure he stayed away from Anna. But who?

Was it one of his friends playing a joke?

No. This was no joke. This was for real. The whispers were filled with true menace, true hatred. The threat was sincere.

Stay away from Anna—or you'll be dead too.

Who was it? The strange, puffy-cheeked young man who answered the Corwins' door? Maybe. It was hard to tell from whispers, hard to tell if it was a man or a woman.

Cory closed his eyes tight and tried to drive the whispers from his mind. He felt a little warmer now, but he was still far from sleep. He turned onto his side, then slid over onto his other side, then tried sleeping on his stomach.

For some reason he found himself thinking about the strange neighbor who had stopped him that night on Fear Street. He had been thinking about that man all week, picturing his worn gray slicker, his stubbled face, the menacing way he had stared at Cory. He said he was a neighbor, but why was he directly outside the Corwins' house so late at night? He had claimed to be walking his dog. But Cory had seen no dog. And why had the man warned Cory to stay away from the Corwins? Was he warning Cory—or threatening him?

Cory forced the man's face out of his mind. He decided to think about Anna instead—those clear blue eyes as bright as a doll's, the dramatically red lips on that pale ivory skin. He remembered the dream where she was kissing him again and again.

The phone rang.

He was still wide awake, but it startled him, making him jump straight out of bed. He picked up the receiver at the beginning of the second ring. "Hello?" The word came out choked and dry.

"Cory—is that you?" A tiny voice, very faint.

"Yes." His heart was pounding so hard, he could barely get the word out.

"Can you help me, Cory?"

He had spoken to her only once, but he recognized her soft, almost childlike voice.

"It's me. Anna. Anna Corwin."

"I know," he said. Then he felt terribly foolish. How would he know that she would be the one calling him in the middle of the night—unless he had been thinking of nothing but her for weeks?

"I need you to help me," she said, speaking rapidly, her voice just above a whisper. "I don't know anyone else. You're the only one I've talked to. Can you help me?"

She sounded so frightened, so desperately frightened. "Well . . ." Why was he hesitating? Was it because of the first whispered call telling him to stay away from her?

"Please—come quickly," she pleaded. "Meet me on the corner of Fear Street, just past my house."

She sounded frightened. But her tiny, breathy voice also made her sound very sexy. The chill Cory felt now wasn't entirely fear. It was mixed with excitement. He looked across the room at his alarm clock. It was one thirty-seven. Was he *really* seriously considering sneaking out and meeting this strange, frightened girl on Fear Street in the middle of the night?

"Please, Cory," she whispered, now more enticing than frightened. "I need you."

"Okay," he said, not recognizing his own voice, not sure it was him saying the word.

"Hurry," she whispered, and the line clicked off.

He listened to the silent phone for a few seconds, trying to figure out if he was awake or dreaming this. Had Anna Corwin really just called and begged him to meet her? He had been thinking about her, searching for her all week. Was it possible that she had been thinking about him at the same time?

The idea was more than a little exciting. But why had she sounded so frightened, so frantic for him to come at once? And why did she want him to meet her out on the street?

The street.

Fear Street.

Cory had started to pull on his jeans, but he stopped as he

remembered where Anna lived, where she wanted to meet.

"I'm sixteen years old," he told himself. "I'm not a child. There's no reason for me to be afraid of a silly street." But he had to admit that the idea of waiting alone for someone on Fear Street in the middle of the night was pretty frightening.

He suddenly remembered another Fear Street story in the newspaper, this one from the previous spring. Two cars going in opposite directions on Fear Street late at night had collided head-on. A Fear Street resident heard the crash, ran out in his pajamas, saw that both cars were filled with badly injured people. Some of them were unconscious. Some were pinned inside the crushed cars.

He ran back to his house and called the police. The police arrived less than ten minutes later. They found the cars crushed together in the middle of the street. But both cars were empty. There was dark blood on the seats and blood on the street. But all the passengers had disappeared without a trace.

No sign of them was ever found. Six people, six injured people, who had been trapped inside two cars, vanished in less than ten minutes. . . .

Cory finished getting dressed. He knew he had no choice. He had to go. He had to go to her. She needed him.

Sneaking down the steps to the front hallway, he tripped in the darkness and nearly fell. He grabbed the banister and steadied himself, hoping his parents hadn't heard. Taking a deep breath, he continued down the stairs. He groped around until he found the car keys on the counter in the entranceway. Then he silently let himself out of the house.

He zipped his down jacket against the cold and jogged to the car. He put the car in neutral and let it glide down the drive. Then he started it in the street as far from the house as he could get it. "I'm getting pretty good at sneaking around," he told himself. "But why am I doing this?"

Because Anna's in trouble.

He turned down Mill Road and headed south toward Fear Street. Clouds had covered the moon, and the streetlamps cast only dim light on this narrow, old street. He put on the brights just in time to see a large gray animal scamper out onto the highway.

Whump.

There wasn't time to slow down. A single bump told him he had run over it. He looked in the rearview mirror but couldn't see anything. He slowed for a few seconds, then decided to keep going. Nothing he could do about it now.

He suddenly felt sick. What was it anyway? A raccoon? A badger? It was too big to be a rabbit. It might have been an opossum. He wondered if it was stuck to his tire. Yuck. He forced himself to think about Anna.

There were no other cars on Mill Road. He passed a few trucks going the other way, their headlights causing him to squint and look away.

A swirling wind seemed to come up the moment he turned onto Fear Street. The wind pressed against the front of the car. The car held back, as if it didn't want to go here.

The inside of the windshield had steamed up, and he struggled to see. He slowed down as he passed Simon Fear's burned-out mansion. Bare trees rattled and creaked in the wind, their low branches scraping at one another.

He stopped and wiped the windshield with a rag he found in the glove compartment. Now the glass was smeared, but he could see a little better.

He passed the Corwins' house. It was completely dark. He stopped and stared at it, looking for any sign of life. But there was none.

Had the call been someone playing a joke? Had he driven here for nothing?

No. It was Anna. He recognized her voice. And she sounded too frightened for it to be a joke.

He pulled to the curb at the corner. The wind rushed through the trees. Leaves swirled and scattered over the street. He turned off the lights but left the engine running.

"Maybe I should get out of the car," he told himself. "She might not be able to find me if I stay in here."

But he remembered his last visit to Fear Street, the strange neighbor, the animal howls, and he decided to wait inside the car. He switched off the engine. Then he switched it on again. "I'll play the radio. At least it will drown out the dreadful wailing of the wind." But then he remembered it might drain the battery. He didn't want to be stuck at two in the morning on Fear Street with a car that wouldn't start. He turned the engine off again.

The passenger door swung open.

He started to scream.

CHAPTER 10

"Anna!"

"Hi, Cory," she whispered shyly, sliding next to him on the front seat. She was wrapped in an old-fashioned lacy gray shawl. Her hair was wild and unbrushed, and her blue eyes sparkled with excitement in the glimmer of light inside the car. Then she pulled the car door closed and the light faded.

"You frightened me," he said, turning to look at her.

She gave him an odd smile, almost a devilish smile. Or was it just the dim light? He couldn't see her very well.

"Why did you call me? What's the matter?"

She slid closer. She was almost touching him. The wind shifted directions. Leaves blew up against the car windows, making it even darker.

"Cory, you're the only one who can help me," she said, her voice barely above a whisper. She was trembling slightly, as if she were holding back her fear, struggling to keep herself together. "You're the only one who talks to me."

"Where've you been all week?" he blurted out. "I looked for you."

She seemed surprised. She turned and looked to the rear window. It was entirely steamed up. She rubbed the side window next to her with her hand, making a clear peephole.

"Were you sick? Are you okay?" Cory asked.

She smiled at him again.

"I—I was at your house before," he said. "I wanted to talk to you." He realized he must sound crazy to her. The words just poured out. He didn't seem to have any control over what he was saying.

He was so glad to see her, so excited. It was exciting that she had called him, that he had come to her in the middle of the night, that they were having this secret meeting. But what was it all about? Why wasn't she answering any of his questions?

"Are you in trouble?" he asked. "Is there anything I can do? I was thinking about you this week. Actually, I've been thinking about you ever since that day in the lunchroom."

The lunchroom. Why did he have to bring that horrible occasion up? How embarrassing!

"Really?" she said. "I was thinking about you too." She peered out through the small circle she had made on the window.

"Is someone following you?" he asked. "Is someone out there?"

She shook her head. "I don't know."

"Your family said—they told me you were—" Oh, no! Here he was, blurting it out. Why couldn't he control himself? Why was he talking so crazily?

He hated being so out of control. As a gymnast, he practiced keeping every muscle in control. Now he couldn't even control his mouth!

"I—I just need to know if you're real!" he heard himself saying.

The words seemed to surprise her. A smile slowly spread over her face, a sly smile. "I'm real," she whispered, staring into his eyes. "I'll show you."

She reached both hands up suddenly and grabbed the back of his head. Her hands were hot despite the cold of the night. She pulled his face down to hers and pushed her lips against his.

Her lips were soft and warm. Her mouth opened a little, then closed. She kissed him harder, still holding his head.

He struggled to breathe. She pressed harder, uttering a soft sigh. It was the most exciting kiss, more exciting than in any dream he had ever had. He wanted it to last forever. It appeared that it just might.

She kissed him harder. He was startled by how needy she seemed. She gripped the back of his neck and pressed her lips even closer.

Cory couldn't believe how lucky he was. "Is this really happening to me?" he asked himself. He tried to slip his arms around her, but there was no room to move from behind the steering wheel.

She kissed him, pushing her lips at his, until the kiss really hurt. Then she pulled her mouth away from his. She slid her warm lips across his cheek and up to his ear. He felt her warm, steady breath against his cheek.

She whispered something. "You're all mine now."

Is that what it was? Did he hear her correctly?

You're all mine now?

No. That couldn't be it. He didn't hear it.

"Do you believe I'm real now?" she asked, her hands still on the back of his neck.

He tried to reply, but no sound came out.

She laughed, a surprisingly loud laugh that startled them both. They had both been so quiet up till now.

The wind shifted again. Large brown maple leaves blew hard against the windshield as if trying to break in. Somewhere nearby an animal howled.

She let go of him and settled back in the seat, a pleased expression on her face. He could still feel her lips on his, still taste her, still feel the pressure of her face against his.

They didn't say anything for what seemed a long, long while. Finally he broke the silence. "Why did you call me, Anna?"

He didn't really want her to answer. What he wanted was for her to kiss him again like that. And again. And again.

"You sounded so frightened," he said, reaching for her hand but not finding it.

She smiled at him, this time a guilty smile. "I just wanted to see if you'd come," she said. She looked away. She started rubbing a fresh peephole in the window.

"You—you weren't in trouble?"

She didn't look at him. "I knew you'd come," she said. "I just knew it."

He stared at the back of her head, at her golden hair which fell in long tangles over the gray shawl.

He wanted to kiss her again. He wanted to wrap his arms around her. He wanted to feel her hands on the back of his neck again. He reached out and put a hand on her shoulder. "That's why you called? You just wanted me to come here?"

She turned around, her face expressionless. She looked at him but didn't say anything.

"When I was at your house, a guy answered the door." He had to ask her about it. He just had to. He knew she was real now. So why did her family say she was dead?

"My brother. Brad," she answered, still expressionless. She stared straight ahead at the clouded windshield.

"When I asked for you, he got real upset. He said you didn't live there."

"Brad'll say anything," she whispered, still staring straight ahead at the fogged windshield.

"But he—"

"Please don't make me tell you about Brad. He—he's unpredictable. Don't make me say any more. Just stay out of his way. He—he can be *dangerous*." Her whole body shook when she said that word.

"He told me you were dead!" Cory blurted out.

For a brief second her eyes grew wide with surprise. Then she pulled the door handle, pushed open the door, and jumped out of the car.

Cory made a grab for her. But she was already gone. He threw open his door and climbed out. The wind blew a clump of leaves onto the legs of his jeans. "Anna!" he called to her. But he knew he hadn't shouted loudly enough to be heard over the wind.

He started to run after her, but she had disappeared into the darkness. "Anna!" he called one more time. But she was gone.

The wind seemed to grow stronger. The tree limbs above his head rattled like bones as the dry leaves circled and spun at his feet.

He tasted blood on his lips. He was filled with longing, longing to understand her, longing to know why she had run away, why she wouldn't answer his questions, why she was so terrified of her brother, longing for more kisses.

He was only a few feet from the car when something big and powerful leapt onto his shoulders from behind.

CHAPTER 11

"Cory—wake up! Come on!"

"Huh?"

"Wake up! Get out of bed! Do I have to get a crane to pull you up?"

"Huh?"

"I've been trying to wake you for ten minutes. What's your problem? Didn't you sleep last night?" His mother grabbed his shoulder and started to shake him.

"*Ow!*" The shoulder throbbed with pain. He jerked it away from her. It was all starting to come back to him. His shoulder hurt because the gigantic dog had jumped on it.

"Cory—come on. You've got a gymnastics meet in two hours. You'd better wake up." His mother was more amused than annoyed. She'd never had this much trouble waking him before.

Of course, he had never spent half the night on Fear Street before. He thought of Anna's kiss.

"What are you smiling about? Cory—you're acting downright weird this morning."

"Sorry, Mom. G'morning." He tried to clear his brain. He smiled at her, only his mouth wouldn't cooperate and it came out all crooked. He tried to look normal. He didn't want her to ask a million questions. If only his back and shoulders weren't killing him.

"What day is it?"

"Saturday," she said, turning to leave.

"Saturday? The meet against Farmingville is today!"

"Didn't I just say that, or am I losing my mind too?"

He sat up in bed with a loud groan. She turned around and looked at him. "Hurry downstairs before your breakfast gets cold."

"What's for breakfast?"

"Cornflakes."

They both laughed. It was one of their favorite jokes.

After she left, he carefully pulled off his pajama top and surveyed the damage to his shoulders. They were just badly scratched. That huge Doberman, Voltaire, had pounced on him as if he were a mouse.

The whole scene with all its horror replayed itself in his mind. He heard the low growls again, felt the dog's hot breath on the back of his head, and then felt the jolt of the giant paws bearing down on his shoulders, pushing him to the ground, pinning him down, the dog's massive jaws snapping loudly as it snarled over him.

It seemed to him he was down on the ground for hours before the strange neighbor in the gray slicker had arrived. "Get down, Voltaire. Sit, boy," he had said calmly, with no emotion at all. The dog obeyed immediately, backing away, silent except for its heavy, excited panting. "You back again, son?"

The guy didn't even apologize. He just stared at Cory suspiciously as Cory slowly, painfully, pulled himself to his feet with a loud groan.

"Visiting the Corwins, were you?" the man asked, petting the Doberman's slender black head as if to congratulate him on a job well done.

"I—uh . . . I was just leaving," Cory stammered, his heart heaving in his chest, his shoulders aching, his head spinning.

"Most folks don't come around Fear Street in the middle of

the night," the man said, his expression as unrevealing as ever. It sounded like a threat to Cory.

Cory didn't reply. Somehow he managed to climb into his car, start the engine, and drive away. The man and dog stood watching until Cory was out of sight.

What was going on here? Cory wondered. Why was that weird guy always there when Cory parked near the Corwins' house? Had he been watching for Cory? Was he really a neighbor? Was he spying on Anna?

It's her crazy brother Brad wearing a disguise!

"Get real!" he had scolded himself.

But who was he?

Now it was the next morning, and he was less than two hours away from the Farmingville meet. He looked at his scratched-up shoulders in the mirror. How was he going to explain them to Coach Welner? How was he ever going to get up on the rings? He swung his arms around, testing them. Not too bad. Maybe he could work out the ache. Maybe they'd be flexible enough to perform.

He got dressed quickly, pulling on a clean pair of jeans and a fresh sweatshirt, and hurried down to breakfast. He decided to get to the gym early and work out, do some stretching exercises. He'd be fine.

He thought of Anna. How soft she was, how warm. At least he had proven that she was alive. Wow! Was she alive!

Yeah. He'd be fine, Cory decided. He'd be perfectly fine.

Disgustedly, Cory tossed a towel over his shoulder. He started pacing behind the team bench and bumped right into Lisa. "Ow!" she cried, rubbing her shoulder. "Watch where you're going."

"Hey—what are you doing here? There's a meet going on," Cory said.

"Really? How would *you* know?" she cracked.

"Give me a break. Did you come here just to insult me?" Cory asked glumly. He picked up his pace.

She hurried to catch up with him. "No. Sorry. It just slipped out." She put a hand on his shoulder to stop him, but he pulled away in pain. "What's the matter?"

"I—uh—strained it, I guess." He didn't have the energy to tell her the truth. He wouldn't know where to begin. "You were watching the meet?"

"No. Not really. I got here just in time to see your bar routine."

"It wasn't a bar routine. It was a clown act," Cory said with genuine sadness.

"Sorry," she said. She started to pat his shoulder again but quickly thought better of it. "I came to tell you something. Something I think you'll be interested in." She looked tense. She was biting her lower lip.

"Can it wait till after? Coach is gonna—"

"It's about Anna Corwin," she said.

"Tell me," he said, tossing the towel to the floor.

She frowned. She took both his hands and pulled him to the side of the gym. "We were at my cousin's house last night," she told him, leaning back against the tile wall.

"Which cousin?"

"What does it matter? You don't know any of my cousins."

"Oh. Right."

"My cousin had a friend over, a girl who goes to Melrose. And I was talking to her, and I asked her if she knew Anna Corwin because Anna used to go to Melrose before she transferred here."

"Yeah. And?"

"Well, when I asked her about Anna, the girl got this funny look on her face. She actually went pale."

"Why?" Cory asked impatiently. "What did she tell you?"

"Well, you're not going to believe this. She said that Anna *had* been in her class—but that Anna was dead."

CHAPTER 12

Cory's face filled with surprise, and then anger. "That's not funny, Lisa. Why'd you pull me away from the meet to tell me such a stupid—"

He started to go back, but she shoved him back against the wall. "*Owwch!*" His shoulders throbbed with pain.

"Oh. Sorry. Just let me finish. It isn't a joke. It was a terrible tragedy, my cousin's friend said. There were rumors about Anna Corwin all over her school. No one was sure what really happened. The story was that Anna had fallen down the basement stairs in her house. She died instantly in the fall."

"But that's impossible," Cory said weakly. He thought of their kiss the night before. He felt Anna's lips pressing so hard against his. "Totally impossible."

"My cousin's friend swore that it was true," Lisa told him. "It happened over the summer vacation, and people were still talking about it in the fall."

"No way," Cory said, bending over to retrieve the towel. "I don't believe it. I just don't."

"There's an easy way to prove it," Lisa said. "Get dressed. Let's go do some investigating."

"Are you kidding? In the middle of the meet?" He glanced nervously over to the coach. Coach Welner was unhappily engrossed in Arnie's bar routine.

"You're finished anyway, aren't you?" Lisa asked impatiently.

"Yeah. In more ways than one," Cory said glumly, suddenly remembering the pathetic performance he had just given. "But if Coach catches me ducking out in the middle . . ."

He changed his mind. He knew he had no choice. He had to find out the truth about Anna—right away. "Okay. Meet you in the parking lot," he said.

Making sure that Coach Welner was still watching Arnie's performance on the bar, Cory slipped out of the door and into the locker room, where he changed into his street clothes as quickly as he could.

This story about Anna couldn't be true.

She couldn't be dead. She *couldn't*!

That wasn't a ghost he had kissed—*was* it?

He suddenly remembered the frightened look on her face the first time he had ever talked to her, when he had mentioned ghosts on Fear Street.

No. Get real. There was no such thing as ghosts. The girl who had kissed him with such heat, such feeling, had to be alive!

A few minutes later he had sneaked out of the building and was with Lisa in her car, heading toward the Shadyside public library. A light snow had fallen during the afternoon, covering the trees, making them look ghostlike in the gray light of evening.

"What's at the library?" he asked her, breaking a long silence.

"The microfilm room. They have all the local papers from all over the state on microfilm there. I use this room a lot to do research for articles I write for the *Spectator*."

They rode the rest of the way in silence.

At the library Lisa asked for the Melrose newspapers from four and five months before. "Here," she said, handing Cory a spool of microfilm. "You take a viewer and I'll take a viewer. It'll go much faster this way."

About twenty minutes later she found what they were looking for. It was a newspaper article from the previous spring. Cory stared at the black type of the headline through the viewer:

ANNA CORWIN, MELROSE SOPHOMORE, DIES IN ACCIDENT

The words to the story all blurred in Cory's eyes. But there was a photograph that he couldn't stop staring at. The photo was very unclear. The reproduction was too light, all in grays, as if the girl had been a ghost to begin with.

It's Anna, he thought. Those eyes. The blond hair. It's Anna. He squinted into the machine, trying to make the gray photo clearer.

"But—how—I mean—how can you explain this?" he managed to say, still staring into the viewer, his thoughts swirling crazily through his mind, thoughts of Anna, of talking to her, of touching her.

"I can't explain it," Lisa said softly. "I don't know what to say."

He stared at the gray photograph and then back at the bold headline.

The question repeated endlessly in his mind . . .

How could Anna Corwin be dead?

How could Anna Corwin be dead?

He felt her lips again, pressing so hard against his, pressing, harder, harder until his lips bled.

How could Anna Corwin be dead?

That night Cory was too restless to do anything. He tried catching up on some of his homework, but he couldn't concentrate. At eight thirty he sneaked out of the house and drove around town for a while. There were small patches of white along the sides of the roads and dotting the lawns, remnants of the light snowfall earlier in the day.

He drove around aimlessly, making the same circle through North Hills, down past the high school, across Canyon Road, and then back up again. But he knew all along where he would end up.

On Fear Street.

He parked at the curb in front of the Corwins' yard and stared up at the rambling house. The sky above it was red, casting down an eerie light that made the old house look unreal, like the set of a horror movie.

The inside of the house was completely dark, as usual. A shutter on the side banged noisily in the wind. A dim light went on in an upstairs window. Cory stared at it, unable to see anyone moving inside, and in a minute or so the light flickered out.

He heard a noise behind him, a loud bark. In the rearview mirror he saw the large black Doberman bearing down on the car, galloping like a horse across the dark street. The neighbor in the gray slicker was close behind.

There he is again, Cory thought. Do he and the dog prowl Fear Street all night? Are they ghosts too?

The Ghostly Guards, he thought. They've been assigned to keep people from discovering the truth about Fear Street—from discovering that everyone who lives on Fear Street is DEAD!

He shook his head hard, trying to shake away the ridiculous thoughts. Then he frantically started the engine and pressed his foot all the way down on the gas pedal. In the rearview mirror he could see the man and the dog pull up short, startled by his fast getaway.

He drove straight home and hurried up to bed. He fell asleep quickly and dreamed about a gymnastics meet. He was up on the rings and realized he didn't know how to get down. Everyone was staring at him, waiting for him to move. But he just couldn't remember how to do it.

He was awakened by someone touching his face.

He sat up in bed, grateful that the dream was interrupted. The hand slid down his cheek again. He blinked himself awake.

Anna!

She was on his bed. She sat beside him, her blue eyes staring down into his.

"What are you doing here? How did you get in?" he asked, his voice a hoarse whisper still filled with sleep.

"Take care of me, Cory. Please," she pleaded, looking frightened and forlorn. She touched his cheek again. She brushed her lips against his forehead.

"Anna—"

She pressed her face against his.

He couldn't believe this was happening. She was alone with him. In his bedroom. He wanted another kiss. He desperately wanted another kiss like the one in the car.

"Anna—" He reached up for her. He wanted to pull her down on top of him.

She smiled at him. Her soft hair brushed over his face.

"Anna—why did your family say you were dead?"

She didn't seem at all surprised or upset by the question. "I *am* dead," she whispered in his ear. "I *am* dead, Cory. But you can still take care of me."

"What do you mean?" He suddenly felt very frightened. She looked very ghostly now, pale and transparent. Her eyes burned into his. They weren't friendly eyes. They were menacing eyes, evil eyes.

"What do you mean?" he repeated, unable to keep the fear from his voice.

"You can die too," she whispered. "Then we can be together."

"No!" he cried, pushing her away. "No—I don't want to!"

The phone was ringing.

He sat up and looked around.

No Anna. It had been a dream. It had all been a dream.

But it had seemed so real.

The phone was real. He looked at his desk clock. It was a little after midnight. He grabbed up the receiver.

"Hello, Cory?" A whispered voice. Anna's voice.

"Hi, Anna," he whispered back.

"Cory—come quickly. Please! You've got to come! Please! But don't park by my house! I'll meet you in front of that burned-out old mansion. Hurry, Cory! You're the only one I can turn to!"

CHAPTER 13

He held on to the phone long after she had hung up. He needed to know that it was real, that he wasn't dreaming this too.

Yes. She had really called him. She was real. She was alive.

Should he go? Did he have a choice?

He thought of her sitting so close to him in the car, pressing her face against his, kissing him, kissing him, kissing him.

Of *course* he had to go!

She needed him.

And he needed . . . to ask her all the questions that were in his mind, to find out the truth about her once and for all.

He got dressed in seconds, turned off the desk lamp, and started to sneak silently down the stairs. He was halfway down when his parents' bedroom door opened, and his father lumbered out into the dark hallway. "Cory—is that you?"

He had to answer. If he didn't, his dad would think it was a burglar. "Yeah, Dad. It's me," he whispered.

"What's the matter? What are you doing?"

Think fast, Cory. Think fast. "Uh . . . I'm just going down for a snack. I woke up 'cause I was hungry."

His father grunted, accepting the story. "Thought I heard the phone ring," he said, yawning.

"Yeah. It was a wrong number," Cory said.

He waited until he heard his father go back in and close the bedroom door. He waited another minute or two. Then he crept silently down the rest of the stairs and out the front door.

It was even colder than the first night he had sneaked out, but there was no wind at all. The ground felt hard and frosty beneath his sneakers. The moon was hidden behind thick clouds. Again, he let the car roll down the drive, then started it on the street.

Mill Road was as dark and empty as before. Cory stared at the curving white line in the center of the narrow road and thought about Anna.

Was she really in trouble this time? She sounded very frightened, very frantic. What could the problem be? Was she afraid to tell him?

Or did she just want to see him? If so, why could she see him only in the middle of the night? And why couldn't he park near her house? Why did she have to meet him in front of Simon Fear's creepy old mansion?

He thought of the disturbing dream he had just had about her. And the photo in the newspaper article flashed into his mind. He forced himself not to think about that. He wanted to kiss her again. And again.

This was so exciting!

He turned onto Fear Street and stopped in front of the burned-out mansion. Across the street the cemetery lay dark and still. He turned off the headlights. The blackness enveloped him. He couldn't see a thing. He suddenly felt as if the blackness had walled him off from the rest of the world, as if he had entered a black tunnel, an endless black tunnel, a tunnel leading to . . .

He turned around to look out the back window for her. No sign of her. Nothing moved. The trees, black shadows against the blacker sky, could have been painted on a backdrop.

He rolled down the window and breathed the frigid air. He

looked for her in the rearview mirror. She still wasn't coming. He reached for the door handle to get out of the car. But remembering the huge Doberman, he decided against it.

It was too cold with the window down. He rolled it back up. Where was she? He held his wrist up to check the time, but he had forgotten to put on his watch. He turned again and peered out the back window. Only blackness.

Despite the cold, his palms were hot and sweaty. He coughed. His throat felt tight and dry. He couldn't sit still any longer. He was too nervous.

He pushed open the door and climbed out. He closed the door quickly so no one could see the light. He listened for the neighbor and his vicious four-legged companion. The Ghostly Guards. Silence.

"This must be what it's like on the moon," he told himself. So quiet. So still. So . . . unreal. The insistent theme music from *The Twilight Zone* ran through his mind.

Where was she?

He started to walk down the long block toward her house. The air was cold and wet, so wet it seemed to cling to him as he walked. He stopped at the edge of her driveway and looked up at the old house.

Dark. Completely dark.

Or was it? Was that a sliver of light escaping from beneath a second-story window blind?

Someone was awake in there. Was it Anna?

Was she waiting for the right moment to sneak out and come down to him? Was someone keeping her from making her escape?

Brad.

Crazy Brad.

He shuddered as a chill ran through his body. He decided to go back and wait in the car. The street was so dark, he couldn't see more than a few feet in front of him. The only sounds were his foot-steps as he trudged over the gravelly road. Finally he climbed into the car and closed the door. It wasn't much warmer inside. He slid down low in the seat, pulling his head down into his jacket, trying to warm up.

Where was she?

He stared at the windshield, watching it frost up from his breath.

Was he shivering from the cold? Or from the fact that he was starting to worry about her?

Maybe something terrible had happened to her. Maybe she had called him because she knew she was in danger—and he hadn't come soon enough.

Staring at the opaque layers of steam on the windshield, Cory's ideas grew wilder and wilder. Maybe Brad was holding Anna pris-oner in that house. She had said that Brad was dangerous. That was the very word she had used. *Dangerous.* Maybe she wanted Cory to help her escape from Brad. Only Brad had found out about her plan, and he had—he had—what?

He pushed open the door and jumped out. He looked back down the block toward her house. She wasn't coming. His breath was forming curtains of smoke in front of him. He realized he was breathing very rapidly, and his heart was pounding.

Where was she?

He had no choice. He had to go to her house. He had to make sure she was okay.

She had called him for help, and all he had done was sit in his car trying to stay warm. Some help.

He began jogging to her house, his sneakers thudding loudly over the hard ground, the only sound beside his gasping breaths. He turned up the gravel drive and picked up speed. Looking up, he saw the thin sliver of light in the upstairs bedroom.

The ground tilted and swayed. He forced himself to keep jogging steadily. Up on the porch now. Then he was ringing the bell, forgetting that it was broken. Then he was knocking on the door, first a normal knock, then, when no one answered, as hard as he could.

Where was she?

What were they doing to her?

The door swung open. Brad, looking sleepy and puffy-eyed, stepped quickly out onto the porch, nearly knocking Cory over backward. His little eyes opened briefly with surprise, then narrowed as anger spread over his pink face.

"You—" he said, and turned his face as if to spit.

Cory tried to say something, but he was too out of breath.

"What do you want now?" Brad asked, leaning menacingly over Cory. "What are you doing here?"

"Anna called me—" Cory managed to get out.

Brad's face filled with rage. He reached out and grabbed the front of Cory's jacket. "Are you trying to torture me?" he screamed. "Is this some kind of cruel prank?"

Cory tried to pull away, but Brad's grip was surprisingly strong. "Wait. I—"

"I told you—" Brad screamed at the top of his lungs, "ANNA IS DEAD! ANNA IS DEAD! Why can't you believe me?"

He was pulling Cory's jacket so hard, Cory was having trouble breathing. In a desperate attempt to free himself, Cory brought both hands up and smashed them down against Brad's forearms.

Brad let go. Cory started to back away.

This seemed to enrage Brad even more. He grabbed Cory by the jacket front again and started dragging him. He pulled him through the open front door and into the house. "Now I'm going to get rid of you once and for all," Brad said.

CHAPTER 14

This isn't happening to me, Cory told himself. This is just another bad dream. Wake up now, Cory. Wake up.

He didn't wake up. He was already awake. This was no dream.

Brad pulled him into the living room. The house felt hot and steamy. The air smelled stale. A small fire was going in the fireplace against the far wall. There were no other lights. Shadows twisted on the dark walls. The fire crackled loudly, startling Cory.

Brad laughed. He was really enjoying Cory's fear.

He loosened his grip on Cory's jacket. Cory took a step back. Brad's rhinestone stud earring sparkled in the firelight. His eyes grew watery from laughing. "You're really scared of me—aren't you?" he demanded, wiping tears from his eyes.

Cory didn't reply. He stared back at the odd young man, trying to figure out how to escape if Brad attacked again. But he was too frightened to think clearly.

"Get out of here," Brad growled. "I'm letting you go. But don't ever come back."

Cory hesitated for a second. He wasn't sure he had heard right. Then he ran past Brad and out of the house. The door slammed hard behind him.

The shock of the cold air revived him quickly. He stopped halfway down the driveway, turned, and looked up to the second-floor window. The blind had been raised and light poured out into the surrounding darkness.

A figure stood in the window looking down on him.

"Anna!" he called, cupping his hands around his mouth. "Anna—is that you?" He waved frantically to her.

The figure in the window pulled down the blind.

The front yard returned to total darkness.

"How far can you spit that?"

"What? This peach pit?" Arnie held up the red pit between his finger and his thumb.

"Yeah. How far?" David asked, his expression serious, as if he were making a scientific survey.

"I can spit it into that wastebasket," Arnie said, pointing to a green wastebasket on the other side of the lunchroom, at least a hundred feet away. "Easy."

"You're crazy," David said. "You'll never make it."

"No problem," Arnie insisted. "In fact, it's too easy. Tell you what. See that kid with the red hair, sort of looks like you? I'll ricochet it off that kid's head and into the wastebasket. Just to make it hard."

"No way," David said, shaking his head. "You can't spit it half that far. What do you think, Brooks?"

"What?" Cory looked up from his ham sandwich.

"Think he can do it?"

Cory shrugged his shoulders. "Sorry. I was thinking about something else." He was thinking about Anna, of course. He'd been trying to phone her for two days. No one had answered the phone.

"Arnie says he can spit the pit into the basket over there," David explained.

"So?" Cory frowned.

"So? Have you lost all interest in sports, Brooks?" David demanded. "Bad enough you've lost your sense of humor. Now you don't care about major-league athletic demonstrations?"

"Why don't you guys grow up?" Cory said wearily. He took a bite of the sandwich, but he felt too tired to chew.

"You're wrecked, man," Arnie said, rolling the peach pit around in his fingers. "What's your problem, anyway?"

"I—I haven't been getting much sleep," Cory told him.

"You been thinking about that blond girl?" Arnie said with an exaggerated leer.

"Leave him alone," David said, turning Arnie around in his chair. "Spit the pit. Five dollars says it doesn't go halfway across the room."

"You're on, man," Arnie said. "That's a bet." He tossed the peach pit into his mouth and took a deep breath.

Suddenly his eyes popped open wide. He grabbed his neck. His mouth fell open. He gasped for breath.

"Oh, no! He swallowed it! He's choking!" David screamed, leaping up from his chair and frantically pounding Arnie on the back.

Arnie's face turned bright red. He was struggling to breathe, but it was obvious that he couldn't.

"Help! Somebody help!" Cory yelled.

"Oh my God! He's choking to death!" David, horrified, went white as flour, looked as if he might faint.

"Help—somebody—"

Cory stopped screaming. He stared at Arnie. He realized that Arnie was laughing now. Arnie winked at him. He held up his hand. The peach pit was still inside it. He had never even put it into his mouth.

"Gotcha," Arnie told his two friends, grinning triumphantly. He collapsed on the table in riotous laughter. David quickly revived and joined him, laughing and pounding the table.

Cory stood up and disgustedly threw the rest of his lunch in the trash. "You guys are just sick," he muttered.

"Hey, come on, Brooks," Arnie said, "what's your problem? It's funny, and you know it."

Cory shook his head and went out the door. He wandered around the parking lot for a while. It was bitter cold and he didn't have his jacket, but he didn't notice.

He was trying to convince himself to stop thinking about Anna, to just erase her from his mind. He knew he'd feel so much better if he could just forget about her and go back to his old life.

Look at me, he thought. I'm totally wrecked. I've had no sleep. My schoolwork is suffering. My gymnastics is suffering. *I'm* suffering! And all because of a girl whose creepy brother keeps telling me she is *dead*!

He *had* to drop her, force her out of his life. He knew that's what he had to do.

But he also knew he couldn't do it.

At least not until he got some answers. About the newspaper clipping. About her brother. About why she had called him and then not shown up . . .

He heard the warning bell ring inside the building. It was almost time for fifth period. Shivering, he felt the cold for the first time and, rubbing his arms to warm them, hurried back into the building.

He and Lisa arrived at their lockers at the same time.

"How's it going?" she asked.

He tilted his hand from side to side to indicate so-so.

"I'm really sorry about Saturday," she said. "I mean, about the gymnastics match, and everything."

He searched her face to see if she was making fun of him, but she looked sincerely sorry.

"There's always another match," he muttered.

"I guess," she said. She was acting strange, he noticed. Awkward.

She wasn't teasing him or putting him down the way she had for their entire lives.

"So, how's it going with you?" he asked.

"Okay." She was having trouble with her combination lock. Finally she pulled it open and opened her locker. "Can I ask you something?" Her voice was muffled behind the locker door.

"Sure," he said. It wasn't like Lisa to be so formal. If she had something to ask, she usually just asked it.

"Uh . . . well . . . You know there's the Turnaround Dance here Saturday night. Want to go with me?" She asked it very fast, as if it were all one word. She was still hiding behind the locker door.

Cory was very surprised. He and Lisa had been friends their whole lives. But they'd never gone out on a *date*!

It was a really good idea, he decided quickly. He had to try to forget about Anna. Or at least not think about her all the time. Going out with Lisa would help him. What a good friend Lisa was. She really was there for him when he needed her.

"Sure," he said. "Great!"

Lisa peeked out from behind her locker door. She had a big smile on her face. "I'll pick you up at eight o'clock," she said. She sounded genuinely excited.

Cory smiled back at her. Lisa was certainly acting weird, as if she had a crush on him or something. He glanced past her down the fast-emptying corridor. Was that Anna watching them in the shadows two classrooms down?

Or was he just imagining that it was Anna?

"I've *got* to get her out of my mind," he told himself, feeling genuinely frightened. "Now I'm starting to see her everywhere!"

But, wait. She stepped out of the shadows. She was walking toward them. It *was* Anna.

She walked quickly between them and gave Cory a warm smile. "Hi," she said softly, her eyes revealing that she was happy to see him. She was wearing a white blouse and an old-fashioned flower-patterned jumper. Somehow she looked even more fragile than usual.

"Hi," Cory said. He took a step back. She was standing a little too close to him. He looked at Lisa, who looked very surprised.

"Hi," Lisa said, sticking out her hand to shake hands. "We haven't really met. I'm Lisa. Lisa Blume. You're in my physics class."

"Yes, I know," Anna said, shaking Lisa's hand and giving her a warm smile. "I've noticed you. You're very funny."

"Unfortunately, funny doesn't get you too far in physics," Lisa said, shaking her head. She pulled at her black curls. She seemed nervous. "When did you move to Shadyside?"

"A few weeks ago," Anna told her. "It's hard being a new girl here. It's such a big school. I used to go to Melrose upstate. We had only two hundred students. Cory's about the only new friend I've made here." She smiled at Cory. He could feel himself blushing.

"Lucky girl," Lisa said with her usual sarcasm. She gave Cory a funny look.

"How long have you two known each other?" Anna asked Lisa.

"Too long," Lisa cracked.

Cory didn't join in their laughter. He couldn't take his eyes off Anna. She was so beautiful. And it was so great having a normal conversation with her, seeing her get along so well with Lisa.

Anna suddenly looked upset. "Gee, I hope I didn't interrupt anything," she said to Lisa. "I'm sorry. I heard you ask Cory to the dance. Then I just barged in here between you two and—"

"No. Don't be silly," Lisa said. She glanced at her watch. "Oh. The bell's gonna ring. I promised I'd be early today. I've gotta run." She picked up her bookbag and slammed her locker shut. "Bye, Cory! Nice meeting you, Anna!" she shouted as she ran down the hallway.

As soon as Lisa disappeared around the corner, Anna grabbed

Cory's hand and squeezed it tightly. "Remember Friday night?" she whispered into his ear, standing on tiptoe to reach it.

Yes, he remembered Friday night. But with her standing so close to him holding his hand, he completely forgot everything else he ever knew.

"Yeah," he said. Brilliant reply, Cory. Very impressive.

She brushed his ear with her lips and whispered something else. He couldn't quite make out what it was. It sounded like "You're all mine now." But that couldn't be it.

"Hey, Anna—" he started. "We've got to talk. I've got to ask you about—"

But she covered his mouth with her hand. Then she replaced the hand with her lips and kissed him. The kiss seemed to last forever. Cory had to struggle to breathe. They were finally interrupted by someone whistling at them.

Anna pulled back. Cory looked up to see who whistled.

The bell rang.

"Bye, Cory," she whispered, giving him a conspiratorial smile, and ran off down the hall.

"No, wait—"

But she was gone. And now he was late for class. He shook his head. He knew he wouldn't hear a word that was said in any of his classes. He'd be thinking about Anna all afternoon.

"Smooth move, ace."

"Huh?"

"You heard me," Lisa said. It was three hours later. School was over for the afternoon. They had met once again at their lockers. "When Mr. Martin stood right in front of you and said, 'Cory, I don't think you've heard a word I said today,' and you said 'What?' Real smooth move."

"Get off my case," Cory snapped. "I just wasn't listening, that's all."

"Guess not." Lisa laughed. "What are you doing now? You got practice?"

"Yeah. I'm still on the team, believe it or not," Cory muttered dispiritedly.

"Well . . . uh . . . do you want to come over after dinner? Maybe study and . . ." She opened her locker and reached inside. "Hey—there's something sticky . . ."

She pulled her hand out. And then she screamed.

Her hand was covered with blood.

"Lisa—what is it?" Cory asked.

A dead cat flopped out of her locker and dropped onto her white sneakers. The locker was splattered with blood. The cat's stomach had been slit open.

Lisa pressed her head against the cool tile wall. "I don't believe this. . . . I don't believe this. . . ." She kept repeating herself, not moving from the wall.

Cory saw something tied around the dead cat's throat. It was a note written on white notebook paper.

He bent down, pulled it off, and read it to himself: "LISA—YOU'RE DEAD TOO."

CHAPTER 15

"Anna!"

"Hi, Cory. I waited for you. How was practice?"

He sighed and tossed his bookbag wearily over his shoulder. "Don't ask. I didn't make it to practice."

"Oh." She hurried to keep up with him as he headed down the walk and toward the street. It was five o'clock, and the sky was already dark. A wet wind blew in their faces, gusting around them, making it hard to walk.

But Cory needed fresh air. He needed to move, to use his muscles, to let off some energy. "I had to help Lisa clean her locker," he said. He spun around and looked into Anna's eyes. He wanted to see if she had any idea what he was talking about.

"What is she—an obsessively neat person?" Anna asked, laughing a light musical laugh. "Whoever heard of cleaning out your locker when school has just started?"

She didn't seem to know about the cat. Or else she was a really good actress.

As they cleaned up the mess, Lisa had insisted that Anna had to be the prime suspect. "She heard that we're going to the dance together. She's jealous," Lisa had said, watching the paper towels in her hand soak up the cat's dark red blood.

"Get real. I've never gone out with her," Cory had insisted.

"I saw the way she looked at you," Lisa said. "The way she stood next to you. Very possessive. She did this. I know it."

"That's just stupid." Lisa's accusations were making Cory really angry.

"Go get more paper towels," Lisa said. "Ucccch. I think I'm going to be sick. It's a good thing I hate cats."

Now, an hour and a half later, Cory was walking in the wind, explaining to Anna what had happened. "It was a dead cat. Someone had slit open its stomach," he told her. He studied Anna's reaction.

Her mouth formed a small O of horror. "No!"

"Someone tied a note around the cat's neck," Cory continued. "It said, 'You're dead too.'"

"How horrible!" Anna cried, raising her hand to her mouth. "Poor Lisa. Who would do such a disgusting thing?"

She seemed genuinely distressed. Cory felt guilty for suspecting her. He knew she hadn't done it.

"Want to go get a Coke or something?" he asked.

"No." She shook her head, her light hair tossing wildly in the strong wind. "Let's just walk. I can't believe that about Lisa. That's so horrible."

"Let's change the subject," he said, trying to brighten up.

"I heard you were the best gymnast at Shadyside last year," she said, obediently changing the subject.

"That was last year," he said quietly.

That was before *you* arrived, he thought.

"All athletes have slumps, don't they?" she asked softly, taking his arm, using him as a shield against the wind.

"Let's change the subject again," he said.

"Maybe we could talk about the Turnaround Dance," she said softly, putting her mouth right up to his ear. It sent a chill down his back.

"What about it?" he asked.

"Wouldn't you rather go with me?" Her voice got tiny and sweet, like a little child begging for candy.

"Well . . . uh . . . yeah . . . I guess."

"Great!"

"But I couldn't do that to Lisa. We've been friends too long and—"

"Oh." She frowned in disappointment, then almost immediately her face brightened again. "Oh, well. Some other time, I guess."

They turned down Park Drive, walking slowly, Anna holding on lightly to his arm, so lightly he could barely feel her touch through his down jacket. It felt great to be walking with her. She was so beautiful. Walking down the tree-lined street, the tall streetlights just coming on to brighten the gray evening, she seemed prettier, calmer, and happier than he had ever seen her.

He felt bad about interrupting this peaceful moment. But he realized he had no choice. There were too many questions he had to ask her, too many things he was eager to know.

"I was at your house again," he started. He could feel her tighten her grip on his arm, as if she expected what was about to come next, as if she expected it—and dreaded it. "Your brother . . . Brad . . . he answered the door again."

"Brad." She mouthed the word without making a sound.

Cory stopped walking and turned to face her. "He seemed very upset, Anna. He grabbed me and pulled me into the house and started to rough me up. He kept saying you were dead."

Her mouth dropped open in shock. She uttered a cry, a squeal of pain and surprise, like a small dog that's been stepped on. "No!"

She slipped off his arm and started to run down the sidewalk, her white moccasins not making a sound.

He wasn't going to let her get away this time. Flinging his bookbag to the ground, he ran after her. He caught her easily, grabbed her arms, and spun her around.

She refused to look at him. "Go away!" she cried, shoving him back. "Go away, Cory. You don't want to get involved."

"I'm already involved!" he told her, refusing to let her go. "I can't stop thinking about you!"

Those words caused her to stop struggling. She stared at him questioningly, as if she didn't believe it, as if she couldn't have heard him correctly. "I'm sorry," she said, her voice a whisper.

As darkness settled, the air grew even colder and the wind picked up. He let go of her arms. She turned and started walking back in the direction of the high school. He followed, walking a few steps behind her. "I have to know the truth," he said. "Why did your brother say that about you?"

"I don't know," she answered without looking back. "I told you he was crazy."

"Someone called me before you did last Friday night and told me not to see you because you were dead, and if I did see you, I'd be dead too. Was that your brother?"

"I don't know," she said. "I really don't know. You've *got* to believe me." She started walking faster. He had to hurry to keep up.

"But why would your brother say a thing like that?" Cory demanded. "Why would he tell people you were dead?"

She spun around, and he almost ran into her. "I don't know! I don't know! I don't know! He's crazy! I told you! He's crazy—and he's very dangerous!" she shouted, tears forming in her eyes. "I really can't talk about it. Don't you understand?"

"Who else lives with you?" Cory asked, deliberately lowering his voice. He didn't want to make her cry, didn't want her to get hysterical. The poor girl obviously had a troubled brother who was making life difficult for her.

"Just my mother," Anna answered, wiping her eyes with the backs of her hands. "But she isn't very well. It's just the three of us."

They walked on a little in silence, side by side. "Don't listen to

Brad," she said finally. "I'm here. I'm here with you. Don't listen to him. Just stay away from him. He mustn't know about . . . about us."

"Sorry for all the questions," he said softly, putting his arm around her shoulder. "I didn't mean to upset you. It's just that I didn't know what to think, and you—you called me Saturday night and then—"

"What? No, Cory. You mean Friday night."

"You called me Saturday night, too, and I came as fast as I could and—"

She turned and stopped him by putting both hands on his chest. She looked very upset. "Someone played a horrible joke on you," she said, her blue eyes burning into his. "I never called you Saturday night."

"Then who—"

"Shhhhh. It's okay," she said, putting her finger to his lips. "Let's not talk anymore." She tilted her head up. He leaned down and started to kiss her.

"No!" she cried suddenly, startling him. She pulled away. She wasn't looking at him. She was looking past him to the tall hedges that bordered the sidewalk. "I've got to go. Don't follow. He's watching me!"

She turned and ran up the street toward the high school. Cory stood helplessly watching her flee for a few seconds. Then he moved quickly to investigate the hedges. He ran around to the other side.

About a hundred yards away someone in a dark fur parka was running at full speed in the other direction along the hedge. Was it Brad?

Could be.

Anna was telling the truth.

Now her crazy brother was spying on them.

"Well, I heard the big news."

"What?" Cory looked up from the new issue of *Sports Illustrated*.

"I heard the big news," his mother repeated. She seemed annoyed that Cory didn't know what she was talking about. "I was just talking to Lisa's mother."

"Yeah?" Cory flipped through till he found the gymnastics article he was looking for. "And what's the big news?"

"About you and Lisa," Mrs. Brooks said impatiently.

"Huh?"

She walked over and stood in front of the couch, forcing him to look up from the magazine. "Am I speaking to Cory Brooks of planet Earth?" she asked.

He rolled his eyes. "Give me a break."

"Well, are you or are you not going out on a date with Lisa?"

"Oh." He suddenly remembered the Turnaround Dance. "Yeah. Yeah, I guess." What was the big deal? Why was his mom smiling like that? Why did she seem so pleased?

"I always knew it would happen," she said, crossing her arms as if hugging herself and going up on tiptoes, then quickly back down, repeating it several times. It was her own peculiar exercise. She always did it instead of standing still.

"What?"

"I always knew the time would come when you and Lisa wouldn't want to be just friends anymore."

"Mom, what planet are *you* from?" Cory asked disgustedly.

"Well, I just think it's nice that you and Lisa—"

"I've got more important things to think about," he said.

"Like what?"

Like Anna, he thought. But he didn't say anything. He just shrugged.

"Like your homework?" she asked.

"Oh. Right. I forgot." He climbed off the couch and started quickly up to his room. "Thanks for reminding me," he called down. "Thanks a bunch."

"Anytime," he heard her say from the kitchen. "Hey, your father and I are going out. So you'll have peace and quiet for studying!"

He sat down at his desk and tried to concentrate on ancient China. But his mind kept wandering. Anna's face kept drifting into his thoughts, taking him away from the fourth Ming dynasty. Again and again he saw the look of terror on her face when she realized that Brad was watching them.

Why was she so afraid of Brad? What hold did he have over her? What was he doing to her?

He realized he hadn't gotten satisfactory answers from her. In fact, he hadn't gotten *any* answers. Anna really seemed too frightened to talk about it.

He decided if he underlined the text, it might help him to concentrate. He opened his desk drawer and began to search for a yellow highlighter. The phone rang.

He stared at it, a heavy feeling forming in the pit of his stomach.

He used to look forward to the phone ringing. Now the sound filled him with dread.

It rang a second time. A third time.

He was alone in the house. He could just let it ring forever. He stared at it, his hand only inches away from the receiver.

Should he answer it or not?

CHAPTER 16

"Hello?"

"Hi, Cory."

"David? Hi." He was very relieved to hear David's voice.

"What's happening?"

"Not much. Studying. Reading stuff."

"What are you reading?"

"I'm not sure," Cory told him. They both laughed.

They talked for a while about nothing at all. It was the most relaxed conversation they had had in weeks, probably because Cory was so glad it was David on the phone.

Finally Cory asked, "What's up? Why'd you call?"

"I thought maybe you'd just like to talk," David said, suddenly sounding uncomfortable.

"Okay. So we talked," Cory said, not catching on.

"No. I mean—" David hesitated. "About why you've been so weird lately. Why you've been messing up, you know, cutting practice and stuff. I thought maybe—"

"Nothing to talk about," Cory said sharply.

"I didn't mean to interfere or anything. I just thought—" David sounded really hurt.

"I'm okay," Cory insisted. He really didn't feel like getting into it. He just didn't have the energy. "I've had other things on my mind, I guess."

"You mean the new girl?"

"Well, yeah. . . ."

"She's really rad," David said, his highest compliment. "She's . . . different."

"Yeah," Cory agreed quickly. But he really didn't want to talk about Anna with David. "Listen, I gotta get off."

"Sure you don't want to talk . . . about anything?"

"No. Thanks, David. I'm okay. Really. I'm getting my timing back, I think. I was much better at the meet on Saturday. And—"

"I guess that wasn't you who slipped off the bars a few seconds into your warm-up."

"Anyone can fall, David," Cory said, becoming annoyed. "I just lost my concentration for a second—"

"Lost your concentration! Cory, you've been in a dream world ever since you met Anna. You've been walking around like you fell off the rings and landed on your head!"

"So? What's it to you?" Cory heard himself whine, surprised at his own vehemence.

"Well, I thought I was your friend," David said, sounding as exasperated as Cory.

"Well, friends don't give friends a hard time," Cory said. "See you around, David."

"Not if I see you first," David said.

Normally they would have cracked up over that stupid old line. But this time they both just hung up.

Cory angrily paced back and forth in his room for a while. He couldn't decide whom he was angry at—himself or David. He finally decided he was upset at himself for letting David get him so annoyed.

He slammed his world history text shut. He paced a little while longer. He knew he should be studying, but he just couldn't concentrate. He leaned down on the windowsill and stared out into the night. Across the yard the light in Lisa's room was on. Cory decided to walk over and see how she was doing.

His sneakers slid over the wet grass. He knocked softly on the kitchen door, then a little harder. After a short wait she appeared in the kitchen, looking confused. "Have you got the wrong house?" she asked, smoothing her long black hair into place as she pushed open the door for him.

"I don't think so."

She made a face. "Your sneakers are wet. Look at the kitchen floor."

He looked at the wet tracks he was making on the linoleum. Then in a quick, easy motion he flipped himself up and stood on his hands. "This better?" He began crossing the floor on his hands.

She laughed loudly. "That's great!" she said, following along behind him. "You're a real chimp. Can you eat with your feet?"

He tumbled over when he reached the hallway and rolled to his feet. "Your turn," he said, gesturing to the floor.

"No way," she said, backing away. "Want a banana?"

He shook his head and plopped down on one of the overstuffed living room armchairs. He suddenly felt exhausted.

"Come in the den," she said, pulling his arm. "I don't want you on the good furniture. What are you doing here, anyway?"

"I don't know. Wrong house, I guess," he said.

She laughed again as she dragged him toward the den. He liked her laugh, he decided. It came from so deep in her throat. It was a sexy laugh. She looked cute, he thought. She was wearing faded cutoff jeans and an old Shadyside High sweatshirt with the collar ripped and frayed.

She pulled him harder, and he bumped into her. Her hair smelled of coconut. She must have shampooed it earlier. He inhaled deeply. He loved that smell.

"How's it going with you?" she asked. "Any better?"

"Better than what?" he asked, shoving some newspapers aside so he could drop down onto the black leather couch. "Better than being hit by a truck? Almost."

"That bad, huh?" she said sympathetically. She sat down beside him, her knee touching his leg.

"If I could just get my timing back on the rings." How many times had he said that lately?

"You'll get it back," she said, putting a hand comfortingly on his shoulder.

"Anna was waiting for me outside school," he said. "That was a surprise."

She removed her hand from his shoulder and sighed. "What did she want—some tips on how to do a handstand?"

He didn't notice her sarcasm. Seeing an article that interested him, he picked up the front section of the newspaper he had shoved aside. A car had spun out of control on Fear Street and crashed into a tree. The confused driver had no explanation for what had happened. The road was dry, and he had been traveling at a very slow speed.

"I love these visits of yours, Cory." Lisa's voice broke into his reading. "You tell me about Anna and then read the paper. You're a fun guy."

Cory put down the newspaper and started to apologize when the phone rang. "Who would call this late?" Lisa asked. She dived off the couch and got to the phone before it could ring a second time and wake her parents. "Hello?"

There was silence at the other end.

"Hello?" she repeated.

"You're dead too," a voice whispered in her ear. "You're dead too. You're dead too."

Just like on the note tied to the cat.

CHAPTER 17

"It was Anna who threatened me, Cory. She killed the cat. She made the threatening phone call."

"No, that's impossible," he insisted. "Come on, Lisa. Let's just dance and not talk about it." Cory pulled her toward the middle of the gym floor, where several other couples were already dancing. The floor vibrated to the music, a Phil Collins record with a driving, machinelike drumbeat and pulsating bass that nearly drowned out the singer's voice.

Lisa made a halfhearted attempt to dance with Cory, but after a minute or two she stopped and pulled him back to the side. "You're just trying to change the subject," she said, holding on to his hands. Hers were cold despite the heat of the gym.

"No, I'm just trying to dance," he said, exasperated. "Why'd you ask me to this dance? If all you wanted to do was talk about Anna, we could have gone to my house, or your house."

"But she threatened my life, and all you do is defend her."

"It wasn't Anna," Cory said. "I know it. When I told Anna about the dead cat in your locker, she was horrified. Really. She felt terrible about it."

"So. She's a good actress," Lisa said, sneering. "Good enough to fool you."

A couple of guys from the gymnastics team waved at Cory from across the gym. He waved back. He wanted to run across the floor and talk to them. Kid around with them. Have some fun. This first date with Lisa was not working out.

"Why would Anna put a dead cat in your locker? Why? Why would she call and threaten you?" Cory asked, shouting over the music, a high-voltage record by Prince that was extremely difficult to shout over. "She doesn't even know you."

"She's jealous," Lisa said. "I told you."

"Get real," Cory told her, shaking his head in disbelief. He turned and started to walk away, but she followed right behind him. "Did she ask you to this dance?"

"Maybe."

"Come on—did she? Tell the truth."

"Well . . . yes."

"And was she standing in the hall spying on us when I asked you to this dance?"

"No. She wasn't spying. She—"

"She was listening, right? She was there in the hall. She saw us together. And then afterward I got the dead cat with the note."

"That doesn't prove anything."

"Boy, are you loyal—to her!" Lisa snapped, her dark eyes filled with anger. Some kids standing nearby were staring at the two of them, startled to see what was obviously a heated argument grow even more heated.

Cory was embarrassed. "Lisa, please." He took her arm, but she pulled it away from him. "I know Anna. She wouldn't—"

"How well do you know Anna?" Lisa demanded. "How well?"

"It's got to be someone else who's trying to scare you. Someone who knows you."

"Who then? Who is it?"

"I don't know, but it isn't Anna!" Cory shouted. "Anna has her own problems. She doesn't have time to be making up problems for you."

"Oh, doesn't she?" Lisa's anger was getting the better of her. She shoved Cory hard in the chest, pushing him backward against the crepe paper streamers that lined the gym wall. "Come on and sit down. Maybe you'd like to tell me all about Anna's problems. Maybe we could spend all night discussing Anna's problems. You'd like that, wouldn't you?"

"Calm down, Lisa. Everyone's watching us."

"What *are* Anna's problems, Cory? Come on. Let's discuss them. What are her problems? Is she too thin? Is that her problem? Is she too pretty? That's it. I've guessed it, haven't I! She's too pretty, poor thing."

"Lisa—please. You're getting crazy over nothing."

"Nothing? Over nothing? Someone threatened my life. I guess that's nothing!"

"That's not what I meant, and you know it. Come on. Don't lose your temper. Let's dance or something. I apologize. Okay?"

"Apologize for what?"

"I don't know. For whatever."

She sighed and shook her head. "I should've known this wouldn't work out." The record had stopped. Her voice seemed to echo through the whole crowded gym. "You're just totally obsessed with that girl. Oh. I'm embarrassing you, aren't I, Cory?" Another record started.

"No. I mean, yes. I mean—"

"So sorry. I won't embarrass you anymore." She turned away from him and ran across the crowded dance floor. He started after her, then decided not to follow her. He watched her push her way through dancing couples until she made her way to the other side of the gym and disappeared through the double doors.

Now what?

Give her a little time to cool down and then go apologize to her? That was probably the best idea. He'd seen Lisa lose her temper hundreds of times before. She always flared up like a fire just taking hold, but her anger always faded as quickly as it came on.

Lisa was the jealous one, he decided. The idea made him smile despite the fight they had just had. She was jealous of Anna. And, of course, she had good reason to be.

Anna. For a split second he thought he saw her across the dance floor.

No, it couldn't be. He pushed her from his mind. He decided to go over to the refreshment table and get a Coke, maybe shoot the breeze with some guys for a while, and then go apologize to Lisa.

He was halfway across the gym when he heard the scream.

It was a girl's scream. A scream of terror.

The music stopped. Everyone heard it.

Cory knew at once.

It was Lisa's scream!

CHAPTER 18

Several kids were already out in the dark corridor by the time Cory got there. A single amber bulb at the far end of the hall provided the only source of light. The kids were shadows, moving and shifting in the dark as they searched for the girl who had screamed. "There's no one here!" someone yelled, his voice echoing off the tile walls.

"Then, who screamed?" someone else asked.

Cory knew who had screamed. But where was she?

"I'm down here! Can somebody help me?" Lisa's voice floated up from the stairwell.

Taking them two at a time, Cory was the first one down the stairs.

"What's going on?"

"Who is it?"

"Is someone down there?"

Voices bounced around the empty hallways.

"Lisa—are you okay?" Cory asked. She was sitting on the floor at the bottom of the stairs.

"No, I don't think so."

He helped her to her feet, but she couldn't stand on her right foot. So he eased her back to the floor.

Several kids were on the stairway now, looking down at them in the dim light. "What happened?" "It's Lisa Blume." "Is she okay?" "Did she fall?"

"I—I'm okay," Lisa called up to them. "Sorry if I scared you. You can go back into the gym now. Really. I'll be okay."

A few kids lingered on the steps. Some guys started whistling loudly, seeing how it sounded in the echoing hallways. Eventually the music started in the gym again, and everyone went back inside.

"It's my ankle," Lisa told Cory, wincing with pain as she tried to stand on it again. "It got twisted. But I think it's okay. I just have to walk it off—if I can walk. Wow, I was lucky. I could've been killed. These stairs are *hard*!"

He let her lean her weight against him as she tested the ankle. "Did you fall?" he asked.

"No. I was pushed."

"What?"

"You heard me."

"But who—"

"Ouch!" she cried, and leaned harder on his arm. "How should I know? It was so dark. I was walking past the stairway. I didn't see anyone. I thought I was alone. It was so quiet out here, it was creepy. Just the sound of the drums vibrating from the gym. I—I think I'd better sit down."

He half carried her back onto the bottom step, where she dropped down heavily, breathing hard from the pain. "Hey—this is some memorable first date, huh?" she asked.

They both laughed, more from tension than from her remark. "So go on," Cory said. "What happened?"

"I don't know. I guess someone was there the whole time. I didn't hear footsteps or anything. Of course, I wasn't paying much attention. I was just concentrating on how mad I was at you."

"Thanks a bunch," Cory said sarcastically. "I knew this had to be my fault."

"Well, of course it is," she said, pulling him down beside her and holding on to his arm. "Suddenly two hands shoved me hard from behind. I saw this guy standing there as I fell down the stairs. I guess I screamed."

"Guy? What guy?"

"He was weird-looking. I couldn't see too well in the dark. He had watery eyes and sort of a puffy face. And he had a shiny earring in one ear."

"An earring?"

Cory's heart dropped to his knees.

"Brad!" he cried.

"Brad? Who's Brad? You know him?"

"He's Anna's brother," Cory said. "He's very wild."

"But—he tried to kill me!" Lisa cried, starting to realize just what a close call she'd had. "Why would Anna's brother try to kill me?"

"I just thought of something," Cory said, jumping to his feet. "Did the door open after you fell down the stairs?"

"What do you mean?" Lisa seemed confused.

"Did the outside door open? Did the guy with the earring run out?"

"No. I—I don't think so. No. I'm sure. The door never opened."

"Well, they keep all the other doors locked at night," Cory said excitedly. "Only the door near the gym is open for the dance. That means—"

"The person who pushed me is still in the building?"

"That's right. Let's take a little look around." He lifted her up off the step. "Can you walk?"

She put her foot down on the floor and tested it. "Yes. It's a little better."

He helped her up the stairs. "We'll search the long corridor first. Then we'll double back and search the shorter one." He was whispering now.

She leaned lightly against him, staying close as they walked. Their shoes clicked against the hard floor, the only sound in the long, dark corridor. "This is silly," she whispered.

"Maybe. Maybe not," Cory whispered back, his eyes straight ahead of him. "Shhhh." He stopped and held her back. He'd heard a noise in the language lab.

Was someone hiding in there?

They crept up to the glass-paneled door, which was pulled open about a third of the way, and listened. They heard it again. A shuffling sound, like the footsteps of someone scampering to a new hiding place.

They stood listening at the door for a few seconds. "Someone's in there," Cory whispered. "I think we're about to find the guy who pushed you."

He pulled the door open the rest of the way. The two of them stepped quickly into the large room. Lisa felt along the wall until she found the light switch, and turned on the lights.

"Who's in here?" Cory called.

The sound again.

They followed it across the room. One of the windows had been left open a few inches. The sound they'd been hearing was the venetian blind blowing in the wind.

"Good work, Sherlock," Lisa cracked, shaking her head. "You've caught the venetian blind in the act!"

Cory didn't laugh. "Come on. Let's keep searching," he said, turning off the lights. "If Brad is still in the building, I want to find him."

They turned the corner near Mr. Cardoza's classroom and walked on silently, Lisa leaning a little harder on Cory as her ankle began to swell and grow more painful. The hall grew darker as they walked away from the light.

Scratchy sounds. They both gasped. Something scampered in front of them, ducking into one of the classrooms. "What was that?" Lisa asked.

"Stop pulling on my sweater so hard. You're taking all the wool off," Cory complained.

"But what was that?" Lisa whispered loudly, gripping his arm even tighter.

"A four-legged creature," he said. "Probably a rat."

"Oh," she said. "Think there are more of them?"

"Probably."

They walked to the end of the corridor, sticking close together, then headed back, opening doors and peering into the dark, silent rooms. Nothing seemed the same. In the dark the familiar classrooms looked so much larger. They became mysterious caverns filled with creaking sounds and shifting shadows.

"Cory, I think you'd better take me home," Lisa whispered, sounding very discouraged. "Look at my ankle. It's about the size of a cantaloupe. I don't think I can walk much farther."

"Sure you don't want to dance some more?" It was Cory's feeble idea of a joke. They both knew it was feeble, but they laughed anyway.

But the laughter was cut short when they heard a voice coming from Mr. Burnette's biology classroom.

A young man's voice.

Very quiet. But definitely a young man's voice.

Lisa leaned against the cool tile wall for support. They crept silently to the doorway, which was open just a crack.

Another sound. A cough.

Someone was hiding in there.

"Brad?" Lisa whispered, putting her mouth right up to Cory's ear.

"We'll soon see," Cory whispered back, his heart pounding.

He pulled open the door and stepped inside.

He flicked on the light.

A girl screamed.

She was sitting on a boy's lap. Her lipstick was smeared across her chin.

Cory recognized the boy—Gary Harwood, a senior, a guy from the wrestling team.

"Hey, Brooks—what do you think you're doing?" Gary barked, squinting at the sudden light.

"Give us a break," the girl said, frowning, her arm still around Gary's massive shoulder. "Can't we have some privacy?"

"Yeah. Get lost," Gary said menacingly.

"Sorry," Cory managed to say. He carefully turned off the lights and backed out of the room.

Lisa was already in the hall, leaning against the wall, laughing and shaking her head. Cory reached out and pulled her hair. "Not funny," he insisted.

She pulled him across the hall into the small music room. She was laughing so hard, tears rolled down her cheeks.

"Don't get hysterical on me," he said, forcing a straight face

"But it is hysterical," she said, wiping her cheeks with her open hands. "A guy from the wrestling team. That's who you pick on? He'll murder you! He cracks walnuts against his neck!" She started laughing all over again.

"It's not funny," Cory insisted. "Come on. We've got to keep searching. If the guy who pushed you is still—"

He stopped in mid-sentence. Someone had stepped into the shadows of the doorway. First Cory saw the sleeve of the black fur parka as the dark figure grabbed the doorknob. Then he saw the hood pulled up to shield the man's face.

Lisa grabbed Cory's arm. "That—that's *him*," she whispered.

The hood slid back as the man entered the room.

It was Brad.

CHAPTER 19

Brad stepped back into darkness. But they had already seen his face.

Surprisingly, he looked more frightened than they did.

He started toward them, pulling the parka hood back up over his head as if he could hide inside it. Cory and Lisa stepped back toward the tall windows. Lisa backed into a music stand, sending it toppling to the floor. The loud crash made them both cry out, startled.

Brad stopped halfway into the room.

His eyes were darting from side to side. He seemed unable to decide what to do next. He muttered something under his breath. Cory could hear only the last word: "Mistake."

Brad said it again. Again Cory could hear only "mistake."

Was Brad threatening them? Was he warning them not to come after him? They couldn't tell. They couldn't hear him.

Brad stood staring at them, his tiny black eyes wide in panic. Inside the parka his forehead was covered with large beads of perspiration. His face was bright red.

Suddenly he turned and, without saying another word, fled from the room. Cory pulled away from Lisa's frightened grip and ran after him.

But Brad slammed the door hard before Cory could get there. And then Cory and Lisa heard a loud bang.

"Hey!" Lisa yelled.

Cory tried the knob. He tried it again. Again. He tried pulling. Then pushing. He turned to her, looking very worried. "It won't turn. He must have shoved something against the door."

"Are you sure? Maybe you're pushing when you should be pulling."

"You want to try it?" Cory snapped.

She slumped down on a folding chair and gently rubbed her ankle. "No. Guess I'll take your word for it. Was that Anna's brother?"

"Yeah."

"Are we gonna call the police when we get out of here? *If* we get out of here," she added, just to show that she could still be her usual sarcastic self.

"I don't know," Cory said, trying the door again without success. "I—I think I'd like to talk to Anna first. She might be in danger. If we send the police after Brad, there's no telling what he might do to Anna."

"Let's just get out of here," Lisa said wearily.

"How are we—oh, I know. Call Harwood. He and that girl are probably still making out across the hall, right?"

Cory shrugged. He put his face against the door and yelled, "Hey—Harwood—let us out of here! *Harwood!*"

No response.

He tried again, louder. Still no reply.

"Oh, how stupid!" Lisa said. "Stop yelling. No one can hear. This is the music room. Everything is soundproof."

Cory stood staring at the doorknob for a few seconds. Then he turned, ran to the window, and pulled up the metal blinds. The room looked down on the student parking lot. It was a clear night. The rows of cars reflected the bright parking lot pole lights.

"Hey—look!" Cory yelled.

Brad was running to a small car on the edge of the lot. Cory watched him climb into the car and speed away, his tires squealing on the asphalt.

"Come on—let's get out of here," Cory said. He unlocked one of the windows and pulled it all the way open.

"But we're two stories up," Lisa protested.

Cory stuck his head out the window and leaned way out. A few seconds later he pulled it back in. "No problem," he said, grinning. "I'm a gymnast, remember?"

"Uh-oh. I don't like that smile on your face. Are you going into your Tarzan act now?"

"Yeah," he said, scratching himself and nodding his head like Tarzan's chimp.

"Well, I don't exactly feel like Jane," Lisa said, wincing in pain as she tried to put weight on her ankle.

"No problem. I'll come back for you," Cory said.

"What are you going to do?"

"There's a three-inch ledge that runs under the windows. I'm going to walk the ledge to that sycamore tree, then climb onto that extending branch, then slide down the trunk."

"Maybe we should just stay here until they open school Monday morning," Lisa said.

"Thanks for the encouragement," Cory said, looking down at the narrow granite ledge.

"We could sit back, relax, and watch my ankle swell," Lisa suggested, hobbling over to the window, taking Cory's hand and pulling him back from the window.

"No problem," Cory told her, pulling away. He lifted a leg over the window and started to ease himself out onto the ledge. "Really. No problem. I could do this blindfolded."

Lisa moved away from the window, plopped down into a chair, and put her ankle up on the attached desk. She couldn't bear to watch.

Cory had both feet on the ledge now. He was still holding on to the bottom of the window frame. He looked to his left. He had to move only ten feet or so and then he would be at the tree.

He carefully turned around so that he was facing the window. He took a sideways step. "Hey! It's slippery!"

"Oh, great!" Lisa called, rubbing her sore ankle. "Get back in here!"

"No. I'm outta here," he said, but he didn't sound quite as confident as he had a few seconds before.

He had to let go of the window frame to take a second step. That meant he was now pressing against solid brick.

Moving slowly, carefully, his palms pressed against the brick wall, he took another sideways step. Then another.

To his dismay the ledge suddenly narrowed. He had to stand on tiptoe to stay on it. But standing on tiptoe made it harder to balance.

He realized he'd been holding his breath the whole time. He exhaled and took a deep breath. He turned his head and looked back over his shoulder at the tree.

The tree seemed farther away than it had from inside the building. And as he edged closer, he realized that the branch he planned to climb on to wasn't as close to the ledge as it had originally appeared. In fact, it was at least four feet away, maybe farther.

He was just realizing that he'd never be able to reach the tree branch when his right foot slid off the slippery ledge and he started to fall.

CHAPTER 20

Using his gymnastics reflexes, Cory reached up as he started to drop and grabbed the ledge as he would a parallel bar.

He missed.

His hands slid off the wet stone ledge and he continued to drop, his body sliding straight down against the brick wall.

"Hey!" His feet hit a ledge on the first floor, and instinctively he dived forward, falling through an open window. He landed hard on his hands and knees on a wood floor.

It took him what seemed forever to catch his breath. Then he slowly got up on his knees and looked around the dark room. He recognized it immediately. He had fallen into the woodshop. "I'll have to thank whoever left that window open," he said aloud.

He stood up and stretched, and tested his body. He seemed okay except that he still had the feeling he was falling. Remembering Lisa, he hurried out of the shop and into the hallway. He could hear the drum rhythms from the music in the gym echoing down the tiled corridor. He turned and took the steps two at a time, and ran to the music room. He saw the hall monitor's desk had been jammed against the door. It was heavy, but he shoved it aside and opened the door to the music room. "That was quick," Lisa said. She was still slumping in the chair with her ankle up on the desk.

"I took a shortcut," he said.

A half hour later they were sitting on the low couch in her living room. Lisa propped her swollen ankle up on the coffee table and settled back comfortably against the cushions.

"Some adventure," Cory said dejectedly. He was thinking about Brad. And Anna. Poor Anna.

"Some first date," she said, staring straight ahead at her ankle. "I'm really sorry. I—"

"No. I'm sorry," he said.

She leaned forward suddenly and started to kiss him, a soft, tentative kiss.

The phone beside the couch rang. They both jumped back.

She picked it up quickly, pushing her hair away from her face with her free hand. "Hello?"

She heard breathing at the other end.

"Hello? Hello?"

"Who is it?" Cory asked her.

She shrugged. "Hello?"

More breathing. Harsh, rhythmic breathing. Meant to sound threatening.

"Why are you doing this to me?" Lisa cried.

The phone went dead.

Lisa tossed down the receiver. Her hands were shaking, but she looked more angry than frightened. "This has got to stop!" she cried.

Cory moved across the couch, intending to comfort her. But she pulled away from him. "We've got to call the police," Lisa said.

"I know. I know," Cory agreed. "Just let me talk to Anna first. I'll go see her first thing in the morning."

"But Brad will be there, won't he?"

"I don't care. I'm not afraid of Brad. I'll get to Anna. And I'll make Anna tell me what's going on. And I'll tell Anna that we have no choice. We have to report Brad to the police."

"Ouch!" She dropped back down to the couch and started rub-

bing her ankle. "Hey, some date. I really know how to show a guy a
good time, don't I?"

"At least it wasn't boring!" he said, forcing a laugh. He got up
and started for the door. "Sure you'll be okay?"

"Yeah. Sure. Call me right after you talk to her tomorrow, you
hear?"

"Right. Don't worry."

"Good luck tomorrow."

"Thanks," he said. "I'll need it."

CHAPTER 21

He turned the car onto Fear Street, cruised the long block, and this time pulled right up the gravel drive to the Corwin house. He had never seen the house in daylight. It looked even shabbier with a bright sun beaming down on its faded shingles and falling gutters.

His parents had wondered where he was going so early on a Sunday morning. He had told them he had a special gymnastics team workout. He didn't like lying to them, especially when it was such a feeble lie. But he couldn't very well tell them he was driving to Fear Street to find out why a girl's brother was terrorizing him and Lisa and had tried to kill Lisa.

He didn't really know what he'd do if Brad answered the door. He'd been up most of the night thinking about it but hadn't been able to come up with a plan. All night he had tried to sort out his feelings about Anna. He felt angry at himself for becoming involved with her and her brother. Yet he also felt sorry for her. And he was frightened for her. And . . . and . . . he was still terribly attracted to her, to her old-fashioned prettiness, to her teasing sexiness, to her . . . everything.

All these weeks he had spent thinking of nothing but Anna. And still, to this very moment, she was a complete mystery to him.

Well, no more.

He was about to unravel the mystery. All of the mysteries. He wasn't going to leave until his every question was answered.

He knocked loudly on the door.

No response. He waited awhile.

Ignoring the pounding in his chest and the impulse to run as far from this house as he could, he raised his fist and pounded again.

Silence.

He knocked again, harder. Then again.

He waited. There wasn't a sound inside the house, no sign that anyone was there.

More angry than disappointed, Cory turned and started back to the car.

"Morning."

It was the strange neighbor. He was leaning on the hood of Cory's car. He was wearing the same rain slicker and white tennis hat, even though it was a bright, sunny morning. Voltaire, the big Doberman, was at his side. Cory jumped back, then was relieved to see that the dog was on a leash.

"Don't ever see you much in the daytime," the man said, grinning at Cory, not exactly a friendly grin, but a more pleasant expression than Cory had ever seen on him.

"Guess not," Cory said, walking slowly to the car.

"They're not home," the man said, pointing to the house. "Left early this morning."

"Oh," Cory said. "Know where they went?"

The man seemed offended by the question. "I'm no snoop," he said curtly.

"You seem to know a lot about them," Cory said.

The man looked at him thoughtfully. "Can't help but notice some things when you're a neighbor," he said finally. "You seem like an all-right young man."

The compliment startled Cory. "Thanks."

"That's why I can't understand your comin' to visit them," he said pointedly. The dog barked. "Okay, okay, Voltaire." The man pulled himself up from Cory's car. "Be seein' you," he said, giving Cory a wave as if they were old friends, and then trotted off to keep up with his pulling dog.

"Not if I see you first," Cory said under his breath. Neither the old guy nor his dog seemed as threatening in the daytime, though. Just a snoopy neighbor out walking his dog day and night, trying to see what he can learn around the neighborhood.

Well, Cory had learned absolutely nothing. He took one last look at the old house, then dejectedly got back into the car. He had spent the whole night going over and over what he was going to say. And now there was no one to say any of it to.

He spent the afternoon trying to do some homework. He was terribly behind. He called the Corwins' house every half hour. There was no one home all day or all evening.

The next morning, feeling nervous and out-of-sorts, he drove to school early and waited by Anna's locker for her to show up. But she hadn't arrived when the bell rang, and he went to his homeroom, disappointed again.

He didn't catch up with her until after school. Then he ran into her by accident outside the biology lab.

She looked for a moment as if she didn't recognize him. Then her expression changed and she gave him a warm smile. "Cory. Hi."

"I—I've got to talk to you."

"I can't. I've got to go home and—"

He grabbed her arm. He wasn't sure why. He wasn't sure what he planned to do. He just knew he wasn't going to let her get away. "No. You're coming with me. I've got to talk to you. I'll take you home after."

She didn't resist. She could see that he was serious, that he wouldn't take no for an answer.

He led her to his car in silence, pulling her as if she were a captive, not letting go of her hand, as if she might slip away and disappear into thin air if he didn't hold on. He drove to the Division Street Mall. She played with the radio, pushing the buttons in order, listening to a station for ten seconds, then moving on to the next.

At the Pizza Oven he guided her to a booth in the back. She slid in across from him, smiling uneasily, her eyes darting nervously to the front of the long, narrow restaurant. It was quiet. Only a few booths were filled. Most of the after-school crowd hadn't arrived yet.

A waitress slouched over to them, cracking her bubble gum noisily. Cory ordered two Cokes. Then he turned to Anna and took her hand. "Tell me the truth about you, and about Brad," he said, staring into her deep blue, mysteriously opaque eyes. "I want to know what's going on. Everything."

She didn't question him. She seemed to know that she had no choice this time. And once she started talking, she seemed eager to get the story out, desperate to tell it to him, relieved to finally have someone to tell it to.

"I moved here last month with my mother and Brad," she began, looking at Cory, then shifting her gaze to the front window of the restaurant, then back to Cory. "My father left us, just disappeared several years ago. My mother is not well. She's very frail. Brad has always been the head of the family.

"About a year ago," she continued, talking rapidly in her soft voice, "something terrible happened to Brad. He was in love with a girl named Emily. Emily was killed in a plane crash. It was just awful. And Brad never recovered from the shock."

"What do you mean?" Cory asked.

"He lost his grip on reality. He just couldn't take Emily's death. For a while he imagined that Emily was still alive. We had a sister. Her name was Willa. Willa was a year older than me. She looked like me, but she was really beautiful. She was the true beauty of the family.

"After Emily died, Brad got very protective of Willa and me. He got very mixed up. He started calling Willa by the wrong name. He started calling her Emily. Soon after that he started telling people that Willa was dead—even when she was standing right there in the room!

"We didn't know what to do with Brad. He was so mixed up. We tried to get him to go to a doctor. But he refused."

"Here's the Cokes. Pay now, please," the waitress interrupted.

Cory pulled out his wallet and found two dollar bills. Anna tore the paper off the straw and greedily drank her Coke almost to the bottom without taking a breath.

"Go on. Please," Cory urged.

"The story just gets worse," she said. A single large tear formed in each eye. Her eyes look like two blue lakes, Cory thought.

"Brad kept confusing Willa and Emily. He kept saying Willa was dead. Then, one horrible day, it happened. Willa was killed. She fell down the basement stairs."

Cory groaned aloud. "How awful—"

"Brad was home at the time. He said it was an accident. Willa was carrying some clothes down to the basement, and she just slipped and fell. But Mom and I never believed him. We suspected that Brad had pushed Willa.

"First, you see, he was telling people that Willa was dead. And then—she really *was* dead!

"We were so frightened. We were terrified of Brad, of what he might do next. But we had no one else to support us. Dad left when we were little. He just took off. Mom was too sick to work and too proud to take welfare. We had no one but Brad. So what could we do? We *had* to believe his story that Willa's death was an accident."

"So then you moved to Shadyside?" Cory asked.

"No. Not yet. This was still last spring. Brad seemed better for a while. But then his mind became confused again. He started telling people that *I* was dead. I was so scared, I didn't know what to do. Was Brad going to kill me next? I was terrified every day."

"I don't believe this. I just don't believe it," Cory said, offering her his Coke since she had finished hers.

She took a long sip. "Somehow Mom got the strength to insist that we move. We moved here to Shadyside. We hoped the new surroundings would help snap Brad out of his shock, his confusion. But it hasn't helped. He keeps telling people that I'm dead. And at the same time he's terribly overprotective. He won't let me go out, or have dates, or anything. Some days he won't even let me go to school."

"So that explains it," Cory said, more to himself than to her. The dreadful details of her story were still spinning through his mind. *This poor girl is living in a nightmare,* he thought. *I've got to find a way to help her. We've got to get Brad out of the house.*

But then he remembered something.

"Hey, wait a minute," he said.

"What?" She looked as if she were dreading what he was about to say.

"I saw a newspaper clipping. From Melrose. It said that you were dead. It had a picture and everything."

"Oh." She flushed. Her hands gripped the edge of the Formica tabletop. She was thinking hard. She didn't seem to have an answer. "Oh, yes. I remember that newspaper thing now," she said, her normal color returning. "I guess I blocked it. Isn't it horrible? Can you imagine seeing your own obituary in the newspaper? Brad claimed that the newspaper got it all wrong. But I think Brad just couldn't face Willa's death, and so he told them it was me."

Cory shook his head in disbelief.

"Cory, I'm so frightened all the time," Anna said, grabbing his hand in hers. "I don't know what to think. Is Brad confusing me with Emily? Is he confusing me with Willa? Since he's telling people

I'm dead, does it mean he plans to kill me too? I'm really scared—especially now that my mother is visiting her sister. . . . Brad and I are alone. . . ."

Cory just stared back at her, at the soft tears forming along the rims of her beautiful eyes, at her golden hair. He didn't know what to say. It was such a sad and frightening story.

Suddenly she leaned across the tabletop and pulled his face close to hers. She began to kiss him, gently at first and then harder.

Then, just as suddenly, she stopped and pulled back.

Her face filled with horror.

Cory turned around in the booth to see what she was looking at. There was Brad outside the front window, his face pressed to the glass, a look of fury on his face.

"I—I've got to go," Anna said, her face filled with panic.

She leapt up from the booth and disappeared out the back door of the restaurant.

Cory turned to the front. Brad hadn't moved from the window. He was staring straight ahead at Cory, his face frozen in hatred, in rage.

CHAPTER 22

He tried to call Lisa as soon as he got home, but she was out with her family. Then, after dinner, he tried to call Anna. The phone rang and rang. He let it ring twenty times. He counted the rings.

Then, his head spinning with frightening images, images of Brad's furious face, images of Anna's fear, images of Anna falling down endless basement stairs, he hung up.

He tried five minutes later, and five minutes after that, letting the phone ring twenty times each call, but with the same results.

What if something had happened to her? What if Brad, in his rage at seeing them together in the restaurant, had done something to her?

No. He couldn't allow himself to think that.

But he had to. Brad had already killed once. Or so Anna believed. Who was to say that he couldn't kill again?

Standing with his red face pressed against the restaurant window, his eyes bugging out, his mouth twisted in fury, Brad had certainly looked like someone who could kill.

Cory picked up the phone and, ignoring his trembling hand, dialed the Corwin house again. Someone picked up on the sixth ring.

"Yeah?"

Cory recognized the harsh voice. "Brad? I know Anna's there. Put her on the phone."

"Anna isn't anywhere. Anna is dead."

The phone clicked off. Brad had hung up on him.

What did Brad mean? Was Anna really dead now? Had Brad just killed her?

No. This was just another of Brad's sick, twisted fantasies.

Or was it?

Cory realized he had no choice. He pulled on his jacket, ran down the stairs two at a time, and grabbed the car keys from the front entranceway table. "Hey—where are you going?" his mom called.

He mumbled an answer. He wasn't sure what he said. He pulled the front door closed behind him, and a few seconds later he was speeding through a thick, wet fog, driving blindly, with Anna's face his only guidepost, driving once again to Fear Street.

"Anna, be alive," he said to himself. "Please—be alive, be alive, be alive." The windshield wipers, clearing the wet fog from the glass, clicked the rhythm to his words: "Be alive, be alive, be alive . . ."

The drive seemed to take hours. Finally he pulled up the long gravel drive to the Corwin house and squealed to a stop. Not turning off the engine or the lights, he threw open the car door and ran up to the porch.

He stopped at the front door, raised his hand, and knocked—and heard a loud scream.

A scream of anger, of fury.

"He's come for me! Let me go!!"

She's alive, he thought.

And without hesitating he pushed open the heavy wooden front door and burst into the house. He found himself in a dark, narrow entranceway with a small coat closet along the wall. He inhaled the powerful smell of mothballs. Beyond the entranceway was the living room, lighted only by a small, flickering fire in the fireplace.

"Let me go!" he heard Anna scream. "He's come to see me! Me!"

His heart pounding, Cory ran into the living room. There on

the floor in front of the fireplace, Anna and Brad appeared to be locked in a desperate fight. She was sitting on his chest, struggling to remove his arms from around her waist so that she could stand up. She managed to pin his arms down, but Brad reached up a hand and pushed under her chin until her head snapped back. Then he quickly rolled out from under her and gave her a hard shove that sent her sprawling toward the fire. With a loud groan he climbed to his feet, prepared to attack again.

Cory hurtled across the room, his arms outstretched, ready to help Anna any way he could.

Hearing Cory approach, Brad turned around, startled. But he turned too late. Cory leapt onto his back. Cory drove a fist into Brad's side, and both of them fell to the floor and began wrestling to get the advantage.

"Cory! You're here!" Anna cried, recovering and moving away from the fire.

Brad swung around, trying to land a punch in Cory's midsection. But Cory scrambled away and the punch went wild.

"Get out of here!" Brad shouted, saliva dripping down his chin, his small eyes wild with rage. "You don't know what you're doing! You don't want to be here!"

"Too late!" Cory cried. He lowered his head and rammed it into Brad's chest. Brad cried out and staggered backward.

"Help me, Cory! Please—help me!" Anna was shrieking from the corner of the room. She was holding her hands over her ears as if trying to shut out a deafening sound.

But Cory and Brad were scuffling in silence now.

Brad was soft and not very powerful, but he was bigger than Cory and seemed to be more experienced at fighting. He spun Cory around and shoved him hard into the wall.

Dazed, Cory dropped to all fours and tried to shake it off. But Brad leapt quickly onto his back and began pulling his head back.

"My neck! You're going to break my neck!" Cory screamed.

But his cries made Brad pull back even harder.

"Help me, Cory. Help me!" Anna continued to scream, wedging herself tightly in the corner of the room.

Still pulling Cory's head back, Brad lifted Cory to his feet. Cory struggled to breathe. He realized he was about to go under, about to lose consciousness. The pain made it so hard to move, so hard to think.

Somehow he grabbed a vase off the table beside the couch. It was heavy and nearly slipped from his hand. But with one last burst of strength he brought the vase down hard over Brad's head.

Brad's eyes shut tightly from the pain. He uttered a short cry that faded as he dropped to the floor. Cory, gasping for air, took a step back, trying to ready himself for Brad's next onslaught. But it didn't come. Brad fell heavily onto the floor and didn't move. He was unconscious.

Before Cory could regain his balance, Anna was in his arms. She threw her arms around him, nearly knocking him over, and pressed her face against his. "Thank you," she whispered. "Thank you, thank you. I knew you would come. I knew it."

Cory's heart was pounding so hard, it felt about to explode. His chest heaved as he struggled to catch his breath. His muscles ached from the strain of the fight, and he began to feel sick to his stomach.

"I knew you would come. I knew it," Anna repeated, pressing against him.

"We—we've got to call the police," Cory said, trying to back away from her grasp, trying to calm himself, slow his breathing.

"Thank you for saving me. Thank you." Her breath was hot against his cheek.

He looked down at Brad, still sprawled unconscious on the carpet. "Anna—please. We've got to move quickly. Brad won't be out for long," Cory pleaded. He wasn't sure Anna was hearing him.

"We've got to get you away from here. We've got to make sure you're safe from him."

"Yes," she whispered. "Yes." She took his hands and started to pull him toward the stairway in the front hall. "Come with me, Cory. We're alone now. He can't bother us." She kissed his cheek, his forehead. She gave him a devilish look. "Come to my room, Cory. He can't bother us now."

"No, Anna—please. We've got to call the police," he insisted. Her eyes were wild, unreal, like big blue buttons. Her face seemed to glow with excitement. "Anna—Brad will wake up soon. We can't—"

She pulled him up the creaking, uneven stairs. "We have to celebrate, Cory. You and me. Come." A sexy, inviting smile spread across her face. Her eyes grew even wider, even more opaque.

Cory gave in. He realized he couldn't resist her. He started to follow her up the stairs.

"I want to show you something, Cory," she said as they reached the landing.

"What? What is it, Anna?"

"This," she said. The smile faded instantly from her face. Her eyes narrowed. She reached down to a low table in the narrow hallway and picked something up in her hand.

What was it?

Cory had trouble making it out in the dimly lit hallway.

She held it up. It was a silver letter opener shaped like a dagger, sharp as a dagger, too, from the looks of it.

"Anna—" Cory felt the fear well up in his chest.

"This will take care of Brad," she said. She plunged it through the air, a practice swing.

"No!" Cory yelled. "I won't let you."

"I won't let anyone stand in my way," she said. "Not even you."

She raised the letter opener above her head. She moved toward him, brandishing it like a knife. In the shadowy light her face became hard, frightening, ugly with hate.

"Put that down!" he cried, backing up, confused, not sure this was really happening. Hadn't he just saved her? Wasn't she just in his arms thanking him, inviting him up to her room? "Anna, what are you doing? Stop. We have to call the police!"

Her eyes were clear and cold. She didn't respond, didn't seem to hear him. She swung the letter opener down fast, trying to stab him in the chest.

Cory leapt backward. The blade missed him by less than an inch.

She lunged forward, raising the blade again, preparing another attack. He backed up, raising his hands to fend her off. "Anna— what are you doing? Anna—please—listen to me!"

His back, he realized, was against an open window. He had no room to move now.

She moved quickly forward, thrusting the silver blade in front of her.

He tried to move back, dodge out of the way.

She lunged at him.

He tried to jump out of the way, lost his balance, and fell back— out the open window.

CHAPTER 23

It was as if it were happening in slow motion. First he felt his feet leave the floor. Then he saw the black sky and felt the shock of the cold night air on his face.

Then he knew he was falling, falling backward, falling down, headfirst.

Instinctively, his legs bent. He caught them around the windowsill. He was a gymnast, after all, he told himself. He had skills. He just had to use them.

He had to use them. Or die.

The backs of his knees hit the windowsill. He clamped his legs tightly and held on. Then he swung himself up, using the strong stomach muscles he had developed through years of practice. He flipped himself up until his head was upright, then slid easily back into the hallway.

Anna hadn't moved. She stood in the hallway, holding the letter opener in front of her, staring blankly at the window.

Cory did a forward flip across the hallway and kicked the letter opener from her hand.

She shrieked and seemed to come out of her shock. He landed on his feet and stared at her. Her face, which had been expressionless as she stared at the window, filled with anger. With a desperate cry, a wild animal cry of attack, she lunged at him.

Dodging to the side, he grabbed her as she moved past him. He spun her around and pulled her arms behind her back.

"Let me go! Let me go!" she screamed. But she was light and weak, no match for him.

He held her arms firmly behind her back and began to move forward, pushing her to the stairs. She struggled with all of her strength, shrieking and cursing him.

He started to pull her down the stairs when he heard a sound. Looking down, he saw to his horror that Brad had revived.

Brad was coming up the stairs after him.

Cory was trapped.

CHAPTER 24

"Stay away, Brad. Stay away!" Cory heard himself shouting.

He wasn't making any sense. Why would Brad stay away?

"I warned you," Brad called up wearily. He was halfway up the stairs.

Anna struggled to free herself, but Cory held on tight. He looked back up to the open window. For a brief moment he considered dropping Anna or tossing her down at Brad, then leaping out the window.

"I tried to frighten you away," Brad said, climbing toward him slowly, deliberately. "I tried to scare you, to keep you from getting involved with her."

"Go away, Brad!" Anna screamed.

Brad took another step closer. Anna struggled. Cory tightened his grip.

"I just wanted to keep you safe from her," Brad said.

"Shut up, Brad! I'll kill you too!" Anna shrieked.

With a burst of strength she pulled out of Cory's grasp. She dived for the letter opener. But Cory caught her again and pulled her back.

Brad sat down on the top step and rubbed the back of his head. Cory suddenly realized that Brad had no intention of fighting him.

"Want to know the whole story?" Brad asked Cory. "You're not going to like it."

"Shut up, Brad! Shut up!" Anna cried.

"I've been telling you the truth. Anna is dead."

"Shut up shut up shut up!"

"She isn't Anna. She's Willa. She's Anna's sister."

Cory was so stunned, he nearly let her go.

"When Anna fell down the stairs and died, Mom and I suspected that it wasn't an accident, that Willa pushed her," Brad said, rubbing the bump on his head. "She was always insanely jealous of Anna. Anna had everything. Anna was beautiful. She had a million friends. She got straight A's without having to study hard. Willa couldn't compete in any way—and Anna never let her forget it."

"Shut up, Brad. I mean it—"

"But I couldn't prove that Willa had killed Anna. And Mom isn't well. I knew she couldn't survive losing both her daughters. So I never did anything about Willa.

"After Anna's so-called accident, Willa seemed to be okay," Brad continued, his voice soft and shaky, so soft Cory had to struggle to hear. "But I kept close watch over her. We moved here. I hoped the new surroundings would help us all forget the tragedy of losing Anna. It was a stupid thing to hope for."

"Shut up, Brad. You're stupid. You've always been stupid!" Willa shrieked, still struggling to free herself from Cory's grasp.

"Like I said, Willa actually seemed okay once we moved here," Brad told Cory, ignoring his sister's outburst. "At least, she acted perfectly normal at home. But when you started coming around, asking for Anna, I began to suspect what Willa was doing. I noticed that she started to dress like Anna. And talk like her. I tried to scare you away, Cory. I did my best to keep you from getting involved with her. I figured out that she was calling herself Anna at school, that she was trying to slip into Anna's identity."

"I'm going to kill you!" Willa shrieked, her eyes on the letter opener.

"I knew I should've gotten Willa professional help," Brad said sadly. "But we just couldn't afford it. I was foolish. I should've done something for Willa. Anything."

"I'm going to kill you too!" Willa screamed. "I'm going to kill you both!"

"I know she's been making phone calls to you and to that girl who's your friend. I know she's been making all kinds of threats, leading you on, forcing you to meet her, drawing you into her web. I guess she can't help herself."

"Wait just a minute," Cory broke in. "I have one little problem with your story, Brad. What about the other night at the dance? That wasn't Anna—I mean, Willa—who pushed Lisa down the stairs. That was you."

"I *told* you that was a mistake," Brad said heatedly. "I told you in the music room it was all a mistake. I followed Willa to the dance. I figured she was going there to make trouble for you. I wanted to stop her. I waited for her there in the hall. It was dark. I couldn't see much of anything. I thought it was Willa who was hurrying past me. I made a grab for her. I didn't really mean to push her, but she fell. Then when I got a good look at her, I realized I had grabbed the wrong girl. I watched to make sure she wasn't badly hurt. Then I panicked and hid. I didn't know what to do. I felt terrible about it. I was just trying to protect you from Willa."

"Anna went to the dance—not Willa. Willa is *dead*!" Willa broke in. "Stop calling me Willa. I'm not Willa. I'm Anna! I'm Anna! I'm Anna!" She began wailing at the top of her lungs.

Brad stood up and held out his arms. Cory handed Willa over to him. She slumped against Brad, exhausted.

"Call the police," Brad told Cory. "We've got to get her some help."

CHAPTER 25

"Cory, you've eaten half a chocolate cake!"

"Don't worry. I'll save you a slice." He cut himself another large chunk and slid it onto his plate. He'd been starving ever since he'd left the Corwins' house.

Lisa sat down close to him on the leather den couch and watched him eat. "So that's the whole story?" she asked.

He swallowed a mouthful of icing. "Yeah. That's all of it," he said, suddenly no longer feeling hungry.

"And I was right. About the dead cat and the phone calls—it was all Anna."

"No. All Willa," he corrected her. "But yeah. You were right." He frowned and put the plate on the coffee table. "Another horror story from the folks on Fear Street," he said bitterly. He felt unsteady, shaky, as if he might burst out screaming—or crying. He stared at the wall, trying to get himself together. He was experiencing so many feelings at once, he couldn't sort them out.

She put a hand gently on his shoulder. "When it comes to girlfriends, you sure know how to pick 'em," she said.

He sighed. "Yeah. Maybe from now on I should let you pick them for me."

Her hand went up to his face. She rubbed the back of her hand tenderly over his cheek. "Maybe I should," she said softly.

He turned and looked at her. "Got anyone in mind?"

Their faces were inches apart. She moved forward to fill in the inches. She kissed him, a long kiss, a sweet kiss.

"Maybe . . . ," she said.

THE SURPRISE PARTY

How easy it was. And how quick.

The rifle popped, cracked like a cheap firecracker.

Bye-bye, Evan.

Pleasant dreams.

It was so easy. And not all that unpleasant, really. Especially if you didn't think about it.

Especially if you locked the whole picture up in some remote corner of your mind—and thought instead about . . . her.

She was so bad.

How else could he describe her? He thought about her all the time. She was always invading his brain, pushing away what he was supposed to be thinking about, until sometimes he thought she might drive him out of his mind.

He would do anything, he realized, for her.

She was so bad. He wanted to crush her, crush her, crush her. He wanted her to be with him, to care only for him, to feel just the way he did.

And now she would.

He wiped the rifle handle off against his shirt and walked quickly along the path through the trees.

The woods were quiet, so quiet now.

Everything was so fresh and leafy green. Everything was so bright and cheerful.

He started to walk more quickly, his boots crunching loudly over dry twigs and weeds. He turned and took one last look at the body.

Would he get away with it?

Of course he would. . . .

CHAPTER 1

SATURDAY AFTERNOON

Meg Dalton pressed the handbrakes and skidded her bike to a stop on the dirt path. She took a deep breath and smiled. "Sure smells like spring," she said.

Sunlight filtered through the tall trees, with their fresh green leaves still unfurling. Dogwoods and cherry trees were already in bloom, blanketing Shadyside Park with splashes of white and pink.

It's so beautiful here in May. It's like riding through a fairy-tale world, Meg thought. Her friends were always putting her down for saying things like that. She decided to keep the thought to herself.

Her two companions, pedaling their bikes leisurely, caught up to her. "Hey, Meg—why'd you stop?" Tony called.

"Let's keep going to the river," Shannon said, gliding past Meg, then turning around. "Come on. I want to ride. I've got to burn off some of the extra pounds I put on this winter."

Meg stared at her friend. Shannon didn't have any extra pounds to take off. Her figure was perfect. With her coppery hair, blue eyes, and full, pouty mouth, Meg thought, Shannon looked just like that actress in the movies, Molly Ringwald.

"I've gotta get a new bike," Tony said. "There's no rubber left on the pedals."

"Ssshhhh," Meg interrupted, pointing to a bed of pink and purple wildflowers just ahead. "Look. A hummingbird."

"Are we gonna keep riding, or what?" Shannon asked impatiently. "If I knew this was going to be a nature field trip, I would've brought my notebook."

Shannon hopped back on her bike seat and pedaled away. Meg hurried to catch up to her. "Hey—wait up!" Tony called. "It's hard to pedal with no rubber on the pedals!"

They rode past a noisy softball game on the public diamond, recognizing several of their friends from Shadyside High. In the sloping, grassy field beyond the diamond, people were sunning themselves, throwing Frisbees, and having picnics.

It's like everyone has burst out of their cocoons and come out ready for fun, Meg thought. She knew her friends would put her down for that thought, too.

Everyone was always teasing Meg for being too gung ho, too enthusiastic, too bright and chirpy. She was short and, to her constant regret, still hadn't developed much of a figure. And with her round face, short blond hair, and big blue eyes, she was sometimes mistaken for a kid, which drove her bananas!

A baby squirrel scampered across the path, and Meg had to swerve to miss it. "That could've been five points!" Tony called from several yards behind.

"Not funny, Tony," Meg called back. She pedaled harder and caught up to Shannon.

"Tony seems to be in a good mood," Shannon said, her eyes straight ahead on the path.

"He's done nothing but complain about his bike the whole afternoon," Meg said with a sigh.

"But for *him*, that's being in a good mood!" Shannon cracked.

Meg forced a laugh. She realized that Shannon was right about Tony. He had been so moody all winter. He was always losing his temper and getting angry for the tiniest reasons, or for no reason at all.

At first Meg thought maybe it was her fault. Maybe Tony was getting tired of her. They had been going together for more than two years. Maybe he was angry because he wanted to dump her and didn't know how. But every time she mentioned it, he got a hurt look on his face and swore that nothing was wrong.

The ground grew soft as the path began to lower itself toward the river. They had to pedal around deep puddles of rain water.

"And how are you and Dwayne getting along?" Meg teased. It was the only thing she could ever think of to tease Shannon about.

"That creep!" Shannon shouted, breathing hard from her rapid pedaling. "He follows me around like a sick puppy, with those dark, mournful eyes. Ugh. He's always flexing his muscles in those tight white T-shirts he wears, you know, showing off."

"Well, he works out all the time. He's really got a great bod," Meg said.

Shannon looked surprised. That was such an un-Meg thing to say. "Well, he's still a creep. He's always hanging out with your cousin Brian, playing *Wizards and Dungeons* in the woods. Oh—" Shannon suddenly realized what she had said. "I didn't mean to say that your cousin is a creep. I—"

"That's okay. Brian is definitely a little weird," Meg said, laughing.

There didn't seem to be any more to say. They rode on for a long while in silence. Meg felt a sudden chill, more from her thoughts than from the wind. It was exactly a year ago, she realized. Exactly a year ago that Brian had found Shannon's brother Evan.

Exactly a year ago on a spring day just like this one that Brian had found Evan—shot to death in the Fear Street woods.

Meg shook her head as if to shake away the memory.

At least Shannon can laugh now, Meg found herself thinking.

At least she can crack jokes again and go biking in the park with her old friends.

What a long winter.

Meg slowed down and let Tony catch up. "How's it goin', slow-poke?"

"I think my chain's slipping," he grumbled. He pulled off the maroon sweatshirt he'd been wearing, revealing a gray T-shirt underneath, and tied the sweatshirt around his waist. Despite the cool winds off the river, he was sweating. "I've gotta get a new bike," he said, climbing off and bending down to inspect the chain.

She loved the way he looked when he studied something closely, the way his dark eyebrows lowered and his forehead wrinkled, his frown of concentration. "You'll be working for your dad as soon as school's out," Meg said. "You'll be able to save up for a new bike."

"Yeah, sure," he muttered, wiping his grease-covered hand on his jeans. "With what the old man's paying me to pump gas, maybe I can afford a pogo stick." He climbed back on the bike and started to pedal away.

She followed along the curving path. Beyond a long field of tall grass and reeds, the narrow, brown Conononka River flowed quickly but silently, high on its banks, since there had been a lot of snow that winter. Meg was surprised to see Shannon down by the river at the end of the bike path, talking to two other kids on bikes.

As she rode closer, Meg recognized Lisa Blume and Cory Brooks. Lisa and Cory had become something of a joke around Shadyside High. They had grown up next door to each other and were lifelong friends. The previous winter they had started dating—and ever since, they hadn't been able to get along at all!

Tony and Meg rode up to meet them. "We were just heading back," Cory said. "It's cold down here."

"What are you two doing tonight?" Shannon asked Lisa.

"I don't know. Cory didn't make any plans," Lisa said with the wry half-sneer that often crossed her face. "I don't think he remembered we had a date."

"I thought we'd just hang out or something," Cory said uncomfortably. He started to put his arm around Lisa, but she stepped away.

"Tony and I aren't going out," Meg said. "I've got to stay home and work on my final report for psych. I am so far behind with it, I—"

"Oh—I almost forgot my big news!" Lisa interrupted. "Guess who's coming back to town for a visit? Ellen Majors."

Shannon gasped and grabbed for the handlebars of her bike as it started to fall. "Sorry," she said quickly. "The bike just slipped." She suddenly looked very pale.

"Ellen's going to be staying at her aunt's," Lisa added.

No one said anything.

Meg knew they were all thinking the same thoughts, all thinking of a year ago, all thinking of Shannon's brother Evan.

Ellen Majors and Evan had gone together since junior high. Ellen, Meg, and Shannon had been inseparable best friends for even longer.

Then when Evan died, it all fell apart.

Ellen moved away a few months later. No one had heard from her since. Until now.

"It will be great to see her," Meg said brightly, breaking the silence. "It's been so long."

"Yeah," Lisa added, trying to copy Meg's enthusiasm but not quite pulling it off. She and Ellen had never been that close.

Shannon didn't say anything. She was staring at the river, a distant look in her eyes.

"Maybe we should have a party for Ellen," Meg said. She looked at Tony, who looked away.

"Yeah," Lisa repeated.

"Why?" Shannon asked sharply.

"To . . . uh . . . welcome her back," Meg said, surprised by Shannon's hostility to the idea. "To show her that we still care about her, I guess."

"Evan's still dead," Shannon muttered, not looking at them.

"But we've got to show Ellen that we don't blame her," Meg said, surprised at all the strong feelings she suddenly had. She hadn't realized how much she had missed Ellen all year.

"I guess. . . ." Shannon said unconvincingly, her voice barely audible over the gusting wind.

"I think a party's a great idea," Lisa said, climbing back on her bike. "A surprise party maybe. You know Ellen. She probably wouldn't come if she knew about it in advance. I'll help you two get it together. In fact, I'll start telling everyone about it right away!"

"Count me in," Cory said.

Meg looked back at Tony. He was staring at the ground. "Tony—are you okay?"

"Yeah. Sure."

"Well, what do you think of the party idea?"

"Good. It's okay."

"We've gotta get going," Lisa said, starting up the path. "See you later."

Meg, Shannon, and Tony stood watching them ride off till they disappeared into the trees. "Guess we should be getting back, too," Shannon said. The color still hadn't returned to her face. She looked washed out, drained.

"I don't believe it!" Tony screamed.

Both girls were startled. "Tony—what??"

"I've got a flat tire!" He lifted the bike up into the air with both hands.

"Tony, don't—" Meg said.

He started to slam the bike to the ground, then thought better of it, and lowered it slowly to the grass.

"Tony, it's just a flat. You can walk it back to—"

"Just go on without me," he muttered. "Go on ahead. See you later."

Seeing that he meant it, the two girls got on their bikes and rode off. When they reached the trees, they could hear him kicking the bike, cursing it loudly.

"What's his problem? Too much raw meat for breakfast?" Shannon asked.

"I don't know," Meg said with a sigh. "Sometimes he just loses it." She wished she did know what his problem was. It wasn't normal to get that angry at a bike—was it?

That night up in her room, Meg was trying to concentrate on her psych paper, but she found her thoughts drifting to Ellen. Ellen with her tall, lanky, blond good looks. She looks so much like Daryl Hannah, everyone always said. Meg wondered if Ellen still looked the same or if she had changed.

A surprise party was a terrific idea. Meg could already see the shocked look on Ellen's face. How happy they all would be again.

The phone rang.

She picked it up, grateful for the interruption.

"Hello, Meg?" A whisper. Like wind blowing into the telephone.

"Who is this?" she asked, a funny feeling forming in the pit of her stomach. "We have a bad connection."

"This is a friend." Still just a whisper.

Who could it be?

"I'm warning you. Don't have a party for Ellen."

"Now, wait a minute—" Meg cried, surprised by her own high-pitched voice, by the fear rising within her. And the anger.

"I'm serious. Dead serious. Don't have a party for Ellen. Don't force me to show you how serious I am."

"Who is this? What kind of a stupid joke—"

She heard a click. The dial tone returned.

She dropped the receiver back onto the phone. The room was silent now. But the whispered voice remained, repeating its threatening message in her ear, the whispers growing louder and louder until she held her ears and forced them to stop.

CHAPTER 2

SATURDAY NIGHT

Meg sat at her desk, staring at the phone until it became a white blur. How did she feel?

Scared? No.

Angry? Yes, that was it. Angry and insulted.

Did the caller really think he could frighten her with that stupid, hoarse whispering?

Whoever it was had seen too many bad horror movies, she decided. *Halloween V! Freddy Returns! Friday the 13th, Part 400!* How dumb. Girls in those films were either traitors or frightened idiots. They'd get one scary, whispered phone call and fall to pieces, frightened out of their wits.

Well, this was real life, not a dumb movie. And whoever it was certainly didn't know Meg very well. Maybe she was small and young looking. Maybe she wasn't as sophisticated as a lot of kids at Shadyside. But she wasn't easily pushed around. She had a stubborn streak a mile long. At least that's what her mother always said. And Meg took that as a compliment.

She realized that her heart was pounding. Okay, she admitted to herself, maybe I am a little upset.

She picked up the receiver and pushed Tony's number. The line was busy.

That was annoying. Who could he be talking to?

She wanted to talk to someone. Her parents? No. They'd make too big a deal about it. They'd probably call the police right away, make a big fuss, forbid her to have the party.

And the call was probably just an obnoxious joke some kid from school had decided to play.

She pushed Tony's number again. Still busy.

She hung up and tried Lisa's number. Lisa picked it up after the first ring, and said, "Where are you?"

"Huh?"

"Cory?"

"No. It's Meg."

"Oh. Meg. I'm sorry. I thought it was Cory. He's a little late. Like an hour."

"Sorry," Meg said.

"It's not your fault," Lisa said quickly. She sounded really angry. "I'm trying to look on the bright side. Maybe he was run over by a truck."

"Right. Keep it light." Meg laughed.

"What are you doing? Waiting for Tony?"

"No. We're not going out tonight. I'm supposed to be writing my psych paper."

"But . . ."

"How'd you know there was a *but*?"

"I'm a mind reader," Lisa cracked.

"But I—"

"See? I told you."

"I just got this creepy phone call."

"Really?" Lisa started to sound interested. "Was it a breather? I got a breather once. I couldn't believe it. It was so gross."

"No. This was a whisperer." Meg was beginning to regret telling Lisa about the call. Lisa would only make endless jokes about it. She had such a dry sense of humor. She never took anything seriously.

"What did he whisper?" Lisa asked. "Sweet nothings?"

"No. He told me not to have a party for Ellen."

"He what!?"

"You heard me. He warned me not to have a party."

"Well . . . who do we know who hates parties?"

"I don't know. I couldn't recognize the voice. It was such a strange, hoarse whisper. I really couldn't even tell if it was a boy or a girl."

"I'll bet it was Cory," Lisa said. "He'll do anything to keep from getting over to my house on time."

That was supposed to be funny, but Meg didn't laugh. She felt annoyed that Lisa wasn't taking it more seriously. "It was kinda scary," she told Lisa. "How many kids have you told about Ellen and the party?"

"A lot," Lisa said. "After I ran into you in the park, I went to the mall. I ran into a lot of kids from school. And then I called some kids tonight while I was sitting around waiting for you-know-who. Hey! There's the bell! That's probably him. Gotta run. Later, Meg." She hung up before Meg could say goodbye.

Meg found herself smiling. Lisa complained nonstop about Cory and was constantly putting him down. But when the bell rang, she went running. She really was crazy about him.

Without realizing it, Meg had pushed Tony's number again. This time it rang through. "Hello?"

"Hi, Tony. It's me."

"Oh. Hi." He sounded strange, sort of far away, confused.

"I just got the creepiest phone call. Someone warned me not to have a party for Ellen."

"Me too!" Tony exclaimed.

"What?"

"Yeah. I just got a call. Someone whispering. I think it was a guy. But I couldn't tell. It could have been a girl."

"And what did they say?"

"Not to help out with the party. He said I wouldn't make it to the party if it did take place. I'd be in the hospital."

"Someone's playing a stupid joke—right?"

"I don't know, Meg. Whoever it was sounded pretty serious."

"Oh, come on, Tony. You think he meant it?" Meg was now suddenly disappointed that Tony was taking this seriously. She wanted him to tell her that it was just a joke, that she should just forget about it. Why did he sound more frightened than she did?

"Who do you think it was, Meg?"

"I don't know. Some kid from school. Someone who's bummed out because he doesn't have a date tonight."

"Maybe." Tony didn't sound convinced. "But we don't know anyone who would do anything that dumb. What if—what if—"

"What, Tony?" Meg asked impatiently.

"I don't know. Maybe we should take it seriously. You know, call the police or something."

"What? Get real!" Meg cried angrily. "I wouldn't—"

"I'm just worried about you. That's all," he broke in. "I don't want some creep doing something horrible to you because of a stupid party."

"It isn't a stupid party," Meg insisted. "It's a party for Ellen. My best friend. And I'm not going to let one gross phone call that's probably just some moron's idea of a funny joke stop me from doing what I want to do."

After a long silence Tony agreed. "Yeah. You're right. I guess I just got a little shook."

"Sorry. I didn't mean to yell," Meg said, forcing her voice down, trying to calm herself and speak softly.

"So . . . should I come over and . . . uh . . . comfort you a little?" Tony asked. It sounded more like pleading than asking.

Meg laughed. "No. I shouldn't even be talking to you. I should be writing my psych paper."

"Was that a *yes?*"

"No. It was definitely a *no.*"

"But you mean *yes*, right?"

Meg laughed. It was nice to hear Tony teasing her again, kidding around. "I mean no. Really."

"You mean you need a little comforting, right?"

"No. Give me a break. I need a little writing time. I—"

"You know you won't be able to concentrate on your paper."

"Yes, I will."

"You said yes! I heard you!"

Meg laughed. "I said no."

"But you meant yes?"

"Well . . . maybe."

"Maybe? I'll take a maybe," Tony said happily. "I'll be right over."

"Okay," Meg said, just as happily.

CHAPTER 3

MONDAY AFTERNOON

Meg propped her Government text in front of her on the table and looked around the study hall. What was all that noise in the back of the room? She quickly saw that it was just Cory Brooks and his friend David Metcalf from the gymnastics team clowning around on a tabletop.

The study hall was a wide, windowless rectangular room kept blindingly bright by long rows of fluorescent lights suspended high over wooden tables that stretched nearly the width of the room. A small desk stood at the front for the study hall monitor. The desk was empty now, Meg saw. Mrs. Frankel was always late, which gave Cory and David time to do their act on the tabletop.

"Hi," Shannon said, giving Meg a weary wave and taking her usual seat in the row behind her.

"Hi," Meg echoed, searching her bookbag for the invitations she had bought.

"Foster doesn't realize school's almost out," Shannon complained. "He started a whole new unit this morning."

"Bad break," Meg muttered. She didn't really know what Shannon was talking about. She just knew that Shannon hated Mr. Foster, hated school, and hated work of any kind. Shannon never failed to come into study hall without one complaint or another.

"What do you think of these?" Meg asked, holding up the package of invitations. They were Day-Glo green and pink with the words COME TO A SURPRISE PARTY in silvery ink.

"What are they?" Shannon asked, deftly applying dark red lipstick to her pouty lips.

"Invitations. To Ellen's party. Is that a new color?"

"Yeah. I saw it in a magazine. What do you think?"

"Very . . . uh . . . dramatic."

"Meg, are you sure this party is a good idea?" She dropped the lipstick tube into her bag and rummaged around for a tissue.

"I don't know. I think so. I just think it would be nice to show Ellen we still care. The three of us were best friends for a long time, after all. And Ellen went with Evan for so long, she was practically part of your family."

Meg immediately regretted saying that. Shannon gave her a bitter look. She blotted her lips with the tissue and didn't say anything. Finally, after Meg had turned back to the front, Shannon said, "How can you send out invitations when you don't know where the party will be?"

"I had a great idea about that," Meg said. "You know, my dad's company did the reconstruction on the old Halsey Manor House. He said we could have it for free if we promised to do a perfect cleanup job."

"That old house in the Fear Street woods?" Shannon cried, surprised. "Yuck. It's creepy back there. Why would you want to—"

"The house has been completely restored. It's like new inside. It's a great place for parties now. And think how nice it'll be not to have any adults around to bug us."

Shannon agreed that the no-adults part was good. But she started to protest about having the party on Fear Street, when Mrs. Frankel showed up and started shouting for everyone to get quiet and start studying.

Meg turned to the front of the room and opened the package of invitations. She started to fill in the first one. All of this talk about Ellen was bringing back a flood of memories. She had a lot of good memories of Ellen. She could remember dozens of exciting and happy times they had spent together since they had met in elementary school.

But now when she thought about Ellen, her mind was drawn to the tragedy of the year before. Ellen and Evan had seemed so much in love. And then, in an instant, Evan was dead. And everything was changed.

Sure, Evan could be crazy sometimes. Sure, he was headstrong and impulsive, always getting himself into one kind of trouble or another. But he could be so lovable, too, so full of fun . . . so full of life.

For a long time it was impossible for any of them to accept the fact that he was dead.

It still was impossible.

Meg looked around the large room. Just about everyone who was involved in the tragic accident, just about everyone who had been involved with Evan, was in this study hall.

Her eyes roamed from face to face. There was Shannon, Evan's sister. She seemed to lose some of *her* life when Evan lost his. She had always been so enthusiastic about everything, so spirited, so ready to have fan. Evan's death had caused her to withdraw. She didn't seem to need her friends as much. It was as if she were pulling into herself, hardening herself, forcing herself not to need anyone else so that she couldn't be hurt by another loss in the same way.

Tony sat near the back, writing intently in a notebook. He and Evan had been buddies. Tony had admired Evan, looked up to him, Meg realized, for his wildness, for the fact that Evan didn't care what people thought of him, for his need to do what he felt like when he felt like it. Tony wished he could be that way. But he was too hung up to be that free and easy, too worried about being poor in a school where most kids were better off, too concerned about being accepted by other kids.

Tony had tried to act tough when he learned that Evan was dead. But at the funeral he broke down and sobbed. Ever since he'd been so moody.

On the other side of the room sat her cousin Brian. With his wavy blond hair, blue eyes, and dimpled grin, Brian looked like an innocent kid. But Meg knew that Brian wasn't as happy-go-lucky as he looked. He was a strange guy who kept mostly to himself.

Right now he wasn't studying. He was reading a copy of *Dragon* magazine. He spent most of his time playing that game *Wizards & Dungeons,* hanging out with his friend Dwayne, talking about Fourth-Level Warriors and dragons and stuff Meg wasn't the least bit interested in.

Brian and Evan hadn't been friends. But Brian had been in the Fear Street woods that awful day. Brian heard the shot and came running. Brian told everyone that he found Evan lying dead on the ground, Ellen sitting beside him, crying, unable to talk, unable to say a word, unable to explain.

What had Brian been doing alone in the Fear Street woods? No one knew. But Brian had changed, too, because of Evan's death. Afterward, he seemed to become even more involved in the strange fantasy games he played. His grades, which had been excellent, began to slip. His parents, Meg's aunt and uncle, were very worried. But they felt helpless. They didn't know what to do about Brian.

One death, Meg thought. One boy dies in the woods, and so many lives are affected.

She didn't know whom to feel more sorry for. Maybe Ellen. Poor Ellen. Ellen probably felt the most guilty. If only she had been able to stop Evan from going into the Fear Street woods.

The story went that he was going to spend the night there on a dare. Who had dared him? He wouldn't tell Ellen. "I just need some excitement," he told her. He grabbed his father's hunting rifle—just in case—and hurried off to Fear Street. Ellen begged him to leave the rifle home. But he refused.

She went home, but she was too worried to stay there. She went to Fear Street and tried to find him in the woods. She heard a shot, the fatal shot, the shot that changed all of their lives. She heard it and followed the sound of it till she found Evan, lying face down, his left shoe tangled in an upraised tree root.

He was already dead. His foot must have tangled in the root. He must have tripped and fallen, and the gun went off. And that was it.

A few minutes later Brian arrived and found them. Nearly in shock himself, Brian managed to help Ellen out of the woods, away from Fear Street.

A tragic accident. Ellen had never been able to talk about it with anyone. A few months later her family moved away. No one had heard from her—until now.

Maybe we can all be good friends again, Meg thought, with her usual optimism.

"Meg! Meg Dalton! Meg!" A voice broke into her thoughts.

She looked up. Mrs. Frankel was calling her. "Meg, you must be reading a very exciting chapter. I've been calling you for five minutes."

Meg could feel her face growing hot. She knew she was blushing. "Sorry."

"There's a message for you at the office. Come up and get a pass."

Meg left the invitations on the table and, still blushing, went up to get the pass. Who had left her a message? Was it from home? Was someone sick or something?

She grabbed the pass off the desk and started to jog down the hall. "Hi, Meg. What's happening? Did you hear about Gary breaking up with Krista?" It was Lisa sitting in the hall monitor's chair.

"Sorry, Lisa. I'll call you later," Meg said. "I'm kinda in a hurry." Lisa looked surprised that she didn't want to stop for some hot gossip, but Meg kept hurrying on to the office.

When she got inside, out of breath, a nervous feeling in the pit of her stomach, there was no one at the front desk. "Anyone here?" she called. No reply. Finally Miss Markins, the office secretary, appeared from the inner office. She looked surprised to see Meg.

"They told me there was a message here for me," Meg said.

Miss Markins pursed her lips and shook her head. She looked through a stack of pink message slips on her desk. "No. None for you, Meg."

"Are you sure?" Meg insisted. "They just told me in study hall."

Miss Markins looked annoyed that Meg hadn't taken her word, but she grudgingly looked through the messages one more time. "Sorry. Must be a mix-up."

"A mix-up. Yeah. I guess so. Thanks," Meg said. She turned and walked slowly out of the office. In a way she was relieved. A message in the office was seldom good news. But why had someone called her to the office if there was no message there for her?

She stopped and chatted with Lisa for several minutes. There was no point in hurrying back to study hall. She wasn't going to get any studying done. That was obvious. And she could work on the invitations after school.

"What are you doing after school?" she asked Lisa. "Want to come over and help me write invitations?"

"I can't," Lisa said, flipping a pencil up toward the ceiling and catching it. "I have a *Spectator* meeting. We're planning our last issue. I know everyone's waiting breathlessly for it, right?" Lisa was assistant editor of the school paper.

"But I'd love to help out with the party," Lisa added quickly. "Ellen and I weren't really close or anything, but I always liked her."

They talked for a few more minutes. Then Meg headed back to

study hall. Lisa's so funny, Meg thought. She has such a sharp sense of humor. Meg liked Lisa's sophisticated looks too. I wish I could be more like her, she thought, instead of such a babyface.

She tossed the hall pass back onto Mrs. Frankel's desk. Mrs. Frankel didn't even look up. Her head was buried in the test papers she was grading. Meg took her seat. She looked around the room for a moment, glanced at her watch, and then looked down at the table.

Oh!

The party invitations.

Someone had cut them all into tiny pieces.

Who would do such a horrible thing?

Meg spun around and faced Shannon. Shannon didn't look up from her book.

"Hey—"

Shannon finally noticed Meg. She closed the book, keeping her place with her finger.

"Did you see anyone come over to my desk?"

"No," Shannon whispered, her eyes on Mrs. Frankel at the front of the room. "I wasn't here. I went to the library to get this book. I just got back a second ago."

Meg stared hard at Shannon. She felt guilty for suspecting her friend. Shannon wasn't happy about having the party for Ellen, but she would never do something like this—would she?

She started to show Shannon the cut-up invitations, then she thought about the whispered phone call she had gotten on Saturday night.

Was the creep who made that call right in the same study hall with her now? Was it Shannon?

No. Of course not. How stupid.

But then, who was it?

She gathered up the pieces of the invitations and began to sweep them into her bag. Then she searched in her bag for a pen. There was ten minutes left to study hall. She could start making a list of all the things she needed to buy for the party.

Someone yawned loudly near the back door, and everyone laughed. Meg found a pen and opened her notebook to a clean sheet of paper. *Things to Buy*, she wrote up at the top.

"Meg, please come up here," Mrs. Frankel called.

Now what?

She closed the notebook and hurried up to Mrs. Frankel's desk. "You seem to have another message at the office," Mrs. Frankel said, looking perturbed.

"Are you sure?" Meg asked.

"I'm not sure about anything around here," Mrs. Frankel said dryly. "But you'd better go check."

Meg hurried back down the hall, passing Lisa with a shrug, as if to say, I don't know what I'm doing back here again, either.

Maybe Miss Markins found the first message, Meg thought. And yes, when she got to the office, Miss Markins had a long, white envelope for her. "I guess someone left this for you," Miss Markins said. "I just found it on the counter. I didn't see who left it."

Meg thanked her and took the envelope out into the hall to open. It was sealed tightly and took her a while to tear open. She put out a piece of lined, white notebook paper and unfolded it.

The words on the paper were written in sloppy block letters with a red crayon. She read them three times.

MEG, I'M WATCHING YOU. DON'T HAVE THE PARTY. I DON'T WANT TO HURT YOU—BUT I WILL.

CHAPTER 4

LATER, MONDAY AFTERNOON

"Hey, Shannon—wait up! I want to talk to you!"

Shannon turned around in the crowded hallway, swinging her bulging backpack over her shoulder. "Can't. I'm late. I have a dentist appointment."

Meg pushed through a laughing group of kids and hurried to catch up to her. The bell had rung before Meg could get back to the study hall. She looked for Tony. She wanted to show him the threatening note. But she didn't see him in the room or in the hall.

"Shannon—wait up!"

"I can't. Really. Call me tonight, okay?" Shannon turned and disappeared around the corner.

"Hey—you see Shannon?" It was Dwayne Colligan. He towered over Meg. All she could see was his blue T-shirt stretched tightly across his muscular chest.

He's so big, he doesn't look like a teenager, Meg thought. Maybe he was held back five or six times. All of the hours he should have been studying and doing homework, he must have been working out.

"You just missed her," she said coldly. She didn't like Dwayne, and she didn't like the idea of Dwayne and Shannon. He wasn't good enough for her. He wasn't good enough for her dog. She was glad that

Shannon agreed. Meg didn't even like Dwayne hanging out with her cousin Brian, but there was nothing she could do about that.

"If you see her, tell her I've got something for her!" Dwayne shouted over the noise of the corridor.

"What?" Meg asked.

He gave her an exaggerated wink and a big, dirty smile in reply, and trotted off, laughing as if he'd just made the best joke in the world.

Ugh, Meg thought. He's so gross. Shannon is going to have to tell him to get lost, once and for all.

She walked back to the study hall to collect her things, then headed up to her locker on the second floor. "Hey, Tony—hi!" He was standing at his locker, leaning against the wall with one hand, reading a piece of paper in his other hand.

When he looked up, she saw that his face was troubled. "Oh, hi, Meg." He looked back down at the paper.

She dropped her backpack on the floor and grabbed the paper out of his hand. It was another note with big block letters scrawled in red crayon. "You got one too?" As she read his, she bent down and pulled hers out of the bookbag to show him.

His read: TONY—DON'T LET THE PARTY TAKE PLACE—OR YOU'RE DEAD MEAT. A FRIEND.

"I found it in my locker," Tony said, reading her note quickly and handing it back to her. He seemed quite shaken. "Who could have done it? It's someone who knows us both, who knows where our lockers are, who knows where we are."

"I don't know," Meg said, shaking her head, re-reading his note. "I haven't a clue."

"Still think it's just a joke?" he asked. He took the note from her hands and crumpled it up into a ball.

"No. I guess not. But who would want to stop this party? Why would someone be so desperate to stop it that they'd do *this*?"

Tony shrugged. He took a maroon sweatshirt from his locker and pulled it over his head. "We don't know how desperate they really are," he said, straightening his hair with both hands.

"What do you mean?"

"I mean, how far will they go to stop us? Will they really hurt us?"

She stared into Tony's eyes and caught the fear inside. "That's ridiculous," she said softly. But now she wasn't so sure. She hadn't been at all frightened. She only felt anger that someone would be pulling something like this. But seeing the fear on Tony's face made her a little afraid, too.

"I really don't want to find out how desperate they are," he said, looking away to evade her staring eyes.

"What do you mean?"

"I think we should forget about the party. We can see Ellen and have a good time without throwing a big surprise party with a hundred kids—can't we?"

"That's not the point," Meg said sharply. "We can't let this creep—whoever it is—push us around. If we want to throw a party, we're going to throw a party. It's a free country, right?"

"But someone really doesn't want us to throw that party," Tony said. He picked up the balled-up note and started tossing it from hand to hand.

"I don't care," Meg said. "I don't care!" She could feel her anger rising. "We're having that party. And we're going to find out who's trying to frighten us—and get them to stop!"

"Meg, please—" He grabbed her shoulder, hard at first, then loosened his grip. "Think about this. Think about it carefully. We both should think about it before we decide what to do."

"No. I've already decided," she said stubbornly. She pulled away from him. She realized that she was annoyed that Tony would give in, would back down so easily. Was he frightened for her, or for himself? she wondered.

He was just frightened.

She had another thought. What about Shannon? Had Shannon received any threatening phone calls or notes?

No.

She surely would have mentioned them.

Shannon was as much behind the party as Meg and Tony, wasn't she? Why wasn't she being threatened too?

"Someone cut up my invitations," she told Tony.

"Huh?"

"I had them in study hall. I was called to the office, and when I got back they'd been cut into tiny pieces."

"Wasn't Shannon sitting right behind you?"

"Yes. But she said she went out. To the library. She didn't see who did it."

"Funny," he said, thinking hard. "I didn't see her leave the room."

"You didn't?"

"No. I was there the whole time. I'm sure she was too."

"Well, that's weird." She leaned back against the lockers. "Tony, you don't think Shannon—"

"I don't know. She didn't really want the party at first, did she? But I don't think she'd—"

"No. Of course not. She's my best friend."

She picked up her note and read it again. Did the big block letters look as if they could have been made by a girl? Hmm . . . maybe. It was hard to say.

Meg felt a chill slide down her spine. She suddenly had the feeling that she and Tony were being watched. She looked up from the note.

Yes. Someone was staring at them from across the hall.

It was her cousin Brian. And he had the eeriest look on his face. How long had he been watching them? Why was he just standing there, staring like that?

"Brian?" she called.

He looked startled, as if he hadn't planned on being seen.

Tony took a few steps toward him.

Brian turned and ran.

CHAPTER 5

MONDAY NIGHT

"Meg, what are you doing up there?"

"Homework, Mom!" Meg shouted. "If I don't finish this psych paper, I'll get an Incomplete in the course."

"I thought you finished that paper days ago," Mrs. Dalton called up the stairs.

"No. I . . . uh . . . I've been working on it. But some other things came up."

"Well, get to work, then."

"Mom, thanks a bunch for the advice. You know, if I have to spend the whole night discussing it with you, I won't get too far."

"Well, aren't you the tense one these days! So touchy!"

"Mom, please—give me a break."

Silence.

She heard her mother walk away from the stairs.

Meg looked down at the sheet of notebook paper in front of her on the desk. She wasn't working on her psych paper. Instead she had written on the top line: LIST OF SUSPECTS.

She started to write the number *1*, but her pencil lead broke. She tossed the pencil across the room and picked up another. Then she wrote the number *1*, and beside it the name *Brian*.

Then under *Brian* she wrote: "Why?"

A) Because he was staring at Tony and me so strangely.
B) Because he ran away when he saw that we saw him.
C) ?

She sucked on the pencil eraser. Why? Why? Why? What reason could Brian possibly have for wanting to stop Ellen's party?

She searched her memory for a clue. Brian and Ellen. Brian and Ellen . . . Nothing. Zero. Zip. She couldn't come up with anything.

Brian and Ellen were only acquaintances, never even friends, really. Brian certainly had no reason to hate Ellen or even dislike her.

Brian had been the one to help Ellen, to rescue her, that day a year ago, that day in the Fear Street woods when Evan shot himself and Brian found Ellen there, crying, dazed . . .

Evan.

Ellen and Evan.

Did Evan's death have something to do with this?

Meg removed the pencil from her mouth and wrote: NOTE: DOES SOMEONE HATE ELLEN BECAUSE OF EVAN?

Then she added a second name to her list of suspects: *Shannon.* And under *Shannon* she wrote: "Why?"

A) Because Evan was her brother. Maybe she blames Ellen
    for what happened.
B) Shannon was in study hall when the invitations were
    torn up.
C) Shannon wasn't enthusiastic about the party from the start.
D) Shannon's been different since Evan died.

She crossed out *D,* drawing heavy black lines through it. It wasn't fair, Meg decided. They had *all* been different since Evan died.

Shannon is my best friend, Meg thought, tapping the pencil rapidly on the desktop. She wouldn't try to scare me, would she? She wouldn't try such stupid horror-movie tricks.

Would she?

Would Shannon be honest with her about the party, about Ellen?

"I don't know," Meg said, not realizing she was speaking aloud. Shannon, she decided, would have to stay on the list of suspects.

And who else?

"Meg—how's the paper coming along?"

Oh, no. Her mother was back already!

"Fine, Mom—till you interrupted!" she shouted. "You made me lose my train of thought."

"Maybe that's because you think with your *caboose*!" Her mother laughed hysterically. She always loved her own rotten jokes.

"Thanks for the support, Mom!"

She heard her Mom walk away again, still chuckling. Her eyes returned to the sheet of paper. She was surprised to see that without realizing it, she had written a name after the number 3: *Ellen.*

Why was Ellen a suspect?

A) Because someone from school could have called her and told her about the party.
B) Because Ellen never liked parties.
C) She never called or wrote to any of her old friends. Maybe she doesn't want to see everyone.
D) She never even explained why her family moved away from Shadyside so suddenly.

Yes, Ellen had to be considered a suspect, Meg realized. But how would she have gotten the red-crayoned notes to Meg and Tony?

A friend. Someone in school could be helping her.

So maybe there were *two* people Meg should be looking for.

She wrote the number 4. Is there a fourth suspect? Is there someone else who knew about the party, knew Meg and Tony had a good reason to stop the party?

She couldn't think of anyone. So she wrote down *Dwayne*.

Why?

"Because I don't like him."

The phone rang.

She stared at it, reluctant to pick it up. Maybe I'll just let it ring, she thought.

But she knew she couldn't do that. If a phone rang, she always had to pick it up, even if it wasn't hers. She couldn't bear to let a phone call go unanswered.

She let it ring one more time, took a deep breath, and picked it up. "Hello?"

"Hi, Meg."

"Tony?"

"You're safe? You're okay?"

"Tony—what do you mean? You sound terrible!"

"I—I was worried about you. I . . . well . . . I think someone was following me tonight."

"Following you? Where?"

"Following me home. I was at my dad's gas station, see, helping out. He had the car, so I walked home. It was weird. I kept seeing these shadows. But every time I turned around, there was no one there."

"And?"

"And then there were footsteps behind me. So I started running. And the footsteps started running too."

"Did you see who it was? Was it a boy or a girl?"

"I never saw. It was pitch black. And whoever it was stayed pretty far back."

"Are you sure there really was someone there?"

"Of course I'm sure," he snapped angrily. "I'm not totally nuts, you know."

"Sorry, Tony. Don't shout at me. Please. I just wanted to know—"

"Listen, this is getting scary, Meg. I think this person really means business."

"Didn't you get a look at whoever it was at all? Didn't you see anything?"

"No."

"Was he tall or short?"

"I don't know. I just ran. I just wanted to get home. *Give me a break—okay?*"

"Sorry. Please don't yell."

"I called you right away. I thought maybe they tried something—maybe they followed you, too, or something."

"No. I'm fine. Really."

"This party, Meg. I don't know."

"What do you mean?"

"I mean, is it worth it? It's just a stupid party."

"Yes, but now it's a principle," Meg said.

"A principle? Aw, come on—forget about principles. Somebody followed me, Meg. I'm really scared. I'm not willing to risk my life for a party—"

"But don't you see?" she cried impatiently. "It isn't just a party. If somebody wants to stop it so badly, there's got to be more to it. There's something else going on here, Tony. And we've got to find out what it is."

"You're really enjoying this, aren't you," he said with some bitterness. "You're a real Nancy Drew, huh? You like being Miss Detective. You think this is exciting."

"Kind of," Meg admitted. "But I also don't like being pushed around by someone who thinks they can tell me—"

"Count me out," Tony interrupted.

"What?"

"Count me out. You heard me."

"Out of what?"

"Out of everything. Out of the party. Out of . . . you and me."

The words seemed to sting her ears. The sting traveled quickly to her chest. It was so . . . unexpected.

"You mean that?"

"Good-bye," he said quietly and hung up the phone.

Meg slammed the receiver down angrily. Of course, Tony was just mouthing off without thinking again, she told herself. Of course he really doesn't mean it. He doesn't really want to break up with me over this.

Or does he?

He did sound really frightened. Meg asked herself if she was frightened too. No, she decided. She wasn't at all scared. She was too furious to be scared. She wasn't going to give up the party. And she wasn't going to give up Tony.

"I'll find out who's doing this and I'll find out why," she said aloud.

She picked up the receiver and started to push Tony's number. But then she thought better of it. "I'll give him a day or two to calm down. Then I'll apologize."

She wasn't going to allow herself to believe that he really had broken up with her. She wasn't going to believe it. No way. She realized she was biting her lower lip and now it was bleeding.

How was she to concentrate on her psych paper? She couldn't. She'd have to try again tomorrow. But what should she do now?

She looked down at her list of suspects. Number 3: *Ellen*.

She didn't want Ellen to be on the list. The party was for Ellen, after all. All of this trouble was for Ellen. It really would be easier if she could cross Ellen off the list.

I'll call her.

The idea seemed to float into her mind from out of nowhere. Such a good idea.

I'll call her and tell her how happy I am that she's coming for a visit.

She felt her throat tighten. A feeling of dread started up from her stomach. No. It won't be hard. It won't be hard to talk to Ellen. We were best friends, after all.

She picked up the phone and pushed Information. She realized her hands were suddenly ice cold. It didn't take long to get Ellen's phone number.

I should have called her sooner, she scolded herself. Why did I wait all these months for Ellen to call me?

She pushed the upstate area code and the number. It rang once, twice, the dull rings sounding very far away. Ellen picked up after the third ring. "Hello?"

"Ellen? It's me. Meg."

"Meg? I don't believe it! Hi!" Ellen shrieked. She sounded thrilled to hear from Meg. Meg let out a sigh of relief. She felt much better.

"So how are you?"

"Fine. Just fine. How are *you?*"

"Okay. Not bad," Meg said. "It's funny to hear your voice. It's been so long."

"I know," Ellen said, sounding guilty. "I've been meaning to write or something. I just got so busy and—"

"How's your new school?"

"Okay, I guess. It's different, really different from Shadyside. I'll tell you about it when I see you. I'm coming down, you know."

"Yeah. That's why I'm calling. I wanted to tell you how glad I am. I—"

"I'll be staying at my Aunt Amy's. I hope we'll have lots of time to spend together."

"Me too, Ellen. I really miss you." Meg blurted that out. She hadn't really meant to sound so emotional. It just came out. It felt so good to be talking to her old friend, so comfortable, as if things hadn't changed at all.

"Me too."

"You want to do anything special, or see anyone, or anything?" Meg asked, talking rapidly, excitedly.

"No, not really. How's Tony?"

"He's okay. The same, I guess."

"You two still together?"

"Yeah." Up until two minutes ago. But why go into that?

"I'm so happy you called, Meg. I can't wait to see you."

"Me too."

They chattered on for a few more minutes, not really talking about anything. Then Meg decided she'd better say good-bye before the call got expensive enough for her father to complain about. Ellen promised to call as soon as she got to Shadyside, and then they hung up.

Meg felt really good. What a nice talk! Ellen sounded the same as ever. And she'd been so happy that Meg had called.

Meg picked up the pencil and started to cross out Ellen's name from her suspect list. But then she stopped. She stared at the paper, thinking hard.

Ellen had seemed so happy, so thrilled, so enthusiastic.

Too enthusiastic.

Too happy.

That wasn't like Ellen at all. It was all so forced, so phony. She was being super-cheery, dripping with sweetness, Meg realized.

She wasn't being Ellen. She wasn't being herself.

What was she trying to hide?

CHAPTER 6

WEDNESDAY NIGHT

"Why don't you hit him?"

"I tried that. He thought it was funny."

"And I guess reasoning with him is out."

Lisa rolled her brown eyes and sighed. "That's all I do is reason with him. Cory and I spend all our time together reasoning with each other. That's one of the main reasons we don't have any fun. We're too busy reasoning with each other and discussing why we're not getting along. We don't have any time left to *get* along!"

Meg tilted the can to her lips and took a long drink of Diet Coke. She slumped down low in the big leather couch, holding the can in her lap. "I like this room," she said after a long silence, looking around at the dark wood-paneled walls, the bookshelves up to the ceiling with the big-screen TV built in to the center, the glass doors that opened onto a backyard terrace. "We don't have a den."

"You're not trying to change the subject or anything, are you?" Lisa asked with a wry grin.

Meg smiled. "I just don't know what to say. Tony and I aren't getting along, either. We had a big fight about the party for Ellen. He's really frightened that whoever's been trying to scare us really means business. But I told him I wasn't going to let some creep frighten me out of what I want to do."

"Maybe you *are* being stubborn about it, Meg. Maybe Tony is right," Lisa said, pulling her long legs over the side of the leather armchair she was sitting in. "At least, Tony's worried about you. If someone was threatening me, Cory would probably say, 'Yeah, but what's on TV tonight?'"

Meg laughed. Lisa did a great Cory impression. "Maybe you should just lighten up on Cory for a while," she said. "He's really a good guy. Maybe you're just expecting too much from him. You two have grown up together. He lives right next door. It's natural he'd take you a *little* for granted. In a way, he should."

Lisa finished off her Diet Coke and crushed the can in her hand. "What's with you, Meg? I didn't want any good advice. I just wanted to complain."

Both girls laughed.

"But I'm being selfish," Lisa said, tossing the crushed soda can toward a wastebasket by the desk across the room. "Hey—two points!" Her face turned serious. "You came over here to tell me about the terrible things that have been happening to you, and all I do is talk about Cory and me. I'm sorry. You've got real problems. You know, maybe you should call the police."

"Sure, Lisa," Meg said, pulling herself up with some difficulty. The couch was so soft, she had sunk down into the cushions. "I'll go to the police and tell them that someone cut up my party invitations in study hall. That'll really get 'em excited, right. They'll probably get the whole police squad out on that case! Maybe a S.W.A.T. team too!"

"How do you get your skin like that?" Lisa asked.

"What?"

"Your skin. It's so perfect. Like a baby's skin."

"Huh? Lisa—" Meg's hand went up involuntarily to her face.

"Your face always looks like you just washed it. Fresh-scrubbed. That's what they call it. You have that fresh-scrubbed look."

"I guess now it's *you* who wants to change the subject," Meg grumbled.

"No. Sorry. I just got distracted." Lisa stood up and stretched. Then she walked to the glass doors and looked out. "Look, Meg, maybe you should just forget about the surprise party. Then all of your problems will go away."

"But I don't want to," Meg told her, not meaning to sound so whiny. "I really care about Ellen. I really want to show her that we still care about her. And. . ."

"And?"

"And I'm really curious now. I want to find out why someone is so desperate to stop this party."

"What do you mean?"

"It isn't just a silly prank. Someone has a serious reason for trying to stop the party. But what could it be?"

"Is it because someone really hates Ellen?"

"I don't know of anyone who hated Ellen. Do you?" Meg asked.

Lisa stared out into the darkness. "No. But then, what else could it be? Maybe it has something to do with Evan."

"Evan. Yeah. I was thinking that too. What made you say Evan, Lisa?"

"I don't know. When I think of Ellen, I guess I automatically think of Evan. You know. Ellen and Evan. We always talked about them together. But Evan has been dead for a year. What could he possibly have to do with someone trying to stop the party?"

"I don't know. It's a total mystery. But it's a mystery I want to solve. That's why I'm not going to give up about this party. I'm not going to quit. If I give up now, we'll never know what this is all about."

"Did anyone ever tell you you're a very stubborn person?"

"Everyone," Meg said. "What are you looking at?"

"Just looking across the backyard. There's a light on in Cory's room. I wonder if he's up there." She stared out a while longer, then backed away from the glass doors and dropped back onto the black leather armchair. "So do you have any idea at all who might be trying to frighten you and Tony? Any hunches?"

"Promise you won't laugh," Meg said cautiously.

"You know me," Lisa replied.

"Yes, I do. That's why I said 'promise you won't laugh.'"

"Okay. I promise. But my fingers may be crossed a little."

"Well, I made a list of suspects."

"And?"

"Well, number one on the list is Brian."

Lisa sat up straight. "Brian? Why Brian? He's your cousin, isn't he?"

"Yeah. Second cousin. But that doesn't rule him out. He may be in my family, but he's still as weird as they come. Always hanging around with Dwayne, playing those fantasy games."

"I don't know," Lisa said doubtfully. "Who else is on your list?"

"Shannon."

"What?!" Lisa's eyes lit up with surprise.

"Shannon sits right behind me in study hall. She could easily have cut up the invitations. When I asked her about it, she said she didn't see anything because she went to the library. But Tony was in the study hall too. He says he never saw Shannon leave the room."

"And what about the phone call and the note?"

"She could have been the one," Meg said, sounding less sure of herself.

"But, Meg, she's your best friend, right?"

"Right. I know it's a crazy idea, Lisa. But Shannon hasn't been the same since Evan died. And she seemed to be very much against this party right from the beginning."

Lisa sighed and shook her head. "Your cousin and your best friend. Who else is on the list—your mom and dad?"

"Come on, Lisa. I—"

"Not very likely suspects, Meg. Why would Shannon try to scare you like that? Why wouldn't she just tell you that—"

"I don't know. I just get weird vibes from her, that's all. Maybe she blames Ellen for what happened to Evan. Maybe she's afraid of something that might happen at the party. I don't really know. I just—"

"Well, go ask her, then."

"What?"

"You heard me," Lisa said, jumping to her feet and starting to pace back and forth. "She's your best friend. You don't want to be walking around with your best friend on your list of suspects. So just go ask Shannon if she's the one. Ask her why she doesn't want a party for Ellen. Talk to her. Straight. That's what friends are for, right?"

"Uh . . . I think maybe I'm like you," Meg said, straightening her sweatshirt. "I didn't want any good advice. I just wanted to complain."

Meg thanked Lisa for the talk and headed out to the car. The cool air revived her, cleared her head. Maybe Lisa is right, she thought. Maybe I will have a little talk with Shannon tomorrow. She slid into her mother's little Toyota and headed for home, rehearsing over and over what she would say.

She pulled up the drive and stopped a few inches from the garage. A light over the garage door cast a dim yellow glow onto the shingles of the house.

Meg started to climb out of the car, then, startled, inhaled sharply. That shadow on the porch—it wasn't usually there, was it?

Was someone waiting for her in the darkness?

CHAPTER 7

WEDNESDAY NIGHT

Meg slumped down in the seat, staring hard at the shadow on the porch shingles. The shadow didn't move.

Her finger was on the ignition key. Her first impulse was to start the car up again, back down the drive, and race away.

But maybe it was Tony waiting for her there. How many times had he done that—waited for her on the doorstep without ringing the bell and going in? Dozens!

Maybe he had come to apologize, to make up.

She pulled the key from the ignition and started to open the door.

Or maybe it wasn't Tony.

Maybe it was the creep who had called her. Maybe it was the creep who had followed Tony.

The shadow didn't move.

How was it possible for a person to stand so still?

She pushed open the car door a few inches. "Who's there?" she called, surprised that she sounded more angry than afraid.

Silence.

"Who is it? Is someone there?"

Silence. The shadow didn't move.

"Tony—is that you?"

It wasn't possible for someone to stay that still for so long.

She climbed out of the car and crept silently across the wet lawn toward the porch. She could feel the fear rise and catch in her throat.

She took another step, another step, her sneakers making soft, squishy sounds in the tall, dew-covered grass. Why am I doing this? she asked herself. Why aren't I running away? Why am I being so stupid?

She stopped at the side of the porch. "Who's there?"

And then she laughed.

The shadow was made by a stack of tall flower pots her father had left on the fence railing.

"Meg, you're losing it," she said aloud, and breathed a heavy sigh.

She hurried inside to get some sleep, locking the door securely behind her.

THURSDAY AFTERNOON

Meg poked her fork at the bright orange substance on her plate. If it was macaroni and cheese, where was the macaroni? If it was just cheese, why was it such a weird color?

The lunchroom wasn't very crowded for some reason. Maybe other kids had heard they were serving this orange sticky stuff today and hurried somewhere else for lunch. Cory Brooks and some of his pals from the gymnastics team were clowning around at a table near the door. "Don't they ever get tired of throwing milk cartons at each other?" Meg asked herself.

The windows along the far wall were open, since it was the warmest spring day yet. The brassy bleats from the band out on the practice field, playing "Pomp and Circumstance" over and over again as they prepared for the seniors' graduation, were annoying everyone.

Meg straightened the sleeves of her white blouse. She took a tentative bite of the macaroni and cheese substance. It had no taste whatsoever.

She looked up to see Shannon carrying a tray toward her table. Shannon made a sour face. She was inhaling the aroma of the food substance on her plate.

Oh boy, Meg thought, taking a deep breath. She knew that confronting Shannon wasn't going to be easy. But now was as good a time as any. She might as well get it over with.

"What *is* this stuff?" Shannon asked, dropping her tray in front of Meg's and pulling out a chair with a loud scraping noise.

"It's just Styrofoam," Meg said. "Like those crunchy things they put in packages when they ship them somewhere."

Shannon poked it with a fork, just the way Meg had. "Hey—I think it tried to bite my fork!"

Meg didn't laugh. She looked Shannon in the eye and stared hard as if searching for an answer to the question she hadn't asked yet.

"What's wrong with you?" Shannon asked, dropping her fork onto the tray. "You're weirder than usual today."

"I . . . I have to ask you a question," Meg said softly.

"Go ahead. Ask. But get that morbid look off your face."

"Sorry." Meg didn't realize she looked so grim. She wanted to toss this off as a light, silly thing. But now that was impossible. "Look. I know this is ridiculous, but I just have to ask."

"Go ahead," Shannon pleaded. "The suspense is killing me."

Meg took a deep breath. She could feel her face growing red. "Did you call me late at night and send me a threatening note?"

"What?"

"Did you? I got this call and a note, and—"

"About what?" Shannon looked genuinely confused.

"Threatening me. Telling me not to have the party for Ellen."

"Threatening you? You think I was threatening you?"

Meg realized she had made a mistake. "No, I . . ." She struggled to think of something to say to get herself out of this.

"Meg—what exactly are you accusing me of?" Shannon's voice rose several octaves. Her hands gripped the edge of the table.

"I wasn't accusing you. I was just asking," Meg said lamely. "I just wanted you to tell me it wasn't you. That's all."

"Well, it wasn't me," Shannon sneered. Her surprise was quickly turning to anger. "Why on earth would I threaten you, Meg?"

"I don't know," Meg said. "Someone's been making horrible threats. Someone followed Tony and . . . I . . . I'm upset, Shannon. I guess I'm not thinking clearly. I—"

"I guess you're not," Shannon said coldly.

"But, Shannon, I didn't mean—"

"I think you did what you meant to do. I don't understand why you wanted to insult me, why you'd accuse me. I always thought we were good friends. I always thought we trusted each other. I'd never accuse *you* of anything like that. But I guess we're different. Very different. More different than I thought." She choked out the last words. She seemed about to lose control.

"Shannon, you're taking this the wrong way. I only meant—"

Shannon, her face knotted up in anger, pushed away from the table, turned, and walked with long, quick strides out of the lunchroom.

Meg sat frozen, staring after her, feeling like a real rat.

Thank you, Lisa, for such good advice, she thought. Now I have no friends at all. No Tony. No Shannon.

She realized she couldn't blame Lisa for what had happened. She never should have done it. She never should have confronted Shannon that way. She never should have accused her.

But wait.

Wasn't Shannon overreacting a bit? Why did Shannon get so

hysterical so quickly? She usually didn't have such a short fuse. Was she trying to hide the fact that it *was* she who was terrorizing Meg? Was she carrying on like that to keep Meg from questioning her, from finding out the truth?

No. Meg knew Shannon. Shannon's shock and anger were real. She wasn't putting it on.

And she had every right to be shocked and angry.

Meg had been a fool. And a cruel one at that. Now Shannon would probably never speak to her again. And why should she?

Meg sat miserably staring at the door to the lunchroom, trying to will Shannon back in so that she could apologize, so that she could explain.

And where was Tony? Why was he being so stubborn? Didn't he know that she needed him now?

After a while she realized she was starving. She shoved the tray of yellow macaroni to the side and lifted the brown paper bag from her lap. She always bought lunch and brought a lunch too. The lunchroom food was just never enough.

She started to unwrap the bag.

That's funny, she thought. There's something leaking in here.

Leaking? How could it be leaking? She had only packed a sandwich and an apple. It must be—

She reached her hand in. She felt something wet and sticky. And thick.

"OH!"

She pulled her hand out fast, tipping over the bag. A dark red liquid oozed out, spilling down her white blouse, onto her skirt. Meg pulled up her hand. It was covered with the warm liquid. It dripped down her wrist and onto her arm and puddled on the lunch tray.

"It's blood!" she cried. "My lunch bag is filled with *blood*!"

CHAPTER 8

THURSDAY NIGHT

Meg couldn't concentrate on her psych paper. She stared down at her desk without seeing it. All she could see was the sticky, dripping lunch bag, which had turned out to be filled with red paint. Then Shannon's face. Then the dripping blood. Then Shannon's face again, the hurt look, the look of complete shock, of betrayal.

"I've got to apologize," she said aloud. She couldn't bear to have Shannon so mad at her. She couldn't bear to feel so guilty, so . . . wrong.

The car was parked in front of the house, but Meg felt like walking. Walking the nine or ten blocks would give her time to think of what she was going to say.

It had rained most of the afternoon, and the air still smelled fresh and wet. Small puddles of water on the pavement reflected shimmering yellow light from the streetlamps. Meg jumped over the bigger puddles, walking quickly.

She reached Shannon's house without deciding exactly what to say. She just wanted to throw herself on Shannon's mercy and beg her forgiveness. Shannon could be cold and hard, she knew. Especially this past year. It might take a lot of begging. But what choice did she have?

The Harpers' house was set back high over a sweeping lawn of carefully trimmed grass, a large, old weeping willow looming over the drive like an ancient servant guarding the entranceway. The front of the house was completely dark, but Meg knew that the family always stayed in the family room and kitchen in the back.

Shannon opened the door a few seconds after Meg rang the bell. Her face fell. "Oh. It's you."

"I came to grovel at your feet," Meg said, trying unsuccessfully to keep her voice steady. "I just want to apologize. I'll do anything. Really. I feel terrible."

"That's good," Shannon said, looking past Meg.

"You've got to accept my apology," Meg said. "You're my best friend and—"

"Come in," Shannon said, pulling back the door. Her voice was flat and unfriendly.

Meg followed her into the entranceway. Shannon was wearing tan Bermuda shorts and a tank top. Her arms and legs looked very pale, almost ivory-pale. Everyone looked really pale in May, Meg decided, after the long winter.

Shannon led her into the dark living room, switched on a brass floor lamp, and took a seat on a narrow red velvet antique loveseat.

Meg hated Shannon's living room. Partly because the furniture was so fancy and so uncomfortable. And partly because of the large photograph of Evan that hung in a dark wooden frame in the center of the front wall. It was impossible to stand or sit in the room without staring at the photograph, and it made Meg even more uncomfortable than the hard, ornate chairs.

It wasn't at all a typical photo of Evan. For one thing, he was wearing a dark sports jacket and a tie. He had just come from some sort of family function, a wedding maybe. His blond hair, usually wild and unruly, was slicked back, his eyes were set in a blank stare, and he was wearing a forced smile that Meg had never seen on him in real life.

Meg figured this was the way Mr. and Mrs. Harper wanted to remember Evan—not the way he was, a troublemaker, a wild man, but the way he looked in this picture, civilized and completely in control.

Staring at the photograph always brought back memories of the other side of Evan for Meg, though. It was as if her mind were rejecting this false image, this smooth stranger, to bring back the real boy she knew with all of his faults and all of his problems.

She suddenly remembered a night downstairs in the game room in Shannon's basement. Who was there that night? All of them—Shannon and Ellen and Meg and Tony and Evan. Tony and Evan were shooting pool on the large table in the center of the room. The girls were trying to play doubles Ping-Pong with only three people.

Meg could hear the sounds in that room again, the shouts, the loud laughter, the pop of the Ping-Pong ball against the paddles, the clicking sound the ball made as the girls chased it across the tile floor, and the solid tap of the pool cues hitting the shiny, colored billiard balls.

Evan was in a particularly wild mood that night. He had accidentally rammed one of the family's cars into the back of a pickup truck that afternoon, and Tony was laughing at him. "It wasn't my fault, man," Evan declared, knocking the three-ball into a corner pocket and grinning at Tony, pleased with himself.

"You plow into the back of a truck, and it isn't your fault?" Tony scoffed.

"No way. That truck was going below the minimum speed on the thruway. So I couldn't help it. He was going too slow!"

Tony laughed and missed his shot.

"So you tried to speed him up by giving him a little bump," Ellen muttered.

"A little bump that totaled your car!" Tony fell on the floor laughing, holding his sides.

"So you're both against me, huh?" Evan said, staring at Ellen. Suddenly he wasn't joking anymore.

"No, Evan. Tony and I—"

"I saw you!" Evan cried, swatting his pool cue hard against the side of the table. "You think it's a big joke, huh? Some idiot truck driver slows down and forces me to crash, and you two think it's a riot!"

"Come on, man—" Tony started, holding up his hands as if in surrender.

"No. *You* come on!" Evan cried. He raised his pool cue like a sword and started swinging it against Tony's cue. *Click-click-CLICK.* Evan, his eyes wild, his blond hair tossed back, started hitting Tony's cue harder and harder, challenging Tony to fence with him.

"Evan—stop!" Ellen cried.

He swung his cue like a baseball bat, meaning to hit Tony. But Tony ducked and the cue hit Ellen on the shoulder. It made a loud, sharp sound. She cried out and backed against the basement wall. "Evan!"

But Evan ignored her. He and Tony were standing on the pool table now, going at each other with grim determination, like a movie swordfight. Meg remembered the look on Tony's face. It was all just a goof to him. He was having a great time.

But Evan looked serious, intent on winning. It soon became obvious to everyone but Tony that Evan was really fighting. The pool cues clattered against each other. Both boys leaped down from the pool table and moved across the floor, attacking and thrusting.

Evan's face grew bright red. He was scowling, and his eyes seemed to be clamped shut. Suddenly he swung down hard. There was a loud crack.

Tony's eyes went wide, then rolled up in his head. He slumped down to the floor. Blood began to pour down his hair from the top of his head.

Evan didn't look down at Tony. He was studying his pool cue. "I think I cracked it," he said, very concerned.

Ellen began to shriek at him. "How could you do that to Tony?"

Meg remembered the surprised look on Evan's face. He didn't seem to realize what he had done. He looked down. His expression changed, his features all seeming to drop at once. He bent over Tony. "Hey—you okay? That was an accident. I guess my arm slipped."

"That's okay," Tony said groggily. He smiled up at his friend. He would always forgive Evan for anything.

Meg and Shannon decided to drive Tony to the Emergency Room at Shadyside Hospital. As they left, they could still hear Ellen down in the basement, yelling at Evan, trying to make him admit that it wasn't an accident. Tony got five stitches.

It was a horrible night. But no one ever knew what to expect from Evan. Some nights he was a lot of fun, the funniest, happiest guy around.

Other nights "his arm slipped." People would get hurt.

"You keep staring at that photo," Shannon said from the small loveseat.

Her words brought Meg back to the present. "Yeah. I know."

"It's a weird photo, isn't it?" Shannon asked, shaking her head. "Evan looks like some kind of Martian."

"He doesn't look like Evan," Meg said with some sadness.

They sat across from each other in silence for a long while. Finally Meg said, "You've got to forgive me, Shannon. It was temporary insanity, I guess. I really do apologize. I was out of my head. Really. I've been crazy for days. I mean, when I got home from Lisa's the other night, I saw shadows of flower pots on the porch. I was terrified! I was sure someone was waiting there to get me."

"Poor kid," Shannon said unsympathetically. "When does the groveling begin?"

"Forgive me and I'll do anything. I mean it. I'll even ask Gary Brandt to go out with you."

"You'll *what?*"

"You know you want to go out with him, but you're too shy to ask."

"Now, listen—"

"So I'll ask him for you. Really. I'll do it to make up for this afternoon."

"Good lord. I think you're serious." Shannon stared at her friend in disbelief.

"Of course I'm serious. I really don't want you to be mad at me."

"Okay. I'm not mad," Shannon said. "But don't you dare ask Gary Brandt anything."

"Okay, I—"

"Promise?"

"Promise," Meg said. She shifted in the seat, starting to feel a little relieved. "Do you really accept my apology?"

"Yeah. Sure. I overreacted a little. I'm sorry too." Shannon came over and gave Meg a quick hug. "Now tell me about these threats. I really don't believe it," she said, shaking her head.

Meg told her about the phone call, the note, and about Tony being followed. "Oh—I almost forgot. I talked to Ellen," she said, happy to change the subject. "I called her. She sounded great. Really good. She's really looking forward to coming back and seeing everyone."

"Glad to hear it," Shannon said. "I have to admit I was wrong about the party. It is a good idea. You were right."

"Good!" Meg said. "I mean *great!* So you'll help me with it and everything?"

"Yeah, sure," Shannon said with a shrug. "Why shouldn't we both risk our lives? Risk our lives for the right to party! Yeah!"

Meg laughed, but she didn't really think it was too funny.

"Oh, before I forget," Shannon said, "Mike will be home that weekend, so we'll have to invite him even though he doesn't know Ellen very well."

Mike was Shannon's half-brother. When Shannon's mother died, her father remarried and a few years later, had Mike. Meg had seen very little of Mike. He went away to school, somewhere up in New England.

"That's good," Meg said. "Mike's real cute."

"He's gotten to look so much like Evan, it's creepy," Shannon said wistfully. "So who do you think wants to stop this party?" she asked, sighing sadly. It was a year later, but she still wanted to avoid talking about Evan.

"I just can't figure it out," Meg said, shifting her legs on the uncomfortable chair. "It's really making me crazy."

"It must be someone who really hates Ellen," Shannon said, shaking her head.

"But who could that be?" Meg asked. "Ellen was just about the most popular girl at Shadyside."

"Beats me," Shannon said. "I just haven't got a clue. Hey— maybe it doesn't have to do with Ellen. Maybe it's someone who really hates *you*." She laughed. The idea really seemed to strike her funny.

Meg was shocked. The idea had never occurred to her. "Huh? Like who?"

"I don't know. Forget it," Shannon said quickly. "Stupid idea. Someone wants to stop this party from happening. Someone wants to keep us all from getting together again. But why?"

"What is this person afraid of?" Meg asked, thinking hard. "Hmmmm . . . Afraid that we'll talk about him? Afraid that some secret will come out? Afraid that Ellen will tell us something?"

"Maybe, maybe." Shannon was tapping her fingers nervously on the antique coffee table. "Now who might have a secret they wouldn't want any of us to know about. . . ." Her face suddenly tightened. Her expression turned grim. "Brian!" she cried.

Meg stared back at her in surprise. "Brian?" Meg thought of her suspect list. Brian, of course, was her number one suspect. "What makes you say Brian?"

"Well . . . he's so weird, Meg. I know he's your cousin and all. But he's so weird. And he's gotten so much weirder ever since . . . ever since that day. Didn't you ever wonder what Brian was doing in the woods, how he just happened to find Evan seconds after—after . . ." She couldn't finish her thought.

"Shannon, you don't think Brian had anything to do with—"

Shannon stared into Meg's eyes. "It's possible, isn't it?"

"Yes, but—" Meg knew Brian was weird. And she had always thought it a coincidence that he had come upon Ellen and Evan just after Evan had accidentally shot himself. But in typical naive fashion, Meg had never suspected that Brian might have had something to do with Evan's death.

"I guess I should go confront Brian," Meg said.

"Try to be a little more subtle than you were with me," Shannon said pointedly.

Both girls laughed. Meg was very glad she had come over. Now maybe she could go home and be able to concentrate on her psych paper.

She said good night to Shannon, walked out the front door and down the long drive, and began jogging over the wet pavement toward home. She realized it must have rained again while she was at Shannon's, for the street was very wet and currents of water were rolling down the curbsides toward the storm drains.

She looked up and saw car headlights and then a dark car behind them. It was coming toward her very fast, its tires splashing up waves of rainwater on both sides as it moved.

Keeping to the curb, Meg continued to jog. But she froze in

place when she realized that the car had swerved so that it was coming right at her.

It seemed to speed up.

She had no time to move, no time to jump out of its path.

Frozen like a frightened deer, she tossed up her hands as if to shield herself, and screamed as the car roared down on her.

CHAPTER 9

LATER, THURSDAY NIGHT

The driver pulled the car to the curb in front of the house and shifted into park. His heart seemed to be pounding in rhythm with the windshield wipers. *Thump-THUMP Thump-THUMP Thump-THUMP.*

He turned off the engine. The wipers came to an abrupt stop in the middle of the windshield, but his heart kept up the insistent rhythm. He didn't make a move to get out of the car. He didn't know if he could walk. He stared out the windshield, waiting to feel better, waiting to feel a little calmer, a little more normal.

Maybe he'd never feel normal again.

The rain had stopped completely. It had been a fast, hard storm and had blown over in a minute.

Where was he?

He looked around. It took a while to remember. He was in front of his cousin Mark's house. He was sitting in Mark's car. He had borrowed the car that morning.

He was returning it when he had seen Meg jogging in the street. And then . . . and then . . .

He ran Meg down.

No, he didn't.

But he nearly had.

What had he been thinking of? What happened to his brain? He realized he was sweating now. The sweat was rolling down his forehead. His T-shirt was drenched. He felt hot all over, hotter than he'd ever felt.

What had happened to his brain?

The windshield was steaming up. Soon he'd be wrapped in this safe cocoon. No one could see him. No one could know he was in there. Maybe he'd stay in there forever.

He had nearly run Meg down. He had aimed the car right at her, and then he had floored it.

He heard her scream over the roar of the engine.

He saw her eyes go wild.

He saw her shield herself with her hands. Still he kept the gas pedal down to the floor. Still he didn't swerve the wheel.

Then he saw her leap to the side, falling hard to the pavement.

Finally he had cut the wheel, squealed to the left. He remembered struggling to regain control. Working the wheel till the car was headed back on the road. Then he sped away. He never even looked back.

Maybe he would never feel normal again.

He had only meant to frighten Meg.

That was all. Really scare her. Show her that he meant business, that he wasn't going to kid around with any more scary phone calls, or notes, or lunch bags filled with fake blood.

But then when he saw her in the street, he forgot what he was doing. He remembered why he had to frighten her. Oh yes. He remembered why he couldn't allow the party to take place. Yes, yes, yes.

But he forgot what he was doing, forgot his foot so heavy on the gas, forgot his hands so rigid on the wheel.

He could have killed her. He only wanted to frighten her.

He had killed once. Now he had almost killed again.

I'm losing it, he thought. I'm losing it bad.

But he had been lucky this time. She had leapt away. She was safe. She was okay.

But was she frightened?

Maybe she was frightened enough to give up the party. Then things could go back to normal—right?

Then he could feel normal again.

He'd just have the other murder to think about. Every day. For the rest of his life.

He slammed his head angrily against the side window.

No. Get control, man. Get control.

Now the left side of his head ached. Good. That felt more normal. A headache made it feel a little more normal.

Take it easy, man. Deep breaths. Yeah, that's better.

You only scared her, after all.

You have to scare her, scare her out of having this party.

You have no choice. You can't let this party take place. You can't let everyone be all together again. You can't let Ellen come back and tell . . .

You can't let her tell what happened last year. . . .

Meg tore off the soaked, mud-stained clothes and tossed them in a heap in the middle of her bedroom floor. Then she hurried to take a hot shower.

Aside from a bruise on her shoulder where she had landed on the curbside, she was fine. Now if only she could get her hands to stop shaking, her heartbeat to slow down, her legs to stop trembling.

A nice, long shower would do the trick. She was so glad her parents had gone to bed early. She didn't really want to explain why she had returned home looking as if she had taken a swan dive into a mud puddle.

How *could* she explain it?

She wasn't sure she knew what had happened herself.

Should she call the police?

And tell them what?

She hadn't really seen the car behind the headlights. She couldn't describe it at all. It had been too dark—and then suddenly it had been too bright as the headlights bore down on her.

But had the car really swerved to hit her? Or had the driver just lost control for a moment?

The street was very slippery because of the sudden downpour just before she left Shannon's house. Maybe the driver was sliding on the street. Maybe whoever it was hadn't seen her at all. Maybe she was making a big deal over nothing.

Nothing?

She had almost been killed.

She shivered. The hot, streaming water wasn't warming her.

She dried quickly, still shivering, and pulled on her warmest flannel pajamas. Then she gathered up the clothes she had tossed onto the floor and put them down the laundry chute.

"What will make me feel better?"

Tony.

Tony would know the right things to say. Tony would know how to calm her down.

She missed Tony so much. She needed Tony now.

She pulled a pink cotton robe over the pajamas and sat down to phone him. She looked up to see a half moon peering through her window. The sky had cleared.

She punched Tony's number. It rang twice, three times, then a few more.

"Come on, Tony. Where are you?"

" 'Lo?"

"Tony?"

"No. This is his fa-father."

She recognized Mr. Colavito's muffled stammer. It meant he had spent the evening at the corner tavern. Big surprise. He spent *every* evening at the corner tavern.

"It's me, Meg, Mr. Colavito."

"M-Meg?" He sounded as if he were trying to remember if he'd ever heard that name before.

"Yes. Meg. Is Tony home?"

"No. Not now."

"He isn't?"

"No. He went somewhere, I think."

Very good. Helpful, as usual. "Oh. I see. Well . . . thanks. Sorry I woke you up."

"That's okay. I was only sleeping."

Meg hung up. Tony's dad had been drinking even more than usual lately. Tony didn't talk about it much. But she knew it worried him.

She stared at the phone. Where could Tony be so late on a school night?

She sent out a mental signal: "Tony—I need you. Call me. Call me, Tony. Are you getting this message?" She concentrated hard, giving full force to any telepathic powers she might have.

Then an unhappy thought interrupted her message-sending.

He couldn't be out with someone else, could he?

Could he?

Tony, walking quickly, did not pick up Meg's telepathic signal. He was six blocks from his home on the Canyon Road. His sneakers were soaked, as were the cuffs of his jeans. He must have walked through rain puddles without noticing them. He couldn't wait to get home and change into some dry clothes.

The street was silent except for the sound of water dripping off the tall trees and the damp sound of his shoes against the pavement as he walked.

Suddenly he heard a loud, insistent thumping sound. Tony automatically felt his chest. But the sound was coming from the driveway of a house halfway down the block. White spotlights attached to the roof lit up the entire drive and side of the house. It's almost as bright as day over there, Tony marveled.

He kept walking till he recognized the guy shooting baskets on a brightly lit garage backboard. It was Brian's *Wizards & Dungeons* buddy. "Hey—Dwayne!"

Dwayne Colligan didn't look up. He dribbled in for a layup, missed, took the rebound, and dribbled back down the drive. "I thought I smelled you in the neighborhood, Colavito" was his cheerful greeting.

Tony ran across the neighbor's lawn onto Dwayne's drive, waited for his moment, and stole the ball from Dwayne. "Hey, Tony—you'll infect my ball, man!"

"Take a lesson, Colligan," Tony said and made a high hook shot. Swish. It didn't even touch the rim.

"Lucky shot," Dwayne scoffed.

"What are you doing out here in the middle of the night?" Tony asked, looking up at the bright spotlights.

"I like to shoot baskets at night, man," Dwayne said, dribbling in and making an easy layup. "It's kinda soothing, you know." He caught his own rebound and quickly shot again, this time a fadeaway hook shot. "Where you comin' from, Tony?"

"Around," Tony said.

Dwayne dribbled in circles around Tony. His biceps flexed when he dribbled. He had powerful arms. His body didn't look like a teenager's. He had spent thousands of hours getting it that way.

"So how's it going?" Tony asked, just making conversation as Dwayne missed an easy jumpshot.

"It's going," Dwayne said with a shrug. He grabbed the rebound and dribbled away from Tony.

"How's it going with Shannon?" Tony asked, grinning.

"Not great," Dwayne said, very serious. He tossed up a wild shot that bounced off the side of the garage. "Truth is, she won't go out with me."

"That's a downer, man," Tony said, chasing the ball down the drive.

"I don't get it," Dwayne said, pushing both hands against the shingled wall of the house and doing some quick stretching exercises. "I know her brother hated me."

"Evan?"

"He hated my guts. He told me to stay away from his sister. He knew I was hot for her. He said he'd make me regret it if I ever came near her."

"Yeah?" Tony dribbled the ball hard against the asphalt drive. He never knew any of this. Evan had never talked about Dwayne to him.

"You know something, man," Dwayne said, a wide smile on his pale face, "when they found Evan shot dead in the woods, that was good news to me. I was glad. That meant I could go get his sister."

Tony felt the rage start in his chest, then spread over his entire body.

"Evan was my best friend!"

He screamed so loud, he hurt his throat.

He pulled back the basketball in one hand and heaved it with all his might, slamming it into Dwayne's stomach.

Dwayne uttered a groan of surprise. Tony started to run, slipping on the wet driveway. He was three houses away when Dwayne called after him. "What's your problem, dork?" he shouted. But he made no move to come after Tony.

Tony kept running, picking up speed as he ran.

"You're a real dork, man!" Dwayne shouted, cradling the ball against his stomach with both of his big, meaty hands. "What's wrong with you, anyway?!"

Tony ran for two blocks before stopping. Now he was drenched with sweat. But he felt much better.

In fact, he felt pretty good.

He didn't like people saying bad things about Evan. In fact, he wouldn't stand for it.

Evan was a great guy.

Dwayne was a first-class sleazoid creep.

He couldn't stand there and let someone like Dwayne say he was glad that Evan was dead. He had to throw the basketball at him. He had to hurt Dwayne for saying that. He had to do something—and he did.

Tony felt good about that. He felt so good, he ran the rest of the way home, four long blocks without slowing down once.

CHAPTER 10

FRIDAY NIGHT

Meg knew she was in big trouble over her psych paper now. It was already three days overdue. She had written only two paragraphs, and she wasn't sure she liked them.

But what could she do? She had so much on her mind.

If only she could talk to Tony, tell him what had been going on, tell him about the lunch bag filled with fake blood, tell him about the car that tried to run her down . . . maybe.

She had looked for him in school. But he wasn't there.

She threw her pen down and crinkled up the sheet of notebook paper she had been staring at. I should be with Tony right now, she thought. It's Friday night. I shouldn't be sitting here alone, writing a boring paper.

What was Tony trying to prove, anyway? That he was as stubborn as she was? Why hadn't he called her?

She jumped up from her desk. "I'm going over there," she said aloud. "Right now."

She told her parents she was going over to Tony's, took the car keys from their usual shelf by the door, and drove to the end of the Canyon Road to the small rowhouse where Tony and his father lived.

Thinking of all she had to say to Tony, imagining how they

would make up, she parked against the curb and ran up the steps to Tony's front stoop.

The door swung open before she could knock. Tony's father stepped out, the Cubs cap he always wore pulled down low on his forehead. He looked as surprised to see her as she was to see him. She was always surprised by how much he looked like Tony, a slighter, gray-haired version.

"Hi. How are you?" they both said at once.

"I was just going out for a . . . uh . . . walk," Mr. Colavito said. That meant he was heading to the corner tavern.

"Is Tony home?"

"No."

"No?"

"No. Sorry. Anything I can do? You okay?"

"Yeah. I'm . . . okay. Do you know where he went?"

Mr. Colavito started down the steps. Meg stayed at his side. Somewhere down the street, a cat was screeching its head off. It started all the dogs in the neighborhood barking, an animal symphony.

"He went with that boy Brian. He's your cousin, ain't he?"

"Brian. Yeah. Tony went somewhere with Brian?"

Since when would Tony have anything to do with Brian?

"Yeah. They went off to play some kind of game together." Mr. Colavito walked quickly. He was eager to get to the tavern.

"*Wizards and Dungeons?*"

"Yeah. That's it. I think that's it. Tony said not to worry. He wouldn't be out too late. You can try callin' him later." He hurried on ahead.

"Okay. Thanks," Meg called after him. "Did they say where they were going?"

"Nope. They didn't tell me," Tony's dad called back, and disappeared around the corner.

Meg slowly climbed back into her car, feeling more confused than ever. Tony wasn't into *Wizards & Dungeons*. And he never could stand Brian. Why on earth would he suddenly go off on a Friday night with Brian to play the game?

Did they go to the Fear Street woods? That was where Brian and Dwayne always went to play it. Would he really go to those frightening woods with Brian, after all that had happened there?

Meg thought she might drive around for a while, but she suddenly felt very tired. She drove straight home, pulled the car up the drive, ran inside, and went up to bed.

It took more than an hour to get to sleep. When she finally did manage to drift off, she had strange, colorful dreams, troubling dreams in which she was chasing people, chasing the wrong people, chasing people she didn't even know.

The ringing phone on her desk woke her up. For a long moment she thought she was still dreaming. Still chasing. Still being chased.

She picked up the receiver reluctantly. "Hello?" Sleep clogged her throat.

"Hello, Meg? Are Brian and Tony there?"

"No. Who is this?"

"It's Tony's dad."

"Oh. Hi. Sorry. I was asleep. I—"

"They're not there?" He sounded strange, very tense. He spoke too clearly, too distinctly, as if he'd been drinking and was trying to hide it.

"No. Of course not."

"It's four in the morning," Mr. Colavito said. "Brian's mother called me. Brian isn't home and neither is Tony. Do you have any idea where they might have gone to play that stupid game?"

"Well . . . uh . . . I don't know. The Fear Street woods, maybe . . ." Meg forced herself to wake up. What was going on here? Why did Mr. Colavito sound so worried?

"I'm calling the police," he told her. "Tony and Brian have both disappeared."

CHAPTER 11

FRIDAY, AFTER MIDNIGHT

Meg was wide awake now. Too awake. Her mind filled with horrifying images of Tony and Brian, of the thick, dreaded woods where so many tragedies, explained and unexplained, had taken place.

Tony, what were you doing there? she thought. Why were you in those woods with Brian tonight?

And why haven't you come out?

She knew she had to go there. She had to see that they were all right. She crept over to her closet and pulled out the jeans she had been wearing earlier. Struggling to pull them up in the dark, she stumbled, bumped her desk, and the desk lamp went crashing to the floor.

"What was that?" she heard her mother ask in the next room.

A few seconds later her father lumbered out to investigate, turning on the hall light and peering into her room.

"Meg—where are you going? What time is it?" He looked like a bear coming out of hibernation, yawning and squinting at her.

"It's late, Dad. But I have to go out."

"Where are you going?" he repeated, rubbing his thick, black stubble. He looked very confused.

"Uh . . . well . . . Tony's missing, you see."

"Missing? What do you mean missing? Where?"

"In the Fear Street woods, I think."

Her father thought about that for a while. Meg pulled a heavy wool sweater down over her head. She had it all the way on before she realized it was backward. She decided to leave it that way.

"Let me get this straight. You're going to the Fear Street woods?" Her father was starting to wake up.

"Yes. I have to. Tony and Brian went there, I think, earlier this evening. Now they're missing."

"Fear Street?" He was trying hard to make sense of what Meg was telling him. But of course it didn't make any sense at all. "Sorry. I'm not letting you go there in the middle of the night."

"But, Tony—Dad, please—I have to! Brian once showed me the cave where he goes to play *Wizards and Dungeons*. I think I can find it. The police won't know where it is. I can help them."

He thought about it, rubbing his dark stubble. "Oh, all right. But I'll have to go with you. Just give me a second." He disappeared back into the bedroom.

Meg stood in the hall. She could hear him explaining quickly to her mother, banging into furniture as he pulled on his clothes. She thought of running to the car, driving away before he could come after her. But something held her back. She realized she was glad he was coming.

The dangers of the Fear Street woods weren't just rumor. People really did disappear in those dark hills that stretched for miles past the end of Fear Street. Strange, impossible accidents were reported in the newspaper. Trees fell, seemingly for no reason at all. Normally fearful animals attacked with bizarre ferocity.

Perhaps the strangest thing of all about those woods was that no birds ever ventured there. No birds chewed the ripe wild berries, or dug for worms in the soft earth, or built nests in the trees. Over the years, teams of scientists from universities around the nation had come intent on explaining why the woods were bird-free. But they all went home as mystified as when they had arrived.

"Ready?" Mr. Dalton reappeared in the hallway in a heavy plaid wool shirt and corduroys. "Let me just get a couple of flashlights. You can tell me the whole story on the way."

There wasn't much to tell. As they drove down the silent, empty roads toward Fear Street, Meg told him about Tony and Brian going off to play *Wizards & Dungeons*. And then about the call she had just received from Tony's dad.

"Tony isn't into that game, is he?" her father asked, turning on the windshield wipers to remove the thick mist from the windshield.

"No," Meg answered quietly. "He isn't."

"I didn't think so. He's not the type."

Meg was too tired to ask her father what he meant by that. She knew he didn't really approve of Tony. He probably meant it as some kind of a dig. But she didn't want to get into any kind of discussion now. She just wanted to concentrate, concentrate on Tony and Brian being okay.

As they turned down Fear Street, the sky seemed to darken. Meg realized it was because of the trees that overhung the street. They passed the old cemetery and followed the narrow, curving street to its end.

Flashing red lights indicated that the police were already there. Two patrol cars were parked at the edge of the woods, the lights on their roofs blood red, circling soundlessly, a silent alarm that made Meg's heart jump and made the fear she had been holding down rise up to her throat.

She jumped out before her father stopped the car and ran across the wet ground, blinking against the harsh red lights, fighting the fear, pushing it back down so that she could breathe.

"Oh. Hi." She bumped right into Tony's dad, who leaned against a patrol car, trying to regain his balance. His eyes looked red and watery in the harsh light.

He pointed into the woods. "They're in there somewhere. The cops found footprints. They're gonna find 'em." It was obvious that he'd had quite a bit to drink. Meg had to struggle to make out what he was saying.

Brian's parents, Sid and Marge, Meg's aunt and uncle, hurried over, their faces tight with worry. "Meg, you didn't have to come," Sid said, squeezing her arm as if making sure she was really there. "I'm sure Brian and Tony are perfectly—Oh. Hi, Todd."

Meg's dad appeared behind Meg, looking grim and uncomfortable. "Any sign of 'em?"

"Not yet. But they're in there," Marge said, her voice a whisper. She looked away.

"We don't know why Brian likes that game so much," Sid said. "He probably just lost track of time. He's been doin' that a lot these days."

"That's probably it," Meg's dad said, not too convincingly. He looked over at Tony's dad, who was still propped up against one of the patrol cars, his eyes swimming in his head. Mr. Dalton frowned and then suddenly remembered the flashlights he was carrying. "Let's go. We can help the police look for them." He offered a flashlight to Brian's dad.

Sid started to take it, but Marge pulled his hand back. "No. Stay here with me. The police said to stay here by the cars, not to go hunting for them."

"I'm not just going to stand here," Mr. Dalton said impatiently. "They didn't tell that to me."

"I'm coming with you," Meg said, reaching for a flashlight. "I know where the cave is where they play. Follow me."

Mr. Dalton hesitated for a moment, pulling back on the flashlight, but, seeing the frantic look on Meg's face, he relented. "Okay. But stick close to me. Stay right with me, you hear?"

Meg nodded agreement, clicked on the flashlight, and followed its narrow beam of light into the woods. The ground was blanketed with dried, brown leaves and fallen twigs. Every footstep made a loud crunch which seemed to echo through the trees. Meg stopped, thinking someone was following them. But it was just the sound of her own sneakers crackling over the leafy ground.

"Someone's gonna have to give those boys a good talkin' to," Mr. Dalton said, aiming his flashlight at his feet but still stumbling over a fallen tree limb. He landed hard on his knees but quickly pulled himself up and continued on. "They've got no right to scare us all this way."

Meg didn't say anything. She was thinking of Evan. Then Brian. Then Brian finding Evan, shot dead in these same woods.

Meg's father wandered off to the left. She could see his flashlight flickering between the trees. Lost in her own thoughts, she didn't realize they were heading in different directions.

She shivered. The air was wet and cold. It didn't feel like spring in the woods tonight. Tree frogs began to chirp, a sudden, deafening symphony of scratching. She heard a flapping sound overhead. It wasn't a bird. It must have been a bat.

"TONY!" she shouted suddenly. Her voice didn't sound like her at all. It sounded like a frightened girl in a bad horror movie. *Nightmare on Fear Street*, she thought. Freddy's coming. Freddy's coming!

No!

Stop thinking stupid thoughts.

"TONY! TONY!" She didn't care what she sounded like. She just wanted to find him.

Something darted behind the wide trunk of an old maple tree. Something—or someone?

"TONY? BRIAN? ARE YOU THERE?"

No. It was an animal, a raccoon, slinking out of her circle of light, seeking the safety of the dark.

Without thinking, she followed the creature, trying to get it back into her light. She stopped when she realized she had become sidetracked, and changed direction, moving the yellow light in wide circles now. The tree frogs stopped their shrieking as suddenly as they had started. Now the only sound was the crackling of the dry leaves beneath her sneakers and—

"Dad?"

Where was he?

She had kept his light in view in the corner of her eye. But now she couldn't find it.

"Dad? Hey—Dad?"

No reply.

She had wandered too far, following that stupid raccoon, lost in her own morbid thoughts. And now she was alone. At least until she could find him again. Or until she could find Tony and Brian.

"TONY? TONY? CAN YOU HEAR ME?"

Where were the police? Where were their flashlights? How far had she wandered? What direction was she going?

She turned around. Then turned around again. Nothing but blackness. "TONY? BRIAN?"

She climbed a low hill, slipping on the wet leaves. The Fear Street woods weren't flat. Low hills and sharp ravines made hiking treacherous in the daytime. At night, she realized, it was impossible not to stumble, not to fall. "TONY? DAD?"

Silence.

I'm not going to get frightened, she thought. But what was that tight feeling in her throat? And why did her legs feel so rubbery? And why could she feel her heart pounding against her chest?

No. I'm not going to get frightened. At least, not any more frightened than I already am. "DAD?" Her voice sounded so weak. She was trying to shout, but she couldn't. Her mouth felt so dry. "DAD? TONY?"

Where were they?

Where was she?

She took a few steps forward, then turned around. She followed her beam of light through the trees. A tall, thick clump of flowering weeds appeared to be a man leaning toward her. She turned away from it, feeling a stab of fright course down her back. She took a few more steps. But was she going forward or back? She moved the light in a circle. She was spinning. No. The ground was spinning.

STOP!

She took determined steps, careful but determined, walking in a straight line, twigs crackling loudly beneath her, another low, gray animal slinking out of the light which she kept directly ahead of her.

"TONY? DAD? ANYBODY HEAR ME?"

She stopped.

But the crackling continued for a few seconds.

She spun around. "Who is it?"

Silence.

Had she just imagined it? It sounded like footsteps.

She started walking again. A twig snapped like a gunshot behind her.

She stopped. Someone was there. "Tony? Is that you? Brian?" She swung the light around, moving it slowly in a wide arc. No one.

Was it the police? Her dad? No. They would've answered her.

Was someone else lurking in the woods—a *stranger*?

She started walking faster. The footsteps behind her came faster. She was up on the balls of her feet, trying to tiptoe away, trying to run over the impossibly tangled ground.

But whoever pursued her was faster.

"OHHHH!"

A hand grabbed her shoulder roughly from behind.

CHAPTER 12

FRIDAY, AFTER MIDNIGHT

Her flashlight was kicked from her hand. It sailed into a deep clump of leaves, its light buried. Meg tried to twist free. But the hand held tight, squeezing her shoulder harder as she struggled. She realized she was gasping for air. The sharp pain from her shoulder was spreading down her arm, down her side, down her entire body.

The grip on her shoulder tightened. She felt hot breath against her cheek. She smelled onions and french fry grease.

"I warned you—don't have the party."

The words were whispered but the whisper was a roar.

With one desperate surge of strength, she pulled herself out of the suffocating grasp. She lurched forward—and screamed as she began to fall. She raised her hands to grab onto something. But there was nothing to grab.

She was falling down a steep ravine, falling face forward, then rolling. Her head hit something hard, a rock or a tree stump.

Lights flashed in her head, flashed in rhythm to the throbbing pain. The lights didn't stop, even though she was unconscious.

She came to quickly, feeling the pain in her head and in her shoulder. She didn't know where she was. She looked for her ceiling, her dresser, her desk. But she wasn't in bed.

She was lying on wet ground, in a deep, foul-smelling pile of decaying leaves and weeds.

She sat up, her head throbbing harder. She remembered now.

"Hey—" She tried to shout, but she didn't make any sound. She reached up and pulled twigs from her hair.

My hair. I must look a mess, she thought.

Of all the crazy things to think about. Am I going crazy?

A leaf was stuck against the back of her neck. She pulled it away and felt a surge of nausea. She fought it back. And sitting up straight, taking deep breaths, fought back the dizziness too.

And stood up.

And saw the body lying at her feet.

At least, she saw part of a body. A sweatshirt pulled up to reveal bare skin. The back of the sweatshirt, torn and stained. Blue jeans. An arm.

Wait a minute. Was she seeing things? Was she hallucinating because of her fall?

She dropped to her knees to get a closer look. No. It was a real body. It moved suddenly, and groaned.

It was alive.

The stains on the sweatshirt. The stains . . .

She reached forward and touched the sleeve, pulling her hand back as she felt the warm wetness. Blood.

She crawled around him, and turned him so she could see the face. Brian.

Not Tony. Brian.

She felt so guilty for thinking that. But she couldn't stop her thoughts. She couldn't hold back the feeling of relief she felt.

"Brian—are you awake? Can you hear me?"

He groaned again but didn't move. His mouth was bleeding.

She saw his face in the light. It was swollen and bloody.

The light?

Someone was shining a flashlight down on them. "Meg? What—what are you doing here?" a familiar voice called from the top of the ravine.

"Tony? Is that you? You're okay? Are you really okay?"

He came sliding down the side of the ravine. Then he ran to her, pulled her up from the ground, and put his arms around her.

"Tony—I was so worried. Oh, I'm so glad to see you! Somebody grabbed me and pushed me and—"

He held her tighter, pressing his cheek against her forehead. "Ssshhhh. It's going to be okay," he said softly.

"But, Brian—" she started. "He—he's—"

She could feel Tony's muscles go tense. He let go of her and took a step back. "I went to get help, but I got turned around, I was heading into the woods instead of to the street."

"But what happened?" Meg cried, feeling her panic return the moment Tony let go of her.

"Brian fell down the ravine. I guess his flashlight went out and he tried to run without it. I didn't see him fall. It took me a long while to find him. Then I went to get help."

"But I don't understand why—"

"How did you find him?" Tony asked. "Meg, what are you doing here?"

"Someone grabbed me. I got away, but I fell," she said, reaching for his hand, squeezing his hand. "Oh—your hand is cut!"

He pulled it away from her. "From branches and things. I was running, trying to get help. I guess I cut myself. Who grabbed you? What happened?" He spoke to her tenderly, his face filled with concern.

He still cared about her. Despite the horror of what had just happened, she felt strangely relieved.

"I couldn't see him. It happened so fast."

"OVER HERE! HERE THEY ARE!"

"YOU KIDS OKAY?"

The shouting voices were accompanied by darting circles of light, and in a few seconds, two policemen appeared, followed by Meg's dad. "You're okay?" he cried, rushing forward to hug her. "I thought you were right with me. I turned away and you were gone."

"Where's the other one?" one of the policemen asked Tony, shining his flashlight into Tony's face. The policeman was very young, Meg saw. He looked as young as Tony, although that was impossible, and he seemed very frantic, as if this were the first excitement he'd had on the job.

Tony turned away from the harsh light and pointed down into the ravine. "Brian's down there. He fell. He's hurt pretty bad."

"Radio for an ambulance," the policeman told his partner as he scrambled down the side of the ravine to examine Brian. The other policeman turned and started to run to the patrol car.

"He's beat up pretty bad," the policeman called, squatting next to Brian, shining his light in Brian's face. The policeman sounded too upset.

Don't they teach them to always sound calm? Meg asked herself.

Brian stirred and opened his eyes. He tried to lift his head, but the policeman gently indicated for him to lie back.

"What happened here, son?" The policeman shined his light in Tony's face.

That's funny, Meg thought. He looks younger than Tony, but he calls Tony "son."

Tony squinted back at him. He looked very tired and very frightened, Meg thought. "He fell. I didn't really see it."

"Pretty bad fall," the policeman said, lowering his light to Tony's chest. The front of Tony's sweatshirt was mudstained and torn.

"I went for help," Tony told him. "But I got lost."

"What were you doing here late at night in the first place?" the policeman demanded. Meg could hear an ambulance siren in the distance.

"Nothing, really," Tony said uncomfortably. "Playing a game."

"Some game," the policeman growled. He took off his uniform jacket and draped it over Brian's chest. "Keep warm, son. You're going to be okay." Brian gazed up at him. He didn't say anything. He didn't seem to know where he was.

A few minutes later the ambulance arrived. Two men in white labcoats dropped down into the ravine and lifted Brian onto a canvas stretcher.

"I'm okay," Brian insisted. "Really. I'm okay." He stared up at Meg but didn't seem to recognize her. "I'm okay. Really." She heard him protesting as they carried him off to the ambulance.

"Your dad is waiting for you," Mr. Dalton told Tony, not bothering to hide his angry feelings. "And I'd better go talk to Sid and Marge. You boys sure caused a lot of trouble and a lot of worry tonight for no good reason."

Tony looked away and didn't say anything.

"If I were your dad, I'd ground you for life," Mr. Dalton said.

"Yeah, yeah," Tony muttered under his breath.

"What did you say to me?" Meg's dad flared.

"Now, come on, Dad," Meg said softly. "It wasn't Tony's fault. He's had a hard night, too. It must have been very frightening being lost in these woods. Give him a break."

"I tried to get help," Tony repeated.

Mr. Dalton scowled at Tony. Then his face filled with surprise as he looked at Meg closely for the first time. "What happened to you? You're covered with dirt."

"I tripped," she lied quickly, feeling her face go red. Luckily, he couldn't see it by the light of the flashlight. "That ravine is impossible to see, and it's so steep."

"Poor Brian," Tony muttered.

"Poor Brian? It's a little late for that," Mr. Dalton sputtered angrily. "It's a little late for everything. Maybe you'll think twice before going off in the woods to play a stupid, worthless game." He stomped on ahead of them, looking like an angry bear who just had a fish stolen away from him.

Meg and Tony followed behind, walking slowly. Meg took Tony's arm and leaned against him as they walked. "Why *were* you here playing the game with Brian?" she asked, whispering so her father couldn't hear their conversation.

Tony shrugged. "I don't know. It looked like it might be fun."

"But you were never interested in it before," Meg said, walking even slower, letting her father get farther ahead.

"Yeah, I was," Tony told her, sounding defensive. "I just wanted to see what it was like. But I didn't know Brian was so serious about it. As soon as we got to the woods, he sort of changed. He became a Third-Level Wizard, or whatever. He was playing a character, but he *was* the character. He's too serious. It's like he lost himself completely. It's scary."

"What character did you play?" Meg asked, holding onto his arm, stepping carefully over a fallen tree limb.

"Uh . . . a warrior, I guess. It was weird."

"The whole thing's weird. You never could stand Brian. Now all of a sudden—"

"That's not true," Tony said angrily. He stopped walking and pushed away her arm. "How many times do I have to say it? I was just curious about the game. That's all. Give me a break! You want to cross-examine someone? Go to law school!"

"I'm sorry," she said quickly, surprised by his anger. "I didn't mean anything. I've had a bad night, too, you know."

He suddenly seemed to remember that she had been grabbed by someone in the darkness. His face softened. He lowered his head. "I'm sorry too," he muttered. "So you didn't see the guy who grabbed you?"

"No. It was so dark. It happened so fast. He took away my

flashlight. Then he grabbed me. Then he whispered something in my ear about the party. Then I fell down the ravine."

"He *what*? What about the party?" Tony put both hands on her shoulders to stop her. "Tell me this again."

"He said, 'I warned you about the party.' Something like that. He sounded very angry, very crazy. I was so scared. He was breathing into my ear. His breath was so hot. And he really hurt my shoulder. It still aches."

Tony looked very upset. "Do you think he followed you into the woods? Do you think he was waiting outside your house and followed you here?"

"I don't know. I don't know what to think. Last night, I was coming home from Shannon's. I think someone tried to run me over in a car. I'm frightened, Tony. I—"

"Oh no. Oh no. No no no. I'm just so glad you're okay," Tony said, pulling her close. "This is all too much, Meg. Too much. You'll forget about the party now, won't you?"

"What?"

"This is just too scary, too dangerous. You'll forget about the party, right?"

"No way," Meg said, a grim frown of determination on her face. "You don't know me very well, do you! A challenge is a challenge. I'm going to have that party for Ellen. It's the only way I can find out who is doing all this to us!"

Tony let go of her. He stood staring into her eyes, then looked away.

I love the way he's so worried about me, Meg thought.

"You look so troubled," she said. "What are you thinking?"

"That you're making a big mistake," he said, suddenly looking very scared. "You've got to think about this, Meg. Really think about it. Whoever tried to run you down, whoever grabbed you tonight—he might have been trying to show you that . . . that he might do something even worse. . . ."

CHAPTER 13

SUNDAY AFTERNOON

On Sunday, a balmy, hazy Sunday that felt more like summer than spring, Meg slept late, had a long, leisurely breakfast of pancakes and bacon, and then walked up to North Hills to visit Brian. It wasn't exactly her idea of how to spend a Sunday afternoon, but both of her parents had urged her, and pestered her, and repeatedly told her how much it would mean to Brian, who wasn't allowed to leave his bed because the doctors thought he might have internal injuries. So finally she gave in and decided just to get it over with.

Brian lived in an enormous white house overlooking the river. With its tall columns on both sides of the double-doored entranceway, it always reminded Meg more of a Southern plantation than a house a normal person would live in. When she was little, Meg would wander off by herself down the long, carpeted corridors, peeking into room after room, until she'd get frightened and run back to where everyone else was, usually in the front parlor or the library.

The house was too big, too creaky, too old, too . . . scary. No wonder Brian grew up to be so weird!

As Meg walked up the long, smooth driveway, lined with

carefully pruned hedges, she saw a familiar blue Taurus beside the house. She saw Cory Brooks and his friend David Metcalf coming out of the house. They weren't smiling or joking around as usual, she noticed immediately.

"Hey, Meg. Hi. How's it goin'?" Cory called. She wondered if he was glad to see her, or glad to be leaving Brian's house.

"Okay, I guess," she said.

"Lookin' good," David said.

Meg was embarrassed. She suddenly remembered she hadn't even brushed her hair. She was only going to see Brian, after all. She hadn't planned on running into anyone else.

"I heard about your lunch bag the other day," Cory said sympathetically.

"Great lunch. We didn't know you were a vampire," David said, laughing at his own joke. No one else laughed.

"It was only red paint," Meg said, making a face at David. "But it sure looked like blood."

"What a bad-news joke," Cory said.

"I'm not so sure it was a joke," Meg said, feeling a sudden chill despite the heat.

"Yeah. Lisa told me someone was trying to scare you," Cory said, shaking his head. Then his mouth dropped open and his eyes nearly popped out of his head. "Lisa! Oh no! I forgot about her! I was supposed to pick her up an hour ago!"

He started running to his car, with David following. "Hey, how's Brian doing?" Meg called after them.

"Not too good!" Cory called, starting the car while David scrambled to climb in.

"He's real quiet. And when he does talk, he doesn't make any sense," David called.

He didn't make any sense *before* his fall, Meg thought. Then she scolded herself for thinking such harsh things about her poor,

injured cousin. She watched Cory speed around the circular driveway and take off toward Lisa's house, which was only a few blocks
away. She watched the car until it turned a corner and, realizing she
couldn't put it off any longer, went up the flagstone walk and rang
the bell.

"Oh, hi, Meg. Your mom told me you were coming. Brian will be
so glad to see you."

"Hi, Aunt Marge. How's he doing?"

Meg's aunt chewed her lower lip. She seemed very nervous.
"Oh . . . he'll be okay, I think. He's just a little . . . distracted. The
shock of the accident. You know."

"Yeah. He must be pretty shaken up," Meg said awkwardly. She
didn't really know what to say. She hurried past the long, mirrored
dining room, down the corridor that led to Brian's room.

"He looks worse than he feels," Brian's mother called after her.

"Thanks for the warning," Meg said. She turned and glanced
back just before she reached Brian's room. Aunt Marge suddenly
looked so much older.

Meg continued to Brian's bedroom door, stopped just outside it,
and forced a smile to her face. She froze it there, determined to keep
smiling no matter what. She had come to cheer Brian up, after all.

She knocked on the heavy oak door and walked in. Brian looked
up but didn't make an attempt to sit up.

"Brian—is that you?" she cried.

Nice going, Meg, she thought. Of all the stupid things to say!
Why did I say that? Why not just walk in and say, "Yecch. Your face
looks like something in a butcher shop window!" Go ahead. Tell
him how horrible he looks. That'll cheer him up.

"Hi, Meg," Brian said. His voice sounded okay, but his right
cheek was so swollen he couldn't move his mouth very well. He had
one black eye which opened only halfway. A cut on his chin, Meg
saw, had required several stitches.

"Brian, you really know how to take a fall. Maybe you should be a stuntman."

He tried to laugh, but it came out a wheeze.

"A wizard doesn't need a stuntman," he said. At least, that's what Meg thought he said. He was talking so slowly and softly, it was hard for her to hear.

"I didn't bring you candy or flowers," she said, sitting down tentatively at the foot of the queen-size bed. "I didn't think you really wanted that stuff."

He stared at her with his one good eye, but didn't reply.

"Is there anything you do want? Anything I can bring you? Your homework, maybe?" She laughed, a forced laugh, but it sounded pretty genuine.

He didn't seem to hear her. "How do I look?" he asked, his voice flat, expressionless.

"You look . . . uh . . . not great." She wasn't going to lie to him. He had mirrors. He could see for himself. "Let's put it this way—you've looked better."

He seemed to be thinking about that answer. Finally he muttered something about not having the power to change things. Meg couldn't really hear him.

"Maybe things will go better for me when school's out," he said clearly, a bit louder, still staring at her with his unswollen eye.

"You'll feel better soon," she said. "Are they giving you some kind of painkillers?"

"Yeah. I guess." He turned his head away.

"You really did it to yourself this time," Meg said, trying to sound light, but it didn't come out that way.

"Did you come here to scold me?" Brian snapped. "Very helpful."

"Sorry. I didn't mean it that way," Meg said, feeling guilty. She was always picking on him, it seemed. From the time they were little kids, she had never been able to tolerate him for more than a few seconds. But she knew she should be a little more understanding now. He really looked as if he'd been run over by a truck.

She suddenly remembered Shannon's suspicions about Brian, about that day a year ago in the Fear Street woods. Did Brian have a secret—a dark, dirty secret he had been keeping from them all these months?

"What were you and Tony doing in the woods so late at night?" she asked. She leaned forward and stared into his eyes, hoping it might encourage a direct answer from him.

But he didn't say anything. Then finally, in a faraway voice, he said, "The Warrior came and fought for his place."

"Brian, really—" Meg felt the anger rise in her again, but this time held it in check.

"But the Wizard has tricks that warriors do not know of."

"Great, Brian. Great. So you and Tony were playing *Wizards and Dungeons*, or whatever it's called?"

"The battle isn't won yet," he said mysteriously.

Meg realized she had better change the subject. Brian obviously did not want to talk about what had happened. "Are you going to get back to school in time for finals?" she asked, forcing a smile.

He didn't reply.

"The seniors are out already," she told him. "Now they just have to wait for their final grades and graduation. It's supposed to rain next Tuesday, so they may have to move the graduation into the auditorium."

Again, he didn't reply. He was staring at her now. He looked as if he were thinking hard, debating something in his mind, trying to decide whether to tell her something or not.

She decided to give him one more chance to talk about the other night. "Did you ask Tony to play the game with you, or did he ask you?"

"I will reveal everything when I reach the Fourth Level and become a full-powered Wizard," Brian said.

How annoying. She just wanted to shake him. All this stupid wizard talk.

Why wouldn't he answer her question? She really wanted to know about Friday night in the Fear Street woods. Was it Tony's idea to go play the game in the woods? Did Brian somehow force him to come along? Tony wouldn't talk about it, and neither would Brian. Why? Were they *both* afraid of something, of someone?

"You look tired, Brian. Maybe I should go." She stood up and stretched.

"Thank you," he said softly. Was it thank you for coming? Or thank you for going?

"You'll feel better real soon," she said. "You just need plenty of rest."

"Thank you," he repeated.

She reached forward and squeezed his hand. It felt soft and lifeless, like an overripe peach.

She started to leave, but he held on to her wrist. He pulled her back with surprising strength. She waited for him to explain, but he stared up at her silently.

She waited a long while, her hand gripped by his, waiting for him to speak.

"I—I should confess," he said finally, letting go of her hand.

"What?" She wasn't sure she had heard correctly. She stared down at the bedspread. It was too painful to look at his swollen, purple jaw from this close.

"I—uh . . . no." He seemed to change his mind. He turned his head toward the window.

The room darkened as clouds covered the sun. The breeze from the window had turned cold and damp. Another storm was blowing up outside.

Meg felt a chill that wasn't caused by the wind. She suddenly had a hunch. A hunch about what Brian wanted to say, about what he wanted to confess.

She took a deep breath. "Brian," she said. "Look at me."
He turned back to face her.
"Brian—did you make a call? Have you been calling me?"
"Yes," he said calmly. "I have."

CHAPTER 14

SUNDAY AFTERNOON

"What?"

She hadn't expected him to confess so quickly, so easily. He was so casual about it, it was hard to believe him.

She waited for him to apologize, to start to explain, but he just stared back at her blankly.

The room grew darker. Nervously, she walked around the bed and clicked on the table lamp beside it. The lamp cast a yellow glow over his face, leaving his black eye and swollen jaw in shadows, making his wounds seem deeper, more ugly.

"You admit it? You made that call?" Her voice came out higher and shriller than she had wanted. But his casualness was unnerving her.

"Yes," he said, a narrow smile forming on one side of his puffy, swollen cheek. "I wanted!—"

He started to add something, but they were interrupted. His father poked his head into the room, looking concerned. "Everything okay in here?"

"Yes. Fine, Uncle Sid," Meg said quickly.

"How are you feeling, Brian?" his dad asked.

"Okay," Brian said after a long pause.

"Can I get you two anything? A Coke or something? A cup of tea?"

"No. No thanks, Uncle Sid. We're fine."

He left reluctantly. Meg listened to him pad down the long corridor, then turned back to Brian. "What were you going to say? About the call?"

"Yes." Brian stared up at her with his one good eye. "Yes, I remember. I've been calling. And I think I can reach Evan."

"Evan?!"

"I have the power, Meg. I have the Fourth-Level power. I think I can call Evan back."

"Cut the crap, Brian!" Meg shouted with sudden vehemence. She stood over him, her face twisted in anger. "I asked you a straight question. I want a straight answer. You're not going to hide behind any of this phony sword and sorcery baloney! You're going to tell me the truth."

Brian suddenly looked very frightened.

He couldn't be that frightened of me, Meg thought. What is he really frightened of? She was determined to find out before she left the room. "Did you call me or not?"

"Yes, I called you," he said, looking to the window. "I called you several times, three or four, I guess."

"What? Several times? Why? Why did you do it?"

"I wanted to warn you—" He stopped. "I can't talk about it. I really can't."

"What did you want to warn me about, Brian?" She wasn't going to back down. "What were you trying to prove?"

That seemed to make him angry. His swollen face turned scarlet. "I wasn't trying to prove anything. I told you. I was trying to warn you—"

"Of?"

"To . . . uh . . . be careful. But I couldn't tell you. I couldn't admit that . . . uh . . . I just couldn't. I hung up each time before you picked up the phone."

"What??" What was he talking about? Wasn't he confessing that he had made the threatening, whispered call, that he had been the one trying to frighten her?

"I was scared, Meg. I don't want to explain. I really can't explain. I'm telling you too much already. I can't tell you. I just can't."

"Can't tell me what, Brian? Can't admit what??"

He shook his head sadly. "You really don't understand anything, do you?"

"Can't admit what?" She felt so confused now, so frustrated. Why wouldn't he tell her what was on his mind?

"I can't, Meg. I just can't tell you. Don't try to force me. It won't do you any good. It won't do either of us any good. I'm warning you—"

"Stop saying that, Brian. Stop saying you're warning me. You're not making any sense. You're not explaining anything."

Suddenly he sat up and grabbed her wrist again. He leaned forward, pulling his swollen, battered face close to hers. Close up, in the dim bedroom light, he looked like a creature from a horror movie. The bitter, sharp aroma of antibiotic ointment rose from his face. Meg felt as if she couldn't breathe.

He pulled her even closer. "I'm warning you," he said, in a low voice she had never heard before. "There are things you don't understand. There are dangers. Real dangers. The woods . . . It wasn't an accident. . . . I mean—I can't . . . I shouldn't. But, listen to me, Meg. Watch out. I'm warning you. . . ."

He's threatening me, Meg thought.

This isn't a warning. It's a threat. But why?

He let go of her wrist and slumped back on his pillow. He suddenly looked exhausted, completely drained.

"Brian—"

He turned his back to her.

Rubbing her wrist, she silently ran out of the room, down the long, thick-carpeted corridor, and out the front door. On the front porch she stopped and leaned against one of the white columns, taking deep breaths, trying to get the smell of Brian's skin ointment out of her nose.

She looked up. Someone was walking across the porch.

"Ellen!"

"Oh!" Ellen's mouth dropped open in shock. "Meg! I didn't—"

"Ellen, what are you doing here?" Meg shrieked, completely shocked to see her.

"Well, I—uh . . ." Ellen looked really embarrassed.

"I didn't even know you were in town yet!"

"Well, yes. I . . ."

Meg ran over and gave her old friend a hug. "You look great!" she cried. She took a step back. Ellen looked exactly the same. She still looked beautiful with no makeup at all. Her hair was lighter and longer, but still tossed back simply behind her narrow shoulders. She was still so tall and lanky, still looked exactly like Daryl Hannah.

Ellen gave Meg an uncomfortable smile. "I just got in . . . a few hours ago. I was going to call you."

"I—I'm just so surprised," Meg said. "I looked up—and there you were!"

"It's really nice to see you," Ellen said stiffly, looking toward the double front doors. "How's Shannon?"

"Good. She's good," Meg said. "She can't wait to see you!"

"I'm at my aunt Amy's. Why don't you come over after school tomorrow? Bring Shannon too."

"Okay. Great!" Meg said brightly. "It's been such a long time. I can't wait to talk to you."

"Me too," Ellen said. She pulled her tan raincoat tighter and shivered. Ellen was always freezing, any time of year.

"What are you doing here?" Meg asked, suddenly remembering they were standing on Brian's front porch.

"I heard about Brian. About his accident. In the woods. I thought I'd just . . . you know . . . stop in and say hi."

"Oh. That's great," Meg said. "He can really use some cheering up. He's not in great shape."

"It must have been awful," Ellen said, closing her eyes. She stepped forward and gave Meg another hug. "See you tomorrow?"

"Can't wait. You look great. Really!"

"Thanks." Ellen turned and walked up to the front door.

Meg stepped off the porch, turned to watch Ellen go into the house, then headed for home, hurrying to beat the rain, thinking about Brian, the awful look on his face, the threats he made to her.

As soon as she got home, she rushed to her room and phoned Tony. "Please be home, Tony. Be home."

"Hello?"

"Tony? Hi. It's me."

"Meg. How are you?"

"Uh . . . I'm not sure. I was just over at Brian's."

"Yeah?" His interest seemed to perk up. "What happened? How come you sound so funny?"

"Well . . . Brian said the weirdest things to me. Frightening things. I really couldn't believe—"

"Brian what!?" Tony's voice stayed cool, but there was an edge to it.

"He said he shouldn't say anything. I mean, he wasn't going to—but he told me—"

There was a long silence at the other end. Finally, in what was almost a whisper, Tony said, "He did? He *told* you?" He suddenly sounded very upset.

"He warned me—"

"Listen—" Tony started.

"My parents are home. I've got to get off," Meg said. "We've got to talk, Tony. Later."

"Yeah," Tony agreed. "Brian told you, huh?"

"Well, yes, he—"

"We've got to talk, Meg. Tonight."

"No. I can't tonight, Tony. I've got to write my psych paper. I—"

"Okay. What about David's party tomorrow night? We'll meet there and then go somewhere, just the two of us."

"Yeah. Okay. That would be good." Meg was pleased. Tony never wanted to talk about anything serious lately. Now, here he was, volunteering to have a real discussion, just the two of them.

"We'll go up to River Ridge. We'll take a walk up there and we'll talk," Tony said.

"River Ridge? You mean the place they call Lover's Leap?"

"It's pretty up there, and we'll be alone," Tony said softly. "We haven't been together for so long. It'll be real nice, Meg. Just the two of us."

"Okay. But isn't it dangerous up there?" Meg asked.

"I'll take care of you," Tony said.

CHAPTER 15

SUNDAY AFTERNOON

Tony didn't realize how tightly he was gripping the phone receiver. When he slammed it down, his hand was tingling. His palm began to itch. He scratched it hard with the fingernails of his other hand, scratching faster and faster until the skin was red and raw, but the itching didn't go away.

The back of his neck felt cold and wet. He realized his legs were trembling. Still scratching his palm, he plopped down on the living room couch, threw his head back against one arm, and stared up at the ceiling.

So Brian had talked. Well, big surprise. Lately Tony had suspected that Brian might talk. He was the weakest one. Ellen's return, the plans for the party would be a perfect excuse for Brian to let go and spill his guts.

That's why Tony had done everything he could to make sure Brian wouldn't talk. Hadn't he taken Brian out to the Fear Street woods and beaten him up as a reminder not to talk?

But he talked anyway.

He *squealed*. That's the word they always used in gangster movies on TV. Brian *squealed*.

And now Meg knew.

Meg knew that Tony killed Evan. Brian had told her.

Tony uttered a loud cry, a moan of regret, of pain, of anger, and slammed his fist into the sofa cushion.

What was he going to do now?

Meg knew . . . Meg knew about last year. . . .

Once again Tony saw himself in those dreaded woods. Saw Ellen. Saw Evan.

Once again he felt the hunting rifle in his hands, Evan's rifle. Once again they struggled for control of it, screaming at each other, pulling with all their strength, out of control, out of all reason, pulling, pulling, pulling. . . .

And the gun went off. Just a loud pop. Like a firecracker, almost.

And Evan fell.

Tony had killed Evan.

And Ellen was screaming. In the background the whole time, Ellen was screaming. Like a wailing siren. Like a broken alarm. She was sitting on a fallen tree, pulling the sides of her straight, blond hair with both hands as if holding on to herself, and screaming, her eyes frozen open, staring straight ahead at Tony, staring at the boy who had just killed Evan.

But Tony hadn't meant to shoot Evan.

Or had he?

That's what he couldn't decide. What was he thinking at the moment? Was he thinking that he wanted to kill his friend, Ellen's boyfriend? Was he thinking that he *had* to kill him?

No.

It was an accident. It was just an accident. They struggled. The gun went off.

Because Tony had *wanted* it to go off.

No!

Tony *wanted* Evan dead.

No!

These thoughts were going to drive him crazy.

Maybe he already was crazy.

What was he going to do now? What was he going to do about Meg?

He didn't have a choice, did he? Meg wanted to talk to him. She didn't want to believe all that Brian had told her. That was so much like Meg. She wanted Tony to tell her that it all wasn't true, that everything was going to be just fine.

If I deny it, she'll believe me, he thought.

But that wasn't the answer. There was still Brian. And there was still Ellen. Ellen could talk. Ellen could give him away just as Brian had.

Maybe I shouldn't have beaten Brian up, he told himself, his mind going back a few nights ago to the woods, pictures of their fight in the darkness repeating behind his closed eyelids, pictures accompanied by the sound of his fist pounding Brian's chest, his shoulders, his stomach, and then his face.

Brian had told anyway. Despite Tony's fierce warning, after nearly a year of keeping the secret, Brian had told.

And now what was Tony supposed to do about Meg?

Didn't Brian realize the danger he was putting Meg in by telling her how Evan had been murdered?

No. Of course not. Brian wouldn't think of that.

What to do about Meg?

He couldn't let her turn him in. He couldn't let her tell everyone that he was a murderer. His life would be ruined. Over. All over.

He couldn't allow that.

She wouldn't keep his secret. She was such a straight arrow. There was no way he could trust her to keep the secret.

But he couldn't kill Meg, too—could he?

"No!" he said aloud. He sat up. Maybe if he sat up, the ringing in his ears would go away. Maybe his palm would stop itching.

He couldn't kill her—but he *had* to kill her. He had to push her off the River Ridge.

It was Brian's fault. Brian left Tony no choice. No choice at all.

Now it was either Meg or him.

And it wasn't going to be him. It was going to be Meg.

One push and his secret would be safe. One push. And what an excellent warning that would be to Ellen—and to Brian—not to say another word. They'd get the message, okay. They'd understand that they'd be next.

But, wait. This was Meg. Meg, Meg, Meg. He loved Meg—didn't he? He cared so much about Meg. Could he really be thinking of killing her? Could he really do it, just push her over the ridge?

Was he really a cold-blooded killer?

No!

Maybe.

Meg had sounded so worried on the phone. So horrified. But not horrified enough.

How could she be so trusting? How could she agree to go with him to River Ridge? She was just such a trusting, naive person. She was stupid. No. Maybe she really didn't believe Brian. Maybe Brian told her, and she refused to believe it.

Why should she believe Brian, anyway? Everyone knew he was wild. Out in the woods all the time playing that stupid game with Dwayne.

I don't have a choice, he decided. I have to kill poor Meg. Let me count the reasons. One. She knows too much. Two. It will be a warning to Ellen and Brian. Three. If Meg is dead, the surprise party will be canceled.

No, I can't. Not Meg. Not Meg.

But I have to.

I already killed Evan, my best friend. I can kill Meg, too.

Sorry, Meg. You understand, don't you? Of course you do.

You're always so understanding.

CHAPTER 16

MONDAY AFTERNOON

"So you didn't call the police after the car tried to run you down?"

"No. Maybe I should have, but I didn't," Meg said. "I mean, what could I tell them? I didn't even get a good look at the car. It was too dark. All I saw was headlights."

"But, Meg—" Shannon started.

"Besides, now I'm not even that sure it was trying to run me down. I mean, the road was real slippery because of the rain. Maybe the driver just lost control for a second. If I call the police, they won't be able to do anything. It'll just be a waste of time."

"But what about the guy who grabbed you in the woods?"

"Same thing," Meg said. "I didn't see him or anything. There's nothing helpful I can tell the police. Don't look at me like that, Shannon. I really think calling the police would be a waste of time."

Shannon shrugged. "Whatever."

They looked up at Ellen's aunt's house. It was bright yellow with freshly painted white shutters. The front lawn sloped up sharply. To get to the house, the girls would have to climb about a hundred flagstone steps built into the sloping grass.

"We should've brought mountain-climbing gear," Shannon complained, motioning for Meg to go first. "And a Saint Bernard." She followed Meg up the crooked stairs. "You want to go to David Metcalf's party tonight? He's having an end-of-school party because his parents are out of town."

"Yeah, I know," Meg said. "I'm meeting Tony there. We can go together. Pass the oxygen, please." They were halfway up the hill.

"Gee, it'll be great to see Ellen again," Shannon said. "Of course, we'll be too winded from the climb to talk to her. We can just make hand signals."

"She looked great," Meg said, suddenly feeling nervous about seeing her old friend.

Shannon was staring straight up. Meg followed Shannon's gaze and discovered that Ellen was standing at the top of the slope, waving down at them.

"Hi!"

"Hi! Hurry up!"

"Throw us a rope!"

Ellen was wearing a sleeveless, wine-colored T-shirt and white tennis shorts that emphasized her long legs. Her hair seemed even lighter, almost silvery, in the sun.

At the top of the hill a lot of hugs were exchanged, and everyone commented with high-pitched delight on how everyone hadn't changed a bit and how wonderful everyone looked and how great it was to be together again.

"Shall we go in?" Ellen asked. "My aunt is out shopping, but—"

"Let's stay out here. It's so pretty," Meg said, plopping down on the grass. "I love being able to look down the street from so high up."

"It doesn't take much to get Meg excited," Shannon cracked. She sat down on the top flagstone, straightening her blue top.

"So how are you?" Ellen asked, grinning at them both, her hair glowing in the sunlight. She took a seat between them and squeezed Meg's hand.

"Fine."

"Okay."

"How about you?"

"Yeah. Good. Real good," Ellen said. She giggled, a high-pitched giggle. Meg recognized it as her nervous giggle. When she was really tense, Meg knew, Ellen would end every sentence with that little jingle of a giggle.

They looked down the hill as a boy rode by on his bike. We were doing fine when we were standing up, Meg thought. Now it's gotten awkward. Come on, please. Somebody think of something to say.

"How's your new school?" Shannon asked Ellen.

Ellen put her hands behind her in the grass and leaned back on them. "It's okay, I guess. It's big. Much bigger than Shadyside. Sometimes I feel kinda . . . lost." The giggle again.

They stared down the hill. "What's happening at Shadyside?" Ellen asked, her fixed grin finally fading.

"Not much," Shannon said.

Meg's mind went blank. She couldn't think of anything interesting to tell Ellen. It's been a whole year, she thought. There must be *something*! "A few new teachers," she said. How lame.

"Cory Brooks and Lisa Blume are going together," Shannon said.

"You're kidding!" Ellen reacted with a little too much surprise, Meg thought. It wasn't *that* shocking, after all.

"That's amazing," Ellen added, followed by her nervous giggle.

"You going with anybody?" Meg blurted out. She could feel her face getting red. Sure, it was a normal question to ask someone—but not Ellen, not after her last boyfriend shot himself to death in the woods.

You're being too sensitive. That was a year ago, she scolded herself.

Ellen did look uncomfortable. "No," she said quickly, putting her grin back on her face. "I haven't really met anyone I like that much. I mean . . . I've gone out a few times. But . . ." She made a face.

"Suki Thomas got caught shoplifting," Shannon said, changing the subject.

"Big surprise," Ellen said, shaking her head.

"It was pretty serious," Meg said. "She has to see a probation officer and everything."

"That's probably made her even more popular with the boys," Ellen said. "Right?"

"Yeah, she's real popular," Meg said.

A green flower-delivery truck rolled by down below. A small cloud drifted over the sun, casting a shadow on the grassy hill. The three girls stared at the truck, each of them trying to think of something to say next.

"There are so many things I want to ask you," Meg told Ellen. "But it's been so long, it's sort of hard to know where to start."

Ellen and Shannon quickly agreed, as if that explained away their awkwardness, their inability to talk freely and easily the way they always had.

"You still going with Tony?" Ellen asked, not looking at Meg.

"Yeah," Meg said, feeling herself blush again. Why did she feel uncomfortable about that? "We're still together. Tony's had sort of a rough time, though."

Ellen shifted her position on the grass. "Tell me about it." Bitterness creeping into her voice. She pulled out a wide blade of grass and began sucking on it, her eyes narrowing as the sun reappeared.

"It's pretty here," Shannon said.

"Yes. Very," Meg quickly agreed. This is horrible, she thought. Why can't we talk about anything?

"Shadyside seems so much smaller to me now," Ellen said, yawning. "Oh. Sorry. I stayed up till two watching a movie on cable. Do you believe we don't have cable at home?"

"How can you live without cable?" Shannon asked, brightening.

Ellen shrugged. "I took my aunt's car and went driving around.

Everything looked the same, only smaller. It takes less than half an hour to drive everywhere."

"Yeah," Meg said, "Shadyside isn't exactly your major metropolis." What a stupid and boring thing to say, she thought.

"You been playing any tennis?" Shannon asked.

Ellen didn't seem to hear her.

"I miss our Saturday morning games," Shannon said.

"Remember the games we used to play when we were kids?" Meg asked. How lame, she thought. When in doubt, start talking about when you were kids.

"Yeah. Remember shadow-chasing?" Shannon said, a bit too eagerly. She was obviously pleased to have something safe to talk about. "What a dumb game that was."

"That wasn't our dumbest game," Ellen said, laughing. "Our dumbest game was 'Eek, A Mouse.'"

"I'd forgotten all about that one!" Meg cried. "It was just a screaming contest, right? We'd pretend we saw a mouse and then see who could make the most terrifying, earth-shattering scream."

"That was a great game," Shannon said. "We should play it right now. Bet I'd win."

"Bet you wouldn't," Ellen said.

But they didn't play the dumb kid's game. They fumbled around, trying to think of other things to talk about for a while. Meg felt more and more awkward. She knew that the other two felt the same, which made her feel even worse.

A gray station wagon started to pull to the curb down at the bottom of the sloping yard. "There's Aunt Amy," Ellen said, climbing quickly to her feet and brushing off the back of her tennis shorts. "I'd better go help her with the groceries." She seemed grateful for the interruption.

"Guess we'd better get going," Shannon said, sounding dejected and not hiding it at all.

"You're . . . uh . . . still coming out for pizza with us Saturday night, right?" Meg asked, trying to sound casual. Saturday night, of course, was the surprise party. Going out for pizza was the excuse Meg and Shannon had dreamed up to get Ellen to the party.

"Yeah. Right. Great," Ellen said with forced enthusiasm. "See ya."

"See ya, Ellen."

"You look great!"

Meg and Shannon descended the flagstone steps quickly in silence. They didn't say a word to each other until they were inside Shannon's red Mazda. "Well, that was just like old times," Shannon said sarcastically.

Meg felt so bad, she thought she might cry. But she took a deep breath and held it in. The visit was so awful, she thought. It was like losing a friend all over again. "We didn't have much to say to one another," she said tentatively. She wasn't sure how Shannon felt about it all. But maybe if she talked about how she felt with Shannon she wouldn't feel so hurt, so . . . abandoned.

"Well, I guess it's natural," Shannon said. Her way of dealing with situations like this was to minimize them, act as if they were ordinary, normal, to be expected.

"I felt so bad!" Meg cried, struggling to keep herself together.

"It *was* a little awkward," Shannon admitted, her eyes on the road. "But we haven't seen her for a whole year."

"Come on, Shannon. Admit it," Meg pleaded, shoving the seat belt out of the way so she could lean her arms on the dashboard and rest her head on her arms. "It was dreadful. We were all totally tongue-tied and miserable."

"Aw, Meg, stop exaggerating," Shannon scolded. "It wasn't all that bad. Really. We were all nervous. But we'll get over it. And so will Ellen. I'm sure it'll go better at the party. We'll—"

"The party!" Meg wailed. "What a disaster! Why did I ever

think it was a good idea? Oh, it's going to be a nightmare! Whoever's been trying to stop it was *right!*"

"Meg—"

"You think Ellen's going to be happy to be dragged to a party to see all her old friends? Shannon—she wasn't even happy to see *us!*"

"Meg—chill out. Please. You're blowing this all out of proportion. Just because we were a little nervous this afternoon doesn't mean Ellen won't like the party. It'll be completely different. We'll be different and she'll be different. You'll see. It'll be fine."

Meg just moaned with her head buried in her arms. Shannon stopped the car. "Why are you stopping?" Meg cried.

"Because you're home," Shannon said, laughing. "Get out. See you at David's party tonight."

Meg muttered some kind of good-bye and ran into the house, thinking about David's party. She realized she was really looking forward to being with Tony. It had been so long since they'd been together, just the two of them. And they had so much to talk about.

Maybe, she thought, Tony had some idea of what Brian was trying to tell her, of why Brian was threatening her. She couldn't wait to tell Tony her suspicions about Brian. Maybe Tony would be able to help her understand what was going on. . . .

CHAPTER 17

MONDAY NIGHT

"Bet you'd never guess that David's parents are away," Shannon said, rolling her eyes.

"What a scene!" Meg said, staring out through the windshield as Shannon parked the car across from David's house.

Stereo speakers on the driveway were blaring out dance music, and couples were dancing in the garage. Kids were sprawled all over the lawn. Two couples were making out on the steps leading up to the front porch. Another couple was entwined under the tree at the side of the driveway. All of the lights in the house were on. There seemed to be even more kids inside.

Shannon climbed out of the car and slammed the door. She was wearing skin-tight white pants and a silky, wild pink top. Some guy sitting on the lawn whistled to her and called out, "Lookin' good, Shannon!" This clever remark was followed by loud appreciative laughter from the other guys on the lawn.

"Maybe we should have Ellen's party on David's front lawn too," Shannon joked. "This looks pretty rad!"

"Let's go in the house," Meg said.

"Glad we got here early before everyone starts throwing up," Shannon said.

Walking up the drive, Meg looked for Tony, even though she knew he wouldn't be there this early.

"Think fast!" someone yelled. A basketball flew by their heads and bounced down the drive and into the street. The guys on the lawn thought that was hilarious.

"Where's David?" Shannon asked a kid they knew.

He shrugged. "Haven't seen him all night. How'd you do on the English final?"

It was Shannon's turn to shrug. Meg led the way past the couples on the front steps into the living room. The room was filled with kids from school milling about, talking and laughing. Arnie Tobin, David's friend from the gymnastics team, seemed to be asleep on the couch, probably passed out.

"This is really gross," Shannon complained. "I love it!"

"Hey—there's Lisa!" Meg cried. She waved to Lisa, who was talking to some kids by the entrance to the dining room.

"Hey, Shannon, you didn't have to dress up just for me."

Meg turned around to see who that was. It was Dwayne, a beer can in his hand, a smile on his face, as he walked up to Shannon, his dark eyes looking her up and down. He walked up very close, forcing her to take a few steps back.

"I see you dressed up too," Shannon cracked.

Dwayne was wearing a gray T-shirt, torn above one sleeve, brown stains down the front, and faded jeans with one front pocket torn off.

He stepped closer and leered down at her. He was about a foot taller than she was. "You come inside to dance with me, huh?"

"Yeah, sure. I've been dreaming about it all week," Shannon said sarcastically.

"Shall we do our dancing vertically or horizontally?" he asked, and gave a dirty laugh at his own joke.

"Dwayne—such big words for you," Shannon said. "Have you been going to night school or something?"

The smile faded from his face. His eyes went cold. "I don't like jokes like that. I'm not dumb, you know." He grabbed her arm.

"Hey—let go of me." She pulled away from him.

He laughed. "You're not scared of me, are you?"

"No. I'm not scared of garden slugs, either. I just don't want them touching me."

His face reddened as his eyes narrowed. "Give me a break, okay? I just want to dance with you. I'm not a bad guy, Shannon." He was moving forward, backing her into a corner.

"Let's get to know each other," he said, his smile returning. He wasn't looking at her face. He was staring at her tight blouse. "You'll see. I'm okay, really."

"Dwayne, please—"

"If we get along tonight, we can have an even better time at the surprise party Saturday night,"

"What? What are you talking about, Dwayne? You weren't invited to that party!" Shannon shouted.

"I was, too. Suki Thomas asked me to go as her date."

Shannon's back was against the wall. Dwayne took a long sip from his can and moved in closer. "Dwayne, don't come any closer. I don't want to dance with you. I mean it."

"Don't knock it if you haven't tried it," Dwayne said with a leer.

Meg decided she'd better do something. "Hey, Shannon—Tony wants to see you!" she called. It was the first thing that came into her head. She ran over and tugged Shannon away. "He's in the kitchen. He wants to ask you something."

Dwayne shot Meg an angry look. "Tony? You mean Lunchmeat? Lunchmeat is here? Isn't this past the little boy's bedtime?"

Meg ignored him and pulled Shannon out of the corner. He started to follow. Shannon turned and flashed him a withering look. He tossed up his hands. "Oooh—the evil eye!" He laughed. "Okay, I can take a hint. Thanks for the dance. See you at the party." He tossed his empty can onto the couch. It bounced off the sleeping Arnie's stomach and rolled to the carpet. Arnie didn't stir.

"Thanks for the help. But I know how to handle that creep," Shannon told Meg. "Just hit his nose with a rolled-up newspaper."

"He's so big. He's kinda scary," Meg said.

"I'm going into the dining room. There seems to be tons of food in there," Shannon said. "You coming?"

"No. I think I'll—Oh! Here's Tony!" Tony stood at the front door, wearing straight-legged jeans and a gray leather jacket.

"Hi, Tony. Bye, Tony," Shannon said. She disappeared into the dining room.

Meg ran over to Tony. She was really glad to see him. "Hi, stranger," she said, taking his hand. His hand was ice cold.

"Great party," he said, looking around. "Where's David?"

They both saw David at the same time. He and Cory appeared in the entrance to the den, walking on their hands for some reason, their feet straight up in the air. Suddenly all of the change fell out of Cory's chinos pocket, and both boys collapsed to the floor laughing.

"Let's go," Tony said, pulling her toward the door.

"You just got here. Don't you want to talk with anyone?"

"No. Just you," he said. "Let's go where we can be alone." He smiled at her. He seemed nervous, she thought. And very pale.

A few minutes later they were in his dad's car, driving north on the River Road, heading toward River Ridge. The weather had grown cool again, and the wind gusted off the river. Meg was wearing layers of T-shirts, but she wished she had brought a jacket. "It's so dark up here," she said, snuggling close to him as he drove.

"Yeah. There aren't many lights on the River Road," he replied, staring straight ahead.

The road grew steep as it climbed toward the high ridge at the spot where the river split in two. River Ridge was actually a trail originally made by Native Americans. It started low on the eastern banks of the

Conononka and followed the river, sloping up until it looked down on the water from tall, granite cliffs. The farthest and highest point of River Ridge was known as Lover's Leap. The Ridge was a romantic place to walk, especially on warm spring and summer nights, but no one really knew why that spot was called Lover's Leap.

They drove in silence for a long while. "You're very quiet tonight," Meg said finally.

"I'm just happy to be with you," he told her. His voice sounded strange to her, tight and tense. Or was she just imagining it because *she* was the tense one?

Near the top of the road, he pulled the car over and parked it between two trees. He switched off the ignition and the headlights. "Let's take a walk," he said.

"I don't have a jacket," she said, already feeling a little chilled. "Can I borrow yours?"

He hesitated. "Come on," he urged softly. "I'll keep you warm."

She got out of the car and followed him onto the path. She could hear the river flowing far below them in the darkness. The dirt path, soft beneath her sneakers, led up higher along the cliff. Tony reached back his hand and she took it.

"It's a little scary up here, don't you think?" she asked. He didn't say anything. She caught up with him and went a few steps ahead, still holding onto his hand.

"Look—we're right on the edge of the cliff," she said, suddenly alarmed. "They should put a railing or something here."

He still didn't say anything. He was standing behind her. He reached both arms around her shoulders, and, holding her tightly, guided her right up to the edge of the cliff.

CHAPTER 18

MONDAY NIGHT

I'll just get it over with, he thought.

It would only take a second. One hard push and over she'd go. Simple. And quick.

So why was he hesitating?

She was so trusting. She seemed so comfortable with his arms around her like that. She didn't even question him when he refused to lend her his leather jacket.

Maybe she didn't know anything after all. Maybe he was going to commit a murder he didn't have to commit.

He decided to find out. "Tell me about Brian," he said softly into her ear, leading her away from the cliff edge and a few feet onto the path.

"He was so strange," Meg said, shivering. "I didn't really understand him."

"What did he say?" Tony asked, allowing a little impatience to enter his voice.

"He said he was warning me. But it sounded like a threat."

"Warning you about what?"

"I don't know. He just said to be careful. He said things weren't what they seemed. He wasn't making any sense. He seemed really frightened. He told me I was in danger."

"From who? From the guy who's been trying to stop the party?" He held on to her tightly. If he had to, he could shove her over the edge from here. She'd probably be too surprised to struggle.

"I don't know. He wouldn't say."

So Brian didn't crack entirely, Tony realized. He wanted to. Brian wanted to tell her it was me. But he was too scared.

Has she figured it out? No.

"I thought maybe you could tell me what he meant," Meg said, leaning back against him.

So trustful, he thought.

"I don't know," he told her. "What else did Brian say?"

He had to push her. He decided he had to push her. Even though she hadn't figured it out, she would sooner or later. And his life would be ruined.

She was leaning back against him. One hard shove. That's all it would take. And he wouldn't have to worry—about her, anyway.

"Brian said I was in danger. That's all. He told me to be careful."

"Who did he mean?" he asked innocently. "Who was he warning you about?"

Get ready. This is it.

Push her and then run. Don't stand there listening to her scream. Don't wait to hear the splash, the sound of her body cracking as it hits the shallow river bed. Just run, Tony. You'll be okay. You'll be fine.

"I think he meant *himself*," she said uncertainly. "I was so confused. I think he was trying to warn me about *him*. But how can that be?"

Again, he hesitated. "I don't know. Brian's such a weirdo," he said.

"But how could it be Brian?" she asked. "That night in the woods, it couldn't have been Brian who grabbed me and made me fall down the ravine. Brian had already fallen into the ravine."

Is she going to put one and one together and realize that I was the only one who could have grabbed her? Tony wondered. "Then who could it have been?" he asked, preparing himself, steadying his legs, closing his eyes. He didn't really want to watch her when she went over.

"Do you think there could be two people trying to stop the party?" she asked. "Brian and someone else?"

She turned around to face him.

No. Don't turn around. Don't make it harder for me. Don't look at me now.

She has such a cute face, like a doll. So perfect. So pretty.

Don't weaken, Tony. Of course you care about her. But you care more about keeping free, keeping alive, keeping your secret . . . forever.

"Brian and someone else? I don't know." His voice trembled. He wondered if she could see how upset he was.

Please turn around. Please don't look into my eyes so lovingly.

"Tony—you weren't involved in it, were you?" Meg asked suddenly.

"What?" Tony's whole body shuddered violently.

She pressed her forehead against his cheek. "I had this dumb thought that Brian might mean you. It's so strange, the crazy things that can go through your mind when you're upset and trying to figure things out."

"Yeah. Strange," he said. "No. He couldn't mean me. No way."

She was figuring it out. Feeling her forehead against his cheek, he could almost hear her brain working, solving the mystery. Could she tell he was lying? Had she already figured out he was Evan's killer?

She pulled away. "I love the sound of the river flowing down there. It's soothing somehow."

Maybe you'd like to listen to it close up, he thought. Her voice was changing, becoming colder, becoming more suspicious. Or was he imagining that?

"I'll tell you something else kind of strange," she said. "Ellen went to see Brian. He was the first person she visited. Don't you think that's odd?"

Tony let out a short gasp. "Ellen? She—what?" He was too upset to control himself, to hide his unhappiness at this news.

He grabbed her arms. He braced his legs. He took a deep breath.

"What's wrong, Tony?" she asked softly.

"Nothing."

One hard shove. That's all it would take. She probably wouldn't even realize what was happening until she was halfway down.

No. No. No.

He wasn't going to do it.

He knew he wasn't going to do it.

I'm not a killer, he thought. I'm not a killer after all.

Or was he? Could he do it?

His mind spun. For a moment he felt so dizzy he thought he might plunge over the side.

He steadied himself, holding on to Meg. What would be the point of killing Meg? She didn't know anything. She hadn't figured out anything. Killing Meg wouldn't help him in any way.

Brian was the problem. Ellen was the problem. Brian and Ellen together were the problem.

Meg was never the problem.

Okay. You get to live, Meg. And you get to have your surprise party.

He had tried to stop the party, and he had failed. But the party wasn't the problem. He had two problems. Brian and Ellen. Brian and Ellen. Brian and Ellen.

I'll be at the party with them, he thought. I'll be there with my two problems. I'll be watching them. I'll be listening to them.

He suddenly remembered the pistol his dad kept in the cabinet next to his workbench in the basement. And the box of shells next to it in the back of the shelf.

The gun. I could bring the gun. Just in case.

Yes. I'll bring the gun Saturday night.

For Brian. And Ellen.

For my own protection.

Brian already tried to give me away. Who knows what he and Ellen were cooking up together. But I'll be ready for them. I'll be ready, willing, and eager.

"Tony, what's wrong? You just had the strangest look on your face." She peered up into his eyes, her face filled with concern. For the first time he saw some suspicion there, too.

"Uh . . . nothing. Guess I'm cold. Let's go back to the car."

"But—aren't you going to kiss me first?"

Why was she looking into his eyes like that? For reassurance? For reassurance that he wasn't a murderer?

"Kiss you? Oh, yeah. Right."

He put his arms around her and kissed her, and thought about the gun waiting for him in the basement cabinet.

CHAPTER 19

SATURDAY NIGHT

Meg pulled the car to the curb and looked up the hill to Ellen's aunt Amy's house. A trail of tiny yellow lights went all the way up along the side of the flagstone steps to the front porch. I really don't feel like climbing those steps again, Meg thought.

She honked the horn. No sign of Ellen up there. She honked it again, longer. Why do they put such tinny horns in these foreign cars? she asked herself.

Success! Ellen appeared on the porch and signaled that she'd be down in a minute.

Meg waved back to her, grateful she didn't have to get out of the car. She felt so nervous, she wondered if she'd be able to enjoy a single moment of the party. I guess I'll feel it was worth it if it makes Ellen happy, she told herself. Meg, Shannon, and Lisa had worked all day, getting the Halsey Manor House in order, cleaning, decorating with balloons and flowers, and putting out the food and soda.

I should be looking forward to the party, she thought. But I just know it's going to be dreadful. Ellen's going to hate it. And she's going to hate me forever. How could I have been so stupid?

But Ellen's smile as she came trotting down the steps reassured Meg. Watching Ellen descend, Meg decided the party might work out after all. Ellen had always been a good sport about everything in the old days. She was sure Ellen would be a good sport tonight. And maybe she'd even be pleased that her friends wanted to make such a fuss over her.

It was a cool and blustery night. The weather just couldn't make up its mind to stay summery. Ellen was wearing a straight, red mini-skirt over black tights. And a long-sleeved black top. She looked beautiful.

I wish I were tall, Meg thought, putting on a smile as Ellen slipped into the car. Meg was wearing a turquoise, patterned Gap sweater—her only expensive sweater—over purple pegged pants.

"Hi. Where's Shannon?"

"Oh. We're going to pick her up," Meg said, shifting into reverse so she could back away from the curb. "You look great."

"Thanks. So do you. You haven't changed a bit, Meg. You still look ten years old."

"Is that supposed to be a compliment?" Meg laughed. She headed west toward the Old Mill Road which would take them to Fear Street.

"Where are we picking up Shannon?" Ellen asked, scooting down in the seat and resting her knees on the dashboard. "At her house?" She had an apprehensive look on her face. She probably didn't want to go to Shannon's house, Meg decided. After all, it was Evan's house, too.

"No. We're picking her up at the Halsey Manor House." Meg tried her best to sound matter-of-fact about it, as if she picked Shannon up there every day of the week.

"What? That old mansion back in the woods?" Ellen was very surprised. "The Fear Street woods?"

Meg nodded, keeping her eyes on the road. She knew she was a very bad liar. She hoped Ellen wouldn't start asking her a lot of questions.

"What's she doing there?" Ellen asked, rolling down the window, deciding it was too cold, and quickly rolling it back up.

"Uh . . . I don't know. She just asked me to pick her up there." Meg decided a simple I-don't-know would get her into less trouble than making up some kind of elaborate story. "How's your aunt? Have you had a good visit?" she asked, determined to change the subject.

Ellen sighed and scooted even lower in the seat. "Oh, I don't know," she said wistfully, watching the familiar houses pass by in the darkness. "Maybe I shouldn't have come back. There are just so many memories. . . ."

Oh, wonderful, Meg thought. I'm about to drag her into a mansion full of memories!

She turned onto Fear Street, driving quickly past the cemetery and the sprawling, rundown old houses across from it. The night seemed to grow blacker the moment she turned the corner and entered Fear Street. For some reason none of the streetlights were on. And most of the houses were completely dark.

Meg saw Ellen shudder and close her eyes. They were driving past the Fear Street woods. "Oh, I hate this place," Ellen said. She opened her eyes. "We're really taking the scenic route tonight, huh?"

"I guess," Meg said. She didn't know what to say. Having the party at Shannon's would also have been a mistake. Let's face it, she told herself, having it *anywhere* is a mistake. Ellen is just not over what happened here. Maybe she never will be. And she doesn't even want to pretend that she is.

She turned down the narrow dirt road that twisted through the woods to the Halsey Manor House. She couldn't think of anything else to say to Ellen. She felt just as awkward as during their first visit on Monday. And as the headlights revealed the massive stone mansion up ahead, a feeling of dread as big and heavy as the mansion came over her.

"Frankenstein's castle," Ellen said. "I haven't been here in years. They used to have birthday parties here when we were little. Very gloomy birthday parties."

Well, welcome to another very gloomy party, Meg thought. She had an impulse to turn around in the circular drive in front of the mansion and take Ellen right back to her aunt's house. Or maybe, just keep driving, keep driving through the night until there were no familiar houses, no familiar landmarks at all . . . and no memories.

This isn't like you, Meg, she scolded herself. You always make the best of any situation. That's one of your finest qualities. This is going to be a great party once it gets going. Well, maybe not a great party—but an okay one. And Ellen will appreciate it. There's no way she won't appreciate it.

She silently thanked herself for the pep talk and pulled the car up to the entrance to the old house. There were no other cars in sight. Everyone else had been instructed to park in back. Two stone torches bearing flickering electric lightbulbs, one much dimmer than the other, lit the doorway, which was arch-shaped and looked like a castle entrance.

"You go get her," Ellen said. "This place gives me the creeps."

Meg pulled the door handle and pushed open the door. "No. Come on in with me. Don't make me go in there alone."

Ellen frowned and pulled her legs off the dashboard. "It gives you the creeps, too, huh? What on earth can Shannon be doing in there?" She climbed out of the car and smoothed down her mini-skirt. "Okay. Come on. We'll go together."

Meg felt so nervous she could barely walk. She'd never surprised anyone at a surprise party before. As she pushed open the heavy doorway and stepped into the front hallway, she vowed she'd never do it again. "After you," she told Ellen, motioning for Ellen to go in.

Their sneakers squeaked over the dark marble floor. The house was silent. An enormous, low chandelier, a confusion of brass and crystal, managed to dominate the room without providing much light.

"This way, I think," Meg said, pretending she didn't know where she was going. She led the way through the wide front chamber and pulled open a heavy door at the back. The room behind the door seemed to be dark. "In here," Meg said.

Ellen reluctantly followed her in. Meg's legs felt shaky, and she realized she was breathing really fast. I've never been this nervous in my life, she thought. Please, please don't let this be a *total* disaster.

"SURPRISE!"

The lights came on, revealing dozens of grinning faces.

Ellen stared at Meg, not understanding what was happening.

"SURPRISE!" The cry was followed by cheers and laughter.

"Look at her!" Shannon shouted from across the room. "She really is surprised."

Meg stared at Ellen, waiting for her to smile, a smile of recognition, of acceptance, of delight.

But the smile didn't appear.

Ellen looked absolutely horrified.

CHAPTER 20

SATURDAY NIGHT

Like snapshots, the scenes of the next few minutes froze in Meg's mind. Shannon hugging Ellen. Ellen finally forcing a smile to her face. Ellen hugging Lisa. Lisa laughing about how surprised Ellen looked. Ellen joking to Meg that she'd find a way to pay her back for this. Half-joking, maybe? Tony and Ellen greeting each other stiffly, each looking more uncomfortable than the other. Tony congratulating Meg for pulling the whole thing off. Kids crowding around Ellen to say hi and welcome her back. Ellen starting to look more comfortable as more kids came up to greet her.

"It's going really well!" Shannon shouted in Meg's ear, trying to be heard over the noise of the crowd.

Meg jumped. She wasn't expecting anyone to come up behind her like that. "You look great," she told Shannon.

"Doesn't Ellen look great? She really was surprised." Shannon wandered off to talk to some other kids. Meg went over to Tony, who was on the edge of the crowd, not talking to anyone. "It's so hot in here. Why don't you take off that heavy leather jacket?" she asked.

"I'm okay," he said, looking annoyed. The jacket bulged out above his waist. He kept both hands in his pockets.

"Doesn't Ellen look great?" Meg said, starting to feel a lot better about the party.

"Yeah. I guess."

"You in a bad mood or something? This is supposed to be a party." Why was she giving Tony a hard time? Just nerves, she figured. She'd gotten through the surprise part of the party, but the evening still had a long way to go.

"Give me a break," he muttered. "You know I don't like parties much."

She impulsively kissed him on the cheek. "Dance with me later?"

"Maybe." He forced a half smile.

After everyone had had a chance to greet Ellen, the large room got very noisy. With school just out, everyone was in a mood to celebrate.

Lisa was chattering animatedly to Ellen, gesturing with her hands and laughing. But Ellen, seemingly distracted, kept looking over Lisa's shoulder. Meg followed Ellen's eyes. Ellen was looking at Tony.

Tony stared back at her, scowled, then looked away.

What's his problem? Meg thought. Then someone called her to help find the paper plates, and she forgot all about it.

When she looked back a few minutes later, Ellen was talking animatedly to a large group of friends. Lisa and Cory were in the center of the room, actually getting along for once. A few feet away from them, Suki Thomas, her peroxide-blond hair spiked in angry punk style, had her arm around Dwayne's waist as Dwayne looked anxiously around the room, probably searching for Shannon. The vast room echoed with laughter and loud voices. All in all, this was a pretty terrific party, Meg decided.

"Quick—crank up some music!" Shannon shouted, startling Meg from behind once again. "And crank it all the way up! This party is *okay!*"

Meg had borrowed Tony's boom box for music. It was nearly as big as her stereo at home. She rushed across the room to put in a tape, but Ellen stopped her in the middle of the room. "Great party, Meg," Ellen said, giving Meg a hug. "What a surprise. I'm a little . . . overwhelmed."

"I thought maybe you'd be furious at me," Meg said, giggling. She had borrowed Ellen's nervous giggle, she realized.

"It was very sweet," Ellen said. "I really don't deserve it."

"Don't be silly," Meg said. "We all wanted to welcome you back. We miss you, Ellen. I do, especially."

"I miss you, too." Was that a tear in Ellen's eye? Meg couldn't believe it. It wasn't at all like Ellen to get that emotional. The party must have really touched her.

"I'm going to put some music on," Meg called to her, hurrying across the room.

Dwayne stepped in her way. She nearly ran right into him. "You seen Shannon?" he asked.

"Not lately," she said coldly. She looked for Suki and spotted her across the room, her arm around some other boy's waist.

"Tell her I'm looking for her, okay?"

"Sure, Dwayne." She hurried away from him. At the table with the boom box, she quickly shuffled through the tapes and grabbed the hottest, loudest dance music she could find, and shoved it into the player.

A few seconds later the music blasted out. It sounded great, booming off the walls and ceiling of the cavernous room. Several couples began to dance. Meg looked for Tony, but couldn't find him. Finally she spotted him sitting on the floor by himself in a corner, sipping a can of soda.

"Want to dance?" she shouted, standing over him, moving with the music.

"Maybe later," he said. He took a long swig from the can and stared past her at Ellen across the room. He still hadn't taken off his leather jacket, Meg saw, despite the heat of the room.

"Great party," Lisa said, stepping between them and giving Meg a hug. "You really did it!"

"*We* really did it!" Meg said happily. "I think we all deserve a—"

She never finished her sentence. A commotion over by the boom box in the corner caught her eye. The music stopped in mid-note. Someone screamed. The few kids who were dancing turned around, confused.

"Hey—what's going on?"

"BRIAN!"

Meg and Shannon started to run toward him. Brian was standing between the boom box table and the doorway. He had white bandages wrapped around part of his head.

"It's the return of the mummy!" someone shouted. A few kids laughed.

"QUIET, EVERYONE!" Brian screamed over the laughter.

"Brian, what are you doing here?" Meg cried.

Through his bandages she could see that his eyes were wild. He had a twisted, gleeful smile on his face. He raised both arms high in the air to signal for quiet.

"Brian, please—" Meg shouted. He didn't seem to hear her.

"What's wrong with him?" Ellen asked, coming up to Meg, a very worried look on her face. "What's he going to do?"

"Listen to the words of a Fourth-Level Wizard!" Brian shouted, his arms still high above his bandaged head.

The huge room grew absolutely silent. No one moved.

"I have the power now! I have reached the Fourth Level! And tonight, I am going to bring Evan back!"

"NO!" Ellen screamed, her mouth dropping into a wide O of horror. She tugged at the sides of her long, blond hair with both hands.

"I'll stop him!" Tony yelled, starting toward Brian, one hand clenched in a tight fist, the other reaching inside his leather jacket.

"No, wait—" Meg held Tony back.

"I am going to bring Evan back—*now!*" Brian shouted. He lowered his arms and then used both hands to point to the door.

The door slowly started to open.

"What is he *doing?*" Shannon cried. "Why is he doing this?"

"No. Stop this!" Tony called, pulling away from Meg to rush at Brian.

The door swung open. Someone was standing in the dim light of the corridor.

Someone walked slowly into the room.

"Is this a joke?" Shannon cried. "Some sort of sick joke?"

Tony froze, his hand inside his jacket.

Brian continued to point, his eyes wild with triumph, as the tall figure stepped into the light.

Some kids gasped. Some screamed.

The figure who stepped into the light was Evan.

CHAPTER 21

SATURDAY NIGHT

"No! IT'S NOT YOU!" Tony screamed.

Evan glared at Tony. His eyes looked white in the harsh light. He pointed a finger at Tony, an accusing finger, and took a step toward him.

"NO! YOU'RE DEAD!" Tony screamed, his features twisted in panic. He pulled his hand out from under his jacket. He was gripping a large black pistol. He swung it wildly, the nose pointed up to the ceiling. "I KNOW YOU'RE DEAD BECAUSE—"

Evan took another step toward Tony.

"Tony—the gun—" Meg cried. "Where did you—why?—"

"Okay, okay!" Tony shrieked, staring into Evan's eyes. "I know why you're here, Evan! I'll tell. I'll tell everyone the whole story! I'll tell everyone who killed you!"

"Mike! Why are you doing this?" Shannon shouted. She turned to Tony. "It's not Evan—it's my half-brother Mike! For God's sake, put away the gun!"

I don't know what he's doing, but I've got to get that gun away from him before he does something horrible, Meg thought. She stumbled forward and made a desperate grab for it. But Tony pulled away from her. He shoved her away hard, raising the gun out of her reach, then pointed it at Mike.

"Okay, okay. I'll tell everything!" Tony cried. "That's what you want, isn't it? Well, all right. Listen, everyone! I know who killed Evan. I'll tell the whole story now. I—"

The lights went out.

Shouts and screams echoed off the walls. Kids were running in panic toward the door. Meg searched blindly for Tony. She wanted to grab him, hold him, take the gun away, find out what was going on, why he was so terrified, why he was about to confess.

Confess?

Yes. Tony was about to confess.

Meg felt herself begin to tremble. She thought of Brian's warning to her. And she realized that Brian and Mike must have cooked up this whole scene.

Just to frighten Tony. . . .

A gunshot just inches away from her made her jump and cry out. Someone screamed in pain. Chairs toppled over as kids tried to scramble blindly out of the pitch-black room.

"NO—PLEASE!" Now it was Meg's turn to scream. "Turn on the lights! Somebody—turn on the lights!"

A few seconds later the lights came back on. Meg looked down. She was standing over Tony. He was curled on the floor, his eyes bugged out in fear, his hand grasping his shoulder. Blood poured down his arm onto the carpet beneath him.

"Tony—"

"I—I've been shot!" He didn't seem to believe it. "I've been shot!" he repeated incredulously.

"Somebody stop him!" a girl's voice shouted.

Stop who?

Meg looked up. Who was that running to the door? It was all happening so quickly, she wasn't sure she was seeing correctly. But she was. It was Dwayne. And he had Tony's gun in his hand.

"Stop him! He shot Tony!"

Dwayne tripped over a folding chair and sailed over it, landing on his stomach on the floor. Still gripping Tony's pistol, he turned quickly and threatened everyone with it. He climbed slowly to his feet, his dark eyes darting back and forth, keeping everyone in view.

"I almost got away," he said. "I'm sorry you turned on the lights."

"Dwayne—why did you shoot Tony?" Meg screamed.

Tony, writhing on the floor, moaned and held his shoulder as his blood continued to flow in a widening circle beneath him.

"Shut up! Just shut up!" Dwayne shouted at her, aiming the gun at Meg. She could see that he was desperately trying to decide what to do next. His plan had obviously been to shoot Tony and then escape in the darkness. But now every person in the room had seen him trying to run away with the gun in his hand.

Why? Why did Dwayne shoot Tony? Why did Tony come to the party with a gun? Meg was as confused as she was frightened.

"I've got no choice," Dwayne said, his eyes still nervously surveying everyone around the large room. "I don't want anybody comin' after me."

He moved forward quickly and grabbed Ellen roughly by the arm. He held the nose of the pistol to her temple. "You come with me. You're the likely candidate, aren't you? You helped to kill Evan too."

Meg didn't think she heard correctly. Ellen help to kill Evan? Ellen *too*? What did Dwayne mean?

"No—please—" Ellen begged.

But Dwayne dragged her to the door, the pistol pressed tightly to her forehead. "Anybody comes after me, and she's history!" Dwayne shouted. No one moved. There was no doubt in anyone's mind that Dwayne meant it.

"Please—listen to him!" Ellen cried to everyone.

Someone has to stop him, Meg thought. We can't let him take Ellen. He's already shot Tony. We can't let him shoot Ellen too.

This is all my fault. My fault. My party. My fault.

She knew she wasn't thinking clearly. She was too frightened to think clearly. But she knew she had to do something. She moved quickly along the wall, keeping in the shadows.

Dwayne didn't see her as he backed toward the door. If she could get to the door first, maybe she could surprise him, maybe she could grab the gun away, at least give Ellen a chance to run away.

Kids were standing in small groups, frozen in fear. Meg moved quickly behind them, keeping low, praying that Dwayne wouldn't see her.

Could she get to him before he got out the door? Could she startle him, surprise him enough to free Ellen?

Her head was spinning. The floor seemed to buckle beneath her feet. The walls tilted. But she kept moving steadily, silently to the door.

"That's it. Nobody move. Don't force me to do something I'd hate to do," Dwayne called. He had his arm around Ellen's waist now as he dragged her across the room. He took the gun away from her head and gestured with it, aiming it around the room as a final warning to anyone who might think of following him.

Meg got to the door first.

She took a deep breath. Dwayne was just a few feet away, backing toward her. The gun was in reach.

She could just reach out and—

He spun around. He saw her.

He shoved Ellen to the floor as Meg made her move.

Meg lunged for the gun. She saw his face. She saw his eyes.

She knew she was too late.

Dwayne caught her arm and spun her around. He slammed her hard against the wall and shoved the pistol against her neck.

He pushed the gun against her throat until Meg cried out in pain. "Let's go, babes. You're comin' too. I always wanted to have two girlfriends!"

Everything seemed speeded up now. Everything went too fast to see, too fast to think about, too fast to understand.

They were in the dark corridor. The three of them. Dwayne pushing the two girls ahead of him, threatening them with the pistol if they hesitated or slowed down. Now they were running. Running too fast.

Ellen stared straight ahead, her face a blank. Was she pretending this wasn't happening? Meg tried to stop, tried to resist, but Dwayne forced her on, shoving the gun to the back of her neck. The metal was cold, so cold. It sent shivers down her back, shivers that didn't stop when he took the gun away, shivers that made it hard to run, hard to move, hard to breathe.

He pushed them toward the front door of the old house, stopped, stood there without opening it, and then pulled them roughly back the other way. Ellen stared hard at the door. For a second Meg thought she was going to try to make a run for it. But Ellen lowered her head and closed her eyes, resigned, waiting for Dwayne to tell her where to go next.

"They'll look for us outside," he said, sounding calm, sounding cold, as cold as the pistol against Meg's back. "So we'll stay inside."

Keeping them right in front of him, he pushed them to the stairs that led down to the basement. Meg stumbled, started to fall forward, but he grabbed her arm and kept her moving. "They'll search the woods all night. But we'll be cozy and safe down here. Me and my two girlfriends. Real cozy." He laughed. He sounded very pleased with his plan.

"Why?" Meg managed to ask. Her voice came out choked and small.

"Keep moving," he ordered, giving her a hard shove that almost sent her sprawling down the tiled stairs.

"Why?" she repeated, too frightened to stop moving, too frightened to resist, too confused not to ask why. "Why did you shoot Tony?"

"I had to. I didn't know how much that stupid moron knew. But I couldn't take the chance. I couldn't let him tell everyone—"

"Tell everyone *what?*"

"That I killed Evan."

CHAPTER 22

SATURDAY NIGHT

"But Tony killed Evan!" Ellen cried. "I saw him!"

Meg stopped and uttered a cry of shock, of horror. "Tony? What are you saying, Ellen?"

"Tony killed Evan," Ellen repeated.

"That's impossible—" Meg started.

"Meg, you don't know anything," Ellen said bitterly.

"Keep moving," Dwayne ordered, gesturing with the pistol.

Where were they? He had pushed them into an area of the house that hadn't been renovated, through endless dark rooms, rooms filled with covered furniture, rooms caked with years of dust, empty rooms, rooms filled with strange tools and equipment.

They pushed open another door and stumbled into another room. Dwayne found the light switch and turned it on. It was a large kitchen. Cobwebbed and dust-covered, it appeared to have been abandoned for a very long time. Grimy copper pans hung on hooks just above their heads. A grease-stained range stood against the wall. Wooden counters were cluttered with dishes and pots that hadn't been used for years. The entire room smelled of mold and mildew and decay.

"Perfect," Dwayne said, looking around. "I like to hang around a warm, inviting kitchen. Don't you?" He laughed to himself. "Ol' Dwayne has done it again. They'll never find us here. We'll hang out a bit, get cozy, and when the excitement dies down, we'll make our escape." He gestured for the girls to sit on the floor beside the range, which they did.

He pointed the pistol at each of them and pretended to shoot them one at a time, making gun noises with his lips.

"Great sense of humor, Dwayne," Ellen muttered.

"Shut up," Dwayne said, and laughed, as if he had just cracked a joke.

"What do you think you're doing?" Ellen demanded. "I saw Tony kill Evan. Why did you go berserk up there? What is in your crazy brain?"

"You never figured out the truth?" Dwayne looked sincerely shocked.

"I *know* the truth," Ellen insisted. "I was there. Tony and I followed Evan into the Fear Street woods. We were worried about him. I had just told Evan I wanted to break up with him."

"You *what?*" Meg cried. None of this made any sense to her. Ellen break up with Evan?

"I'm sorry, Meg. I'm real sorry," Ellen said, seeing the confusion on Meg's face. "But you've got to grow up sometime, kiddo. Tony and I were going out behind your back. I wanted to go with Tony. So I told Evan."

"You and Tony?" Meg tried to keep her voice steady, but this was all too much.

"Yeah. Me and Tony. Well, you can imagine how Evan took the news. He threw a fit. He went bananas. He grabbed his father's hunting rifle and bombed off to the woods. He said he just wanted to shoot something. Anything. Well, Tony and I followed him. We were worried about him. He was so crazy. We wanted to try to calm him down. But the first thing we knew, Tony and Evan were fighting, fighting over the rifle. It went off and . . . Evan was dead. Tony killed Evan."

"I don't believe it," Meg said, feeling dazed. She pulled up her knees and curled up, resting her head against them. "Tony was there? That can't be! Brian said—"

"Brian came running up a minute or so after Tony shot Evan. He found Tony and me there, trying to decide what to do. He was scared out of his mind. He said he had it all figured out. He was going to make it look like Evan shot himself, like it was an accident. Then he threatened Brian and me. He said he'd kill us both if we ever told anyone that he was in the woods with us. Brian and I saw the look on Tony's face. We knew that he meant it."

"I—I don't believe this. I just don't," Meg insisted.

"You might as well hear the rest," Ellen said. "Tony ran off after making it look like an accident. I—I was hysterical. I couldn't think straight. I was so frightened. So was Brian. As soon as Tony was gone, we went for help. All of these months Brian and I kept our secret. That Tony killed Evan. All of these months we were too frightened to talk."

"No wonder Tony's been so weird all year," Meg said.

Dwayne laughed. Meg looked up. She had almost forgotten that he was there, standing over them with the pistol. Why was he laughing? What could possibly be so funny?

"Hey, let's give a little credit where credit is due," he said.

"What are you talking about, Dwayne?" Ellen asked.

"I thought Tony found out the truth. I thought he was going to tell it all upstairs when that Evan clone showed up. I thought he was going to tell everyone that I did it. That I did Evan." He laughed and shook his head. "I guess the joke's on Tony. That stupid moron."

He started pacing the room, twirling the pistol in his hand.

"How could you kill Evan?" Ellen persisted. "How? I saw Tony and Evan fight over the rifle. I saw Evan fall. I saw him die."

Dwayne shook his head. "You're stupid too. Tony didn't kill Evan. I did. Brian and I were playing *Wizards and Dungeons* in the woods when we heard a gunshot. Brian said we had to go see what it was. I said no. I told Brian I was going home. Brian went to see what the shot was. I followed him, keeping behind so he wouldn't see me."

"So you were there too?" Ellen cried.

"I watched everything. The whole scene. I thought Tony had killed Evan. But after he ran off, and after you and Brian went to get help, I went up close and took a look. Evan wasn't dead. He wasn't even hit. He had hit his head on a rock and was knocked unconscious."

"Oh, no," Ellen moaned. "Evan was alive. And you—"

Dwayne nodded his head. "I hated Evan. I always hated Evan. He wouldn't let me go out with his sister. He wouldn't even let me talk to her. I wasn't good enough for her. He always made me feel like a worm. So . . . here was my chance. I picked up the rifle. And taught Evan a lesson. A final lesson. He was dead already, right? At least three other people thought so. So . . . I just made it official."

"That's the most cold-blooded thing I've ever heard," Meg cried. She realized she was trembling. Her mouth was so dry, she thought she might choke. Her hands and feet were freezing cold.

Dwayne giggled, a sick, high-pitched giggle. "Yeah, it is, ain't it!" he said boastfully. "Funny thing is, it was so easy. And kind of fun, in a way."

He'll kill us next, Meg realized. He killed Evan as easily as swatting a fly. He's laughing about it, not the least bit sorry. He shot Tony upstairs. And now we have to be next. He's told us too much. We know everything.

We're not getting out of here alive.

Dwayne grinned down at her. It was as if he could read her thoughts. He twirled the pistol menacingly and stared at them both.

I've got to do something, Meg thought. I can't just sit here. I've got to at least try to get us out of here.

"How could you kill somebody like that?" Ellen screamed at Dwayne, her voice filled with disgust, with loathing—and with new fear.

"Like this." He pointed the pistol at her and pulled back the hammer.

"No, don't—" Ellen raised her hands as if to shield herself.

Dwayne laughed and made a shooting noise again with his lips.

He isn't always going to pretend to shoot us, Meg thought. One of these times—very soon—he's going to pull the trigger for real.

"Can we stand up?" Meg asked. "My legs are falling asleep."

"Yeah. Sure," Dwayne said, still staring at Ellen. "Whatever." He twirled the pistol and dropped it. It clattered against the hard concrete floor.

Meg helped pull Ellen to her feet. And as Dwayne bent over to retrieve his pistol, she whispered in Ellen's ear, "Eek! A Mouse."

Dwayne grabbed the gun and turned back to them quickly. "You two are pretty slow," he said with a pleased sneer. "You could have made a run for it just now."

"We're not going anywhere," Meg said dispiritedly.

She wondered if Ellen had heard her. She wondered if Ellen understood. She didn't dare look at her to see. Dwayne was watching them too closely.

She just knew she had to do something. Killing Evan was so easy, Dwayne had said. She didn't want to make it easy for him. She didn't want to die in this filthy, abandoned cellar kitchen.

Her back pressed tightly against the cold tile wall, she moved an inch closer to Ellen and gave her arm a light tap. Your turn, Ellen. Remember the game? Eek, A Mouse. Did you hear what I whispered? Please, Ellen.

Please.

"What's going on?" Dwayne shouted suddenly, raising the pistol.

"YAAAAAIIIIII!" Ellen screamed at the top of her lungs, a

deafening scream of pure terror, and pointed behind Dwayne. "A MOUSE!"

Startled, Dwayne turned.

Meg knew she had an instant. Less than an instant.

She reached up and grabbed a big, copper frying pan off the wall. It was heavier than she had imagined. But she didn't think about that.

In one motion she grabbed for it, reached it, pulled it down.

And as Dwayne turned back to them, she swung it.

And hit him hard in the face.

So hard the frying pan clanged, metal against bone.

Dwayne didn't utter a sound.

His eyes closed. Two teeth dropped out of his mouth. Blood gushed from both nostrils.

And he fell.

Meg picked the gun up from the floor. "Let's get upstairs," she said, breathing hard, so hard. But breathing. Grateful to be breathing. "Someone upstairs must have called the police by now."

They took a final look at Dwayne, lying face down in a dark pool of blood. Then they ran out of the dank kitchen and headed through the maze of dark, empty rooms toward the stairs.

"Hey!" Ellen called, struggling to keep up with Meg. "You sure know how to throw a party!"

CHAPTER 23

SUNDAY AFTERNOON

"So it was Tony the whole time trying to stop the party?" Shannon tossed a pair of socks across the room to Mike, who dropped them into his suitcase. Shannon and Meg were up in Mike's room, helping him pack to go back to school.

"Yeah, it was Tony," Meg said, shaking her head. "What an idiot I was."

"You weren't an idiot," Shannon said quickly. "You were . . . uh . . ."

"Trusting," Mike said helpfully. He folded a pair of jeans into the suitcase.

"That's just another word for *idiot*," Meg said.

"Meg, please—that doesn't sound like you," Shannon said. "You've been through a horrible time. We all have. But you can't let it make you . . . uh . . ."

"Bitter," Mike said. He always liked finishing Shannon's sentences for her.

"I—I guess I've learned a lot from all this." Meg sighed wearily.

"Is Tony going to be okay?" Shannon asked.

"He lost a lot of blood, but the ambulance arrived quickly last night. They got him to the hospital in time. The doctors there said he'll be okay," Meg said quietly. That part of her life was over, she knew. She was so used to Tony. She wondered what it was going to be like without him now.

Shannon held up a pair of dirty sweatsocks. "You're not going to pack these, are you, Mike?"

"No. I was going to give them to you. Happy birthday."

Shannon tossed them into the suitcase. "They don't smell any worse than the rest of your clothes."

"I talked to Tony's dad," Meg said. "He's going to get him help. You know, to get his head straight. Some friends know a really good shrink in New York. Poor Tony's very mixed up. It's going to take a long time."

"Think of what a year Tony must have had," Mike said, shaking his head. "He went a whole year thinking he had killed Evan, a whole year scared to death that people would find out, scared to death his life was ruined forever. And then it turns out he didn't kill Evan after all. That's pretty heavy."

"Poor Tony. And poor Ellen," Shannon said. "And poor Brian. Poor everyone."

"Where is Ellen?" Mike asked.

"Went back home this morning," Meg told him. "I wonder when we'll ever see her again."

They were all silent for a while, each thinking about the horrifying scene the night before at the party. Bright sunlight filtered through the curtains, which fluttered in a warm breeze. Baby robins chirped from a nest just beyond the window.

"Your cousin Brian's quite a guy," Mike said finally. "When he came to me with that idea about pretending to be Evan, I thought he was nuts."

"We all thought he was nuts," Meg said. "Poor Brian. He was just so frightened of Tony. He lost himself in that fantasy game world of his just so he wouldn't have to face the real world."

"But if it wasn't for Brian and Ellen, we might never have known the truth," Mike said wistfully.

"Brian and Ellen?" Meg asked, surprised.

"Yeah. They cooked up the idea together for me to appear at the party as Evan," Mike said.

"That's why Ellen went to visit Brian!" Meg realized. "To plan that little scene."

"So Ellen knew all about the surprise party," Shannon said.

"Brian told her," Mike said. "They both couldn't stand the guilt any longer. They had to let the truth out. They had to let everyone know about Tony, about them, about what really happened in the Fear Street woods. They had wanted to go to the police for months. But they had waited so long, they weren't sure the police would believe them.

"And they were so frightened of Tony. They thought they'd be safer if they exposed him in front of everyone," Mike continued.

"Brian put on a really convincing act," Meg said.

"He was really brave," Mike said, slamming the suitcase shut.

"You were brave too," Meg told him. She turned away. She suddenly had tears in her eyes. It was all starting to catch up to her.

Shannon came around to where Meg was sitting on the bed and put an arm around her shoulder. "You'll be okay," she said tenderly. "We'll all be okay now."

Meg wiped away the tears with the back of her hand. She and Shannon accompanied Mike down the stairs.

He stopped in the front hall and put his suitcase down. "Please go tell Dad I'm ready to go to the airport," he told Shannon.

"Aye, aye, sir." She hurried to the backyard.

He turned to Meg and smiled. "You know, I'll be back in July," he said. "Maybe we could go out or something."

Meg returned his smile. "That would be nice," she said. "I'd like to go out with you, Mike. Only . . . uh . . . one thing . . ."

"What's that?"

"Please—*no parties!*"

THE OVERNIGHT

CHAPTER 1

Della O'Connor tugged the combination lock, wondering why she could never get it to open on the first try. All the way down the long hall, locker doors slammed and kids laughed and shouted to each other, the daily celebration of school letting out.

The lock pulled open on the third try. She removed it and swung open the locker door, groaning as the heart on the inside of the door came into view. Last September someone had scratched the heart, and the words DELLA & GARY inside it, into the gray paint.

For the hundredth time Della told herself to find something to cover it up. She didn't want to be reminded of Gary every time she opened her locker.

She had angrily broken up with him three weeks ago, never dreaming that he would take her seriously, that they wouldn't make up in time for the spring prom. But the prom had come and gone— and Gary was just gone! He hadn't called her since their fight. And whenever she ran into him in the halls at school, he passed right by without giving her a chance to say anything.

Della was looking forward to the Outdoors Club overnight. Gary would be there, and she would be able to apologize to him then. She pictured him smiling at her. Staring at the heart on the locker door, she pictured his wavy blond hair, his lively brown eyes, the way they crinkled when he smiled at her, the tiny freckles on his cheeks. The overnight will be so romantic, she thought. Camping out all night under the stars. Just the two of us . . .

Of course, the other members of the Outdoors Club would be there too—including Suki Thomas, who had obviously joined just to be close to Gary. But Della wasn't worried about Suki. She was confident she could get Gary back if she could talk with him. Well . . . fairly confident.

She tossed her books to the floor of the locker and fixed her hair, peering into the small, square mirror she had attached to the locker door above the heart. With her pale skin, her bright, green eyes, her long, straight black hair, Della was very pretty. She always looked calm, cool, and together, even when she didn't feel that way.

Slamming the locker shut, she was surprised to see her friend Maia Franklin standing beside her. "Maia—how long have you been standing there?"

"Not long. How do you get your hair to do that?" Maia asked.

"Do what?"

"Be straight."

They both laughed. Maia had short, auburn hair, the curliest hair anyone had ever seen, probably curly enough to make the *Guinness Book of World Records!* With her round eyeglasses and her short, boyish figure, she reminded Della of Orphan Annie.

"Are you going to the Outdoors Club meeting?" Maia asked.

"Of course." Della jammed the combination lock shut. "Hey—did your parents give you permission to go on the overnight?"

"Yeah. Finally. After calling Mr. Abner five times and making him reassure them that it was going to be properly chaperoned and making him promise he'd keep his eye especially on me at all times."

Maia's parents were so strict with her. They treated her like a ten-year-old. "What's their problem, anyway?" Della asked, shaking her head.

"I don't know. I guess they think if I spend the night camping out on an island where there are boys, I'm going to behave like a rabbit in heat."

"And what's wrong with that?" Della asked.

Both girls entered Mr. Abner's classroom laughing. Three other members of the Outdoors Club were already there, sitting together in the front row. Gary was talking to Suki Thomas. He looked up for a split second, and when he saw that it was Della, he quickly turned his attention back to Suki.

Suki seemed very pleased to have his attention. She was smiling at him and resting a hand on his arm. At first glance, Suki seemed an unlikely candidate for the Outdoors Club. She was very punky looking, with spiky platinum hair and four earrings in each ear. She was wearing a tight black sweater with a long, deliberate tear in one sleeve, and a very short black leather skirt over dark purple tights. The purple of the tights matched her lipstick perfectly.

Look at Gary making goo-goo eyes at Suki, pretending he doesn't see me, Della told herself. What do boys see in her anyway? She didn't have to ask that question. Everyone in school knew the answer. Suki had quite a reputation.

Pete Goodwin said hi and flashed Della a smile as she and Maia headed to join everyone in the front row. He's kind of good-looking, Della thought, sitting down next to him, even though he's so basic. Pete had short brown hair and serious brown eyes. He was very preppy looking. Some of his friends even called him "The Prep," which he didn't seem to mind.

"Where's Abner?" Della asked him, lowering herself into the seat, resting her arms on the flip-down desk. She watched Suki patting Gary's arm.

"He was called to the office, said he'd be right back," Pete said. "How's it going, Della?"

"Fine, I guess."

The windows were open. A soft spring breeze floated in. The

sweet smell of fresh-cut grass blew into the room. Della could hear the *thwack thwack* of tennis balls being hit from the tennis courts beyond the teachers' parking lot.

"Guess we'll be planning the overnight today," Pete said awkwardly.

"Guess so," Della replied just as awkwardly.

Della cleared her throat loudly and scooted her chair forward, trying to get Gary's attention. But he refused to turn around, keeping his gaze firmly fixed on Suki, who was pulling at the threads of his sweater sleeve as she talked to him.

"Uh-oh. Look what just climbed out from behind his rock," Maia warned Della in a loud whisper.

Everyone looked up as Ricky Schorr bounced into the room. Ricky was wearing an oversized white T-shirt with big black letters across the front that read: NOTHING TO SAY. This pretty much summed up Ricky's sense of humor, in the opinion of most Shadyside High students. Ricky tried so hard to be funny all the time, and the fact that he tried so hard was the only funny thing about him.

He was short and thick. His clothes always seemed to be a size or two too big for him, and his black hair, which was never combed, fell down in tangles over his forehead. He was always pushing it back with his hand.

Walking quickly, Ricky headed to the front of the room. "Don't applaud. Just throw money," he said, and laughed an exaggeratedly loud laugh.

The other five members of the Outdoors Club groaned in unison. It was a response Ricky was accustomed to. The smile didn't drop from his face.

"Okay. Quiz time," he announced. "Take out a sheet of paper and number from one to two thousand. No—only kidding," he added quickly. "Here. Take a look at this." He held up a sprig of leaves, which he dropped onto Gary's desk.

"What's this supposed to be?" Gary asked, looking away from Suki for the first time.

"This is the Outdoors Club, right?" Ricky asked, grinning. He pointed at the leaves on Gary's desk. "Identify those. I bet you can't."

Gary looked confused. He picked up the leaves. "You want me to identify these?"

"Yeah. You're the club president. Identify them."

Gary held the leaves up close to his face and turned them over and over in his hands, studying them.

"Come on, Gary. You can do it," Pete urged.

"No, he can't," Ricky said, leaning over Gary's desk.

"Uh . . . it's from some kind of tree, right?" Gary asked. "Beech tree? Sassafras?"

Ricky shook his head, very pleased with himself.

Gary hated to be wrong. He slapped the narrow leaves against his hand. "Aw, who cares?" he said grumpily.

"You *should* care," Ricky told him. "It's poison ivy!" He burst out laughing.

"Huh?" Gary angrily jumped up from the chair, the leaves still gripped tightly in his hand. Ricky tried to get away, but Gary was too fast for him. He wrestled Ricky down to the floor and started rubbing the leaves on Ricky's face and forehead.

Ricky was laughing and screaming at the same time, struggling helplessly to get away. Della, Suki, Pete, and Maia were loudly cheering Gary on.

"What's going on here?" a voice called loudly from the doorway.

Everyone turned to see Mr. Abner stride into the room, his long legs bringing him quickly to the scene of the wrestling match. "Gary, get off him. What are you doing?"

Gary, breathing heavily, backed away. "Just getting ready for the overnight," he told the tall, lanky teacher. "We're having a little poison-ivy identification here."

Ricky groaned, rolled over, and slowly struggled to his feet. His T-shirt had rolled up and white belly protruded.

"Poison ivy?" Mr. Abner looked confused. He reached out and took the leaves from Gary's hand. "These are from a house plant—grape ivy," he said, looking quizzically at Gary, then at Ricky.

"April Fools," Ricky told Gary, a wide grin spreading across his face. He shoved his hair back out of his eyes.

Everyone laughed, mainly because of the shocked look on Gary's face. "He got you," Suki told Gary, pulling him back to his seat. "He got you that time." Gary forced a smile to his face, more for Suki's sake than anyone else's.

"Take your seats. Afraid this is going to be a short meeting," Mr. Abner said, walking over to the window and looking out at the parking lot.

Everyone became silent. What did he mean? He had a very serious look on his normally cheerful face.

"I have a personal emergency back home in Nashville," he told them, still looking out the window. "I have to go home this weekend. So I won't be able to take you on the overnight Saturday."

Suki and Ricky groaned out loud. No one else made a sound. Della looked at Gary, then down at the floor, disappointed.

"We'll have to postpone it," Mr. Abner said, turning around and sitting on the window ledge. "But there'll still be time. It's only May. We'll reschedule it when I get back. Okay?"

Everyone muttered agreement.

"I've got to run," Mr. Abner said, glancing up at the wall clock over his desk. "Sorry about this. See you guys next week." He hurried out the door with even longer strides than usual, a worried, preoccupied look on his face.

Della and her friends sat in silence until he was gone. "What a shame," Della said, starting to get up.

"Saturday's supposed to be a beautiful day too," Pete said. "At least, that's what they said on the radio."

They all started to get up.

"Hey—wait. I've got an idea," Suki said, motioning for the others to come back. "Listen. Really. I've got a good idea. Let's *go* on the overnight."

"What?" Maia cried. "Suki, what do you mean?"

"Let's go on the overnight anyway. You know. Without Abner."

"Go without an advisor?" Maia seemed to be appalled by the idea. "My parents would kill me! I'd be grounded for life. For *two* lifetimes!"

"They'll never know," Suki said.

"Yeah. Right," Ricky cried enthusiastically. "Neat idea! We'll go by ourselves. It'll be terrific. No one to bother us or tell us what to do." He stared at Suki. "Who wants to share my tent?"

"Get real, Schorr," Suki said, rolling her eyes. "You won't get *mosquitoes* to share your tent!"

Everyone else laughed. Ricky looked really hurt.

"Our parents will think we're being chaperoned. They'll think Abner is with us," Suki said, lowering her voice even though there was no one around to overhear. "And what they don't know won't hurt 'em." She put a hand on Gary's arm. "What do you think? You're the club president."

"Well—" Gary started.

"But my parents will kill me!" Maia protested.

"I think it's a good idea," Pete said, looking at Della. "After all, we're very responsible. We're not going to do anything crazy, right?"

Suki grinned up at Gary. "Not if we can help it," she said meaningfully.

"What do you think, Della?" Pete asked.

Della was eager to go. "It could be fun," she said. "We really don't need Abner." It could be a lot of fun, she thought. Especially if

I can pry Gary away from Suki long enough to make up with him.

"What do you say, Gary?" Suki demanded.

"Well . . . okay." He grinned at her. "Let's do it. Let's go Saturday morning, just as we planned."

That brought a cheer—from everyone except Maia.

"I can't," she said unhappily. "If my parents ever found out . . ."

"They won't find out, Maia," Della said. "Really. Everything will be fine. We'll have a great time, even better than if we had a chaperone. We'll come home Sunday morning as scheduled. And none of our parents will ever know."

"You promise?" Maia asked Della, her voice filled with doubt.

"I promise," Della told her. "Trust me, Maia. Nothing bad will happen."

CHAPTER 2

"Did you pack a toothbrush? What about your toothbrush?"

Della silently counted to three. Then, in a controlled voice, she said, "Yes, Mom. I packed my toothbrush. Do you think I should take my hair dryer too? And another three or four changes of clothing? It *is* overnight, after all."

"No need to be sarcastic," Mrs. O'Connor said, squeezing Della's rolled-up sleeping bag. "Is this rolled tightly enough? Will you be able to carry it, do you think?" Della's mother was short and very thin—she weighed just under one hundred pounds—and she always moved and talked quickly, asking ten questions in the time it took most people to ask one. She reminded Della of a butterfly fluttering from flower to flower without ever resting. Now, Saturday morning, she was busily fluttering around Della's room as Della prepared for the overnight.

"Mom, what are you so uptight about?" Della asked. "We used to camp out a lot when Dad was still here." She felt a sudden pang of regret. Maybe she shouldn't have mentioned her father so casually. Her parents had divorced two years before, and her father had immediately remarried.

Her mother didn't react. She was too busy squeezing the sleeping bag. "This Mr. Abner," she said. "You never talk much about him."

"That's because I don't have him for any classes. He's just our club advisor. He's great. Really. You shouldn't worry, Mom."

"But why Fear Island?" Mrs. O'Connor asked. "It's such a creepy place."

"Well, that's the point," Della said, walking over to the mirror and pulling the hairbrush down through her long, straight hair even though it didn't need it. "It's supposed to be exciting, see."

"But Fear Island . . . There've been such awful stories." Her mother straightened some books on a shelf and then fluffed the pillow on Della's bed.

Fear Island was a small, uninhabited island, covered with pine trees, in the center of the lake behind the Fear Street woods. Even though it was a perfect spot for picnics and camping, and only a few minutes' boat ride across the lake, few people ventured there because of the dreadful stories about it.

Some said that strange animal mutations, hideous, dangerous creatures that didn't exist anywhere else, roamed the woods. Others said the island was infected with poisonous snakes. And there were stories that the island had been used long ago as an Native American burial ground, and that ghosts walked the woods at night, seeking revenge for their fate.

Della didn't really believe any of the stories. She was sure they were made up by campers to discourage others from crowding onto the island. But they certainly added an air of adventure to an overnight there.

"We didn't want to camp in a boring state park," Della told her mother. "We wanted to be somewhere more exciting."

"Well, I hope it isn't *too* exciting," her mother said, walking up behind her and straightening the bottom of her sweatshirt. "If anything bad happens, you'll call me right away, right?"

Della spun around, laughing. "Call you? On what? I'll tell you what—I'll send up a smoke signal, okay?"

"You're not funny," Mrs. O'Connor said. But she was laughing too.

The honking of a car horn from the driveway ended their conversation. "That's Pete," Della told her mother. She lifted her backpack onto her shoulders and picked up the blue sleeping bag.

"Who's Pete?" her mother asked suspiciously. She wasn't used to the fact that Gary wasn't always hanging around.

"A boy from the club." Della leaned over, kissed her mother on the cheek, and lumbered out the door under the weight of the bulging backpack.

She waved to Pete, who climbed out of the blue Subaru station wagon to help her with her stuff. He was wearing tan chinos and a plaid flannel pullover shirt. "Hi," he said, pulling up the rear door. "Nice day." The sun was high in a solid blue sky.

"Yeah. It's so peaceful out here."

"Peaceful?" He looked confused.

"My mother isn't out here asking a million questions."

He laughed. He has such perfect teeth, she thought. Too perfect.

Then she scolded herself for being so hard on him. He was a nice guy, after all. It was nice of him to offer her a ride to the lake. He couldn't help it if his teeth were too straight, and his nose was too straight and perfect, and his hair was too smooth, and he dressed better than anyone else.

He really seemed to like her. Maybe, she thought as she climbed into the front seat beside him, she should try to like him too.

But their conversation as they headed to the lake was awkward. Pete was telling her about some camping trip he had gone on with his family, but she couldn't concentrate. His voice kept drifting in and out of her consciousness. She was thinking about Gary. She kept thinking of what she would say to him, how she would start to make up with him when they were alone together in the woods.

"Did you?" Pete asked.

"Huh?" She realized she hadn't heard a word he'd said for at least a mile.

"Did you and Gary break up?" He stared straight ahead at the road.

"Well, yeah. I guess. I mean no. I don't know."

Pete laughed uncomfortably. "Should I choose one of the above?"

"Sorry," Della said. The question had gotten her all flustered. "Gary and I . . . I mean, we haven't really settled things."

"Oh." Pete didn't hide his disappointment. "This overnight should be fun," he said, changing the subject. "You're not scared about spending the night on Fear Island, are you?"

"No. I don't think so."

"Stick with me. I'll protect you," he said in an exaggerated, deep he-man voice.

"Protect me from what? From Ricky's bad jokes?"

"I think he's kind of funny," Pete admitted, turning down Fear Street and heading toward the woods. "In a gross, unfunny kind of way."

The car bumped over the road, which ended at the edge of the Fear Street woods, fifty yards or so from the water. "Everyone's here already," Della said. Pete honked the horn as the others came into view.

She could see Gary and Ricky arguing about something. Maia was sitting by the water. Suki was standing next to Gary. Pete stopped the car and cut the engine. Della could see backpacks and sleeping bags piled up beside the two canoes Gary had brought.

She waved to her friends and helped Pete carry their equipment from the back of the station wagon. "The lake looks so pretty today," she said. The water was very still and very blue, reflecting the clear sky above. Two ducks squawked and bobbed their heads as they swam near the shore. Fear Island was a low mound of green on the horizon.

"Okay. We're all here. We can get going," Gary said, looking at Della. He was wearing a faded denim jacket over a red T-shirt. His blond, wavy hair sparkled like gold in the sun.

He looks terrific, she thought. She gave him a warm smile, and he smiled back. "Gary, I want—" she started.

But Suki quickly stepped in front of her. "I've never paddled a canoe. Will you show me how?" she asked Gary in a kittenish voice.

"Sure," he told her. "Just sit in the middle and watch. The person in the middle doesn't paddle."

"I'll take this canoe. You guys can all take that one," Ricky said. He jumped into the one on the left and stretched out on his back, taking up the whole canoe.

"Very funny, Schorr. Remind us to laugh later," Suki said.

Della had to smile at Suki's outfit. It wasn't exactly outdoorsy. Her jeans had silver studs up the pants legs. She wore a long black T-shirt with a shorter white Guns-N'-Roses T-shirt on top of it. As usual, she had four different earrings in each ear.

"Hi, Della. I'm here." Maia hurried over to Della, smiling but looking worried just the same.

"Great," Della said. "Did your parents give you a hard time?"

"No. Not really," Maia said. "Only, when they dropped me off here, they wouldn't leave. They wanted to talk to Mr. Abner first."

"Oh, no. What did you do?"

"Schorr made a few jokes, and they decided they'd rather go," Suki cracked.

"Give me a break," Ricky cried, still lying in the canoe. "Hey—where's the gas pedal in this thing?"

"They changed their minds," Maia told Della. "But I just know they're going to find out what we're doing." She nervously squeezed her hands into tight fists at her sides.

"Don't be ridiculous," Della said. "How will they ever find out?"

A few minutes later they were paddling, three to a canoe, over the still blue lake, out to Fear Island. "The water's so clear today, you can see fish in there," Pete said, leaning over the side and peering down.

The canoe started to tip. "Oh. Sorry about that." He straightened and continued to paddle.

"Going for a swim, Pete?" Ricky called from the other boat. "You didn't bring your rubber-ducky inner tube!"

No one laughed. The two canoes cut through the water side by side. Pete and Della paddled one canoe with Maia sitting in the middle. Gary and Ricky paddled the other, with Suki practically sitting in Gary's lap.

Is she going to leave him alone for one second? Della asked herself. She was determined to talk to Gary as soon as possible. She had rehearsed over and over what she wanted to say. She knew he would want to go back to her once she talked with him, once she apologized. Suki could just find someone else. That wouldn't be a problem for her.

Patient, be patient, Della repeated silently as she rowed. But it was so hard to wait. Why was there so much waiting in life? Even when you were supposed to be having a good time, you spent most of it waiting!

The slap of the paddles against the water was the only sound now. Della began to feel really warm despite the cool air. She moved her paddle smoothly, keeping in rhythm with Pete's paddle. The island grew larger as they glided closer. She could make out a rocky beach in front of a line of pine trees. A few more minutes . . .

"Whoa!" She heard Ricky cry out and looked up to see him standing up in the other canoe. His eyes were wide and he was covering his mouth with his hand. The boat tipped from side to side.

"Sit down!" Gary yelled to him.

"Seasick! Seasick!" Ricky shouted, struggling to stay on his feet as the canoe bobbed violently beneath him.

"Don't be a dork. You're going to tip us over!" Suki cried, very alarmed.

Ricky held his paddle up over his head with one hand and kept his other hand over his mouth. "Seasick! Ulllp! Seasick!"

"Sit down and be seasick!" Gary yelled again.

"Oh. Good idea." Ricky plopped back down in his place. He grinned at Gary and Suki. He had been faking the whole thing.

"Not funny, Schorr," Gary said, shaking his head.

"You should change your name to that," Suki added, still looking shaken. "Not-Funny Schorr."

"Come on," Ricky said, resuming his paddling. "You guys got a laugh out of it, didn't you? Didn't you?"

They didn't answer him.

The canoes began to bob up and down as the current became stronger near the island's shore. Della was enjoying the ride, the feel of the paddle in her hands pulling the canoe forward with each stroke, the cool wind against her face, the splash and tumble of the rolling water.

A few minutes later they were pulling the canoes onto the beach. "I want to keep on going," she said to no one in particular. "It felt so good on the water."

"It feels much better to be on dry land," Suki said. "Hey!" She let go of the canoe to examine her hand. She had broken one of her long, purple press-on nails. "Now what am I going to do? I didn't pack any replacements," she grumbled.

"I guess that's what's called roughing it," Ricky cracked.

She stuck out her tongue at him.

Suki walked alongside the others, examining her broken nail as they pulled the canoes across the narrow strip of pebbles to where the trees began. "They should be okay here," Gary said, dropping the front of his canoe at the foot of a tall pine tree.

"Is it lunchtime yet?" Ricky asked. "Can we order a pizza or something?"

"Good idea. Why don't you go get it?" Suki said, throwing the broken nail onto the sand. "We'll wait here for you."

Ricky looked hurt.

"I love campfires and making hot dogs over a fire," Maia said, looking a lot more cheerful.

"Hey—it's still morning, remember?" Gary reminded them. "We've got a lot to do before it's campfire time. Come on. Pick up your packs and stuff. We've got to find a good campsite."

"Aye, aye, chief," Ricky said, giving Gary a backward salute.

Pete helped Della on with her backpack and handed her sleeping bag up to her. She thanked him and hurried up to walk with Maia. Pete was being really sweet. Too sweet. She really didn't want to encourage him.

They walked along the beach for a while, keeping near the tree line. The sun was higher in the sky now and it was becoming really warm. Della looked up to see what was causing the loud, discordant squawking she heard. Two blue jays on a low tree limb seemed to be having an argument. "Look how big they are!" she said to Maia, pointing.

"Blue jays are the noisiest birds," Maia said disapprovingly. "They're not at all like bluebirds. Bluebirds are so sweet."

"Welcome to Nature Studies 101," Ricky interrupted.

"Come on, Ricky," Della scolded. "Why'd you come on this trip if you don't like to look at nature?"

"To get close to *you*, babes," Ricky said, flashing her an evil grin. "You know, I brought a king-size sleeping bag. Big enough for me— and a friend."

"What an irresistible invitation!" Della made a face and started walking faster. A dirt path led into the trees, and they followed it. It curved through thick woods, still deep with brown winter leaves. After a while they came to a circular clearing of tall grass and weeds.

"This looks good," Gary said, tossing the tent he'd been carrying over his shoulder to the ground. "Let's set up here."

They all gratefully removed their packs and placed them on the ground. There were two tents to be set up, one for the boys and one for the girls.

"No. Turn them around this way," Pete instructed after they had started to stretch the canvas over the poles they had put together. "The wind usually comes down from the north. So the backs of the tents should face north."

"Very impressive, Pete," Gary said, only half joking. He looked up at the sun, which was directly above them. "But how do we tell which way is north?"

"It's that way," Pete said, pointing. "I have a compass on my watch." He held up his wrist, displaying one of those calculator watches with a dozen different functions.

"Do you think Daniel Boone had one of those?" Ricky asked.

Once again, everyone ignored him. They worked to turn the tents around and get them tightly pegged to the ground. Then they set off in different directions to gather enough firewood to last the night.

Pete started to follow Della, but again she hurried to catch up with Maia. "This is kind of scary," Maia said, stepping carefully over a deep puddle.

"But fun," Della added. She was very excited, she realized, but she wasn't sure why. Maybe it was the fact that they were really on their own, with no adults in sight. Anything could happen. Anything. Just the six of them, alone in the woods for the night. It could be so romantic. . . .

She headed away from Maia and started in the direction Gary had gone off in. This is my chance to talk to him, she thought. She realized that her heart was pounding. Her mouth felt dry. She didn't think she'd be this nervous.

Gary must mean more to me than I let myself admit, she thought. She stepped quickly over the dry brown leaves and fallen twigs, looking for him through the birch and pine trees.

It smelled so sweet and fresh in the woods. She couldn't wait to talk to him, to be with him again, to feel his arms around her. How could she have been so stupid as to lose her temper like that and break up with him? She didn't even remember now what the argument was about.

A squirrel stopped halfway down a tree trunk. It stared at her as she hurried past, then scampered over the leaves to the next tree.

"Gary, I want to apologize." Those were going to be her first words. No fancy introductions. No excuses or explanations. She'd just apologize and get it over with.

She stopped. There he was. She could see him through a gap in the trees. She stifled a horrified gasp.

He was leaning back against a broad tree trunk. Suki was pressed against him. They had their arms wrapped tightly around each other. Their eyes were closed. They were locked together in a long, long kiss.

CHAPTER 3

No one was surprised later that afternoon when Ricky pulled a gun from his pack.

"Come on, guys—everybody take one." He pulled out five more pistols, one at a time.

"Great! Let's do it!" Pete cried enthusiastically.

"Okay!" Gary was just as gung ho. He grabbed a gun from Ricky and pretended to fire it at Pete. Pete hit the ground and pretended to retaliate with his gun.

The three girls groaned in unison.

"Not another ZAP war," Della sighed.

"I hate war games," Suki complained. "They're so . . . competitive."

What a long word for her, Della thought bitterly. In the hours since she had seen Suki and Gary in the woods, her hurt had turned to anger.

"I've never played," Maia said. "Do you divide into teams, or is it every man for himself?"

"We'll do teams," Ricky said, pulling out the paint for the ZAP guns.

"Include me out," Suki said.

"Come on, girls. It'll be fun," Gary pleaded. "A bunch of us had a ZAP war a few weeks ago in Shadyside Park. We ended up covered in paint. It was hilarious."

"Sounds like a real laugh riot," Suki said sarcastically.

"Okay. I'm game," Della said, suddenly changing her mind. If Suki was against it, then she was going to be for it! Let Gary see who was the better sport.

"Me too, I guess," Maia said, looking at Della for reassurance.

"Great!" Gary cried. "Come on, Suki." He put a hand on her shoulder. "You're the only holdout."

"I told you, I don't like war games," Suki insisted, pulling away from Gary.

"It's not a war. Think of it as just a game—with shooting," Ricky suggested.

Suki glared at him and poked his stomach with her finger. "Will I get a chance to shoot *you* with paint, Schorr?"

"Yeah. I guess," Ricky said. "Ooh. Poke me again. I love it!"

"Shut up!" Suki said, making a fist and shaking it at Ricky playfully. "Okay, you win. I'll play. But only because I'll get to massacre you, Schorr."

"Girls against the boys," Pete suggested.

"Good deal," Gary agreed quickly.

Della was disappointed. She wanted to be on Gary's team. And she didn't want to be on the same team with Suki.

Ricky was busy loading the ZAP guns with paint, yellow for the girls, red for the boys. "Remember, two hits and you're a prisoner. Three hits and you're dead," he said seriously.

"I should've known you were bringing these," Pete said, rolling his loaded gun around in his hand. "Your backpack was so much bigger than everyone else's."

"I bring them everywhere," Ricky said. "I brought them to my cousin's wedding!"

"How long are we going to play?" Maia asked, looking at her watch. "Not when it's dark, are we?"

"We'll have creamed them by then," Suki said, taking her loaded

ZAP gun from Ricky. She squirted a stream of yellow paint into the air. Ricky glared at her. "Just testing," she said.

"No shooting for ten minutes," Ricky said. "That gives us time to scatter and take positions."

ZAP wars were the only times Ricky was ever serious. Della decided she liked him better this way, not cracking horrible jokes, not trying so desperately hard to be funny. Unfortunately, according to Gary, Ricky wasn't too good at the game. He made too big a target and was always getting hit.

A shadow passed over the campsite. Della looked up at the sky. A few puffy gray clouds interrupted the clear blue. The air suddenly got colder.

The boys left camp first, traveling south in a group. The girls decided to wait a few minutes and then go west. Then they'd split up and circle in on the boys. After the boys left, laughing and joking, Suki changed into an olive-green sweater, saying it was better camouflage.

Wow, another big word. Two in one day, Della thought. She never had liked Suki. Actually, she had never thought much about her at all. They didn't hang out with the same crowds. But now Della had plenty of reason to think about Suki, and plenty of reason to dislike her.

Or was she being unfair? She had broken up with Gary, after all. Sort of.

"Come on. Let's get going," Maia said. The pistol looked really big and out of place in her little hand.

They started walking together into the woods. "This is kind of sexy," Suki said.

"Huh? Sexy?" Della didn't get it.

"Yeah. You know. Hunting and being hunted."

"Oh."

"It's kind of exciting," Suki said, carefully stepping over a fallen tree limb.

A gust of wind made the new green leaves on the trees whisper and shake. A large cloud rolled over the sun, and the woods suddenly grew dark.

"Is the paint washable?" Maia asked. Her enthusiasm was short-lived. She sounded like her old worried self again.

"Yes, of course," Della said sharply. "Ricky *told* us it was washable. It'll come right out."

Maia looked at her, recognizing the impatience in her voice. Della reminded herself that it was Suki she resented. She shouldn't take it out on Maia.

"Let's split up here and circle around," Suki said, gesturing with the large gray pistol.

"Okay," Della agreed quickly. She realized she was looking forward to being on her own, away from everyone.

"How do I find you if I get lost?" Maia asked, tugging at the sleeves of her sweatshirt.

"Walk away from the sun. East. And you'll be heading back toward camp," Della advised.

Maia looked up at the sun, as if to make sure it was still there. "Okay. See you later." She turned and walked off slowly through the trees, holding the pistol in front of her.

"Listen for footsteps," Della called after her. "No one will be able to come up behind you without making loud footsteps."

"Thanks!" Maia called back.

"She's such a little girl," Suki said quietly.

She didn't say it scornfully, but Della didn't like the idea of Suki putting down her friend. "She's okay," she told Suki, sounding angrier than she had intended.

"Gary's really nice," Suki said suddenly.

Della wasn't sure she had heard correctly.

Suki was staring into her eyes, as if searching for a reaction. Della forced her face to go blank. She wasn't going to give away her feelings to Suki so easily.

"You broke up with him, right?" Suki asked.

But before Della could answer—and what would she answer?—Suki headed off into the woods, pushing tall brambles out of her way so that she could pass through, her white Reebok hightops crunching over the dead leaves.

Della leaned against a smooth white tree trunk, watching Suki until she disappeared into the woods. What was she trying to prove, anyway? Was she trying to excuse her moving in on Gary so quickly? Was Suki challenging her? Was she trying to be friendly? Was she making fun of her?

Della wandered in the general direction the other two girls had gone. Her mind was spinning, trying to figure out what Suki had intended with her surprising, casual remarks. She didn't really pay attention to where she was going. She completely forgot about the large plastic gun in her hand, the gun she was supposed to hold at the ready in case she came upon any of the boys.

The crunch of a footstep brought her back to reality. She spun around and ducked as a spray of red paint flew over her head. She dropped to her knees, raised her pistol, and fired without aiming.

"Hey!" she heard Ricky shout.

Peering through tall weeds, she saw him rubbing at a splotch of yellow paint on his sweatshirt. "Missed me!" she yelled, laughing. Keeping low, she darted to the left and ducked behind a broad tree trunk.

"Lucky hit!" Ricky shouted, running toward her at full speed. He fired, sending a stream of red paint up into the air. It died before it reached the tree.

Della fired back, once, twice, missing both times. Then she took off, running along a narrow path through the fir and pine trees.

She turned back in time to see Ricky, the splotch of yellow paint bright on the front of his dark sweatshirt, fall over a low stump and go sprawling face forward into the dirt. His ZAP gun bounced out of his hand and over the ground.

With a triumphant smile on her face, Della turned off the path and kept running. She pushed branches and brambles out of her way, moving at top speed. This was fun, she decided. Ricky would never find her now.

Suddenly, the clouds thickened and covered the sun, making it nearly as dark as night in the dense woods. Screeching birds circled, then settled onto high tree limbs. The wind swirled dust and dry leaves around her sneakers.

She shivered, realizing that she hadn't kept track of the direction she was heading in.

Where am I?

She looked to the sun to gauge her position, but the dark clouds blotted it out almost completely. Some great advice I gave Maia about watching the sun, she told herself. Poor Maia was probably lost too.

"Hey—Maia!" she called aloud. She didn't care if the boys heard her or not.

There was no reply.

"Maia! Suki! Can you hear me?"

No reply.

The birds suddenly became silent. It was eerie, Della thought, as if someone had just turned them off, like turning off a TV set.

The silence was strange, unnatural.

"Now, don't start getting morbid," she scolded herself.

The wind shifted direction. A branch cracked somewhere behind her. She jumped as it hit the ground with a loud thud. She spun around, thinking someone was there.

"Maia? Suki?"

Where were they?

She turned and started walking back to camp. She wasn't sure it was the right direction, but it felt right. She had a pretty good sense of direction. Of course, she'd never been alone in the middle of the woods before.

There was one good thing about being on an island. The woods wouldn't go on forever. If she kept walking in a straight line, she'd eventually come out of them. But was she walking in a straight line? She couldn't tell.

The terrain sloped up, then down again. She realized she hadn't walked here before. Thick green moss grew up the side of a tilted old tree. Moss. Moss on a tree. It only grows on one side of the tree, she remembered. But which side? She stared at it. The north side? The east side? She couldn't remember.

"Maia? Suki? Anyone?"

Where *was* everyone?

A crunching sound. Behind her. A footstep?

She turned. No one there.

She turned back, walked past the mossy tree. The ground was hilly now, the inclines growing steeper as she walked.

Another crunching sound. Then another.

Someone was definitely following her. She didn't turn around. It was probably one of the boys, planning a sneak attack. But there was no such thing as a sneak attack when every step you took made a sound.

What should she do?

Count to ten, spin around, and fire.

She walked on, stepping through tall ferns bent low in the strong wind. Three . . . four . . . five . . .

The footsteps behind her were louder. Whoever it was was coming closer.

Eight . . . nine . . . ten!

She wheeled around, dropped to her knees, and pulled the trigger.

A stream of bright yellow paint flew through the air, splattering leaves and tree trunks, dripping down onto the dark ground.

A squirrel turned and darted away, making loud crunching sounds over the leaves as it ran.

A squirrel. It was only a squirrel.

She laughed out loud and sent another spray of paint high into the air.

She had been followed by a squirrel. And she had shot at it.

Good move, ace.

Guess I showed *him* not to mess with Della O'Connor.

She fired another shot at a tree trunk, missing by nearly a foot.

It was really dark now, but she didn't feel bad. The squirrel had cheered her up. She wasn't afraid anymore. It was silly to be afraid.

What was there to be afraid of?

She eased herself down a steep slope and began making her way across a flat area, the ground thick with fragrant pine needles and dried-up pinecones.

Suddenly, just a few feet ahead of her, someone stepped quickly out from behind a tree.

"Pete? Gary?"

She stopped short.

It wasn't one of her friends. It was a man she had never seen before. And he was moving toward her very quickly.

CHAPTER 4

He stopped a few feet in front of her, his hands in the pockets of his brown leather bomber jacket. His hair was sandy colored, cut very short. He smiled at her. He had a nice smile, she thought. In fact, he was really handsome, movie-star handsome.

She realized she was holding her breath. She let it out quickly. Her heart was pounding. "Hi," she said weakly. "You scared me. I didn't—"

His smile didn't fade. His dark eyes looked her up and down. "Sorry. You scared me too." His voice was smooth, mellow. She guessed he was about twenty-one or twenty-two.

"I didn't expect—"

"Me either," he said, shrugging, with his hands still in the jacket pockets.

He's really cute, she thought. What a smile!

"What are you doing here?" she blurted out. Then she quickly added, "I was looking for my friends. I seem to be lost. I mean—" Why was she telling him this?

"Lost?" That seemed to amuse him. His smile grew wider, revealing straight, white teeth. He removed a hand from his jacket and swept it back over his short hair.

"Are you lost too?" she asked.

He laughed quietly to himself. "No, I don't think so."

"Oh." Then why was he here in the middle of Fear Island by himself?

"You from Shadyside?" he asked.

"Yeah. I'm on an overnight. We're camping out."

"Are we?" He laughed.

He's the most handsome guy I've ever seen, Della thought. Look at those dimples when he laughs. He really could be a model or something.

"Are you camping out too?" she asked.

"Sort of."

He was obviously playing a game with her, deliberately not telling her why he was there. "Like to answer questions?" she asked teasingly.

"Sure. Ask me anything. Want to know my social security number?" His eyes grew wide as he challenged her.

"No. I just—"

"Want to know my height and weight? My shoe size? My mother's maiden name?" He was talking rapidly, excitedly. She couldn't tell if he was joking or not.

"Yes, I think that would be very interesting," she said, making her own joke and watching to see his reaction.

He laughed. It was a warm, reassuring laugh. She felt drawn to him because of his laugh, because of his dark eyes, because of his clean, good looks.

"So why are you here in the middle of the woods on Fear Island?" she asked, leaning against a narrow tree trunk.

"Well, I came back, you see," he started.

"Back from college?"

"Yeah. Right. Back from college. I go to B.U. Up in Boston." He kicked at a thick, upraised root that curled along the dirt.

"But it's awfully early for school to be out," she said.

"Well . . . yeah. It's not out. I'm here on kind of a project. You know. About trees." He patted the trunk of the tree he was standing next to. "Lots of trees to study on the island. I'm doing my paper on tree reproduction."

"Reproduction?"

He grinned. "Yeah. You know what that is, don't you?"

They both laughed. "That sounds very . . . interesting," she said, staring into his eyes. Why did she feel like flirting with him? She didn't know a thing about him. She didn't even know his name.

"I'm Della. What's your name?"

"Della? That's funny. That's *my* name too!"

"Oh, get real . . ."

"No. I mean it." He raised a hand as if swearing he was telling the truth. He came a few steps closer. He was standing right in front of her now.

"I like your jacket," Della said. She reached out and touched the sleeve. "Real vinyl?"

He laughed. "You're very funny." His eyes peered into hers, as if he were looking for something there. "A sense of humor is important, don't you think? I think so. Some people don't have a sense of humor. How do you deal with them? You know? What can you do about it? Sometimes it's the only way to reach someone. When you want to reach someone and they don't know where you're coming from. Follow my meaning?"

"No," she said, laughing.

He didn't laugh with her. He bit his lower lip. His face turned serious. He looked down at her. She realized for the first time how tall he was, about a foot taller than she.

"I'm talking about communication," he said, shouting the last word. "I'm talking about getting through to people when they don't want you to reach them. Know what I mean?"

"Yeah. I guess." He was starting to frighten her. What was this ridiculous rap about communication? He wasn't making any sense. Why was he getting so worked up?

She took a step back. She decided to change the subject. "So you like trees, huh?"

"Trees?" For a second he looked as if he didn't know what she was talking about. "Oh, yeah. Sure. I like your hair."

"It's all blown by the wind."

"I like that." He looked up at the sky. "Pretty cloudy. Hope it doesn't rain." He was calm again.

"Yeah."

He moved closer and fingered the sleeve of her sweatshirt. "Nice sweatshirt," he said.

"It's real vinyl." She could feel his breath on her neck. She stepped back, but he didn't let go of her sleeve. "I guess I should get back."

"Back?"

"Back to my friends. They're probably wondering where I am."

"Where are you?" he asked. It didn't exactly sound like a joke. There was something unpleasant about the way he said it, something threatening.

"My friends. I have to get back to camp."

"Send this girl to camp," he said, unsmiling, staring into her eyes.

She noticed for the first time that he was sweating.

How weird, she thought. It's too cold to be sweating like that. His leather jacket can't be *that* warm!

"Nice to meet you, Della," she said, trying to keep it light, but eager now to get away from him.

He didn't say anything. He stood staring at her, expressionless. He seemed to be thinking hard, concentrating on something. "Are those *real* gold?" he asked, reaching for one of her hoop earrings.

"I don't know," she said, quickly backing away from him.

Suddenly, he grabbed her hair and held it tightly, pulling her head back.

"Hey!" she cried. "What are you doing?"

"I guess they *are*," he said. "Solid gold. You're a real *princess*, aren't you."

"No. Let go!" She tried not to let her panic sound in her voice, but she couldn't help it.

He tightened his grip on her hair.

"Come on—let me go. I'm *serious*!"

"Me too," he said in a low voice filled with menace.

Still pulling her hair with one hand, he grabbed her arm above the elbow with his other hand and pulled her against him. She could smell the leather of his jacket, the leather smell mixed with sweat.

"Hey—stop!" she pleaded. "You're *hurting* me!"

"Sorry, Princess." He tightened his grip.

She tried to pull away from him, but he was too strong. He dragged her up a brushy slope. At the top, she looked down into a deep ravine.

"What do you want?" she cried. "What are you going to do with me?"

CHAPTER 5

Still holding her tightly with one arm, he unzipped his jacket. It was one of the loudest sounds Della had ever heard, and the most frightening.

"Pete! Gary!" she screamed.

He laughed quietly to himself. "No one can hear you," he whispered. He pushed her closer to the edge of the ravine.

"No, wait," she begged.

"What does waiting get you?" he said. His voice was smooth, calm; terrifyingly calm. "I've been waiting here. Too long. I've been waiting for a lot of things. Finally, I decided just to take something. Something for me. Know what I mean?" He was talking rapidly again, crazily, his eyes wild, spraying her with spittle as he leaned in close to her face.

"Just let go of me," she said, forcing her voice not to tremble. "I won't run away. I promise."

"I don't ask a lot. But I want *something*," he continued, ignoring her request. "That's what I told the old man. But he wouldn't listen. I couldn't communicate, see. That's what we're talking about. Communication. I found a way to communicate with him okay. I found a way. But it didn't do him any good. I mean, you don't learn a lesson if you're dead. Know where I'm coming from?"

"Uh . . . yes. Please let go."

"You don't know what I'm talking about, do you? Well, you'd better not. Just play dumb, okay? *Okay?* You like me. I can tell. I think I can communicate with you. Yes?"

"Yes. No. You're hurting me!"

Breathing heavily, his chest heaving, he loosened his grip a little. Backing away, Della saw the silver chain around his neck, three silver skulls hanging from it. "Oh!" she gasped. They were so ugly, so realistic, so evil looking.

He stared into her eyes. He seemed to be trying to read her thoughts.

"What do you want?" she asked.

He didn't reply. He didn't blink. His silence was scarier than his wild talk.

She suddenly remembered the ZAP gun. She had shoved it into her back jeans pocket. She reached for it now, felt the barrel first, then grabbed the handle. She jerked her arm back, raised the gun, and fired.

A spray of yellow paint shot onto his forehead.

He sputtered, surprised, then cried out angrily and let go of her to wipe his forehead.

She took off, racing, stumbling, flying along the ground. Where was she going? She didn't know. She didn't care. She was getting away.

She tripped over an upraised root, but climbed quickly to her feet. She was running blindly now, thick foliage rushing by in a blur.

And he was right behind her.

He lunged. His arms went around her legs. He tackled her.

She hit the ground hard. Her knee throbbed with pain, which shot up through the rest of her body.

His arms circled her waist.

Before she even realized she had been recaptured, he had pulled her to her feet. Angrily, he gave her a hard shove. He grabbed the ZAP gun from her hand and shoved the barrel into her back.

"Let me go! Let me go!" she wailed.

He stared at her, struggling to catch his breath, perspiration dripping down his forehead, down his smooth cheeks.

He pushed her ahead of him, back up to the top of the ravine. She struggled to break away, but he held on tightly, bending her arm behind her, poking the sharp nose of the ZAP gun into her back.

At the top of the ravine he stopped. He grabbed her by the shoulders and shook her hard. "You shouldn't have done that," he growled.

As he brought his face down closer, she pulled back both hands and gave him a fast, hard shove with all her might.

His eyes opened wide in surprise as he lost his footing.

"Hey!"

He tumbled backward. His feet flew out from under him as he began to topple down the side of the steep ravine.

His hands, desperately reaching for something to stop his fall, grabbed only air.

She closed her eyes.

She heard him scrape against the ground, once, twice. She heard him cry out. She heard a thud. A groan. And then silence.

It took three or four seconds at most.

It seemed like a year.

She opened her eyes. Everything seemed so much darker. The trees, the ground, the sky. She took a deep breath and held it. Sometimes that calmed her down.

This time it didn't work.

Her first instinct was to run. But she knew she couldn't run away until she had looked down to the bottom of the ravine.

The ground seemed to tilt. The trees seemed set at strange angles, warring with each other. She shook her head, trying to shake away the dizziness.

She looked down the ravine. It wasn't as deep or as steep as she had imagined.

He was lying at the bottom, his body twisted, his head in such a weird position, as if it had come off and been carelessly replaced by someone who didn't know which way a head was supposed to fit.

She took a couple of cautious steps down the slope.

He didn't move. His mouth was opened wide. His eyes were closed. His head was bent nearly sideways. It appeared to be resting on his shoulder.

"No!"

Had he broken his neck?

She felt sick. Everything started to spin. She sank to the ground and waited for the woods to stop moving.

What should I do? she wondered. This isn't really happening—is it? Her mind was spinning faster than the trees. She wanted to wake up and forget this dream. She wanted to run away. She wanted to stop the panic she felt. If only she could think clearly . . .

Before she realized what she was doing, she was on her feet, tumbling and sliding down the side of the ravine. At the bottom she stood over the unmoving body, staring at the chain with its three silver skulls that seemed to stare back at her.

His mouth was locked open in an expression of horror. He seemed to be saying, "*You* did this to me. You killed me, Della."

"No!" she screamed. "Get up! Get up!"

She grabbed his arm and started to pull him up. The arm felt limp and lifeless. She dropped it, feeling a wave of revulsion roll up from her stomach.

"Get up! Get up!"

It was so dark, so hard to see. If only everything would stop spinning. If only she could breathe normally, think normally.

What should she do? What??

He's got to be alive, she thought. This can't be happening. It can't.

Her hands shaking, she sank to her knees in the dry leaves and reached for his hand. She moved her fingers around his wrist, trying to find a pulse.

Where is it? Where *is* it? Come on—there's *got* to be a pulse. . . . Yes!

She found it. The soft, insistent thudding in his wrist, so fast, so strong. Yes. He had a pulse. He was alive. He—

No.

She shuddered. It was her own pulse she was feeling.

Her hands were shaking. She reached for his throat. She had seen this in movies. You find a pulse by pressing on the side of the throat.

The head rolled lifelessly back. She pressed hard against the throat. Nothing. She moved her fingers. Nothing.

Nothing. Nothing. Nothing.

She grabbed up his wrist.

Nothing.

"Ohh." She climbed to her feet, her hands covering her face.

He was dead. She had killed him.

Self-defense, she thought. It was self-defense.

But what did that matter? She had killed a man, another human being.

Now what?

Now her life would be *ruined*.

Now her parents would know she went on the overnight without Mr. Abner. Now *all* of the parents would know. She thought of Maia, of the promise she had made Maia that nothing would go wrong.

And now everything had gone wrong.

The whole town would know that she had killed a man. For the rest of her life she'd be haunted by this moment. Her life was ruined, *ruined*.

No.

Why ruin her life for this . . . this creep?

Why ruin all of their lives?

She turned her back to him so she could think better. Her mind was racing crazily, she realized. It was so hard to think clearly, to think in a straight line.

But she knew she had decided.

She wasn't going to tell anyone about him.

There was no reason to tell. And there was *every* reason not to tell.

It was an accident, anyway. Just an accident. He could have slipped and fallen down the ravine and hit his head and broken his neck or whatever he did to himself all by himself.

Suddenly she knew what she would do. It was easy, actually. And it was smart. She was being smart.

And she wasn't just protecting herself. She was protecting her friends. They didn't deserve to have their lives ruined forever because of this . . . accident.

She bent over and filled her arms with dry leaves, dead leaves from the winter just passed. Then she dropped the leaves over his legs. Another armful of leaves. She dropped them over his boots. Another armful.

It won't take long to cover him with leaves, she thought. Then I'll go back to camp and pretend this never happened.

She scooped up another armful of leaves. As she started to drop them onto his chest, she looked up to the top of the ravine.

Ricky and Maia were staring down at her.

CHAPTER 6

"He *attacked* me!" Della cried, struggling up the side of the steep ravine. "I didn't mean to do it! I mean, I didn't mean to push him. He just fell, you see. It was an accident!"

Maia looked even more upset than Della, but she hurried forward and put an arm around Della's shoulder, helping her away from the ravine and trying to calm her. "Take your time," she whispered into Della's ear. "Take your time. Tell it slowly."

"Who *is* that guy?" Ricky demanded, standing on the edge of the ravine, peering down at the half-covered body.

"I don't know," Della said, forcing herself to stop shaking, to stop breathing so hard and fast. "That's what I'm trying to tell you. He just came at me. He wanted to . . . he wanted to . . . I pushed him away, and he fell. He—He's dead. He's really dead."

Maia let go of her shoulder and backed away.

"Della, you promised me—" she started, but she was too upset to finish her sentence. "My parents—they're going to . . ."

Pete came up from behind Della and put a hand on her shoulder. "Take it easy. It's over now," he said gently. "We'll figure out what to do."

Della smiled at him. She was beginning to feel a little calmer.

"This is really gross," she heard Suki telling Gary. "I've never seen a dead body before."

"But who is he? What was he doing out here?" Ricky demanded, looking very serious for once.

"Just some creep," Della muttered, shivering.

"But what was he doing out here all by himself?" Ricky repeated, his voice high and whiny.

"Ricky, how should I know?" she snapped. "He wasn't a close personal friend, you know. He was some guy who attacked me in the woods. He didn't tell me his life story first."

"Sorry," Ricky said softly. "You don't have to shout."

Shout? She felt like screaming at the top of her lungs.

"Are you sure he's dead?" Gary asked suddenly.

"What?"

"Are you sure he's dead?"

"Well, yes," Della said, picturing again in her mind her frantic, unsuccessful attempts to find a pulse. Thinking about it, she began to feel dizzy again. She sat down on the ground, leaning back on her hands, closing her eyes.

"Maybe we should double-check," Gary said.

"I just don't believe this is happening," Maia cried. "All of our lives wrecked because of a stupid overnight."

"Just *shut up*, Maia!" Della screamed, losing control, not caring.

"But my parents are going to *kill* me!" Maia insisted. Della looked up at her. Tears were streaming down her cheeks.

Why is *she* crying? Della wondered. How can *she* have the nerve to cry? *I'm* the one who just killed a man!

"Chill out, Maia," Suki said sharply. "This isn't going to do any of our reputations any good."

"I don't feel so well," Ricky said. "My stomach . . ." He ran into the trees.

"I'm going down there," Gary said.

"What for?" Suki grabbed his arm.

But he pulled out of her grasp and slid down the side of the ravine. "Wait—I'll go with you," Pete said. But he made no attempt to follow.

Della stood up and watched Gary make his way to the bottom of the ravine. The wind had picked up, blowing the leaves she had piled on top of the young man, making it look as if he were moving. Somewhere off in the distance she heard crows cawing loudly. The crows made her think of buzzards. She pictured large black buzzards voraciously attacking the stranger, pulling him apart.

She shook her head hard, trying to erase the hideous picture from her mind. Gary was bending over the body now, brushing away some of the leaves Della had piled on.

"He feels cold," Gary shouted up to them, his voice trembling, sounding higher than usual.

No one said anything. Ricky returned, sweating hard, looking very shaken.

"I can't find a pulse," Gary called up.

"What are we going to do?" Ricky asked, sitting down on the ground, crossing his legs and propping his head up with his hands.

"We're going to finish covering him with leaves," Suki said, as if it had all been decided.

"We are?" Maia asked, more hopeful than surprised. "We're going to pretend we don't know about this?"

"What do you think, Della?" Pete asked, standing very close to her, starting to put his arm around her shoulders, then hesitating.

"Can we keep a secret like this?" Della asked, staring off into the trees, not looking at them.

"We *have* to," Maia insisted.

"Yeah, we have to," Ricky repeated glumly, his head down.

Gary reappeared, breathing heavily, looking shaken. "No pulse at all," he said.

"We've decided to cover him up and pretend it didn't happen," Suki told Gary.

"I guess." Gary shook his head. "Anyone disagree with that plan?"
No one replied.

"Let's go," Gary said, looking at Pete.

"I'll help," Della said, starting after them.

"No." Pete held up a hand. "Gary and I can do this."

They disappeared down into the ravine. Della didn't watch, but she could hear the scratch and rustle of leaves as they buried the young man's body in them. She knew it was a sound she would never forget.

A few minutes later all six of them headed back to camp in silence. Somehow Della was surprised to find the tents, the backpacks, the equipment, and firewood all just as they'd left them. Her whole world had changed in that instant back on the edge of the ravine. She found herself expecting everything to be different now. It was reassuring, somehow, to see the campsite looking the same.

Maybe everything *will* go on as before, she thought. Maybe the secret will be left behind here on Fear Island and the memory of it will eventually fade.

"Let's pack up and get out of here," Suki said, picking up her backpack.

"Right," Maia agreed. "I don't want to spend another second on this horrible island."

"No, wait," Della insisted. "We can't go back now. Our parents will all want to know why we came back so early, why we didn't spend the night."

"She's right," Gary said quickly.

"You mean we have to spend the whole night here?" Maia cried. "No! I won't! I won't!" She picked up her backpack and angrily heaved it at the pile of firewood.

"Maia, if you don't chill out, we'll cover you with leaves too," Suki threatened.

Maia gasped. Ricky laughed. He was looking a little more like his usual self.

"Let's everybody try to stay calm," Gary said. "Della's right. We have to stay here till tomorrow. We have to make everything look like normal. We can't give our parents any reason to suspect that the overnight wasn't a great success."

"What a bummer," Suki muttered. "I don't think anyone's in the mood for this anymore."

"I know," Gary replied. "But we have no choice—do we? We have to stay."

"But I'm so cold," Maia whined.

"Let's get the fire going," Gary said. "A warm fire will make everyone feel better."

"A warm dinner will make *me* feel better," Ricky said. "Especially since I just blew lunch!"

They built a large fire and roasted hot dogs over it. Della was surprised to find that she hadn't lost her appetite. No one said much. Even Ricky ate in silence, hungrily wolfing down his food.

It was a clear, cool night. The wind gusted and swirled, making the campfire flicker and bend. Della looked up to find the sky filled with bright yellow and white stars. "How are you doing?" Pete asked, scooting down onto the blanket beside her.

"Okay, I guess." She smiled at him. He really was being nice to her. Gary and Suki sat across the campfire from her, sharing a blanket but not saying anything as they ate.

Maia sat as close to the fire as she could get. She was rubbing her hands together, trying to warm them. "I just can't get warmed up," she said, seeing Della and Pete staring at her.

"Guess no one wants to tell ghost stories around the fire tonight," Ricky quipped after they were finished eating. It was his first attempt at a joke, and it received the same silent reception most of his jokes received.

"I think we should get to sleep as early as possible," Maia said. "Then when we wake up, it'll be time to go home." She shook her head miserably, staring into the orange glow of the fire. "I just want it to be time to go home."

She stood up and started to drag her blanket toward the girls' tent.

"No—wait," Gary called, taking his arm off Suki's shoulder. "First we have to take an oath."

"Huh? What kind of oath?" Ricky asked, wrapped in his blanket so that only his face showed.

"An oath of secrecy," Gary said. "The secret of Fear Island must stay here forever. We all have to hold hands and swear to it."

The wind howled as the six of them stood solemnly in a circle. They each reached a hand forward over the fire. All six hands touched together.

Suki pulled her hand away. "This is stupid," she said.

"No, it isn't. A ceremony makes it official," Gary told her.

Suki rolled her eyes, but put her hand back with the others. They all leaned together, their faces orange in the firelight. "The secret shall be kept," Gary said slowly, his voice a whisper.

And as he said it, a rush of wind blew out the fire.

Maia screamed. It took a few seconds to get her calmed down. Pete and Suki quickly got the fire relit. Maia was the only one who had reacted, but everyone seemed pretty shaken now.

"At least there isn't a full moon," Ricky said. "We probably don't have to worry about werewolves." His joke was half-hearted. No one reacted.

They piled up their backpacks near the fire since there was no room for them in the small tents. Then Della led Maia to the girls' tent. As she reached the opening, she turned and saw Gary wandering away from the campsite with Suki, their arms around each other's waists.

Inside the tent the air was warm and wet. Della began to unroll her sleeping bag, then stopped. Outside she could hear the wind and the rustling of leaves.

The rustling of leaves, leaves being dropped over a young man's body. Buried in leaves. In leaves. Buried in the rustling leaves.

"No!" She held her hands over her ears, but the sound of the rustling leaves didn't go away.

"You okay?" Maia asked, climbing into her sleeping bag fully dressed.

"What?" It was hard to hear Maia over the sound of the leaves. So many leaves, dry, brown leaves, piled so high.

"I asked if you're okay."

"Yeah, sure. I guess."

"We never should have come here," Maia said. "I knew we never should have done this." She turned her head away from Della.

Della didn't say anything. She finished unrolling her sleeping bag, listening to the wind and the leaves, thinking about the young man, feeling his forehead pressed against her cheek again, smelling the leather of his bomber jacket, then seeing him fall backward as she shoved him, shoved him, shoved him to his death.

She forced herself to think about something else. Gary. No. She couldn't think about Gary either. He was off in the woods now, making out with Suki. Why had she agreed to go on this overnight? The whole point was to try to make things up with Gary. But that was out of the question now. Finished. Done. Done for.

Like the young man in the woods.

Stop it, Della. Stop thinking about it.

No, I can't. I can't. I'll never be able to stop.

A few hours later she awoke from a dreamless sleep. Her arm tingled and felt numb. She realized she'd been sleeping on it. She pulled it out of the sleeping bag and tried to shake it back to life.

Her face felt wet and cold. Everything felt damp. She sat up, her eyes adjusting to the darkness. Maia was asleep, curled deep in her sleeping bag. Suki was asleep too, breathing noisily through her open mouth. When did she come in?

Della swept a hand back through her hair. Wet, wet, wet. Weren't tents supposed to keep out the dew?

She heard a sound just outside the tent. A chill ran down her back. Was someone out there?

She listened.

The wind had died down. It was silent now.

A crackling twig broke the silence. Was it a footstep? She heard a scraping sound. Yes. Someone was there.

Was anyone else awake?

She listened. Another crackling noise, like a footstep on twigs or dry leaves.

She pulled herself up, her arm still tingling. She was wide awake now.

"Maia! Suki! Wake up!" she whispered. "Maia—please! Somebody—wake up!"

Her two tentmates stirred. "What time is it?" Maia finally asked, her voice raspy from sleep.

"Ssshh," Della warned. "Listen. I think there's someone out there."

That startled Suki and Maia into consciousness. They both climbed onto their knees. "Huh? Probably the wind," Suki whispered. But she looked as frightened as Maia.

"What should we do?" Maia asked, pulling her sleeping bag around her to keep warm.

"Sssh. Listen," Della whispered.

They heard a crunching sound. A sound like a shoe scraping over dirt. Then another sound.

What was that? A cough?

Della got to her knees and started making her way cautiously to the tent opening. Her side ached. Her neck felt stiff. Whoever said that sleeping on the ground was comfortable?

"Della—get back," Maia pleaded. "Where are you going?"

"To see who—or what—it is," Della whispered. "Are you coming with me?"

Suki ducked down into her sleeping bag, pulling it up around her head. Maia made no attempt to move.

"Looks like I'm going by myself," Della sighed.

"Go back to sleep." Suki's voice came out muffled through the sleeping bag. "This is all just a bad dream."

Another crunching sound outside the tent, this one a little louder, a little closer.

"Here. Take this." Maia, looking guilty, handed Della a flashlight.

Holding the flashlight in one hand, Della struggled into her sneakers. She hesitated at the tent opening, then stepped out, shining the flashlight in a quick circle around the campsite.

No one there.

She took another step out of the tent. The fire had nearly burned out, red-blue embers crackling weakly in front of her. She stopped and listened.

A footstep. Just beyond the boys' tent.

"Who's there?" she called, but her voice came out softly. She knew it didn't carry past the tents.

She heard another footstep.

"Anybody there?" A little louder this time.

Keeping the light ahead of her and down low, she walked past the boys' tent, stepping gingerly since her laces were untied. She was at the edge of the clearing now. There was no wind at all. The only sound was that of her breathing. And of another footstep over dry leaves.

She took a few steps into the trees. "Who's there?" She shined the flashlight in a wide circle.

She shivered, more from fear than from the cold. What am I doing out here? she asked herself. Who do I think I'll find? Why am I being so brave?

Shivering again, she turned back.

It was probably just some animal anyway, she thought.

Of all the stupid things. Wandering off into the woods in the middle of the night, chasing after a stupid animal. I'm losing my mind, she thought.

She stepped carefully past the fire and was about to climb back into the girls' tent when something caught her eye. The backpacks. They had been piled so neatly by the fire. Now they were scattered on the ground.

Had someone knocked them over?

She took a few steps toward them and shined the flashlight on them. They didn't seem to have been opened.

No. It must have been the wind. Or maybe an animal. A raccoon searching for food. That's all. The footsteps she heard heading into the woods—they must have been the same raccoon.

Maia and Suki were sitting up by the tent opening, nervously awaiting her return. "Just a raccoon, I guess," Della said with a shrug.

"I knew it," Suki said, shaking her head. She slid back down into her sleeping bag.

"Thank goodness," Maia breathed in relief.

Della kicked off the sneakers and slid back into the sleeping bag. It was cold in there now. She knew it would take a long while to warm it up. She listened. But now all she could hear was Suki's loud breathing.

She listened to Suki's snores and Maia's tossing and turning for the rest of the night. She couldn't get back to sleep.

In the morning they all emerged groggy and stiff, like bears coming out of a winter-long hibernation. Maia seemed constantly on the verge of tears, although she never gave in and cried.

They ate a quick breakfast and packed up in near silence, eager to get away from the island, eager to end the overnight, eager not to see each other for a while, to be able to go off somewhere and think silently, by themselves, about what had happened.

The red morning sun was still climbing over the trees when they stepped out of the woods and onto the rocky beach. The lake looked flat and purple in the morning light. The air was clear enough for them to see the town stretching along the bank on the other side of the water.

"Oh no! My backpack!" Ricky cried. "I left it back there." He turned and headed back to the campsite, running at full speed.

The others hurried toward where they had left the canoes, their sneakers crunching over the pebbles.

A few seconds later they all stopped. And stared.

"The canoes!" Della said.

They were gone.

"Oh no!" Maia cried. "We're trapped here!"

CHAPTER 7

"Someone must have taken them," Della said. "I know this is where we left them." She shifted the heavy backpack on her shoulders and looked across the lake to town. It was so close, but so far away.

"Now, don't anybody panic," Gary said, looking very worried.

"Don't panic? What do you *mean*, don't panic!" Maia cried, her face red, her eyes wide with fear. "Who could have done this? What are we going to do? I've got to get home! My parents will *kill* me!"

"We won't be here long. When we don't get home on time, they'll send somebody to look for us," Gary said.

That was supposed to reassure them, but it didn't reassure Maia at all. "Then everyone will know that we came here without Mr. Abner!" she cried.

"Are you sure this is where we left them?" Suki asked, kicking at the sand.

"Yes, of course," Gary said. "Look. You can see the tracks in the sand."

"So somebody had to steal them," Della said quietly. She thought of the dead young man buried in the leaves. They were trapped on the island, trapped with him.

"What's going on?" Ricky called, lumbering up to them, dragging his backpack.

"The canoes—" Maia started.

"Oh no." Ricky turned white. "Oh, wow. I'm sorry. I moved the canoes."

"*You what?*"

"Why?"

A guilty grin spread over Ricky's face. He backed away from them, dropped his backpack on the sand and raised his hands as if preparing to fend off an attack. "It was supposed to be a joke. I did it yesterday, before the . . . uh . . . accident."

"I don't believe this." Suki scowled at Ricky. "You've got a great sense of humor, Schorr."

"I'm sorry. It was just a practical joke. Yesterday, I doubled back during the ZAP war and moved them," Ricky said. "So sue me. When I did it, I didn't know Della was going to kill a guy!"

Della gasped. "Ricky—"

"Give her a break, Schorr," Pete said quickly.

"Give us all a break," Gary said impatiently. "We all just want to get away from here. Where'd you hide the canoes?"

"Right over here." They followed Ricky about a hundred yards down the beach. The canoes were resting in some tall weeds behind a low dune.

"You really are a dork, Schorr," Suki said, looking at him as if he were a piece of dirt.

"I said I was sorry." He shrugged.

They pulled the canoes to the water, tossed their equipment in, and climbed in. The trip back to town seemed to take forever. No one talked. No one looked back at Fear Island.

One day later and we're all different people, Della thought. We all have a secret now. We all have a nightmare that we share, that we must hide.

She looked at Maia. Her auburn hair was a mess of matted-down tangles. Her eyes were red-rimmed, with dark circles around them. She looked as if she'd been crying all night. Pete, who was always so perfectly neat, was wearing a stained and wrinkled sweatshirt. His unbrushed hair fell down over his eyes.

The occupants of the other canoe looked just as worn out. Suki's spiked hair was plastered flat against her head. She hadn't even tried to comb it. Her face was pale, white as cake flour, as if all her blood had been drained. Ricky paddled silently in the rear of the canoe, breathing heavily, sweat dripping down his face despite the cool morning air. Only Gary looked almost normal, except for the tense, worried look on his face as he paddled rhythmically, never moving his eyes from the approaching shore.

I'm going to be home soon, Della thought. But it isn't going to be the same. Nothing is ever going to be the same again.

The slap of the paddles against the water gave way in her mind to the sound of rustling leaves. Again she saw the dry brown leaves being piled onto the lifeless form in the ravine. The leaves were everywhere, so dry, so dead. She looked down. The lake was filled with them, filled with dead leaves, filled with death.

"Della—are you okay?" Pete's voice interrupted her thoughts. The rustling leaves vanished, replaced by the sound of the paddles and the water lapping against the sides of the canoe.

"Yes. I'm okay. I was just . . . thinking." She forced a smile. She knew it wasn't terribly convincing.

"Everything will be okay," Pete said. "You're almost home."

Almost home. Maybe I *will* feel better when I get home, Della thought.

But when, less than an hour later, she pulled open the back door and saw her mother dressed for church, finishing breakfast at the kitchen counter, she was overcome by a feeling of dread.

How could Della face her?

"Well?" Mrs. O'Connor asked, after tilting the coffee cup to her mouth to get the last drop. "How was it? You're home so early."

"Yeah. Well, we got up early," Della managed to say. She

wondered if her mother could see how nervous she was. Mrs. O'Connor was usually a mind reader. She could read more into Della's eyes and expressions than was scientifically possible.

"You look like you didn't get much sleep last night." Her mother shook her head disapprovingly.

"Not much," Della said. She walked to the refrigerator and took out a carton of orange juice. She had a sudden urge to cry. She hoped that maybe, just maybe, an activity like getting orange juice for herself would help her keep control.

But how can I keep control? I killed a man last night!

Did her mother see her hand shaking as she poured the juice into a glass? No.

"Guess you don't want to come to church with me," her mother said.

"I'm going to go to bed. I could sleep for a week," Della told her.

"Was it fun?" Mrs. O'Connor asked, standing up and straightening her dress.

"Kind of," Della said, drinking the orange juice at the sink, keeping her back to her mother.

"Were you really up the whole night?" Mrs. O'Connor asked.

"No. Not the whole night."

"Want breakfast?"

"No. I don't think so."

"Did you talk to Gary?" Her mother knew Della hated questions about her boyfriends, but that never stopped her.

"Not too much." Della drank half the glass. She poured the rest in the sink.

"I was just asking," Mrs. O'Connor said with a shrug.

Ask me if I killed somebody last night, Della thought.

"You look exhausted," her mother said, frowning with concern.

I'm going to tell her everything, Della decided. I can't keep it in. I just can't. "Mom, I—"

"Yeah?" She was halfway out the door.

Della hesitated.

"What is it, Della?"

"See you later," she said.

The door closed behind her.

Della slept all morning and most of the afternoon. When she came downstairs a little before four, her mother was out. She made herself a tuna sandwich and ate it hungrily, washing it down with a Coke.

She felt a little better. All of that sleep helped a lot.

Taking a bowl of potato chips with her, she went back up to her room and did some Government homework. To her surprise, she was able to concentrate on the chapter she was reading. She thought about the young man in the ravine only once or twice, and even then it seemed like a distant memory, like something that had happened and was over.

When her mother got home, Della realized she no longer had the urge to tell her what had happened. At dinner she told her some stories about the overnight, some of them made up, some of them true. She told her about the ZAP war, about how good the hot dogs tasted over the open fire, how Ricky had hidden the canoes and how alarmed they were about it.

I may be able to do this after all, she thought. I may be able to put it behind me and go on with my life.

She began to feel confident, relaxed, almost good about herself—until the phone rang at seven thirty, and she picked up and heard Maia's trembling voice.

"Della, can you come over? I'm not doing so well."

"What do you mean? Are you sick?"

"No. It's just—well, I'm sure my parents suspect something."

Della suddenly had a cold feeling on the back of her neck. Her neck muscles tightened. "Maia, you didn't tell them anything, did you?"

"No, of course not," Maia replied quickly, her voice tense and high. "Of course not, Della. But I think they suspect . . . I mean, I just have a hunch. And I don't—I mean, I don't know how much longer I can—"

"Okay. Try to calm down," Della said, sounding irritated when she meant to sound comforting. "I'll be right over."

"Thanks, Della. Hurry. Please."

Della hung up, feeling more annoyed than sympathetic. It seemed to her that Maia wasn't even trying to get over this. Well, maybe she was. Maybe she was doing the best she could.

In a way, she had gotten Maia into this mess. Maia wouldn't have even gone on the overnight if she hadn't urged her so strongly.

I've got to stop thinking about her so harshly, Della decided. I'll go over there and give her a pep talk, make her feel better. That's what friends are for, after all.

Friends.

Were her friends going to come through for her? Were they going to keep the secret as they had vowed?

They *had* to, Della decided. They *had* to.

She slipped into a clean pair of jeans and a light sweater, brushed her hair until it fell straight and smooth behind her shoulders, put on a little clear lip gloss, and then looked around the room for her wallet. It wasn't on her desk. It wasn't on the shelf by the door, where she usually kept it.

My wallet, she thought. When did I have it last? Did I bring it on the overnight? Yes. It had been in her backpack.

She hadn't unpacked her backpack, she realized. She had just tossed it down by the bed and forgotten about it.

She wanted to forget about it, of course. Now, as she picked it up and dumped the contents onto her bed, the old feeling of dread swept over her. The sound of the crackling dry leaves seemed to pour out of the backpack.

She tossed it to the floor and searched through the wrinkled clothing and toilet articles she had packed. Where was the wallet?

I know it was in there, she thought.

But it's gone.

Could someone have taken it? No. That was impossible.

Everything from the pack felt so cold. She had carried the chill of Fear Island home with her. And now she too felt chilled, pawing through her stuff again and still not finding the wallet.

How mysterious.

She decided to go to Maia's without it. Maia lived only a few blocks away in the North Hills section of town. Della told her mother she was going there to study, and headed out the door.

It was a warm night, almost balmy, a pleasant contrast to the night before. On a front lawn down the block a group of kids was playing baseball, even though it was already dark. A few doors down, Mrs. Kinley was shouting for her son that it was time to come home, and was being completely ignored.

North Hills was such a quiet, peaceful neighborhood, the nicest neighborhood in Shadyside. For some reason, seeing the kids playing ball, walking past the large, quiet houses, past the manicured, carefully tended lawns, made Della feel sad. Somehow she didn't feel a part of that quiet, peaceful, respectable world anymore. Her secret made her an outsider.

Stop it, Della, she warned herself. Just stop it right now. It's natural that you feel sorry for yourself right now. But that will pass.

Maia opened her front door the instant Della rang the bell, and, without saying a word, pulled Della upstairs to her room and closed the door.

Della never could get over Maia's room. It looked like a little girl's room, with lacy white curtains on the windows, shelves of dolls, and stuffed animals everywhere.

"Maia—you look terrible!" Della cried, and then immediately regretted saying it. What a way to cheer someone up!

Maia burst into tears. "I keep crying, then stopping, crying then stopping," she sobbed. She pulled a handful of tissues from a box on her dresser and covered her face, blotting up the tears. When she took the tissues away, her face was bright red.

Della walked over and put her arm around Maia's shoulder. "Maia, everything will be okay. I promise," she said softly.

"You promised me before," Maia said, not looking at Della.

Della didn't know what to say. "What are you worried about? Tell me in words," she said, leading Maia to the bed. Maia sank onto the gray and pink quilt. Della sat down in the small gray corduroy armchair across from the bed.

"My parents. I know they're suspicious."

"How do you know? What did they say to you?"

"Well . . . nothing exactly. But my mom looked at me funny."

"I don't blame her," Della said. "You don't exactly look your best. What did you tell them about the trip?"

"Not much. Just that I had a fun time and that I didn't spend the night making out in the boys' tent, and that it wasn't the wild orgy they imagined it would be."

"That's for sure," Della muttered. "Well, it sounds like you did okay. Did you take a nap or anything?"

"I tried, but I couldn't sleep," Maia wailed. "I just kept seeing that guy lying in the ravine."

"You need some sleep," Della said. "You'll feel much better. Really. I slept almost all day. And I'm feeling . . ."

"What?"

"I'm feeling better. Really, I am. You know, what happened to that guy last night was an accident."

"I know," Maia said, wiping her running nose with her hand.

"He attacked me. It's not like he was some innocent kid."

"Yes, I know," Maia repeated edgily.

"He fell and he was killed. It's not like I intentionally tried to kill him. It was an accident. You have to remember that. An accident."

"I know."

"Well then, what has you so upset, Maia?" Della asked patiently.

"It's just that . . . we're going to be caught. Everyone's going to find out. About the accident. About us being there by ourselves without Mr. Abner . . . about everything."

"That's just not true," Della insisted. "It'll be weeks or months before the body is discovered—if ever. There won't be anything to tie us to it."

Maia started to cry again. It took Della a long time to calm her down. They talked for more than two hours, with Della doing her best to reassure Maia that all their lives would soon return to normal and that their secret would remain one.

At first she felt angry that Maia was acting so much more upset than she was. After all, Della had been the one who was attacked, the one who shoved him, the one who . . . killed him.

But looking around at the frilly room filled with dolls and stuffed animals, and thinking about Maia's strict, overbearing parents, Della became more understanding. Maia didn't have much of an opportunity to act like a grown-up. Her parents were doing everything they could to keep her a child.

By the time Della had finished talking to her, Maia seemed much calmer. "Now, get some sleep," Della told her, heading toward the bedroom door. "You'll feel much better tomorrow. I know you will."

"Thanks, Della," Maia said, smiling for the first time. "Sorry I'm being such a drag."

Della waved good-night and headed downstairs and out of the

house. It felt good to breathe some fresh air. Maia's room had been hot and stuffy. Della was surprised to see the pavement wet. It must have rained while she'd been inside.

She walked quickly along the street, which seemed to glow from the streetlights being reflected on the wet pavement. The wet lawns glowed too, and Della suddenly had the feeling she was walking on a different planet, a green, wet, glowing planet of soft light and eerie silence.

Her house was dark except for the yellow porchlight. Her mother must have gone to bed early. She pulled open the screen door and something dropped at her feet.

An envelope.

She bent down and picked it up. She examined it under the yellow light. There was no writing on the outside of it. Just a black smudge, probably a fingerprint, in the lower right corner.

She felt something bumpy inside.

She let the screen door close and stepped back to open the envelope. She tilted it and let the bumpy object drop into her hand.

It was a tiny silver skull.

A skull from the chain around the dead man's neck?

Peering into the envelope, she saw a small square of note paper inside. Her hand shaking, she pulled it out.

A single line was scrawled in pencil on one side.

It said: I SAW WHAT YOU DID.

CHAPTER 8

"My first thought was that it was one of your tricks, Ricky," Della said, jabbing his chest with her index finger.

Ricky backed away, looking terribly hurt. "Della, give me a break. I wouldn't pull anything that stupid."

"You mean as stupid as hiding the canoes?" Suki chimed in.

They were sitting tensely around Della's living room, everyone from the overnight except for Pete, who'd be late because his family always ate dinner late. It was Tuesday night, two nights after Della had found the skull and note tucked in her door. Her mother was playing bridge at the Garrisons', up the street.

Although they really didn't want to get together, especially so soon after the overnight, the six members of the Outdoors Club realized they had no choice. They couldn't just ignore the envelope. They had to try to figure out who had put it there—and why.

"Are you sure you didn't do this?" Suki accused Ricky, glaring at him with obvious dislike.

"Cut Ricky some slack," Gary broke in. "He isn't totally insensitive, you know."

"Yes, I am," Ricky said, grinning at Gary. "But I didn't grab the skull off the dead guy's neck and leave it for Della."

"Look," Gary said, standing up and reaching into his jeans pocket. "I got one too." He pulled out an identical silver skull.

"Gary—how? Where'd you get it?" Della asked.

"I went out for the mail after school yesterday afternoon, and it was in the mailbox," Gary said. Suki grabbed the skull out of his hand to examine it.

"Was there a note, too?" Della asked.

"No. No note."

"This is weird," Ricky said.

"He's very deep, isn't he?" Suki cracked.

"Lay off, Suki!" Ricky cried heatedly.

"Make me," Suki muttered. She handed the skull back to Gary.

"Please. We've got to cool it," Gary said, looking at Suki. "We can't start going at each other's throats. We've got a real problem here. Whoever dropped off these skulls knows where we live!"

The room grew silent. Della shuddered, thinking about someone standing on her front porch, opening the screen door and tucking in the envelope. Someone standing right outside her front door. Someone who saw them that night in the ravine. Someone who watched them cover the man's body with leaves.

And then? And then this someone, this witness to their crime, did what? Uncovered the body? Pulled the silver skulls off the chain? Delivered them to Della and Gary? For what reason?

"Did anybody else get anything?" Ricky asked. "I didn't."

"I didn't either," Suki said.

Maia shook her head no. Sitting in an overstuffed armchair in the corner with her legs tucked tightly beneath her and a frown frozen on her face, she hadn't said a word the entire time.

"Where's Pete?" Suki asked.

"He'll be here soon," Della said. "But he told me this afternoon he didn't get anything."

"Why just us two?" Gary wondered. He got up from where he was sitting beside Suki on the leather couch and walked to the living room window. "Why just us two?"

He stopped suddenly and turned around. "Hey—I just thought of something. I lost my wallet. Did anybody else lose a wallet?"

"I did," Della answered, raising her hand as if she were in school. No one else said anything.

"It was in my backpack. I'm sure of it," Della said, walking over to Gary at the window.

"Mine too," he said. "Maybe that explains how the guy got our addresses."

Della suddenly remembered the noises she'd heard from the tent late at night, the footsteps she'd followed. Maybe they weren't caused by a raccoon after all. Maybe someone had been there, just a few feet from where she had slept. Maybe this someone had gone through the backpacks and stolen the two wallets.

Della looked out into the dark front yard. He could be out there right now, she thought. She walked quickly to the side of the window and pulled the curtains shut.

"We've got to go to the police," Gary said suddenly, looking at Della.

"No!" Maia cried, her first word of the night. "You can't! I mean, we can't."

"But, Maia—" Gary started.

"We've all got too much to lose. Our parents will never trust us again," Maia shouted, tensely gripping the side of the armchair. "Everyone in town will know that—"

"*But this guy knows where we live!*" Gary shouted back at her. He tossed the silver skull high in the air. It hit the ceiling and dropped to the beige carpet at Maia's feet.

"Gary, cool your jets," Suki said. She patted the couch cushion beside her. "Come back and sit down. Let's all try to think about this calmly, okay?"

Gary shook his head. "I'm calm," he insisted. But he came back and sat down next to Suki, leaning forward on the couch, putting his hands between his knees and loudly cracking his knuckles.

"Yeah, you're real calm, okay," Suki said. "So what do you think this guy with the skulls wants anyway?"

"I don't know," Gary said, cracking the knuckles of his other hand.

"To frighten us, I guess," Della said.

"But not to turn us in," Suki added. "If he was going to turn us in to the police, he would've done it already, right?"

"Probably," Gary admitted.

"If he was going to report the body, he would've reported it," Suki continued. "But that's not what he wants. He just wants to make us squirm, to frighten us. Why?"

Gary shrugged.

"Just for kicks, right?"

"Maybe."

"Well, what if we don't scare so easy?" Suki suggested. "What if he doesn't frighten us, and we don't go running to the police? What if we just ignore his stupid skulls? He'll probably just go away."

"She's right!" Maia cried, perhaps the first time she had ever agreed with Suki.

"But you're forgetting a few important things," Della interrupted, standing behind the couch. "For one thing, maybe he wants to do more than scare us. Maybe he wants to blackmail us or something. If he really saw what we did, if he really was there in the ravine watching us, he could hold it over us. He could blackmail us, blackmail our parents."

"Yes, but—" Suki started.

"Let me finish," Della insisted, hitting the arm of the couch with her open hand. "Even more important, look what this guy did. He stood by and spied on us. Then he unburied the corpse. Then he robbed it. He stole the dead man's necklace. This guy is a creep, some kind of weirdo. He could do *anything*. We could all be in danger."

"But if he really wanted to hurt us, to do something awful, he already had his chance," Suki argued. "But all he's doing is leaving little skulls around. I don't think that's enough to—"

She was interrupted by a loud knock on the front door.

"That must be Pete," Della said, hurrying across the room. "Hi," she said, pulling open the door.

But no one was there.

"Hey!" Surprised, she opened the screen door and stepped out. She didn't see anyone. She came back inside, pushing the door closed and locking it.

"Am I hearing things?" she asked. "You all heard a knock too, didn't you?"

"Maybe it's him. Maybe he's come back," Maia said, looking very frightened. "Are all the doors locked?"

"I think so," Della said. "I'll go check." She ran to the kitchen to make sure the back door was locked. It was. Then she checked the sliding glass doors in the den. They weren't locked. She struggled to pull down the lock. This door was always difficult, but she managed it.

She looked out through the glass into the dark backyard. A pale sliver of a moon was just climbing over the red garage roof. She pressed her forehead against the cool glass.

What was that shadow moving across the lawn? Had she imagined it? No.

She pulled back from the window and pressed herself against the wall. Carefully, she moved her head forward just enough so that she could see out.

It was just a cat.

She took a deep breath and let it out slowly. Her heart was pounding. Her hands suddenly felt ice cold.

That was stupid, she thought. Frightening myself over a cat.

She realized the others must be wondering where she was all this time. Checking the back-door lock one more time just to be sure, she headed down the hall.

She was nearly to the living room when she heard the loud knocking on the front door again.

CHAPTER 9

"*Who's* there?" Della called.

No reply.

Gary joined her in the hallway. "Who is it?" he shouted.

Silence on the other side of the door.

Impulsively, Gary turned the lock and started to pull the knob. "No, Gary—don't!" Della cried. But she was too late. He had already pulled open the door.

There was no one on the front porch.

Gary pushed open the screen door and stepped outside. Down on the street, a car with only one headlight squealed around the corner and sped past, going much faster than the thirty-five mph speed limit. As it passed under a streetlight, Della could see that it was packed with teenagers.

That's what we should be doing, she thought wistfully. Out cruising around, having a good time.

"Gary—please. Come back in," Della called, watching him through the screen door as he explored the front yard.

"No one out here," he said, sounding relieved. He stepped back onto the porch. "The ground is soft, but I don't see any footprints." He scratched his head of wavy blond hair.

"Maybe it's a ghost," Della joked.

"Someone's playing a little joke," Gary said, reentering the house and walking past her in the hallway. "An unfunny joke."

Della closed the door and carefully locked it. They walked back into the living room.

Ricky, Maia, and Suki were standing tensely by the window. "Is he—is he out there?" Maia asked.

Gary shrugged. "I didn't see anyone."

"But who's knocking?" Maia demanded, clenching her hands into tight fists at her sides.

"The Ghost of Christmas Past," Della said.

No one laughed.

"Maybe we *should* go to the cops," Suki said, looking worried for the first time. She was wearing an oversized turquoise sweater that came down nearly to her knees. She wrapped her arms around herself, nearly disappearing into the voluminous sweater.

"No!" Maia insisted. "We still have no reason to. It may be some neighborhood kid playing a stupid prank on us."

"I used to play this joke," Ricky admitted, smiling.

"Big surprise," Suki said sarcastically.

"I used to think it was pretty funny," Ricky said. He walked over to the couch and stretched out, laying his head on the soft arm cushion. "Now I'm not so sure."

"We're sitting ducks here," Della said glumly.

"Look, let's not go over the edge," Gary told her. "The guy's just playing a joke. If he wanted to get in or do something really terrible, he had two chances when the door was open. He just wants to make us squirm."

"We're squirming," Ricky said. "We're squirming!"

"Let's be ready for him the next time he knocks," Gary said.

"What are you talking about, Gary?" Della asked warily. Gary was a great guy and everyone liked him. But one reason why people liked him so much was that he wasn't perfect—sometimes he did crazy, foolhardy things, things that kids would talk about for weeks afterward.

Della knew Gary really well. She had gone out with him for a long time, after all. And she knew the look on Gary's face. It was a look she wasn't happy to see. It was his *daring* look. It was his fixed expression of *daring* anyone to stop what he was about to do next.

"Come on, Gary. What are you thinking?" Della demanded, following him across the living room.

"Nothing much. Don't look at me like that, Della. I'm not going to do anything crazy. I just want to get a look at this joker."

"Let's just go home," Maia said, joining them in the hallway. Ricky and Suki nervously followed her.

"But the party's just starting!" Ricky exclaimed, and then laughed as if he'd made a hilarious joke.

"Come on, Maia. We've got to wait for Pete," Della said.

"And besides, we haven't settled anything," Suki added. "We haven't decided what to do about the skulls and the note."

"Do? What can we do?" Maia whined. "One thing we can do is not sit around this house and let that creep terrorize us."

Gary had disappeared up the stairs. Now he returned carrying Della's Polaroid camera in his hands. "How about a group portrait?" he asked, smiling.

"That's the only way you'll ever get this group to smile," Ricky cracked.

"Here's another way you can get me to smile, Schorr—leave!" Suki scowled.

"Knock it off, Suki," Gary warned. "Stop picking on Ricky."

"Ricky's picking on *me* by existing," Suki muttered.

"Remind me to laugh at that one later," Ricky said, rolling his eyes.

"Come on, you two," Della pleaded.

"I'm going. Really. I have to go home," Maia said, pushing past them to the door.

"No! Don't!" Gary said, pulling her back. "You'll chase him away before I can get his picture."

"That's your plan?" Della cried. "When he knocks, you're going to pull open the door, yell 'Smile!' and take his picture?"

"Yeah," Gary said defensively. "That's my plan. You got a better one?"

"Yeah. Forget it."

"What if he doesn't want his picture taken?" Suki asked.

"What if it makes him mad?" Ricky asked.

"Let me go home—please!" Maia begged.

"After I flash the picture, Della, slam the door and lock it. He'll be too stunned to react quickly," Gary said. "Then we'll call the police." He looked at Della. "What do you think?"

Della rolled her eyes to the ceiling. "Dumb," she said. "But I can see that you're going to do it anyway."

Gary smiled. "Right."

"Please—let me go," Maia repeated.

"Maia, stop. We're all in this together. We have to stick together. We have to help each other," Della said.

"Then let's *all* leave!" Ricky said. He quickly held up both hands. "A joke. Just a joke!"

Maia scowled and angrily walked back to the living room. "You can't keep me a prisoner here," she called.

"You're not a prisoner," Suki said. "But you can't be a deserter either."

"But you're all acting crazy!" Maia insisted, her voice high and tense. "I just want this all to be over."

"That's what we all want," Suki said. "But running home to Mommy won't do that, Maia."

"Ssh. We've got to be ready," Gary said, ignoring her and positioning the camera. "The instant he knocks, Della, pull open the door. You've got to be fast or we'll miss him."

"But how—" Della started to say.

But before she could finish her question, they all heard a loud knock on the door.

Della jumped in astonishment. Time seemed to freeze.

Her breath seemed to freeze.

Everyone in the hallway seemed to freeze.

The knock was repeated.

Somehow she got herself breathing again. Somehow she got her brain to work, her arm to move. Somehow she turned the lock and, with one swift motion, pulled the door open wide.

Gary stepped forward and clicked the camera. The flash sent a burst of white light through the hallway and out onto the porch.

CHAPTER 10

The flash of light revealed movement, a face, a blur of hair, dark clothes. It was a man. He disappeared as quickly as the light.

He leaped off the side of the porch. Della heard him hit the bushes and keep moving.

He must be around the side of the house by now, she thought.

The surprise of it, the fact that some stranger really was on the porch, froze both Della and Gary. It was almost as if *they* had been caught by the camera and frozen on film.

By the time they pushed open the screen door and peered out, there was no sign of anyone.

"The film. The picture. Look. It's developing." Gary's hand was trembling as he held the Polaroid picture and watched the colors darken.

Maia, Suki, and Ricky were standing behind them now. All of them stared in silence as the picture sharpened and filled in.

"Nice shot of the screen door," Ricky said, shaking his head.

The screen door looked shiny and silvery in the photo. Beyond it was only darkness, not even the blur of the man moving off the porch.

"We didn't get him," Della said.

"Back to the drawing board," Gary muttered, disappointed.

Someone stepped suddenly onto the porch.

Oh no! We didn't close the door! Della thought. He's circled the house and come back!

She grabbed the door and started to slam it.

"Hey—what's the big idea?!" the shadowy figure on the porch screamed.

"Pete!" everyone cried, very relieved.

Pete looked confused. "Sorry I'm late. Nice of you to all come to the door to greet me. I see the party's going full swing."

"It hasn't been much of a party," Della said with a sigh. "We've had a visitor." She reached past him to lock the door. "Did you see anyone out there?"

"No. No one." Pete stared at the camera. "Taking pictures?"

"Yeah. We're starting a family album," Ricky quipped.

"Count me out. I don't want Schorr in *my* family!" Suki said.

Maia headed back into the living room and slumped down in the armchair, looking more glum than ever. "Can I go now?" she groaned.

"Guess it isn't much of a party," Pete agreed as the rest of them trooped after her.

Maia made a face. "I'm leaving," she said. But she made no attempt to get up from the chair.

"Wait, Maia," Pete said. "I brought something. I think you'll want to see it."

He pulled a folded-up newspaper clipping out of the pocket of his chinos and spread it out on the coffee table. Everyone gathered around to look at it.

It was from the Shadyside *Beacon*. The headline read:

NEIGHBORS WITNESS BURGLARY,
FATAL SHOOTING

A smaller headline underneath read:

POLICE HUNT TWO MEN IN KILLING

"Read it out loud," Suki said to Pete.

"That's because she can't read," Ricky cracked. Suki gave him a hard poke in the stomach with her elbow.

"You read it, Della," Pete said, handing the clipping to her. "I still have a big, flashing light in my eyes."

The news story reported that neighbors had seen two young men break into a local gardener's home. There were gunshots, the witnesses said, then the two men ran out of the house, empty-handed.

The gardener was found shot dead inside his house. Rumored to be an eccentric millionaire, he had supposedly hidden a fortune in cash in his small cottage—the goal of the intruders, police guessed. When the burglars didn't find the money, the police continued, they must have attacked the gardener and killed him.

The two men were still at large, the article concluded, and finding them was the number-one priority of the police. A neighbor had gotten a good look as they fled. The police sketch of the burglar was beside the article.

"Oh no! Look at the face!" Della cried, holding the clipping up so everyone could see it.

It was the man on Fear Island, the man she had buried in the ravine.

"So he was a killer," Suki said, taking the clipping, staring at the sketch as if memorizing it, then passing it back to Della. "So we don't have to feel so bad."

"He said something to me about an old man," Della said, suddenly remembering. "He started talking really fast, really crazy, and he said something about not being able to communicate with an old man, having to teach him a lesson or something. It didn't make any sense at the time. I was so frightened, I really couldn't hear what he was saying."

"Well, now we know who he is," Pete said, folding up the clipping and shoving it back into his pocket, "and we know who watched us bury him in the leaves. And we know who left the silver skull for Della. It's his partner."

His partner.

So that was the explanation, Della thought. The young man wasn't alone in the woods. He and his partner must have been hiding out there. Who would think of looking for them on that uninhabited island?

And the partner had been hiding in the woods on the edge of the ravine. The partner saw everything.

"What do you think this guy wants?" Maia asked softly.

They had all become very quiet as they thought about the news Pete had brought. They realized their secret was not entirely secret anymore. Someone else was in on it, someone who had murdered an old man. Someone who knew where Gary and Della lived. Someone who had been right outside the door.

"He obviously doesn't want to thank us," Suki said dryly.

"Maybe he wants revenge," Ricky suggested.

Everyone looked at Ricky, as if to make sure he was serious. He was.

A feeling of gloom settled over the room. No one said anything for a while.

"Which is worse—having him want to blackmail us or having him want revenge?" Gary asked, breaking the silence.

"How could he blackmail us?" Maia asked. Her face was red. She looked as if she were about to start crying.

"Not us. Our parents," Pete said, looking at the floor. "They didn't get anything from that robbery. The partner probably sees us as a way to cash in."

"Most of our parents are pretty well off," Gary said.

"Speak for yourself. Mine don't have a dime," Suki snapped with some bitterness.

Gary ignored her. "This partner could tell our parents everything. He could threaten to expose us to the police if our parents don't come up with big money."

"No! That's impossible! That's *horrible!*" Maia cried.

"Whoa. Hold it a minute," Della said, jumping up from the piano bench where she'd been thinking about all this in silence. "That doesn't make any sense at all."

"Nothing makes sense," Suki muttered.

"This partner—he can't go to the police. He killed an old man, remember?" Della said.

"Della's right," Maia broke in, sounding a little relieved.

"He can't go walking into the police station and tell the cops he saw us kill his partner."

"The police would probably thank us, anyway," Ricky said, brightening. "They'd probably give us a reward or something."

"That's not true," Della said, shaking her head impatiently. "But there's no way the partner is going to the police."

"He could threaten to tip off the police. It would be easy for him just to phone them and tell them what he saw," Pete said.

"He's right," Maia cried, horrified.

"So take your pick," Della said mournfully. "Blackmail or revenge?"

"We're dead meat either way," Suki said glumly. "He could blackmail us for the rest of our lives."

"We'd better call the police," Gary said firmly.

"The police won't be able to protect you and Della," Maia argued.

"Oh, Maia—stop thinking about yourself for once!" Della exploded, finally losing her patience. "You're only worried about your parents finding out that you went on the overnight without a chaperone. You don't care *what* happens to the rest of us!"

Maia's mouth dropped open and her face turned as red as a tomato. Della immediately regretted blowing up at her friend. Now she'd be spending months apologizing to her. And what had she accomplished by yelling like that? Nothing at all. She wasn't going to change Maia.

"That's not true!" Maia protested. "I just . . . I just . . . Okay. I won't say another word." She crossed her arms defiantly in front of her and glared furiously at Della.

"But Maia's right," Pete said suddenly, looking at Della. "What are the police going to do to protect you—to protect any of us—from this creep? Nothing. Are they going to put a full-time guard around your house? Or escort you to school and back? No way."

"With our help, the police might be able to catch the partner," Della said.

"When?" Ricky broke in. "After we're all murdered in our sleep?"

"Stop it! Don't *say* that!" Maia screamed.

"Please—we're all getting hysterical," Suki said. "We've got to chill out. So far, all the guy has done is—"

She stopped when she heard the knock on the front door.

They all froze. Maia let out a little cry and sank deep into the armchair. Della looked to the front door as if waiting for someone to come bursting in.

"I, I left the camera on the stairway," Gary said in a loud whisper.

"I'm not going to answer it," Della whispered. "I don't think we should answer it."

No one agreed or disagreed. They were all staring toward the front hallway in frightened silence.

Another knock, this time longer and louder.

"Why is he *doing* this?" Maia cried.

"Come on, let's answer it," Gary said, moving toward the door. "There won't be anyone there anyway."

"No, Gary—" Della started.

But he had made up his mind. He jogged to the front entrance, hesitated for a second, then put his face close to the door and yelled, "Who is it?"

There was a brief silence. And then a man on the other side of the door said, "We're back!"

CHAPTER 11

Gary looked confused for a second. Then he turned the lock and pulled open the front door.

Della's mother and a tall, bald man walked in.

"Oh, hi, Gary. What a nice surprise," Mrs. O'Connor said, looking a bit startled. "This is Mr. Garrison. He walked me home."

"Your mother forgot her house key," Mr. Garrison explained to Della.

Mrs. O'Connor poked her head into the living room and was further startled to see that Della had even more visitors. "Della—a party on a school night?"

Some party, Della thought. "What are *you* doing here?" she blurted out. "I mean, why are you back so early?"

"No one was much in the mood for bridge tonight. So we decided to break up early," Mrs. O'Connor said. "What's going on here?" she asked, tossing her pocketbook down on a side table and striding into the center of the room.

"Mom, I'd like you to meet the members of the Outdoors Club," Della said, regaining her composure. She introduced everyone to her mother.

"I like your hair," Mrs. O'Connor said to Suki. "How do you get it to stand up like that?"

"I use a gel," Suki said, trying to figure out if Della's mom was putting her on or not.

"It's very . . . what do they call it? Very . . . rad," Mrs. O'Connor said.

Ricky started to laugh, then quickly stopped.

"No, I really do like it," Mrs. O'Connor insisted. "Of course, if Della did that to her hair, I'd murder her!"

"Mom, please . . ." Della interrupted.

"And why the special club meeting?" Mrs. O'Connor asked, ignoring her daughter's protest.

"Oh . . . we were just talking about the overnight," Della answered, thinking quickly.

"I hear it was a great success," Mrs. O'Connor said, straightening a pile of magazines on the coffee table. She never could just stand and talk. She always had to be doing something useful at the same time.

"Oh, yes. Great," Gary said.

"It was rad," Ricky added. No one laughed. If Mrs. O'Connor realized that he was making fun of her, she didn't let on.

"We were just finishing, actually," Della said, looking at the others to make sure they understood it was time to leave.

"Yes. Meeting adjourned," Gary said. He smiled at Mrs. O'Connor. "I'm the president. If I didn't say that, they couldn't go home."

Della's mother laughed her high-pitched laugh. "It's so nice to see you, Gary," she said. "We've missed you around here."

Gary turned bright red and looked very embarrassed. Della would have enjoyed his discomfort, except that she felt equally embarrassed.

Everyone said good-bye and walked out into the night, except for Pete, who lingered uncomfortably in the doorway. "Uh . . . Della . . . can I talk to you for a minute?"

"Sure," Della said, wondering why he looked so nervous. Was he afraid to go outside because the dead man's partner might be lurking out there? No. She hoped he didn't want to talk more about the partner and everything else, not with her mom so near.

"I was wondering . . ." he said, leading her out onto the front porch for privacy, "if maybe . . . you'd like to go out with me Friday night?"

"Oh." It wasn't at all what she had expected. She took a deep breath. The air felt cool and sweet. She could smell the apple blossoms from the tree across the driveway. "Yes. Okay." She smiled at him. "Sounds okay."

He smiled back. "I'll pick you up after eight, okay? Maybe we'll go to a movie. Or maybe to The Mill."

"Fine."

The ancient, collapsing mill, built at the end of Old Mill Road before the town of Shadyside even existed, had recently been resurrected and reopened as a teen dance club called The Mill. A lot of Della's friends from Shadyside High went there just about every weekend to dance and meet guys. But she had a hard time picturing Pete there in his crisply pleated chinos and Ralph Lauren polo shirts.

Maybe he isn't such a stiff after all, she thought, watching him head down the driveway to his station wagon. He's been so sweet to me. Maybe he's just what I need to help me forget about Gary.

She shivered suddenly, remembering that someone might be out there. Someone might be hiding in the darkness, staring at her, watching her right now, plotting against her, hating her.

Still shivering, she turned and bolted into the house, slamming the door loudly behind her, so loudly that dogs began barking and howling all down the block.

"I can't believe I'm having such a great time!" Della said to herself. It was Friday night, and she and Pete had already been dancing at The Mill for more than an hour. She laughed and slapped him playfully on the shoulder as he attempted a ridiculous dance maneuver on one leg.

Actually, Pete wasn't a good dancer. In fact, he had no sense of rhythm at all. But at least he tried. He even made jokes about his dancing. I never even knew he had a sense of humor, Della thought, scolding herself for having such a wrong impression of him.

The club was hot and crowded. Teenagers packed the dance floor, bumping into each other as they moved to the deafening music, the insistent drums pounding out a steady rhythm through the massive speakers suspended in every corner of the huge room. Swirling blue and magenta lights made it seem as if the floor were spinning. Crowds of kids watched the dancers from the refreshment bar that ran the entire length of the building, or from the low balcony that overhung the dance floor.

Della and Pete danced nonstop. It was far too noisy to talk. A little after midnight she pulled him out into the parking lot. "Enough! I'm totally wrecked!" she cried happily.

He laughed. Even though it was a warm night, the air felt cool against their hot faces. When she looked up at the sky, Della could still see the swirling colors of the lights. The pounding rhythm floated out from the dance club, drums and bass guitar driving to the same beat as her heart.

"Want to get something to eat?" he asked.

"I don't know. It's so late." She knew she should be tired, but she felt just the opposite, keyed up, eager to keep moving, totally wired.

"Let's go get a hamburger," he said, pulling her by the hand. His own hand was hot and wet.

She pulled back suddenly, catching him off guard, and he stumbled close. Impulsively, she reached her hand up behind his neck, held him, and gave him a long kiss.

When she backed away, he looked stunned.

"That was a good-night kiss," she said, laughing at his shocked expression. "I just wanted to get it over with. Now let's go get a hamburger."

They climbed into the front of the station wagon and immediately rolled down the windows, trying to cool off. Pete backed out of the parking space and headed out of the still-crowded parking lot.

Another car, its brights on, followed close behind. Pete pulled out onto Old Mill Road, squinting into the mirror. "Wish he'd turn his brights off," he muttered.

The road was empty, nothing but darkness up ahead as far as Della could see. There wasn't much reason to drive on this far edge of town so late at night unless you were on the way to or from The Mill.

Della settled back into the seat, resting her knees against the dashboard. She felt great, relaxed and happily tired. But she could see that something was troubling Pete. "What's wrong?"

"This guy won't get off my tail," Pete complained, looking into the rearview mirror.

"Slow down. Maybe he'll go around," she suggested.

Pete slowed down. Della turned around to look out the back window. The car behind didn't pass them. Instead, it slowed down too.

"Maybe it's someone we know," Della suggested. "I can't tell. The bright lights are blinding me." The back window was filled with light, so it was impossible to see anything through it.

Pete slowed down even more. Then he pulled to the side of the road onto the soft dirt shoulder. "Hey, what's the big idea?" he shouted out the window.

The other car pulled over too, and stopped just inches behind them. Pete reached for the door handle, to climb out. "No, wait," Della said, grabbing his other arm. She suddenly felt fearful.

What if this wasn't someone they knew? What if this was . . . someone they *didn't* want to know? She hadn't thought about the dead man and his partner all night. But now the whole thing flashed once again through her mind.

"Don't get out, Pete. Lock your door."

He gave her a funny look, but followed her advice.

They watched the car behind them, he through the rearview mirror, she through the back window, waiting for someone to open the door, to step out so they could see him or her.

But the door didn't open. Whoever it was in the car behind them gunned the engine until it roared.

"I'm scared," Della admitted. "Let's get out of here, Pete."

Obligingly, he put the car into drive and floored the gas pedal. The tires spun loudly on the soft ground and the car lurched back onto the road. Pete lost control for a moment as it skidded onto the pavement. Then he quickly guided it back into the lane and, keeping his foot down hard, sped away.

Della sank back onto the seat, trying to force herself not to panic. She looked over at the glowing green speedometer. They were doing 85.

"Please," Della said aloud without realizing it. "Please go away, whoever you are."

They heard a squeal behind them, followed by the roar of the other car's engine. Bright yellow lights reflected off the rearview mirror again, filling the car with light and fast-moving shadows.

"I don't believe this!" Pete cried. The wheel was bouncing in his hand. It was taking all of his skill and concentration to steer along the curving old road at such a high speed. "He's still on our tail! This is crazy!"

He pressed harder on the gas pedal. Della saw the needle go up to 90.

"What are we doing?" she cried. "This is insane! I hate car chases in the movies! I never expected to be in one in real life!"

"Check your seat belt," Pete said. "Sometimes that one slides loose."

"Oh, thanks for telling me!" she cried. "You picked a fine time to mention it!"

Pete looked into the mirror, and his expression became more worried. "He—He's speeding up!"

"But he's right behind us. He'll crash into us!" Della screamed, ducking down low and closing her eyes.

"My dad'll kill me," Pete said. "He loves this wagon."

"How can you worry about the car?" Della shouted over the roar of the engine. "What about your life!"

"You don't know my dad," Pete said, veering into the left lane, then swerving back into the right. "He really cares about his possessions."

"Oh!" Della cried, as she felt the impact, then another bumpbumpbump, as the car behind them banged into their rear bumper.

"What the—" Pete's eyes stared straight ahead as he struggled to keep control of the car. "Is he really trying to ram us off the road . . . or is it just a game, or what?"

Della shut her eyes tight and gripped the sides of the bucket seat. She cried out again as they were bumped hard from behind, the car seeming to bounce up off the road and then come down with its tires spinning.

"Turn off!" she cried. "Turn onto another road. Maybe he won't follow."

"I can't turn," Pete said, his voice revealing his fright. "I'm going too fast. I don't know if I can keep control."

They were bumped again, this time even harder. The bright lights seemed to circle the car, infiltrating every corner, surrounding them in a harsh yellow glare.

"It's a Taurus," Pete said, his eyes on the mirror. "Know anybody who has a black Taurus?"

"No," Della said. "What are we going to do?"

"Hold on tight," Pete said. "This may be stupid, but I'm going to try it. If it doesn't work . . . well . . . it's been real."

"What are you going to do?" she asked.

But instead of answering, he slammed his foot on the brake and spun the wheel. The car squealed and slid for about a hundred yards, then spun around. The other car veered wildly to the right to get out of the way, then roared past.

Pete frantically moved the wheel, trying to bring the wagon out of its spin. They had completely turned around now and were facing the way they had come. He floored the gas pedal again and they moved forward.

"That's an old Kojak trick!" Pete exclaimed, obviously relieved that he was still alive to tell her that. "You okay?"

"I don't know. I guess. Did we lose him?"

Pete looked into the mirror. "Yeah. I think so. We—"

They heard the squeal of brakes and tires.

"He's turning around!"

Then they heard a crash, so loud Pete's hands flew up in the air. Della screamed but couldn't hear herself.

The crash was followed by a hideous crunching sound, the sound of glass shattering and metal hitting wood.

Pete eased the wagon to a stop. Della's heart was pounding. At first she had thought *they* had crashed! It was all so unreal. It took a long time for her to realize that the other car had slid off the road and smacked into the trees.

"We've got to go back," Pete said. "Whoever it is has got to be in bad shape after that."

"I guess," Della said with a shudder. She turned to Pete. "Are you okay?"

"Yeah," he said, turning the wagon around. "I'm okay. This is a pretty exciting first date, don't you think?"

"Shut up," she said teasingly.

He eased the car around and drove slowly back until they saw the Taurus. Its headlights were still on but they were shining up toward the sky. The car was tilted against a massive tree trunk.

With its tires still spinning, it looked as if it were trying to climb the tree.

As they drove closer, Pete and Della saw that the right side of the car was completely smashed in. Surprisingly, the driver's side was relatively unharmed. Shards of glass lay scattered across the road.

"Let's go see how bad he's hurt," Pete said.

Della grasped his arm tightly but didn't move.

"You don't want to come with me?" he asked softly. "That's okay. No problem. You can stay in the car."

"No," she said, suddenly feeling a wave of nausea. "No. I want to get out of the car. I want to see who it is in there, who was doing that to us."

Pete opened his door and stepped out. He walked around the front of the station wagon and opened the passenger door for her.

Della climbed out unsteadily and they made their way, following the beam of their headlights, to the driver's side of the wrecked car.

"Now let's see exactly who it is," Della said. She gripped the handle and pulled open the door to the Taurus.

The car was empty.

CHAPTER 12

"So who was it in the car?" Maia asked. "Who was chasing you?"

"I don't know," Della told her with a shrug.

It was Monday afternoon, and they were leaning against the yellow tile wall just outside the door to Mr. Abner's room. School had let out ten minutes earlier and already the halls were nearly deserted.

Della had just told the whole frightening story about the Friday-night car chase to Maia, the first person from the Outdoors Club she had seen. She was reluctant to talk about it, but she just *had* to tell someone. Now she regretted it because Maia looked pale and shaky.

"You don't know who was in the car?" Maia asked, not understanding.

"There was *no one* in the car," Della explained, whispering even though the corridor was empty.

"You mean—"

"Whoever it was must have run off into the woods before we got to the car."

"That's so scary," Maia said, pressing the back of her head against the wall and closing her eyes. "Do you think it was—"

"The partner? Maybe," Della said. "It wasn't a kid from school or anything. No one we know would try such a dangerous stunt."

"But why would he—" Maia started. She stopped when Ricky bounced up beside them.

"Talking about me again, huh?" he said, putting his arms around them both. "Well, I'm sorry. You both can't have me. You'll have to fight it out among yourselves."

He laughed and walked past them into the classroom. Maia frowned with disgust. They could hear him greeting Suki, Gary, and Pete.

"He's not so bad," Della said.

"Not so bad as what? Not so bad as bubonic plague?" Maia exclaimed. Then her face filled with concern. "So are you okay? You weren't hurt or anything?"

"No," Della assured her. "Pete and I were okay. Just a little scared. We drove home *very* slowly." She swung her bookbag from one hand to the other and shifted her weight. "I haven't been able to sleep too well, though. Every time I fall asleep, I see headlights and I dream I'm being chased again."

"That's awful," Maia said, shaking her head sadly. "I've been having bad dreams too. What a mistake we all made. If only we'd stayed home instead of . . . Uh-oh. Here comes Mr. Abner."

"Hi, girls. Sorry I'm late," he called to them from down the hall. He strode quickly up to them, his brown leather cowboy boots clicking loudly on the floor as he walked. With his straight-legged jeans and red-and-black-checked flannel shirt, he looked more like a tall, lanky cowboy than a teacher. All he needed was a bandana around his neck, Della decided.

"What are you two talking about so seriously?" he asked.

"Nothing much," Maia said quickly, blushing.

"Did we look serious?" Della asked teasingly. "That must be a first, right?"

He followed them into the room. They took their seats in the first row. Pete smiled across at Della. Suki was playfully slapping Gary's hand.

Mr. Abner lowered a window blind, blocking the bright sunshine that had been flooding over his desk. "Nice day," he said to no one in particular. "Too bad we were in here and missed it."

"I didn't want to miss it," Ricky said. "So I cut my morning classes!" He laughed loudly so Mr. Abner would know it was a joke.

Mr. Abner gave him a weak smile. Then he sat down on the front of his desk, crossing his legs and looking down at his cowboy boots. "I'm back," he said. "Let me apologize again for having to postpone the overnight. I know you had all worked very hard getting ready for it, and I know how much you were looking forward to it."

Della shifted uncomfortably in her seat. She pulled at a long strand of her dark hair, a nervous habit. She'd been doing it a lot lately, she realized. She had a lot to be nervous about.

Now she was worried that somehow one of them was going to give away the fact that they had gone on the overnight without Mr. Abner. If only he would change the subject, she thought. This is just too dangerous. Of course, no one would deliberately reveal anything. But what if one of them should make a slip. . . .

". . . these family problems. I'm sure you know what I mean," Mr. Abner was saying. Della realized she had missed the whole story he had been telling.

The teacher uncrossed his long legs and re-crossed them the other way. "Anyway, I'm back," he said, smiling, "and I have very good news for you."

Everyone was listening very intently now.

"I've been able to reschedule our Fear Island overnight for this coming Saturday," Mr. Abner said. He leaned forward expectantly, awaiting their pleased reaction to his announcement. His smile quickly faded when no one said anything.

"Oh. That's great!" Della exclaimed finally, hoping she sounded just a little bit genuine.

With all of the terror they had experienced in the past two weeks, everyone had forgotten that Mr. Abner would be eager to reschedule the overnight.

"Yeah. Terrific," Ricky said, not being the least bit convincing.

"This weekend? Gosh, I don't know if I can make it," Maia said. "My family is going upstate, I think. To visit . . . uh . . . relatives."

"Yeah. Mine too," Gary said. "I mean . . . not upstate. But I'm pretty sure we have plans, Mr. Abner."

Their advisor looked hurt. "I knew you guys were disappointed before. So I pushed aside some plans of my own." He looked toward the window but couldn't see out because he had closed the blinds. "I have to admit I'm a little surprised by your reaction," he said, scratching his left cheek with his fingernails. "Or rather, your lack of reaction. This *is* the Outdoors Club, right? And you guys have been after me all winter to organize an overnight, right?"

"We're still excited about it," Gary said. "Really."

"I've still got all my gear packed and ready," Della added.

Come on, everyone, she thought. Show a little enthusiasm. Mr. Abner is becoming suspicious. We can't let him start to ask questions about why none of us want to go back to Fear Island. We just can't.

"I'm still crazy to go," said Suki, who had been silent and pensive the whole time. "But I've got to check and see what the plans are for the weekend too." She looked at Gary, as if expecting him to back her up or say something to help.

Gary looked back at her uncomfortably. Then he turned to Mr. Abner and said, "Maybe the club should meet again later in the week. You know, on Wednesday or something. Then we'd all know if we're free or not."

"Well, I guess we'd better," Mr. Abner said, not hiding his disappointment. "I must say, I'm underwhelmed by your enthusiastic response. Is there something going on here that I don't know about?"

A cold chill ran down Della's back. She looked over at Maia, who was tightly gripping the sides of her chair and staring down at the floor.

"I think it's just spring fever," Gary said, grinning reassuringly at Mr. Abner.

"We're all just wrecked from the weekend. I know I did a lot of partying. Too much partying," Suki said.

Everyone laughed uncomfortably.

"We're still looking forward to it," Pete said.

We're looking forward to it like a math test, Della thought. There's no way any of us are ever going back to Fear Island. If only we could level with him. He's not a bad guy. But he's still a teacher. There's no way we can explain anything to him.

"Okay then," Mr. Abner said with a resigned shrug. He stood up quickly. "We're agreed. We'll meet again after school on Wednesday, and you'll let me know if you can fit the overnight into your busy schedules."

He stood up, gathered some papers from his desk, and strode quickly out of the room.

As soon as they were sure he was gone, Gary jumped up, walked to the front of the room and motioned for everyone to stay in their seats. "We've got to talk," he said, nervously looking toward the door. "What are we going to tell Abner?"

"Yeah. How are we getting out of this stupid overnight?" Suki asked, sounding angry for some reason. "There's no way I'm ever camping out again, that's for sure."

"Right on!" Ricky shouted.

Gary motioned for him to lower his voice. "I'm sure we all feel the same way," he said. "So we have to figure out—"

There was a noise out in the hallway, the sound of someone opening a locker.

"We'd better not talk here," Della said.

"Let's go down behind the parking lot," Gary suggested.

"I only have a few minutes," Maia said, looking at her watch. "I told my mom I'd be home at four."

They hurried out the side door and then circled around to the student parking lot behind the building. There were only two cars on the lot. Everyone else had gone home. On the practice field behind the tennis courts, members of the Shadyside baseball team were doing warm-up calisthenics.

"We just have to stall him," Pete suggested as they leaned against the tall metal fence that separated the parking lot from the practice field. "School's out in four or five weeks. If we're all busy on weekends, the overnight just won't take place."

"Maybe we should explain what happened, tell the whole story to Abner," Gary suggested. "It would be good, I think, to tell it to an adult. He wouldn't go to the police or anything. I don't think."

"No!" Maia protested immediately. "It's our secret. We have to keep it our secret. We took a vow, remember?"

The others all quickly agreed with her. There was no telling what Mr. Abner would do if he found out what they had done.

"We can stall him," Suki said with certainty. "We just have to make sure that our stories—"

"Hey, I just remembered something," Ricky interrupted. He turned to Della and poked her on the shoulder with his finger. "My ZAP gun. I came back from the overnight with only five ZAP guns. You never gave yours back to me. Can you bring it over to my house tonight?"

"Oh no," Della gasped, grabbing the fence. She suddenly felt cold all over.

"Not tonight? Well, can you bring it to school tomorrow?" Ricky asked, not noticing her horrified expression.

"I—I left it," Della managed to say.

"What?"

"I had the gun in the ravine. Then the man . . . he . . . he took it from me and . . ." She shook her head hard as if trying to shake away what she was remembering. She stared at Ricky. "I left the gun with the body. On Fear Island."

"No! That's impossible!" Ricky cried. He slammed his fist against the fence, making it clang. Several of the baseball players looked over at them.

"Shhh. Lower your voice, Ricky," Gary warned.

"But my gun! I mean, you can't leave it there!" he screamed at Della, ignoring Gary. "When the police find the body in the leaves, my gun will be there."

"They won't know it's yours, Schorr," Suki told him with a look of disgust.

"*Everyone* knows I'm into ZAP wars," Ricky said heatedly, turning away from Della and shouting in Suki's face. "Everyone knows I'm the one in school with all the ZAP guns. All the cops have to do is ask any kid at Shadyside who has ZAP guns, and they'll be coming right to me. That gun will lead them right to Ricky Schorr! And I'll tell you one thing—"

Gary pulled him back away from Suki. "Cool your jets, man. Come on, Ricky."

Ricky pulled out of Gary's grasp. "I'll tell you one thing, I'm not taking the blame for that dead guy. If the police come to me, I'm telling them about all of you too."

"You dirty—" Suki's eyes grew wide with hatred.

Gary quickly stepped between them.

"Wait! Stop! Everybody—stop!" Della screamed. They turned to her. "Ricky's right. This is my responsibility. All of it."

"Now wait, Della—" Pete started, but she reached up and put a hand over his mouth to quiet him.

"The gun was my responsibility, and I left it there. So I guess I have no choice. I'll go back . . . back to Fear Island . . . and get your gun for you, Ricky."

"Well, okay," Ricky said, still glaring at Suki.

"Whoa! Hold on!" Pete cried. "You can't go back there alone, Della. I'll go with you."

"Thanks," Della said softly, smiling at him.

"Maybe we should all go," Gary said suddenly.

"What?" Maia cried, looking very upset.

"Yeah. Maybe we should go on the overnight. Then Della could slip away and get the gun back. We're all in this together, after all."

"And if we all go, it won't be so bad," Pete added.

"Well . . . I guess . . ." Suki said, thinking it over. "I guess if anything bad happened this time, Abner would be there. He could stomp on any stranger with those baaad cowboy boots of his."

Everyone laughed. Except Maia.

"But—But what do we do if the partner is there?" Maia asked, holding onto the fence and looking down at the ground.

"I hope he is," Gary said, his face hardening with anger. "I'm fed up with all this stupid partner business. I'd like to pound the guy. I really would."

Della looked doubtful. She hated it when Gary started talking tough. "You guys really don't have to come," she said, her voice shaky.

"We're in this together," Gary said. "Of course we'll come. Right, guys?"

The others, except for Maia, murmured their agreement. Finally Maia said, "Well, maybe. I guess . . . It couldn't be any worse than the last overnight—could it?"

CHAPTER 13

As they set off across the lake in three canoes—Mr. Abner and the equipment in one canoe, three club members in each of the other two—the weather was not promising. High clouds had drifted across the sun, and both the sky and water were an ominous gray. A light fog made it hard to see where the water left off and the sky began.

No one said anything. Only the sound of the paddles splashing rhythmically in the water and the raucous honking of two large ducks flying overhead broke the silence.

Della leaned forward, looking past Maia to Pete in the front of the canoe, matching her paddle strokes with his. The waves were stronger this trip, tossed by a warm but gusting wind, and it was more difficult to keep the small canoe moving forward.

"Is this a silent movie, or what?" Mr. Abner called from his canoe, several feet ahead of them. "How about some noise, you guys? Anybody know any songs?"

"No!" Ricky, Gary, and Suki called in unison.

"It's too early on a Saturday morning for songs," Suki added.

"Anybody ever tell you guys you're a lot of laughs?" their advisor asked, paddling harder against the current.

"No," Gary called. "Nobody."

"Well, they were right!" Mr. Abner retorted.

Everyone offered him a half-hearted laugh.

"I can't believe we're doing this," Maia muttered. "I can't believe we're going back to that dreadful island."

"Maia—shhh," Della warned. "The wind could carry your voice. You know why we have to go back. Let's just try to make the best of it."

Maia frowned, closed her eyes and slipped her hands under her sweatshirt to warm them.

A light drizzle began to fall. The gray sky grew darker. The thickening fog made everything seem eerie and menacing.

Perfect, Della thought. This is just the perfect atmosphere for a return to Fear Island, a return to the scene of a . . . murder.

Stop thinking that way, she scolded herself. It wasn't a murder. It was an accident. She thought of the body lying there under the crackling, brown leaves. She thought of someone—the dead man's partner—going to the body, tearing the silver skulls from the chain around the dead man's neck. She thought of the plastic ZAP gun lying there beside the body.

Would she really have the nerve to go back to the ravine and retrieve the gun?

Yes. She had no choice. She couldn't leave it there for the police to find.

She thought of the dead man, of his body under the leaves, decaying, decaying, decaying. Would she have to look at him?

No. She'd grab the gun up off the ground and run.

Maybe Pete would come with her. Yes, he probably would.

She looked at Pete, rowing at the front of the canoe, his dark hair blowing in the strong breeze. She realized she was really starting to like him. When she had arrived at the lake an hour before and had seen Gary arrive with Suki, it hadn't bothered her. She had looked at Gary and not felt those pangs, those feelings of "why aren't we together." Now Gary had become just another guy, just another guy from school. And she was glad.

The rain stopped and the cloud cover lightened a bit as they climbed out of the canoes and dragged them onto the rocky beach. The whole island appeared in shades of gray—the trees, the dunes, the beach. Della felt as if she had stepped into a black-and-white movie.

"Pull the canoes over by the trees," Mr. Abner instructed, not noticing that they already were.

We'd better be careful, Della thought. We'd better not give away the fact that we already know the island.

"Is this whole island solid woods?" she asked. "I haven't been here since I was a little girl."

"As far as I know," Mr. Abner said, tugging his canoe with all of the tents and equipment inside. "I've never been to the other side of the island. Don't know what's over there." He let go of the canoe. "Hey, that's a good idea. Let's hike to the other side of the island. It's a great morning for a hike!"

"Oh no," Suki groaned.

No one else showed much enthusiasm either. "Don't we have to set up the tents and get firewood and stuff first?" Ricky asked hopefully.

"We'll leave everything with the canoes," Mr. Abner said, choosing to ignore their reluctance. "We'll set up when we get back. Come on, everyone. Drop everything and take your backpacks. It won't be a long walk. Just two or three hours at most."

He picked up his blue backpack and swung it onto his shoulders, an excited smile on his face. Della and her friends could see that there was no use grumbling about it. They were going on a hike across the island to the other side.

"Great day for a hike," Pete said, walking next to her, an ironic grin on his face. "How you doing?"

"Me? Okay, I guess. I sure wish this weekend were over." She picked up her backpack. He held it for her while she shoved her arms through the straps.

"You and me both," he said, sighing. The drizzle began again, not exactly rain, but a fine mist that made everything feel wet, even the air they breathed. "I'll go with you to get the ZAP gun. Maybe we can sneak away during the hike."

Della looked up and saw Mr. Abner staring at them. "Maybe we'd better do it after the hike," she whispered.

"We'll go later, when everyone's gathering firewood."

"Thanks," she whispered. "I just hope we're not hiking the whole weekend. Mr. Abner is a lot more gung ho about this than I thought he'd be."

They followed the others into the woods. Della pulled up the hood on her sweatshirt. It covered her head and hair, but it didn't keep out the cold or the increasing sense of dread she was feeling. She didn't want to be walking again through these woods, her sneakers crunching over the dead brown leaves.

The ground sloped sharply up. Her sneakers slid on the mud. The footing was getting slippery from the rain. She grabbed Pete's arm and he helped pull her up a steep incline.

They stepped carefully over a fallen tree and followed the others deeper into the woods. Suddenly Mr. Abner came jogging hurriedly back to them, holding a video camera up to his eye. "Don't look at the camera," he instructed, pointing it at Della and Pete, walking backward to keep them in the picture.

They stopped to stare at the camera.

"No—don't stop," he cried. "Keep walking. Act natural."

"Mr. Abner, what are you doing?" Della asked.

"I'm making a complete record of our overnight," he said, still taping them. "When we get back home, I'll make a copy for everyone to keep."

The poor guy, Della thought. He just doesn't know what's going on. He has no idea that this isn't an experience the rest of us are going to want to remember. This camping trip is something we're all going to want to forget as quickly as possible.

"You can at least smile," Mr. Abner urged, walking backward, keeping the video camera fixed on them. Della and Pete made a feeble attempt at smiles. Then, suddenly, Mr. Abner's heel caught on an upraised root and he toppled over backward into the mud.

The six club members tried their best not to laugh. But the sight of him falling onto his backside, video camera leaping out of his hands, his long legs flying into the air, was too hilarious, and they all enjoyed a good laugh. He climbed up slowly, looking embarrassed, and checked over the video camera to make sure it was still functioning.

"Hiking rule number one: Don't face the wrong way when you walk," he said, brushing wet leaves and dirt off the seat of his jeans. Then he added, "I just did that to wake you guys up. That's the first laughter I've heard all morning."

He was right, Della realized. They weren't doing a very good job of acting normal. But what could they do? None of them, not even Ricky, felt like joking around. It was hard for Della to even think straight. She just kept thinking about how she had to sneak away and what she had to do.

They hiked for what seemed like days, stopping only once to eat the sandwiches they had brought. Finally, feeling tired and extremely edgy, they reached their destination. The other side of the island, not surprisingly, looked exactly like the side they knew. The pine trees gave way to the low dunes of a rocky beach. If there was land across this side of the lake, they couldn't see it. Low clouds and fog blocked the view.

"It's kind of pretty," Della said to Pete, staring out at the lake. "So gray and mysterious. It's almost dreamlike."

"I guess," Pete said, shifting his backpack. He groaned. "This thing was light when we started out. Now it weighs a ton."

Mr. Abner finished videotaping the shoreline and lowered his camera. "Doesn't look as if those clouds are going to lift," he said, making a visor with his hand on his forehead to shield his eyes from the glare.

"What do we do now?" Ricky asked him grumpily.

"We head back, of course," Mr. Abner said, still staring across the lake.

"You mean we have to hike back through the woods?" Maia moaned.

"Do you want me to bring the car around?" Mr. Abner asked, laughing. "I'll tell you what, let's go back along the beach. We'll walk around instead of through."

That idea seemed to please everyone. But by the time they made it back to their canoes and supplies, it was late afternoon, their sneakers were soaked, they were chilled through and through, and their legs ached from trudging so far over sand.

Ricky plopped down in one of the canoes. Della and Maia dropped to their knees on the cold, wet, pebbly sand.

"Aah, that was exhilarating!" their advisor cried, smiling happily as he carefully packed away his video camera. "Hey—don't sit down, guys. Fun time is over. Now it's time to start working!"

Muttering and complaining, they carried the tents and supplies to a clearing beyond the tree line. Della realized that they weren't far from their old campsite, a hundred yards or so farther into the trees.

After the tents were put up, Mr. Abner sent them out for firewood. "Try to find dry wood," he instructed.

"Everything's soaking wet," Suki snapped. "Where are we going to find dry wood?"

"I think I have some at home," Ricky offered. "I'll go home for it."

"Ricky—" Mr. Abner said sternly.

"No. Really. I don't mind," Ricky joked. "I'll go get it and be right back."

"Look for wood that's under leaves or under other wood," Mr. Abner said, ignoring Ricky's plea. "It'll be drier than wood that's been exposed. We can burn wood if it's damp. It'll just take a little longer to get going."

The six of them started off in different directions. "Maia, stay here and help me unpack the dinner supplies," Mr. Abner said. Maia immediately turned and headed back into the center of the camp-site, looking relieved. "Get lots of wood," their advisor shouted. "Looks like it's going to be a cold, dreary night."

"I don't know about cold, but he's right about dreary," Suki muttered to Gary as they headed off together.

"Bet I can cheer you up," Della heard Gary say to Suki.

"Stop it, Gary. Get your hands off me!" she heard Suki protest, not too convincingly.

Della found Pete tossing wet sticks across the ground. "Nothing is dry," he muttered. "Abner's crazy." A sudden wind came up, shaking tree branches and sending leaves flying in different directions.

"This is the longest day of my life," Della sighed.

"You'll feel better once we . . ." Pete's voice trailed off. He looked around. No one was in sight. "Hey—let's go."

"Huh?"

"Let's go get Ricky's gun. Right now. While there's still a little light."

Della hesitated. She could feel her throat tighten and a heavy feeling begin to grow in her stomach. "I guess . . ."

"Abner's busy with Maia in camp. He won't notice. We'll go grab the gun and be back here in a couple of minutes."

"Okay," Della said, pulling up her sweatshirt hood. "I guess this is as good a time as any."

They started off together in the general direction of the ravine.

"Hey, where are you guys going?" It was Abner.

They turned around, startled to see him in the woods. "We were just, uh—"

"Come on, guys," Abner scolded, shaking his head. "You know the rules. No hanky-panky."

"But we weren't . . ." Della protested.

"Of course you were," Abner insisted, laughing. "Come back closer to camp. You don't have to go this far for wood."

"Okay," Della and Pete said in unison. They followed him back to the campsite and started gathering firewood at the edge of the tree line.

"We'll never get away. Never," Della moaned.

"Shhh. Look." Pete pointed. Abner and Maia had gone to the other side of the clearing. "Come on. He can't see us. Let's try again."

"Okay. Quick," she said, her eyes on Abner.

"Do you remember exactly where the ravine is?" Pete asked. Her sweatshirt hood was caught in her hair. He helped her straighten it out. His hand felt cold as it brushed against her forehead.

"I . . . I'm pretty sure."

"Then let's go," Pete said.

They hurried into the trees.

As they quickly made their way over the wet, slippery ground, he reached for her hand. He dropped it when they heard the scream.

It came from the campsite, a shrill, ear-piercing scream, a scream of absolute horror.

Della recognized it immediately.

"It's Maia!" she cried.

CHAPTER 14

A second scream tore through the trees, a scream for help.

Della and Pete got to the campsite together, just as Gary and Suki appeared, looking frightened and confused.

"Maia! Where are you?" Della called.

Ricky stumbled into the clearing, carrying a stack of sticks in his hands. He tossed the sticks next to one of the tents. "What's all the racket?"

"Over here!" Maia cried. Her voice came from near the edge of the woods on the other side of the tents. "Help, please!!"

Her heart pounding, Della ran around the tents toward Maia's voice, followed by the others. They found Maia on her knees beside Mr. Abner, who was lying on his back. She was cradling the advisor's head in her arms. As the others drew closer, they could see that his eyes were closed, his mouth open, a rivulet of blood trickling down from his scalp.

"Maia . . . Mr. Abner . . . what . . ."

"He's out cold," Maia told them. "I can't bring him to."

"But who did it?"

"Did you see it happen?"

"Did he fall? Was he . . . shot?"

Pete and Gary knelt down beside Maia. Gary put his hand on Mr. Abner's sweatshirt, above the chest. "His heart is beating okay," he said. "What happened?"

"He was . . . hit," Maia said, her voice trembling. "Hit over the head. I saw someone . . . a man . . . He ran off into the trees." She looked past them to the woods. "That way."

"A man?" Della cried. "Did you get a good look at him?"

"Who was it?" Gary asked.

"I don't know. He was like a blur," Maia said. "A dark blur. He was wearing a black jacket, I think."

Mr. Abner groaned and turned his head, but his eyes didn't open.

"We've got to get help for him," Maia said. She placed his head gently on the ground and backed away. The sleeves of her sweatshirt were stained with dark blood. "He's hurt bad, I think."

Della was surprised at how well Maia reacted in an emergency. She's stronger than anyone gives her credit for, Della thought.

"Who did it? Why?" Suki asked, hands on her hips. She looked more angry than frightened.

"Maybe it's the dead man's partner," Pete said, looking at Della. "Maybe he's followed us back here."

"And now he plans to croak us, one by one," Ricky said, staring into the trees, his round face suddenly tight with fear.

"Shut up, Schorr," Suki snapped. "You always know how to make things worse."

"What could be worse?" Maia said quietly. She ran around to the other side of the tent. A few seconds later she reappeared carrying a rolled-up sleeping bag, which she tucked under Mr. Abner's head. "Someone unfold another sleeping bag and cover him up," she ordered.

Pete ran to get one.

"We're helpless here," Della said, thinking out loud. "We can't help Mr. Abner. And we can't do anything to protect ourselves if— if whoever did it comes back."

"Some of us have got to go to town for help," Maia said, helping Pete spread a sleeping bag over the teacher.

"I'll go!" Ricky cried immediately.

"Not too eager or anything, are you, Schorr?" Suki said.

"Get off my case," Ricky snapped angrily at her.

"Who's gonna make me?" Suki made a face back at him.

"Stop it. Come on, knock it off," Gary said heatedly. "We've got an emergency here."

"He's losing a lot of blood," Maia said, pressing a handkerchief against the side of Mr. Abner's head, trying unsuccessfully to stop the flow.

"Okay. We'll go get help," Gary said. "Come on, Ricky, Suki. Let's go. You three stay and watch him."

Della watched the three of them hurry toward the canoes. Suddenly, Ricky stopped and turned around. "Hey," he called back, "my ZAP gun. What about my ZAP gun?"

"I'll go get it now," Della answered. She took a deep breath and watched until they disappeared into the trees. "I guess I have no choice," she said to Pete. "I've got to get the gun back. Before they come back with the police."

"Okay. I'll go with you," Pete said, looking down at Mr. Abner. "We'll be back as soon as we can, Maia."

"No!" Maia cried, grabbing his arm. "You can't!"

"What?"

"You can't leave me here alone."

"But Maia—" Della said.

"No. I mean it. That's not fair. What if the man comes back? There won't be anyone here to help me. You can't leave me like that. You just can't."

"She's right," Della told Pete.

"But, Della—"

"I'll have to go get the gun by myself," Della said. "You stay and help Maia."

"But I don't want—"

"We don't want to come back and find Maia hit over the head too. Or worse. It would be our fault, Pete. You've got to stay with her. I'll be right back. I'll run right to the ravine, grab the gun, and run right back."

Pete pulled out of Maia's grasp. "No. I can't let you."

"Look," Della said. She held up the whistle she was wearing around her neck. "See this? I have a whistle. It's real loud. If I'm in any kind of trouble, I'll blow it. Okay?"

"A whistle?" Pete didn't look convinced that this was a good plan. But he looked at Maia, pale and trembling beside him, and realized he had no choice but to let Della go on without him.

"I'll be right back. Really," Della insisted, thinking that maybe if she kept repeating that, she'd start to believe it. She leaned over on tiptoes and gave Pete a quick kiss on the cheek. For luck. Then she turned and forced herself to jog into the woods.

"Wait—stop! Della!" Pete came running after her. "Here. Take this." He handed her a big metal flashlight. "It's getting kind of dark."

She took it from him, surprised by how heavy it was. They turned and walked in opposite directions. She heard Maia calling to him, afraid that he had changed his mind and had left her there.

Maia's such a baby, Della thought.

But then she argued with herself, Maia's right. She has good reason to be scared. And so do I.

She gripped the flashlight tightly. I can use it as a weapon if I need to, she thought.

A weapon?

What am I thinking of? Have I completely lost my mind? Is this really me, walking through these woods to find a dead man, to retrieve a stupid plastic gun? Alone in the woods while some creep prowls about, some creep who hit Mr. Abner over the head and now might be following me, might be watching me, might be ready to—

Stop!

Just stop thinking, she told herself. Don't think about anything. Keep moving, keep walking till you find the ravine. And shove everything out of your mind. There's nothing you can think about now that will make you feel better. Nothing you can think about that will make you feel any safer.

What about Pete? I'll try thinking about Pete.

But she pictured Pete being hit over the head. Pictured a man in a black jacket running through the trees. Pictured Pete lying on the ground like Mr. Abner, blood trickling down to the ground from his head.

Blood, blood on the ground. Blood everywhere.

No. I can't think about Pete.

I'll think about home. Safe, warm, quiet.

But the dead man's partner was right on my porch, leaving his envelope with the silver skull and the frightening note. Right on my porch. He was practically inside my house. He knows where I live. He knows me. He . . .

Is he watching me now? Is he watching me push my way through the woods? Is he waiting for me to stumble, waiting for me to fall so that he can pounce?

Is he waiting for his revenge, waiting to pay me back for killing his friend, for burying his friend in leaves and running away?

No!

Stop thinking!

Della looked around and realized she had lost her sense of direction. It all looked the same to her, the rustling trees, the clumps of brown weeds, the floating, shifting dead leaves.

Had she been here before? Was she walking in circles?

No. This had to be the right direction. She remembered that large, square rock at the bottom of the low hill.

Yes. She was heading to the ravine. She was nearly there. Maybe.

She just had to concentrate on where she was going, chase these other thoughts from her head.

It suddenly grew darker, as if someone had turned off some lights. She clicked on the flashlight, throwing a narrow beam of white light on the ground ahead of her.

Yes. That was better. At least she could see the ground now, could see to step over that fallen branch and step around that hole and walk away from those clumps of thorns.

It's right up here, I think. She stared over the beam of light, trying to see through the trees. She was climbing a steep slope now. Yes. She remembered it. She remembered how steep it suddenly became, how surprisingly steep and—

What was that light?

To her right she saw a flash of white light through the trees.

Was that just my light? A reflection of my light?

No. She saw it again, a narrow beam, cut off by a branch.

Thinking quickly, she clicked off her flashlight. Why give away where I am?

A chill went down her back. She struggled to catch her breath.

Who was it?

The light disappeared, then reappeared a few feet away, a few feet closer. The light seemed to flicker and float, as if free of gravity, as if emitted by some giant firefly hovering among the trees.

Maybe it's Pete.

Yes, of course. It's Pete. He got Maia settled down and came after me.

Should she call to him?

Yes. No. Yes. But what if it isn't Pete? What if it's the creep who hit Mr. Abner?

No. Don't call to him.

The light moved closer.

"Pete?" Her voice came out tiny and frightened. The word just slipped out. She hadn't meant to say it. But now that she had, she repeated it. "Pete?" A little louder this time.

The light floated closer. She could hear footsteps now.

"Pete?"

A cough. She heard a man's cough.

It wasn't Pete.

He was coming toward her now.

She froze. How stupid. How stupid to call out and let him know where she was. To bring him right to her.

No! Stop thinking! Stop thinking—and run.

She turned and started to flee. She wasn't thinking about anything now. Her mind was empty, clear. All thoughts had been chased away by her fear.

She was just running, listening to the crunch of fast-approaching footsteps behind her, and running, running over the slippery brown leaves, over the fallen limbs and branches, through burrs and brambles and clumps of tall, stringy weeds.

She gripped the flashlight tightly in her hand, but she hadn't turned it on. She hadn't time. And she didn't need it. She was running on radar now, the radar of fear. It carried her through the darkness.

But the light behind her was floating closer, closer.

She was climbing now, up a steep slope, climbing away from the light, toward—

Before she realized it, she was near the top of the incline. Before she realized it, she was at its crest. Then over it. She didn't stop, didn't see the fallen tree in her path.

She stumbled, didn't cry out, didn't make a sound, too frightened to scream. She knew where she was. She knew where she was falling.

She knew she had found the ravine. And as she fell forward, almost diving down the side, she saw the dreadful, dreadful pile of leaves—and knew she was falling right onto it.

CHAPTER 15

She was right on top of him.

I'm going to be sick, she thought. A wave of nausea rolled up from her stomach. She took a deep breath and held it, waiting for the feeling to pass.

Dizzy. I'm so dizzy.

She tried to push herself up with her arms, but her hands slipped on the wet leaves.

I'm right on top of him, on top of his dead, decaying body.

She forced herself to her feet, still holding her breath, still feeling dizzy.

I was lying on top of a dead man.

The flashlight. Where was the flashlight?

That's it, Della. Think about the flashlight. Think about finding the ZAP gun and getting out of this ravine. Don't think about the leaf pile. Don't think about the decaying, rotting body you were just lying on. Don't think—

Wait. The leaf pile. It was so flat. She remembered the mound of leaves they had left there.

Well . . . maybe a lot of the leaves had blown away.

Gingerly, she kicked at the leaves with her sneaker.

They fell away at her touch.

She kicked again, probing deeper into the pile.

Nothing but leaves.

Breathing heavily, she stepped onto the leaf pile. Her sneaker sank down deep until it touched . . .

. . . the ground!

She kicked at the leaves, again, again, sending them flying in all directions.

He was gone. The body was gone. He wasn't in the leaf pile.

The body had been moved.

She stood staring at the scattered leaves. She didn't know how to feel. She felt relieved that she hadn't been lying on top of the decaying body. But the fact that he'd been moved brought a flood of questions to her mind.

Shaking her head as if that could clear it, she bent down low and searched in the leaves for the ZAP gun. She shoved the leaves aside with both hands, pawing at them like a dog trying to dig up a lost bone.

Not finding the gun, she stood up and began plowing through the whole area, dragging her sneaker slowly in straight lines, kicking into clumps of matted leaves.

No success.

"I've got to find it," she said aloud. "I've got to."

She dragged her shoe across a wider area, with no success. "It's *got* to be here," she muttered to herself, bending low and scrabbling among the leaves.

Her hand hit something hard.

Startled, she picked it up. It was her flashlight.

This should be a help, she thought. She clicked it on. No light. She clicked it again. Again.

It must have broken during her fall.

Frustrated, she banged it against the side of her jeans leg.

"Ouch!"

Take it easy, girl. Don't lose control.

The light still wouldn't come on.

She was about to toss the flashlight away when she heard the cough.

Behind her.

She spun around.

Someone was standing above her in the darkness. First she saw his black, mud-splattered boots. Then she saw his straight-legged jeans.

Her eyes went up to the leather bomber jacket.

"NO! IT CAN'T BE!" she screamed in a voice she didn't recognize. "YOU WERE DEAD! I KNOW YOU WERE DEAD!"

With a growl more animal than human, he leaped off the side of the ravine, hurtling himself at her and grabbing her throat with both hands.

CHAPTER 16

Della dropped backward, slipping away from him.

Breathing loudly, growling with each breath, he took a step back and lunged at her again.

Without thinking, without realizing she was even doing it, she raised her arm. And when he came near enough, she brought the flashlight down on his head as hard as she could.

It made a loud *thud*. Metal against bone.

The flashlight came on, sending a white beam of light to the ground.

She suddenly felt as if someone else had done it. Someone else's arm had swung down. Someone else's hand had gripped the flashlight. Someone else had cracked it over the man's skull.

But her fear was real. She could taste it now.

Fear tastes bitter, she realized.

She dropped down to her knees in the leaves. Everything was spinning about her, the trees, the ground beneath her, the man lying so still at her side. Spinning, spinning. If only she could get the bitter taste out of her mouth . . .

She waited, keeping her head low, taking deep breaths. She waited for the spinning to stop, waited for her heartbeats to slow.

After a while she began to feel better. She climbed back to her feet. She raised the flashlight and shined it into the unconscious man's face.

"Ohh!" She stared at the face, so pale in the white beam of light, at the closed eyes, at the curly blond hair, at the short, upturned nose, at the long, straight scar across the chin.

It wasn't the same man.

It wasn't the dead man, the man she had shoved down the ravine during the first overnight.

She kept the light on his face until her hand began to shake so badly she couldn't keep the beam steady. Then she turned away from him to think.

This must be the partner, she realized.

Of course. Of course this is the partner.

And then she thought, I just want to get away from here.

She no longer cared about Ricky's ZAP gun, about where the dead man's body had been moved, about the partner, about *anything*. She just wanted to run away, run back to camp, to get Pete and Maia and paddle away from Fear Island and all of its terrors—forever.

Without looking back at the man on the ground, she aimed the light ahead of her, up the steep, muddy side of the ravine, and began to climb. It was too slippery to walk up, so she used her hands too, climbing like an animal, struggling to keep hold of the flashlight as she pulled herself up to the top.

When she made it to the top, the knees of her jeans were soaked through with mud. They felt cold and wet against her legs as she started to run back toward the campsite, keeping the beam of light low in front of her. Her hands were raw and caked with wet mud.

Branches slapped at her face as she ran. A large thorn ripped a long tear in her sweatshirt. She cried out, more in surprise than in pain, but didn't slow her pace.

"I've got to get back, got to get back," she said aloud, the words coming between gasps for air.

The others were probably back from town by now. And they'd have brought the police or a doctor or someone.

Not far to go. Not far to go and she'd be safe.

"Ohhh!"

She fell headfirst over a fallen tree limb.

"I'm okay. I'm okay. Got to keep going."

She pulled herself up quickly. Her left hand was cut. She could feel the warm blood trickling down her wrist.

Got to keep going.

The trees thinned out. She was almost there.

Then she heard the footsteps behind her.

The partner?

No. He couldn't have followed her that easily, couldn't have caught up to her that fast.

It must be Pete, she realized.

As soon as the others got back from town, Pete must have set out to look for her.

Slowing to a stop, she reached for the whistle around her neck, brought it to her lips, and blew it. No sound came out. She shook it. The whistle had no little ball inside.

"Great protection," she sighed, and dropped the whistle disgustedly.

"Pete!" she cried out. "Pete! Over here! I'm okay, Pete! I'm over here!"

She ran toward the sound of his steps.

A foot kicked out from behind a tree, and she tripped over it, crying out in surprise as she landed on her hands and knees in soft mud.

A laugh.

She turned quickly and looked up at him.

The dead man. The man she had killed.

"You're dead," she blurted out, staying down on the ground, staring up into his angry, dark eyes. "You're dead. I know you're dead."

"Okay. I'm a ghost," he said quietly. He shrugged and stepped out from behind the tree. He was wearing the same leather bomber jacket.

"But . . . no! You had no pulse. I checked it. Gary—he checked it too."

The young man stood over her, his handsome face twisted in a sneer, his hands poised in case she tried to move away. "I'm a medical freak," he said softly, calmly. "No lie. I have a very faint pulse point. Even doctors have trouble finding it."

"Really?" she asked weakly. She glanced quickly to either side, trying to figure out the best escape route.

"So it was you all along," she said. "But why? Why were you trying to scare us? Just for revenge?"

"Revenge?" He laughed, a dry, bitter laugh. "What a stupid word."

"Then why?" she repeated.

He shrugged. "We didn't get anything from the old gardener. Not a dime. If he had money hidden away, we sure didn't find it. That was very disappointing. So when you came along and did your little burial number on me, we got an idea. First, we wanted to scare you a bit. You know, soften you up, make it easier to squeeze a little money from you and your kind parents. How much would *you* have been willing to pay to keep things quiet about the murder—my murder?"

He kicked the trunk of a tree, unable to hold in his anger. "Your parents have a lot of dough. They'd probably part with some of it . . . to keep it quiet that their daughter was a murderer."

"But I wasn't!" Della protested. "You weren't dead."

"Details." He grinned.

"Was that you in the black Taurus, out on Old Mill Road?" she asked.

"That was my buddy." He chuckled. "Just having some fun. But I guess you gave him more fun than he bargained for. Poor guy had to walk back through the woods."

"So the skulls . . . the note . . . all to scare us so we'd pay you?"

He grinned. "I guess you could say that. Yeah. We wanted to have a little fun first. Then get down to business."

They stared at each other. Della had spotted a clear path through the trees. If she could only catch him off balance for a second, she figured, she could make a run for it.

As if reading her thoughts, he grabbed her. "You stupid fool," he said, pulling his face close to hers. "Why didn't you check to see if I was breathing?"

"Ow. My arm! You're hurting me!"

He tightened his grip instead of loosening it.

"Why?" he demanded. "Why didn't you check to see if I was breathing?"

"I—I was scared," she said, trying to pull away from his grasp, trying to pull away from the pain. "I was too scared. I just couldn't—I couldn't think clearly. Everything was spinning around. I couldn't figure out *what* to do."

"That's not true!" he screamed in her face, his eyes wild and crazy. He loosened his grip on her arms just a little. "You didn't care," he sneered. "You didn't care enough to see if I was breathing or not!"

"No!" she protested.

"Shut up!" He let go of one arm, brought his hand back and slapped her face hard with the back of his hand.

"No!"

"Shut up! Shut up! Shut up!" He was in a rage.

She stood still, looking down at the ground, her cheek throbbing with pain, and waited for him to calm down. He still gripped one arm, his face close to hers, his hot breath on her face.

Finally he let go and took a step back.

"I'm not a bad guy, really. Some girls say I'm pretty good-looking. What do *you* say?"

His rage had cooled. He was playing with her now, teasing her, testing her.

She didn't want to say or do anything to make him explode again with anger. But what was the right answer?

If only she could break free, she was sure she could run away. The campsite couldn't be far. But right now it seemed as if it were on the other side of the world!

"Well?" He was waiting for an answer.

"Yes. Yes, you're good-looking," she said, looking away from him, trying to avoid his eyes, which were burning into hers. "Very good-looking."

"Say it sincere," he said.

"What?"

"You heard me!" he screamed. "Say it sincere!"

"I *was* sincere," she said weakly, seeing his temper flare.

"Well, maybe this will help you feel a little more sincere." He reached into his pocket, then held something up in front of her face.

It was a pistol.

"No!" she screamed. She hadn't meant to scream, but in that instant she realized that he meant to kill her.

Her fear made her act. She jerked away from him, started to run.

But he caught her quickly, grabbed her arm, and spun her around.

His dark eyes were wild with fury. "No!" he screamed. "No! No! No! You're supposed to be *friendly*! Don't you know *anything*?"

He raised the pistol and pressed its barrel against her temple.

"No, please . . ." she managed to say, her voice a whisper.

"You had your chance!" he screamed.

He pulled the trigger.

CHAPTER 17

She didn't have time to scream.

First, she realized she was still alive. Then, she felt the stream of liquid trickling down the side of her face.

Paint. He had shot her with the ZAP gun.

She reached up and rubbed her fingers in it just to make sure. Yes. Yellow paint.

He let go of her and began laughing, pointing and shaking his head, finding her fear, the frozen look of horror on her face, hilarious. He laughed louder, harder, closing his eyes, pointing, the crudest laugh she'd ever heard.

He twirled the ZAP gun on his finger and shot a stream of paint into the air. This made him laugh even harder. He had tears in his eyes. His laugh became high-pitched. He was laughing so hard, he had to gasp for breath.

This is it, Della thought. This is my chance.

She turned and started to run. She had already picked the route for her escape. His laughter was the distraction she needed to try it. She knew she would have only a few seconds' head start—but maybe, just maybe, a few seconds would be all she needed.

She moved quickly, almost floating over the ground. As she ran, the sudden freedom made her feel light. She had the surprising feeling that if she wanted to, she could fly.

Fly away, Della. Fly away.

I've never run this fast, she thought.

She was startled when he tackled her around the waist and brought her crashing to the ground.

Landing hard on her side, she groaned in pain as he fell on top of her. It felt as if she'd cracked a rib.

He got up slowly, looking down at her, all of the mirth gone from his face. It was as if the laughter had never existed. Now his face revealed only anger.

He pulled her up roughly and gave her a hard shove backward. "You shouldn't have done that," he said, breathing heavily. He shook his head. "No, you shouldn't have tried that."

He looked down at the ZAP gun. He had dropped it before tackling her. She held her aching side. The pain was starting to fade. Probably nothing broken.

"I've got a real gun too," he said softly. "I used it on that old guy in the house. I can use it again."

"No," Della said, wiping wet dirt off her hands. She didn't see any real gun. But she wasn't about to challenge him.

"I can use it again," he repeated, his eyes growing wild as his anger rose. "I don't have any problem with it, really. If that's what it takes to communicate. I only want to communicate, you know. It shouldn't be so hard. People to people. That kind of deal. You know what I mean? So why should it be so hard? Why should it be so hard for people to understand? Why should I have to use a gun? You know where I'm coming from, don't you? You look like a smart girl. You see what I mean, don't you?"

He stopped, as if waiting for an answer.

She stared back at him. She didn't know what to say. "Yes, I see," she said finally.

He's crazy, she realized. He's totally off-the-wall.

She suddenly felt like screaming.

I'm trapped here with a total crazy person. He could do anything to me. *Anything!*

"What are you going to do to me?" she blurted out.

He blinked, surprised by the interruption. His angry expression faded, replaced by a blank stare. "What does it matter?" he asked bitterly. "I'm dead anyway, right?"

"No," she stuttered.

His anger flooded back. He grabbed her arm. "I'm dead anyway, right? You buried me under a pile of leaves, remember? I'm not even here—right?"

"No! I mean—"

"I'm dead. I'm a dead man, a dead man," he repeated, pulling her close.

"No! Please!"

The bright light startled Della almost as much as it did her captor.

There were moving shadows, the crunch of footsteps, and then a triangle of bright, white light.

The light beamed into the young man's eyes. He made a face and let go of Della. "Hey—I can't see!" He raised his hands to shield his eyes.

Another hand pulled at Della's arm. "Come on—let's go!"

"Pete!" she cried, everything coming into focus at last.

Pete was shining his bright halogen lantern into the man's eyes. "Come on!" he cried.

But Della didn't follow immediately. Thinking quickly, she bent down and picked up the ZAP gun. The man lowered his hands to see what was happening. And she fired twice, three times, four.

He cried out. The paint burned his eyes. He covered them again, screaming blindly in pain.

It was time to run.

"No—this way!" Pete yelled.

She had been heading in the wrong direction all along.

She turned and followed him, stumbling over a low tree stump. "Hurry, Della! He's coming after us!"

Della turned, saw him running after them, still rubbing his eyes. Did he have a gun, as he had boasted? If he did, she knew he'd use it. He had certainly made that clear to her.

She pulled herself up and started running again. "Pete—don't wait for me! Just run!" she called.

But Pete waited for her to catch up. "It took me so long to find you. I'm not going back without you!" he cried.

They ran together, side by side, each looking back every few seconds. Their pursuer was still chasing them. He was no longer rubbing his eyes. But he was running uncertainly, carefully, as if he couldn't really see where he was going.

"Almost there," Pete cried, breathing hard.

"I . . . I can't . . ." she moaned. "I can't . . . go any farther. I . . ."

He grabbed her hand. "Come on. You can make it."

They looked back. The man in the bomber jacket was gaining on them. "Come back! I want to talk to you!" he screamed at the top of his lungs.

The sound of his voice, so loud, so close, so out of control, made them run even faster.

"Stop! I just want to talk! That's all—really! Stop! I just want to *communicate* with you!"

Della's side ached and she felt she couldn't breathe, but she kept pace with Pete. Finally they reached the clearing, and seeing the tents and her friends and the small campfire, she leaped forward, lunged with her whole body. She was flying now, floating above the ground, above the pain, because she was back in camp and safe.

Gasping for breath, she dropped to her knees in front of the fire. Maia and Suki came running over to help her, to comfort her.

And the young man in the bomber jacket stepped into the clearing.

"There he is!" she heard Pete yell.

She heard running feet. There was a lot of movement, a lot of confusion.

She looked up, startled to see three policemen burst into the campsite. At first Della thought it was a dream, a hallucination brought on by her long run, her exhaustion, her fear.

But the policemen were real.

The young man stared at them in disbelief. He didn't move, made no attempt to escape.

They circled him and grabbed him easily. He didn't even try to resist. He was too surprised, too winded, too weary to fight back. "Where'd *you* come from?" he asked, looking very bewildered.

"Cincinnati," a red-faced young policeman cracked. "Where'd *you* come from?"

"Mars," was the bitter reply.

"I don't care where he came from," another policeman said, giving him a hard shove. "But I know where he's going."

"You cops know everything," the man in the bomber jacket said under his breath.

"Read him his rights," the third policeman said. Then he hurried over to Della. "You okay, miss?"

"Yeah. I guess," Della said uncertainly. "He was holding me in the woods. He wanted to—"

"That's okay." The policeman put a hot, heavy hand on her shoulder. "You can tell us about it later. Take a little while to catch your breath." He started back to the others.

"His partner—" Della started.

The policeman turned quickly, very interested. "Yeah?"

"His partner's in the woods. In the ravine. I'll take you there."

"Okay. Let me radio the station first." He called to his two buddies. "Hey . . . the partner's here too. In the woods!" Then he turned back to Della.

"You know, there's a reward for these two guys."

Della smiled at Pete, who was pouring a canteen of water over his head, trying to cool down. He smiled back at her through the water trickling down his face.

"The best reward," she said, "is that this nightmare is over."

"Where are you going tonight?" Della's mother asked, straightening Della's hair with her hand.

Della pulled away. Her mother was always rearranging her hair after she'd gotten it just the way she wanted it. "To a movie, I guess. Or maybe to Pete's house to watch some movies. Pete didn't really say."

"Well, a movie's okay," her mother said, straightening a sofa cushion. "I don't want you staying out too late." Her mother stared at her from across the room, a thoughtful look on her face.

She's probably thinking about all the horrible things I told her, Della thought. After confessing to their parents—and the police— all that had happened since their first unchaperoned overnight, it was hard for any of them to think about anything else.

Della had spent most of the week thinking about it all, reliving it, even dreaming about it at night. Now, a week later, it was time to shove it out of her mind, go out, have a great Saturday night.

The doorbell rang and she hurried to answer it. "Hi, Pete."

"How's it going, Della?"

"Great." She called good-night to her mother, stepped out, and closed the front door behind them.

A few minutes later, they were heading toward town in his family's station wagon. "Hey—wait a minute!" Della cried, alarmed. "What's *that?*"

She was pointing to the folded-up green tent in the back of the car.

"Oh, that," Pete said, grinning. "I thought you might like to go camping out!"

She slugged him on the shoulder as hard as she could.

"Just a joke! Just a joke!" he protested, cowering, trying to edge away from any other punches. "I'm taking that in to be patched for my brother's scout troop."

"Well, okay," she said, laughing and settling back in the seat. "From now on, the only camping I want to do is in front of the TV set in the den!"

"That sounds good to me too," Pete said, motioning for her to move closer to him on the seat. "But can you roast marshmallows in front of the TV?"

"We can try," Della said, moving close. "We can try."

MISSING

CHAPTER 1

The first night Mom and Dad didn't come home, Mark and I weren't terribly upset about it. In fact, we had a party.

It didn't start out to be a party. We were feeling kind of lonely, so Mark invited Gena over. Then I called my new friends from school, Lisa and Shannon. And they invited some kids, and before we knew it, there were about twenty of us partying all over the large living room that was still so new and uncomfortable to Mark and me.

We had just moved in two months before at the beginning of September, just in time to start school at Shadyside High. And even though the house was twice as roomy as our old house in Brookline, it was older and kind of run-down.

The kids we met at school always acted surprised when we said we lived on Fear Street. They were always telling us stories about horrible things that happened around Fear Street and in the thick woods that ran behind the houses—stories about strange creatures, unexplained disappearances, ghosts, and weird howls and stuff.

I think Mark believed the stories. He always believes everything people tell him. Even though my brother is a year older than I am, I think I'm a lot more cynical than he is.

Mark is just a straightforward guy. I mean, what you see is what you get. Sure, he looks like a jock with those broad shoulders and the big neck, the blond, wavy hair, and those green eyes, the cute dimple in his chin that he hates to be teased about. But he isn't dumb or anything. He just trusts people. He never kids other people, and I don't think he realizes it when other people are teasing him.

Mark makes friends in a hurry. Kids like him right away. I think my sense of humor, my cynical way of looking at the world turns some kids off. So most of the people at the party were new friends Mark had made at Shadyside in the two months we'd been going there.

I'd become pretty good friends with Lisa and Shannon, who were in my homeroom. But we weren't exactly best buddies yet. And I certainly hadn't found a guy I was interested in—not the way Mark had found Gena Rawlings.

Gena was the reason for the big fight at our breakfast table that morning. Yeah, Mark had a big blowout with Mom and Dad before school. Mom and Dad just didn't approve of Gena, and they didn't want Mark to see her. He was seeing a *lot* of Gena. I mean, like, every day. They were what you could call inseparable. It was kind of sweet, really. Mark is always really intense, but I don't think he ever felt so intense about a girl.

So when he asked Mom and Dad what it was they didn't like about Gena, and they couldn't really tell him, he just blew up.

He had good reason, I think. Mom and Dad are pretty smart people, and they've always been really good at saying what's on their minds. So what was their reason for disliking Gena?

"It's gonna hurt your schoolwork," Dad said. Pretty lame. Mark has always had a solid B average. He works really hard in school, much harder than I do, and takes it as seriously as he takes everything else.

So I don't blame Mark for jumping all over Dad for that one. Of course Dad started screaming back and said a lot of things he shouldn't have. Which forced Mark to turn real red in the face and scream a lot of things *he* shouldn't have. And then Mom got into it, and it got so noisy I thought the peeling yellow kitchen walls might crack and fall!

I just slumped down in my seat and stared at my Pop-Tart. The strawberry stuff was oozing out onto the plate. I didn't really feel like eating breakfast, anyway. I'm not that crazy about Gena, but I don't think Mom and Dad had any business giving Mark a hard time about her—at least not first thing in the morning when we were trying to have breakfast.

It was the worst screaming match we'd had in a long time. The last one, I guess, was back in Brookline, when Mark and I borrowed the car without telling our parents, and they reported it stolen. We were both grounded for two months for that little episode. No big deal.

But this one *was* a big deal to Mark. "I'm sixteen. I know what I'm doing!" he screamed.

Mom and Dad laughed, which was a really horrible thing to do.

Mark was really furious now. He picked up his Pop-Tart and started to throw it across the room. I pictured it hitting the wall with a *splat*. I'm really bad.

But Mark stopped himself just in time and instead tossed it back onto his plate, turned, and stomped out the kitchen door, slamming it as hard as he could behind him. The window glass in the old door shook inside its frame, but it didn't fall out.

Mom and Dad had gone very pale. They looked at each other across the table and shook their heads, but didn't say anything. "You'll be late for school," Dad said to me a while later. His voice sounded shaky. I guess the screaming had him really upset.

Our parents had both been really nervous ever since we moved to Shadyside. I figured it was just the strain of moving and everything—although they should be used to it. Because of their work, we move all the time. We've lived in six different places in the last eight years.

That's not easy on them—or on Mark and me. I've always found it hard to make real friends knowing that in a year or so I'd be moving away and leaving them behind. My mom puts me down a lot for being a loner, but what choice do I have? I mean, why get involved with people when you're only going to know them for a short while?

Anyway, I got my bookbag and looked out the kitchen window. There was Mark, a scowl on his face, in the backyard with his bow, shooting arrows one after the other into a poor, defenseless maple tree.

My brother is an archery freak. The first thing he did when we moved here—even before he took a look at his room—was to search out the right tree in the backyard to hang his target. He's really very good at it. He's a great shot, but of course he should be when you consider the hours and hours he spends doing it.

"It's a good way to let out your frustrations," he always tells me. I guess he was pretty frustrated this morning because he was looking really intense, even for him, shooting an arrow and not even looking at where it went before pulling another from the sheath.

"He's going to shoot his eye out one day," Mom always complains. Sometimes she tries extra hard, I think, to sound like a mom because it doesn't come naturally to her. She's pretty young and pretty cool. And when she's home—which isn't very often because of work—she's a lot of fun to be with.

Dad's okay, too, although he's very serious and intense—like Mark. Sometimes I think he's really hard to talk to. It's like he always seems to have something else on his mind. But maybe that's just my problem.

Anyway, we don't have too many fights like the one this morning. We get along pretty well, I think. Or maybe it's just that Mom and Dad are away at work so much, we don't have time to fight.

I grabbed Mark's jacket and bookbag, ran out the back door, and somehow managed to pull him to the bus stop. We didn't even say good-bye to Mom and Dad.

We didn't realize that it might be the last time we ever saw them.

"What's wrong with Gena, anyway?" Mark asked as we waited for the South Side bus.

"Maybe they think she's too short for you," I joked. Gena *was* about a foot shorter than Mark.

"Huh?"

"Just joking," I muttered. Why do I always have to tell Mark when I'm joking?

Gena was short, but to put it bluntly (which I'm good at), she had a great bod. She also was really pretty, with long, straight black hair down to her waist, creamy white skin without a blemish, and beautiful black eyes that absolutely drove boys crazy. All of the guys at school think Gena is really sexy—and she is.

Now, at ten o'clock at night, with no Mom and Dad around and with the impromptu party in full swing in our living room, there was sexy Gena sitting on my brother's lap on the sofa.

I thought about the fight that morning, and I looked at my watch and wondered where Mom and Dad could be. They usually called if they were going to be late at work.

The speaker was really cranked up. Someone was playing some heavy metal group at top volume. Lisa's boyfriend Cory was having a tug-of-war over a can of soda with some guy I'd never seen before. The can seemed to explode in their hands, a foam of soda erupting over the living-room carpet.

Oh, please, I thought, don't let this party get out of control.

Mom and Dad should be home any minute. And then . . .

I looked back to the sofa at Mark and Gena. She had her hands wrapped around his neck and she was leaning down over him and kissing him, her eyes closed. It was quite a kiss.

I didn't mean to stare—but give me a break! *You could be*

arrested in some states for a kiss like that! I told myself.

And then I thought I heard the front doorbell.

There was loud laughter in the corner by the den. Gena and Mark didn't move. They were in their own world. No one else seemed to hear it.

I ran to the living-room window and looked out. There was a big blue Chevy Caprice in the driveway. Twisting my head against the glass, I could see a tall man wearing a dark shirt and wrinkled chinos standing under the porch light. He saw me peering out at him and held up a badge, a police badge.

Surrounded by all the music and noise and laughter, I suddenly went numb. My heart seemed to stop. Everything seemed to stop.

I knew why the policeman had come.

Something terrible had happened to Mom and Dad.

CHAPTER 2

The policeman smiled as I pulled open the door. "Good evening," he said, looking me up and down.

The porch light sent a glare onto the screen door, and it took me a while to focus on his face. He wasn't young. There were streaks of gray on his mustache. He was staring hard at me through the screen door with the coldest blue eyes I've ever seen, icy blue like a frozen lake in winter. "I'm Captain Farraday," he said.

"What's wrong?" I asked. "My mom and dad—are they—"

"Are they home?" he asked, and he smiled, revealing straight white teeth.

"No. They—"

"They're not here?"

"No. They're working late, I think."

He stared past me into the hallway.

"You didn't come to tell me something about them?" I asked, feeling relieved.

He didn't seem to understand the question. "No. Uh . . . I'm investigating a burglary in this neighborhood."

"A burglary?"

"Yeah. Three houses down. I'm going house to house, seeing if anybody saw anything suspicious. You know, a strange car or something."

"Oh. Well . . . no, I haven't see anything."

A burst of laughter from the living room was followed by a crash of shattering glass. The heavy metal music sounded even louder here in the hallway.

"You notice anyone on the street? You know, anyone you haven't seen before?" His blue eyes stared into mine.

I looked away. "No. No one. I never see too many people on this street, Captain. We're pretty new in the neighborhood, so—"

"Expecting your parents soon?"

"Probably. I don't know. Sometimes they work really late."

We stared at each other for a long moment. Then he reached into the shirt pocket of his uniform and pulled out a little white card. "Here. Take this." He opened the screen door and handed me the card. "It's got my special direct line on it. If you see anything suspicious, call me—anytime."

I took the card and thanked him.

"Keep it near your phone," he said. "Just in case the burglar decides to try this neighborhood again." Then he turned and stepped off the porch.

I stood there listening to his boots crunch over the gravel drive-way. I watched him climb into his big old Chevy. I wondered why he wasn't driving a police car. "He must use it to trap speeders," I told myself. The big car didn't make a sound as it pulled off the curb and disappeared into the night.

I shoved the card into my jeans pocket and walked back into the living room. It struck me that the room was suddenly very quiet. I glanced over to the sofa. Gena was still in Mark's lap, but she had turned around to face me. Both of them were staring at me. Some-one had turned the music down.

"I'm really sorry, Cara," Cory Brooks, Lisa's boyfriend, said qui-etly. He looked very upset.

"What?"

What on earth is going on? I wondered. What happened in here while I was talking to Captain Farraday?

"I was just clowning around with David Metcalf over there, and I guess I . . . well . . . I wasn't feeling too well, and I guess I got a little sick."

I glanced over at Mark, but he had his face buried in Gena's hair.

Then I saw it. A disgusting puddle of green-and-brown vomit dripping down over the side of the coffee table.

"Nice move, ace," Cory's friend David muttered from against the wall.

"Ohh, I'm gonna be sick, too," a girl I'd never seen before groaned, covering her mouth with her hands.

"I'll help you clean it up," Cory said, looking really embarrassed.

"That's okay. Just get a spoon," I told him. "I'll eat it before it clots!"

"Ohh! Total gross-out!" Gena cried.

I bent down and picked up the phony rubber vomit. And then I heaved it at Cory.

Everyone laughed. Cory looked really disappointed.

I had believed it was real for a few seconds, but I'd never give him the satisfaction of telling him that.

"Cory, what a nerdy thing to do," Lisa said, giving him a hard shove on the shoulder.

Cory is big and solid. Her shove didn't move him. "It was David's idea," he said, laughing. He tossed the disgusting rubber joke at his friend.

"I think we should end the party on this high note," I said. A lot of kids groaned in protest. My brother had wrapped his arms around Gena and was nuzzling her neck. I could see that he was going to be no help at all.

"Come on. It's a school night. And the police were already here once."

They all uttered cries of surprise. They were so busy partying, they hadn't even noticed the policeman at the door.

"My parents will be home any minute," I said. I hoped that wasn't a lie. I was beginning to get worried about them. It was nearly eleven.

Kids reluctantly started to leave. I said good night to Lisa and Shannon. They were the only friends I had actually invited, and I hadn't had two seconds to talk to them.

I noticed a big wet stain on the edge of the carpet. This one was real, not rubber. "Oh, well. It's good for the carpet," I muttered to myself.

From the front entranceway, I watched everyone head down the front lawn to their cars, laughing and joking.

"See you tomorrow."

"Not if I see you first."

I hoped the grouchy neighbor down the block was enjoying all the shouting and loud laughter.

Feeling a little chilled, I closed the front door and walked back to the living room, rubbing the sleeves of my sweatshirt to get warm. I couldn't believe it—Mark and Gena hadn't moved from the couch!

I'm gonna have to turn a hose on them! I thought.

"Hey, guys," I said, raising my wrist and taking a long look at my watch. A subtle hint.

The two lovebirds ignored me.

"How's Gena going to get home?" I asked.

Mark actually looked up at me. "I'll drive her," he said. He had lipstick smeared all around his mouth. He looked like Bozo the Clown.

"In what?" I asked. "Mom and Dad took the car to work, remember?"

"Oh." He thought about it. An evil smile spread across his usually innocent-looking face. "I guess she'll have to spend the night."

"You pig!" Gena laughed, and tried to smother him with one of the crushed-velvet sofa pillows. They started wrestling around as if I weren't even there.

Maybe Mom and Dad are right about her, I thought, feeling annoyed—and jealous—at the same time. Why didn't I have some guy to wrestle around with and act like a jerk with? A loud knock on the door interrupted my peevish thoughts.

"That's probably Mom and Dad," I said, just to scare Mark and Gena.

It didn't work. "Why would they knock?" Mark asked.

I ran to answer the door. It was Cory Brooks. "I forgot my vomit," he said a little sheepishly.

He followed me into the living room. He searched for a while, then found his treasured item under a chair cushion. He carefully folded it up and stuffed it into the pocket of his jeans jacket.

"Hey, Cory, can I have a ride home?" Gena was actually standing up. She straightened her blue cashmere sweater, which had become twisted.

"Sure. If you don't mind riding in the backseat with Metcalf."

Gena made a face. "Maybe I'll walk."

"Don't sweat it. I'll tie him up with the seat belts," Cory said. She followed him out the door after standing up on tiptoes to give Mark a last long, lingering kiss.

A few seconds later, Mark and I were alone in the cluttered living room. "You'd better wash the lipstick off your face," I told him, trying not to laugh at how ridiculous he looked. "Then we've got to clean up."

He didn't say anything, just hurried off to wash away the evidence. He came back to the living room a few minutes later, looking somewhat dazed.

As I said, he'd never had a girlfriend like Gena before. I was going to say something to him about it, but of course I didn't. Brothers and sisters can't really talk about stuff like that. Only on TV. In all the sitcoms, brothers and sisters have these long, serious heart-to-hearts. Then they hug each other and go to the kitchen for snacks.

But it isn't that way in real life. If Mark ever hugged me, I'd call a doctor!

"Some party," he said, shaking his head. I think he actually looked a little guilty. "How are we gonna clean all this up?"

"Quickly," I said. "Before Mom and Dad walk in and see it."

"I don't think they're coming home tonight," he said, picking some crushed cans up off the floor.

"Huh? Of course they are."

"It wouldn't be the first time." He sounded a little bitter. "I'll get a big trash bag in the kitchen."

I stood there, suddenly feeling very tired, listening to the old floorboards in the hall squeak as he walked to the kitchen. He was right about Mom and Dad. This wouldn't be the first time they had stayed out all night, either working or partying.

As I said, my parents were young and didn't really like the idea of having to act like parents. I'm not putting them down. They were perfectly good parents, more fun than most when they were around. But they just didn't take being parents as seriously as most other parents did.

They found a lot of other things more important. Their work, for example. I don't completely understand what they do. They're mainframe computer specialists. That means they go into huge companies and install enormous computer systems for them. It takes months, sometimes years. Then they move on to another big corporation, often in another city.

That's why we move so much.

And wherever we move, Mom and Dad get involved in all kinds of things—community things, I mean. You know, clubs and organizations of all kinds. Sometimes I have to admit that I feel hurt that they immediately rush out and find all these clubs to join. I mean, it's like they don't want to stay home and spend time with Mark and me.

But now that I'm older, I realize that's silly. And selfish. They have the right to their own lives, their own interests.

But they could at least call and tell us when they're going to be out late, couldn't they?

Mark came back, carrying a large green plastic trash bag. "I'll hold the bag. Just dump everything in," he said, and yawned.

"How come I never get to hold the bag?" I complained, not really serious.

"What if something happened to them?" he asked, suddenly sounding worried.

"Huh?"

"What if they were in an accident or something?"

"If they were in an accident, they'd call," I said. It was a standard joke between us. Only it wasn't very funny tonight.

"What if the car stalled on Fear Street, back in the woods, and they're lost in the woods? You know those stories about how people go into the woods and come out looking different and not remembering who they are."

"Who told you that story?" I asked, making a face.

"Cory Brooks. He said it was in the newspaper."

"That's about as funny as his rubber vomit. He was messing with you, Mark."

He didn't say anything for a while. But I knew the look on his face. It was his worried face. I'd seen that look a lot. Someone has to be the worrier in every family, and in our family it was Mark.

"Stop looking like that," I told him.

"Looking like what?"

"Looking like that. If you keep looking like that, I'll start to worry, too."

"Let's call them," he said.

"Yeah. Okay." Why hadn't I thought of that sooner?

I followed Mark into the kitchen. We had their number written down on a pad by the phone. It was a direct line right to their office, so we could call it at any hour of the day.

"You call," Mark said, leaning against the Formica counter. He looked very worried.

"Sure," I said. I leafed through the pad till I found the office number. Then I pulled the receiver off the wall and started to dial. Then I stopped.

"What's wrong?" Mark asked.

"There's no dial tone," I told him.

The phone was completely dead.

CHAPTER 3

We both stood there staring at the phone, as if it were going to come to life or something. "That's weird," Mark said finally. "Why is it out? There hasn't been a storm or anything."

"Well, at least that explains why Mom and Dad haven't called," I said. "They couldn't!"

I put the silent receiver back. We were both smiling, feeling a little less worried. Mark started to say something, but stopped.

We both heard the sound. Footsteps above our head. The ceiling creaked.

Someone was walking around upstairs.

I caught the look of fear on Mark's face as the footsteps pounded down the front stairs. I probably looked just as frightened.

We stood listening to the padding sounds grow louder. And then he walked into the kitchen.

And we saw that it was only Roger.

I laughed out loud. Mark was still too shaken to laugh. He was sweating bullets, and he'd become about the same color as the faded gray wallpaper; which made me laugh even harder. I was so relieved.

How could we have forgotten about Roger?

Well, he was so quiet and so *invisible* most of the time, it was easy to forget about him.

Roger was a distant cousin of my mother's, and he was boarding with us. He had arrived a few days after we moved in at Fear Street, and my parents told him he could have the attic room all to himself. This was pretty funny, actually, because the attic room is so small, two people couldn't squeeze into it. Roger *had* to have it all to himself!

Even Roger by himself didn't quite fit into the room. He's so tall, and the ceiling slants at such a low angle, he has to stoop when he stands up in there. But he has a bed and a desk, and he seems pretty happy living with us.

We don't really see him that much. Mark and I try to be friendly. He *is* a relative, after all, and since we move around so much, we're kinda lonely for relatives.

But Roger is hard to get to know. He's so quiet. He's the shyest person I ever met, I think. He's really handsome. He has sandy brown hair and dark, intense eyes. He looks just like a model in a magazine, but I don't think he has any idea how good-looking he is. He's just so shy. He goes to the junior college in the next town. So he spends most of his time up in the attic studying and writing papers.

I don't really know why Mom and Dad took him in. It can't be for the rent he pays. We really don't need the money. Strangely enough, he isn't the first boarder we've had. Other young guys have boarded with us in other towns we've lived in. I guess Mom and Dad just like to help college students out.

"Hi, Roger. You scared us," Mark said, the color starting to return to his face.

A look of alarm crossed Roger's handsome face. "Sorry. Didn't mean to."

Mark and I headed back to the living room to clean up, and Roger followed. "When did you come in?" I asked, starting to gather up soda and beer cans that littered the room.

"Little while ago. I heard all the noise, so—"

"You should've joined the party," Mark said, holding open the trash bag and following me around the room.

"No, that's okay." Roger looked embarrassed for some reason. It must be hard to be that shy. I couldn't picture Roger at a party. I tried to imagine him dancing. He was so stiff and uptight, he probably never danced.

He bent down and grabbed a handful of goldfish pretzels from a bowl beside the sofa. "I was going to do some reading, but I wanted to ask your parents something."

"They're not home," I told him.

He looked very surprised. He looked at his watch.

"Did they mention to you they'd be working late?" I asked him.

"No." He shook his head. He scratched his chin. "Well, no big deal. I guess I can ask them later."

He tossed some of the goldfish into his mouth. "You guys okay?"

"Yeah. Sure," I told him.

He gathered up some paper plates and stuffed them into the trash bag Mark was holding.

"They stay out late a lot," Mark said.

"They called?" Roger asked, reaching for another handful of the goldfish.

"No. The phone's broken."

"Huh? That's weird. Your parents leave a note?"

"No, but I'm sure they're just working late," I said. "Sometimes they get so caught up with their computer problems they lose track of the time."

"Sometimes they work twenty-four hours straight," Mark added, taking a long drink from someone's half-empty soda can, tilting it over his mouth till soda trickled down his chin.

"You're a pig," I told him.

"Hey—I'm thirsty!"

"So they didn't leave a note or anything?" Roger asked, sounding impatient. I wondered why he was asking so many questions. It really wasn't like him. I guess he wanted to see my parents about something important.

"No. They might be at one of their club meetings," Mark said, crushing the soda can in his hand and tossing it into the trash bag.

"They usually come home for dinner before their club meetings," I said.

"Did you look in their room?" Roger asked.

"Huh? What for?" Even Mark was becoming suspicious. This was very strange behavior for Roger.

Roger blushed. "You know. To see if they left a note or anything."

"They always leave notes on the refrigerator," I told him. "You know Mom and Dad. They're computer people, right? They do everything by a system, everything the same way all the time."

It's true. My parents like to think they're such free spirits. But you should see them if I put the Frosted Flakes back in the wrong cabinet!

Roger yawned and stretched. He's good-looking even when he yawns, I thought. "Guess I'll talk to them tomorrow." He grabbed another handful of goldfish, nearly emptying the bowl, and turned toward the stairs. "G'night."

"Night," Mark and I called, and looked at each other.

"He's weird," Mark said.

"He's Mom's cousin, so he *has* to be weird," I cracked. "He certainly seemed nervous tonight."

"Yeah. He looked like he wanted to borrow money or something."

"Maybe you're right," I said, suddenly feeling really tired. "He did look like he wanted *something*. Where are you going?" Mark was heading into the den.

"It's almost twelve. Thought I'd watch *Star Trek*."

"Mark, you've seen them all ten times!"

"No. These are the new ones. I've only seen them twice."

Mark is a real *Star Trek* freak. He watches the reruns whenever they're on, usually after midnight. He isn't much of a reader, but he reads all the *Star Trek* novels as soon as they come out. He thinks it's hilarious to give me the Vulcan salute when no one's watching. Like I said, my brother doesn't have much of a sense of humor.

"Maybe we *should* take a look in Mom and Dad's room," I said.

He gave me a funny look. "You okay?"

"Yeah, I know. It's not like me to be a worrier. I just have a weird feeling about this, you know."

"Okay. Let me just see what episode they're showing." He plopped down on the leather couch, picked up the remote control, and clicked on the TV.

I sat down wearily on the arm of the couch, too tired to do any more cleaning up. A few minutes later, *Star Trek* came on.

"It's an old one," Mark said, "but it's pretty neat. Kirk, Uhura, and Chekov get captured, and the guys that captured them make them wear these dog collars and train for combat."

"Thrills," I said. I'm not into *Star Trek*. "Come on. Let's go upstairs and check out Mom and Dad's room."

"Oh, all right." He aimed the remote control and turned off the TV. "Help me up." He raised his arms over his head and expected me to pull him up.

"No way," I told him. "You weigh a ton."

He looked hurt. Groaning, he pulled himself to his feet. We were both really tired. It was nearly one o'clock in the morning and we had to get up in six hours to go to school.

I followed Mark out of the den and up the stairs. I hated the way the old wooden steps creaked and squeaked when we stepped on them. Mom and Dad were going to get carpet for the stairs, but they just didn't have time.

Our house in Brookline had been brand-new. It was hard to get used to all the creepy noises an old house like this one made. I'm not a nervous person. Mark is the nervous one in the family. But I always have the feeling that someone else is in the room, or someone is coming down the stairs, or someone is creeping up behind me—all because of the creaks and groans and weird noises the house makes.

I guess I'll get used to it. But I do have to admit, I feel a lot more comfortable in this run-down old house when Mom and Dad are home.

Where could they be? I wondered.

Their bedroom door was closed. That wasn't unusual. They often closed it when they went out. Neat and tidy. Everything in its place. Everything in perfect order.

I turned the knob and pushed open the door.

I was surprised to see light. A lamp on the far bed table had been left on.

"Oh!"

I didn't mean to scream. A noise frightened me. It was just a window shade flapping in the wind against the open window.

Then I saw their bed and cried out again.

It was obvious that something terrible had happened. . . .

CHAPTER 4

I'm not sure why my sister went bananas. What's the matter with her, anyway! She never saw an unmade bed before? I mean, give me a break. Sure, Mom and Dad are neat freaks, and sure they *always* made their bed before going to work. But one unmade bed is no reason to freak out and start screaming that something terrible has happened!

I got Cara calmed down in my usual way. I yelled at her and told her to shut up. I mean, I saw right away that there was nothing to be so pushed out of shape about.

Hey, I'm supposed to be the worrier in the family. Cara's supposed to be the calm, cool, and collected one. Well, she was blowing her whole image, that's for sure.

"I'm sorry," she said, biting her lower lip the way she always does when she's done something wrong, which is most of the time. "I didn't mean to scream like that. It's just . . . just—"

"Just what?" I asked. I wasn't going to let her off the hook so easily. I mean, she scared the you-know-what out of me when she screamed like that.

Her voice got tiny and soft. "I guess it was the way the bedspread is half on the floor and the sheet is all balled up like that. It—it just looked like there's been a fight or something."

"You've got to chill out," I told her, sitting down on the edge of the bed. "I don't know what's got you so shook. I mean, you act like Mom and Dad have never stayed out late before."

Cara was so worked up, I decided I had to act supercalm. I was a little worried, too, but I decided not to let Cara know. Actually, I was worried and I was glad. I was glad they had stayed out late because that meant I could invite Gena over, and Gena was really h-o-t tonight!

Sitting on the unmade bed, I thought about the big fight I'd had with Mom and Dad that morning. What was their problem, anyway? Gena was a fox! She was real smart, too, and nice, and she really likes me—a lot. I've only met her dad a few times, but he seems like a good guy. I think he's a doctor. So what is Mom and Dad's problem? Why the big objection to my seeing Gena?

It was so strange how they couldn't give any reasons.

Mom and Dad are always real big with the reasons. They always have at least two or three reasons for everything they do. They're always putting Gena and me down for doing something just because we felt like doing it and then not being able to explain why we did it.

Like everything in life should have a reason, right?

So when I asked their reason for telling me not to see Gena, all they could say was, "Trust us. We know more than you do about things."

What kind of reason is that? Trust us!

I suppose I shouldn't have lost my cool the way I did. But they're used to me blowing my stack. Besides, I had good reason. For once, I was right.

Of course, I realized, sitting in their room, if something terrible had happened to them, I'd feel pretty bad about having had a fight with them this morning. But I shook away that thought. No point in thinking like that. It wouldn't do anyone any good.

"They've worked very late before," I told Cara.

"They usually call." She didn't look any calmer. She was standing over me with her arms crossed over her sweatshirt. "I know, I know. The phone is busted. But they could've called and left a message with Mrs. Fisher next door, couldn't they?"

"Cara, you've got to stop this worrying," I said. "It's just not like you."

But instead of listening to me, she suddenly let out a little gasp. Her mouth dropped open and her eyes grew wide with fright.

I realized she wasn't looking at me. She was looking past me to the window. "Mark—" Her voice came out a whisper. She leaned forward and grabbed my shoulder. Her fingers gripped my sweater. "Mark . . . there's someone—"

"Huh?" I really couldn't hear her.

She pushed my shoulder until I spun around. At first I couldn't see what had frightened her. I saw the window, which was half-open. I saw the darkness beyond the window and a narrow sliver of pale white moon. I saw the patterned floor-length curtains billow a little from the gusting night breeze.

And then I saw them. The two shoes sticking out from under the curtain to the right of the window.

Suddenly I understood my sister's sudden fright—and felt it myself. I stared at the shoes beneath the curtain and at the slight bulge that made the curtain appear to blow in the wind.

And I realized—as Cara did—that someone else was there with us in our parents' bedroom.

CHAPTER 5

If I had thought about it, I probably wouldn't have done it. But, like I said, I don't always have reasons for the things I do. Sometimes I just do them. Then I think up my reasons later, when it's too late.

Anyway, I jumped off the bed. And I ran toward the window.

I could hear Cara yelling to me to stop. But it was too late. I couldn't stop now.

I don't know what I thought I was going to do. I was feeling more anger than fear. I know that. I mean, what was someone doing in our parents' room like that, hiding behind the curtain?

Was it a burglar?

I didn't stop to think that it might be someone really dangerous. I didn't stop to think that it might be someone who would blow me away just as soon as look at me. I guess I didn't think at all.

I just ran—and then stopped when Roger stepped out from behind the curtains, looking real embarrassed.

"It's only me," he said. I guess he saw the fierce look on my face. He held up both hands, as if surrendering.

"Roger! What were you doing there?" Cara cried.

"Uh . . . just looking out the window. I . . . uh . . . thought I heard something outside, but it was just a dog or something."

"But what are you doing in here?" I asked, my heart still pounding.

"You really scared us," Cara said angrily, crossing her arms over her chest.

"Sorry. I just came in to see if your parents left a note or something. Then I went to the window when I heard something outside. I didn't hear you come in."

I believed him, but Cara seemed to have her doubts. My sister never believes anything anyone tells her. "But how could you not hear us? We were talking and everything."

"I . . . uh . . . guess those curtains are very heavy. They keep out the sound," Roger said. He pushed a hand through his wavy brown hair. He was sweating. It was hot in our parents' room, but not *that* hot.

"I really didn't mean to scare you," Roger said, looking past me to Cara. She still had her arms wrapped tightly in front of her. "I was just concerned about your parents and—"

"What's that in your hand?" Cara interrupted.

Roger held up a small black box. "This? It's just my Walkman." He started toward the door.

"No headphones?" Cara asked suspiciously.

"I . . . uh . . . left them upstairs," Roger said. He put the Walkman into his pants pocket.

The window curtains suddenly billowed out into the room.

All three of us cried out in surprise.

They had just been blown by the wind. Somewhere down the street in the Fear Street woods, an animal howled. I had a sudden chill. Guys at school had told me stories about wolves that roamed wild in the woods behind our house.

"Really. I'm sorry if I scared you two," Roger repeated, yawning. "Guess we're all pretty tired." He was halfway out the door, then turned around. "Listen, don't worry about your mom and dad. I'm sure they'll be back when you wake up in the morning."

"Yeah. Probably," Cara said. Her shoulders slumped and she let out a loud sigh. "Sorry if we frightened *you*," she added, making peace with Roger. "We didn't know it was you."

"Night."

"Good night."

Roger disappeared out the door. We listened to his footsteps as he climbed the stairs to his room up in the attic. Then Cara dived onto the bed, sliding on her stomach and burying her face in Mom's pillow.

I walked over and closed the window. Down on the ground the wind was swirling the dead leaves across the front yard. Something on the street caught my eye. It was a gray van, parked directly across from our house. I hadn't remembered seeing it there before. There was no writing on the side. It was too dark to see if anyone was in it or not.

What was it doing there?

I pulled the heavy curtains closed and stepped away.

"Think Roger was telling the truth?" Cara asked, her voice muffled because her face was still buried in the pillow.

"I don't know. Maybe," I said. "Why wouldn't he be?"

"He looked so embarrassed."

"You'd be embarrassed, too," I said. "He felt stupid, that's all."

I don't know why I was defending Roger. I had nothing against him, but I didn't really like him all that much. We didn't have anything in common. That was part of the problem. He wasn't into sports and I wasn't into nineteenth-century English lit. He was so good-looking. Too good-looking, I thought. Cara's girlfriends always started giggling and carrying on whenever Roger walked into the room. Maybe I was just a little jealous.

But I really didn't understand why we needed him around. Sure, he was a distant cousin or something. But that didn't mean he had to live with us, did it? It made me uncomfortable to have someone else in the house. The creepy old house was uncomfortable enough as it was, especially compared to the neat house we'd had back in

Brookline. We didn't need some college guy lurking about, hiding behind the curtains.

So I don't know why I was taking Roger's side. I guess it's because I just like to argue with Cara.

"What was he looking for in here?" she asked, rolling onto her back, her face hidden in the fat pillow.

"Same thing we were, I guess," I said, walking over and sitting down at the far end of the big queen-size platform bed.

"But if he was looking for a note, why was he hiding behind the drapes, staring out the window?"

I groaned. Cara could be really exhausting sometimes. "Give me a break. He explained it, didn't he? What do you want me to say?"

"You're right. I'm just tired." She closed her eyes.

"You're going to sleep here?"

She yawned. "No. I'm getting up." She stretched out her arms and smiled. It was a very comfortable bed.

"See ya," I said. I thought about Gena. I wondered if it was too late to call her. Probably. I thought maybe I'd call anyway.

Suddenly the smile dropped from Cara's face. She sat up quickly.

"What is it?"

"I found something under the sheet."

She had a small object in her hand. It looked like a tiny, white skull. I walked over to get a closer look. "What is it? A human skull?"

"No." Cara held it up close to her face to examine it in the dim lamplight. "It's . . . it's a monkey."

"What?"

She held it up and turned it around so I could see it better. It was a carved, white monkey's head about the size of a Ping-Pong ball. There were rhinestones deep in the eye sockets. They glowed yellow in the light from the bed-table lamp.

I took it from her and rolled it around between my fingers. "Strange. It feels so cold."

"I know," Cara said, and I could see a flash of fear cross her face. "There's something creepy about it."

I held it up and turned it so that it was facing me. As I stared into its shimmering eyes, it seemed to stare back into mine. It was carved ivory, the monkey's twin nostrils deep and dark, its teeth pulled back the width of its face in an ugly, frightening grin. It was so smooth, so cold.

And those rhinestone eyes seemed to peer into mine—seemed to radiate—what?—radiate evil!

I know, I know. Maybe all those rotten horror flicks Cara and I have rented have rotted my brain. Maybe I was just tired. Maybe I was upset because Mom and Dad weren't home.

But there was something ugly, something evil, about that tiny white monkey skull, about those strange, sparkling eyes, about that frozen monkey grin.

I stared at it as if hypnotized for the longest time. Then I couldn't stand it any longer, and I wrapped my fingers around the mysterious object, buried it in my hand, and shut my eyes. Even though I had been holding it tightly, it remained ice-cold, the cold burning my hand the way dry ice can burn. I tossed it back to Cara, who looked at it again, then tossed it onto the bed table, her face filled with disgust.

"What is it? Where did it come from?" she asked.

Just two more questions that I couldn't answer that night.

CHAPTER 6

I didn't sleep well that night. Big surprise. I stared up at the shadows crisscrossing the ceiling, thinking about Gena and how neat she was. I thought about kissing her that night, holding her on the couch. She smelled so great. She was so warm. It seemed like we were the only ones in the room, even though the house was packed with kids.

And of course I thought about Mom and Dad. It felt strange knowing that they weren't downstairs in the den, reading or watching TV, or doing whatever they did after Cara and I went to bed. I didn't feel scared. It just felt strange.

I felt bad about the fight we had had in the morning. But that wasn't my fault, I told myself. Lying there, twisting this way and that in the dark, I got all worked up, having the argument all over again in my mind.

When I looked at the clock it said 1:42, almost two in the morning and I was still wide awake. I got out of bed and walked over to my bedroom window. I don't know why. Maybe I thought I'd see Mom and Dad's car in the drive.

I looked down over the front yard. The yellow porch light cast strange, shifting shadows over the lawn. It was very foggy. I could barely make out the streetlight across the street. Beyond it, the dark woods disappeared into gray-blue mist.

I pressed my forehead against the windowpane. The glass felt cool and soothing on my hot head. From somewhere in the woods I could hear two animals howling in unison. I listened carefully, even more wide awake now. The howls didn't sound like dog howls.

I looked out again. That gray van hadn't moved. It was still parked directly across the street.

The howls seemed to grow louder, closer. Suddenly I saw someone running across the lawn toward the street.

I blinked once, twice. I was only half-awake. I thought maybe my eyes were playing tricks on me.

No. It was Roger. I could see him clearly in the yellow porch light. His tan safari jacket flapped behind him in the wind as he ran. His long, thin shadow seemed to stretch back across the leaf-covered lawn.

He ran quickly in a straight line. As he crossed the street, the side door of the van slid open, and he disappeared into it, two hands helping to pull him up. Then the van door slid closed.

"What's going on?" My voice came out in a choked whisper.

I stared out into the fog. The van was dark and silent now. Shadows shifted on the front lawn. The surrounding darkness seemed to grow even darker.

I realized I was shivering and stepped back from the window.

What was going on? Why was Roger running out to that van in the middle of the night? Who was he meeting there?

Still shivering, I turned toward the door. I decided to wake Cara. But then something beside the bed caught my eye.

It was a soft white glow. Something was glowing on my bed table. I started toward it, stumbled, and stubbed my toe against the leg of my bed.

"Ow!" I hopped on one foot waiting for the pain to subside.

Angrily, I made my way to the bed table, grabbed up the glowing object, and turned on the lamp.

It was the white monkey head.

Its rhinestone eyes glowed even brighter in the light. Its tight smile seemed to be grinning up at me, laughing at me.

Had I carried the monkey head into my room? I didn't remember putting it on my bed table. But I must have. I was so tired last night, I just didn't remember. . . .

I tossed it onto the bed and then walked back to the window. The van was still there across the street, dark and closed up. Roger was still inside.

Something very weird is going on here, I thought, now fully awake. I decided to run up to Roger's room while he was outside. Maybe I could find something up there, some clue as to what Roger was up to. He'd been acting strange all night. But running out to a van in the middle of the night was too strange to ignore.

As I pulled on my flannel robe, I struggled to come up with a logical explanation. He's buying drugs, I thought.

No. Roger was a total straight-arrow. I'd never seen him drink more than half a beer in an evening. He wasn't into drugs.

Then what? A girlfriend?

Yes, that could be it. He could be meeting a girl.

But that didn't make sense, either. Why wouldn't he just invite her in? And I'd seen the van parked out there hours earlier. If he *was* meeting a girl out there, why would he keep her waiting for so long?

He had obviously waited to make sure that Cara and I had fallen asleep. Whatever he was doing, he didn't want us to know about it.

But what could that be?

I stepped out into the hallway and headed toward the attic stairs. The floor creaked and squeaked as I walked. I hesitated outside Cara's door. Should I wake her?

I decided not to. I was just going to slip up to Roger's room, have a quick look around, see if I could find anything helpful, and then hurry back into bed. Whatever I found could wait until morning. At least one of us was getting some sleep.

I was on the first step up to the attic when I heard Roger right behind me. "Hey, Mark, what are *you* doing up?"

CHAPTER 7

I spun around. The hallway was lit by a small, dim night-light down by the floor across from Cara's room. But even in the dim light, I could see that Roger was sweating and his face was flushed.

"You scared me," I whispered.

"Sorry. I seem to be making a habit of it tonight." He didn't smile. "What are you doing up?"

"I . . . well . . . I just went to the bathroom," I replied, thinking quickly.

"The bathroom is that way," he said, pointing back down the hall.

"I know. I—" I didn't know *what* I was going to say next. "Hey, where were *you?*" I asked.

"I couldn't sleep," he said, wiping his forehead with his hand. "Too much studying, I guess. I took a walk to clear my head."

He was lying. He took a walk right into that gray van.

"It's so warm out," he added quickly. "I can't believe this is November." Then he pushed past me and started up the attic steps.

"Well, good night," I whispered. I decided not to call him on his lie, not to tell him I'd seen him climb into the van. I was just too tired and too confused. I wanted to tell Cara what I'd seen and then decide what to do about Roger.

"Night," he called back. He hurried up the steps, eager to get away from me and my questions, I guess.

And I sure had a lot of questions now. But it was too late. The questions all swirled around in my head like clothes in a washing machine, heavy, heavy clothes.

Suddenly, I felt very heavy, too. I lumbered back to my room and fell onto my bed without bothering to take off my robe. When I finally fell asleep, I had strange, uncomfortable dreams.

In one dream, I was abandoned in an endless parking lot. There were gray cars as far as I could see in all directions. I was all alone in the center of the lot. I didn't know which direction I was supposed to go. I didn't know which car was mine. I didn't know where to look to find a way out.

I had been left there by somebody. I remembered that. I had been abandoned there. But what was I supposed to do next?

When the alarm went off at seven, I awoke feeling very out-of-sorts. My muscles all ached. My head felt heavy. I didn't remember any of my other dreams. I just remembered that they were unpleasant.

"Give me a break!" I shouted, not at anyone or anything in particular—just at the world in general.

I stretched and turned onto my side. I was startled to see the white monkey head on my bed table beside the clock radio.

Again it seemed to be staring at me, grinning at me with that ugly, leering grin. The rhinestone eyes gleamed brightly even though there was little light in the room.

I picked it up and heaved it across the room. I heard it hit the wall and bounce across the carpet. "That'll teach you to stare," I said aloud.

Then, remembering Mom and Dad might be downstairs, I forced myself out of bed. I skipped my usual shower, pulled on yesterday's jeans and a striped pullover shirt that I thought was clean enough, and ran to the stairs.

Cara was right ahead of me. "Morning," I said.

She didn't reply. "Hey, Mom! Dad!" she called, as we both took the stairs two at a time. "Where *were* you two?"

We hurried into the kitchen. It was empty. Our dirty dishes from last night were still stacked on the counter beside the sink. "We didn't do a very good cleanup," Cara said.

"Who cares? Where are they?" I shouted.

"Don't yell at *me*. I don't know!"

"I wasn't yelling," I told her. Why was she trying to pick a fight?

"Maybe they're still asleep," she said, pushing past me. "I'll go up and see."

"I'll go with you." I don't know why I followed her. It certainly didn't take two of us to go look in their bedroom and see if they were back. I guess I just wasn't thinking clearly. I was feeling really worried, and when I start to worry, I go into high-gear worrying!

I stopped at the foot of the stairs and watched Cara run up to their room. A lot of horrible things flashed through my mind, horrible things that could've happened to Mom and Dad. "But if something horrible had happened," I argued with myself, "the police would've called by now." That thought made me feel a little better. But I knew I wouldn't feel a *lot* better until I knew where they were.

"Are they up there?" I shouted up the stairs to Cara.

She appeared above me at the top of the stairs. I noticed that her hair was unbrushed, which was really unusual for my sister. She shook her head dejectedly. "Nope. Not home."

My stomach growled. I suddenly realized I was starving. I wondered if there was anything in the house for breakfast. Then I felt bad thinking about food when I should've been worrying about Mom and Dad.

Cara slumped down the stairs and I followed her into the kitchen. We were both feeling pretty miserable. She found a box of cornflakes in the cabinet, but there was no milk. So we poured a bottle of Coke on it instead. "Every day should start with a balanced breakfast," Cara muttered.

Actually, it didn't taste that bad.

I had just about downed the entire bowl when I jumped up. I suddenly remembered the gray van.

"Hey! Where are you going?" Cara called after me as I ran to the living room and peered out the window. It was still dark out. The sun was just beginning to burn through the clouds. The van was gone.

"What are you doing, Mark?" Cara had followed me into the living room.

I motioned for her to sit down on the couch. Then I told her everything that had happened last night.

"And you definitely saw Roger run into this gray van?" she asked. "You're sure you weren't asleep?"

That's just like Cara. Always doubting everything.

"No, I wasn't asleep."

"And you're sure he didn't run past the van and it only looked like the van opened up because of shadows from trees or something?"

Now she was beginning to make me doubt what I'd seen with my own eyes. "No. I saw just what I said. Roger climbed into the van and the door closed."

"He definitely lied to you about taking a walk?"

"Cara, you're really starting to steam me!" I said, trying to control my temper.

"Okay, okay." She threw up her hands. "I'm sorry. It's just that if we're going upstairs to accuse Roger, we should be sure of what we're accusing him of."

"Well . . . it was dark on the street, and very foggy. But I'm sure I saw him climb in."

"Then let's go," Cara said, jumping off the couch and pulling me up. "We'll just put it to him—Roger, what were you doing in that gray van last night?"

"I guess." Cara had asked so many questions, I was beginning to think I'd dreamed the whole thing. Or maybe I was just reluctant to get into a big thing with Roger.

"Uh . . . Cara . . ." I said as we started up the stairs. "Maybe what Roger did last night isn't any of our business. He is entitled to a private life, after all."

Cara sighed and rolled her eyes. "Mark, our parents are missing, right?"

"Well . . . they didn't come home last night."

"And ever since they've been missing, Roger has been acting extremely weird. Wouldn't you agree?"

"Yeah, I guess."

"So we have every right to ask him why he's been acting so weird. Agreed?"

I thought about it for a short while. "Agreed." I had to give in. I never win any arguments with Cara unless I start shouting a lot. And this morning I just didn't have the strength to shout.

Besides, she was right—for once.

We climbed the narrow stairs to the attic. It was about ten degrees warmer up here. Roger's door was closed.

"Should we wake him?" I whispered. "Or should we wait?"

Cara gave me a dirty look. "Of course we'll wake him. You *do* plan to go to school this morning, don't you?"

I knocked on the door softly, then harder.

No reply.

I had a sudden chill, a feeling of dread in the pit of my stomach. Something horrible has happened in there, I thought. I shook my head as if shaking away the thought. I knew I was just being stupid.

I knocked again. Still no reply.

So I pushed open the door and took a step inside.

Gray light filtered in through a small, dirt-smeared skylight. Roger's small cot was made, the thin green blanket tucked in tightly at all four corners. The room was empty. He had left already.

"I don't believe it," Cara said, disappointed that we wouldn't have our confrontation.

"He has morning classes," I said, moving toward the wall to make room for her.

"Not this early," Cara said, biting her lower tip. "Well . . . while we're here, let's take a look around."

"That won't take long," I said. I had to keep my head bent down so it wouldn't bump the ceiling.

I looked through a pile of stuff on Roger's desk, just a bunch of notebooks and texts. Cara got down on her hands and knees and looked under Roger's bed. "See anything?" I asked, whispering for some reason.

"Dust balls," she said, getting up quickly.

The bookshelf next to the desk was mostly empty, a few books and magazines tossed on the middle shelf. A cardboard cup containing marking pens and pencils was on the shelf below it.

"What a grim place," I said.

"Yeah. You'd think he'd put up some posters or something."

I looked at the bare gray walls. This was more like a prison cell than a college guy's room.

Cara started looking through the things on the top of the desk. "I already looked there," I said impatiently. I started to feel really nervous. I wanted to get out of there. What if Roger came back and found us snooping around in all his stuff?

"Hey! Look at this." Cara was holding up an empty notebook.

"A notebook. Big deal," I said.

"Right. An empty notebook." She picked up another one. "Look, Mark. This one is empty, too." I picked up the remaining notebook from the desk. Empty. Not a word written in it.

"So? What does that mean?" I asked. "He hasn't used these yet."

Cara was flipping through Roger's textbooks now. "Look. No underlining. Not a mark."

"So he doesn't like to mark up his books," I said, sighing. "I don't, either. I really don't think this is very interesting, Cara."

"But he hasn't taken a single note! None of this stuff looks like it's ever been opened!"

Suddenly I heard a creaking sound down in the hall. I glanced at Cara. She heard it, too.

We both froze. And listened.

Silence.

I peeked out the door. There was no one there. I tiptoed to the steps and looked down. No one. It was just the old house creaking.

When I got back to Roger's room, Cara was pulling out desk drawers and riffling through them. Since there was no dresser, Roger kept his clothes in the desk drawers. One entire drawer was filled with pairs of navy blue socks all neatly rolled into balls!

"Come on, Cara. Let's get out of here," I pleaded. "We're not going to find anything interesting. There's nothing here at all. It's as if Roger doesn't have a life."

She looked at me. "That's right. That's what's so weird. Don't you think that's interesting?"

"No," I said.

She pulled out the bottom desk drawer. It was filled nearly to the top with underwear. "Let's go," I said.

"We've found zip. Nada. Nothing." I started out the door.

"Wait, Mark! Oh, good Lord!"

I hurried back in. "Cara—what?"

She had pulled the underwear out of the drawer. Underneath it lay a shiny black snub-nosed pistol.

CHAPTER 8

Mark, what are you doing? Put that down!" I shouted. He had pulled the gun out of the drawer and was examining it.

"It's loaded," he said softly.

"Well, don't point it at me!"

"I'm not pointing it. I'm putting it back, okay?" he snapped.

"Just be careful."

He replaced the gun, handling it very gently. Then I shoved Roger's underwear back in on top of it and closed the desk drawer.

"Why do you think Roger keeps a loaded pistol in his room?" Mark asked, squinting his green eyes, thinking hard.

"Maybe he likes to shoot at cockroaches," I cracked.

He looked at me. He didn't seem to understand that I was joking. "Come on. Let's get out of here," I said, shoving him out the door.

Back in the kitchen, Mark started to pace. I sat down at the Formica counter. "Now what?" he asked.

I glanced up at the clock over the sink. It was seven forty. If we didn't leave soon, we'd be late for school. "The phone," I said. "Maybe it's fixed."

We both raced to the wall phone. I got there first and grabbed the receiver. Silence. "Still dead," I sighed.

"We have to call the phone company," Mark said. "Mom and Dad have probably been trying to call all night."

"I know. I'll go down the block to Mrs. Fisher's house," I told him. I picked up my parents' little phone book. "Maybe her phone is working. I'll call Mom and Dad and then I'll call the phone company."

"I'd go with you, but Mrs. Fisher doesn't like me," Mark said. "She came over once when I was practicing my archery in the backyard, and ever since she's always giving me funny looks. She thinks I'm weird or something."

"She's right," I said, and quickly headed out the backdoor. I love getting the last word.

It was still chilly out. The sun hadn't managed to burn through the low, overhanging clouds. I should've put on a sweater or something, but Mrs. Fisher's house was just halfway down the block.

I walked quickly along the side of the street, past the nearly bare maple and sycamore trees. It was beginning to look like winter even though it didn't really feel that cold yet. When Mrs. Fisher's rambling old shingled house came into view, I picked up speed and jogged the rest of the way.

The front doorbell didn't seem to be working, so I used the brass knocker in the center of the door. She came to the door after my second knock. A fairly attractive woman in her late forties or early fifties, she was wearing tan corduroy slacks and a plaid man's shirt. Her jet-black hair was tied behind her head with a blue rubber band.

At first she stared at me. She looked very surprised to see me. "Cara?"

"Good morning, Mrs. Fisher. I'm sorry to bother you so early."

She held open the door so I could come in. "It's not early for me. I'm up at six every morning." The house smelled of coffee and stale cigarettes. "Is everything okay?"

She looked away when she asked that. Something about the way she asked it, with so much concern in her voice, made me suspicious. But of course I was being ridiculous. I think I'd suspect *anyone* this morning!

"Is your phone working? Ours is dead."

"Why, yes. It's working fine. I just spoke to my sister a few minutes ago. That's strange that yours is out."

"Yes," I agreed. "Can I use your phone?"

"Of course." I followed her through the living room, which was filled with heavy, dark antique furniture, into the kitchen, which wasn't much brighter.

"First I'm going to phone my parents," I said, searching the little directory for their direct number.

"Your parents?"

I looked up to see an odd expression on her face. It was more than surprise. It was shock. She saw me looking at her, and the expression quickly disappeared. She picked up a pack of cigarettes and forced one out of the pack. When she lit it, her hand was shaking.

"Yeah. They probably worked all night," I told her. Was I imagining that weird, shocked expression? I must have been. "They're not home."

With the cigarette dangling from her lips, Mrs. Fisher turned and walked over to the sink and started to rinse off some plates. "They didn't call you?"

"They couldn't. The phone's broken."

"Oh. Of course. Where do your parents work?" She didn't turn around. The dishes she was rinsing looked perfectly clean to me.

"At a place called Cranford Industries."

"Oh, yes. Cranford. They make airplane parts or something. I read about Cranford. They do a lot of work for the federal government, don't they?"

"I don't really know," I told her, picking up the phone receiver. "My parents install computer systems."

"Oh. That's interesting." She dried her hands and turned around. She put the cigarette down, then nervously picked it up again. "Cranford is pretty far away. At least two towns from here. Why did your parents buy a house here in Shadyside instead of nearer their work?"

"I don't know, Mrs. Fisher. I never really thought about it. I guess maybe they thought the high school was better here. You know. For Mark and me."

"Cara—" she started, but then she suddenly stopped.

"What?"

"Never mind," she said quickly. "I forgot what I was going to say." · She tossed the dish towel down on the counter. "I'd better hush up and let you make your calls." Looking nervous, she hurried out of the room, leaving the burning cigarette on an ashtray by the sink.

What's her problem? I asked myself. She'd always seemed so calm and normal whenever she came over to visit my parents. She was the only neighbor who was the least bit friendly. All of our other neighbors on Fear Street kept to themselves and never even waved or looked up when we went past.

I pushed my parents' direct line at Cranford Industries and then listened to the low ring. I let it ring six times, seven, eight. . . . No answer. The switchboard message center didn't pick up, either. It was too early, I guess. No one there yet.

I slumped against the counter, suddenly feeling sick. I was so disappointed. I really thought they'd be there.

Now what?

What could I do? Who could I call?

We had no relatives in Shadyside. We'd only been here since September. We hardly knew anyone!

What should I do? I couldn't go to school without knowing where Mom and Dad were, without knowing that they were okay. I couldn't sit there, class after class, wondering, just wondering what was going on.

I felt panicky and sick to my stomach. Maybe the cornflakes in

Coca-Cola was a bad idea. My heart was pounding. I stared at the phone.

And suddenly I knew what Mark and I had to do. We had to go to Cranford Industries. We had to track my parents down.

But how? We could borrow a car. Or maybe there was a bus that went somewhere near there.

Yes. That's what we had to do. We had to cut school and go there. If Mom and Dad were there, we'd find out why we hadn't heard from them. And if they weren't there . . . well . . . They *had* to be there!

"Thank you, Mrs. Fisher!" I called.

There was no reply, so I ran out the door. I was halfway down the walk when I realized I'd forgotten to call the phone company about fixing our phone. So I hurried back into the house and called.

"No service at all?" a friendly woman on the other end asked, sounding truly concerned.

"No. It's totally silent," I told her.

"Strange. We haven't had any other complaints from your neighborhood," she said. "I'll notify the service guys right away."

"Thank you," I said and hung up, feeling a little better. I called my thanks up to Mrs. Fisher, who still hadn't reappeared, and hurried home, eager to tell Mark my idea about cutting school and going to Mom and Dad's office.

I ran up the drive and headed toward the backyard. But something caught my eye as I was about to pass the garage. Our garage doors have long, rectangular windows in them. And through the windows, I thought I saw something strange.

I stopped and walked up to the front door of the garage and peered in. Yes. I was right.

My parents' car—the blue Toyota they drove to work every day—it was there in the garage.

CHAPTER 9

Mark opened the garage door and we stood in the drive gaping at the car as if we'd never seen one before. "How did Mom and Dad get to work?" Mark asked, stepping into the garage and looking into the car windows.

Of course there was another question that both of us were thinking but didn't dare say aloud: *Did* they get to work?

There was only one way to find out.

"We've got to go to Cranford—right now," I said.

Mark kicked a rear tire. "I can't, Cara. I've got a math test this morning. And I wanted to see Gena and—"

He stopped and made a face. He knew those things weren't as important as finding Mom and Dad.

"Oh, I don't know *what* to do!" he cried angrily and slammed his hand against the trunk. He looked just like a little boy having a tantrum. "Ow!" He'd hurt his hand.

"Stop kicking and slamming things," I said. "You're upset. I'm upset. The only way we're going to be less upset is to take some action."

"Okay, okay," he grumbled. "Lay off the lectures, okay? Let's get the car keys and our coats and get going. At least we have a car to drive."

We both looked at the car again. I felt weak. I turned away. That car shouldn't have been there. Something was wrong. Something was seriously wrong.

"Maybe they got a lift to work," Mark said as we hurried into the house to get our coats. "Maybe there was an emergency at Cranford, and someone came to pick them up."

"Maybe," I said. Neither of us believed it, though.

But what *could* we believe?

I grabbed my down coat, the extra set of car keys, and a road map from the desk in the den, and a few seconds later, Mark backed down the drive. The sun had given up its attempts to break through the clouds. It was gray and very windy. November was starting to look like November.

At the end of the block, Mark slammed on the brakes. "The van!" he cried.

The unmarked gray van he had told me about was parked in front of us. A man with very short, white-blond hair sat in the driver's seat.

Mark pulled the Toyota right up to the van. The blond man stared straight ahead, pretending not to notice us.

Mark unrolled his window and stuck his head out. "Hey! You waiting for Roger?" he yelled to the guy.

The guy in the van rolled down his window. "Sorry. I had the radio cranked up. What did you want?" He flashed us a wide smile. He had rows and rows of perfect white teeth. I guess he was handsome with his white-blond hair, pale skin, and sparkling white teeth.

"You waiting for Roger?" Mark repeated.

"Who?"

"Roger."

The guy in the van shook his head. His smile hadn't faded an inch. "Sorry. You've got the wrong guy. I don't know any Roger."

Mark stared back at him, disappointed. "Oh. Sorry."

"No problem," the guy said, and rolled up his window.

Mark floored the gas pedal and we took off with a roar. "He's lying," Mark said.

"How do you know?" I asked.

"From his smile."

We both laughed. It wasn't really funny. We just needed to laugh. Then we both got very silent.

We had the car heater turned way up, but I felt really cold. I guess it was partly because I was so nervous, so worried about what they might tell us at Cranford Industries about our parents.

Mark drove with one hand. He stared straight ahead, driving like a robot or something.

Finally I couldn't stand the silence any longer. "What's the worst thing they could tell us?" I asked.

He didn't react. I couldn't tell if he was thinking about his answer or if he hadn't heard me.

"The worst thing?" he repeated finally, turning onto Division Street. "I guess the worst thing would be if they said, 'Your parents left work at the normal time last Tuesday. We've been wondering where they are, too. Why didn't they come in to work yesterday morning?'"

I didn't have to think about it. Mark was right. That *was* the worst thing they could say. "And what's the best thing they could say?" I asked, just making stupid conversation.

"That's easy," Mark said. "The best thing they could say is, 'Here come your parents now. Guess they've been really tied up here.'"

"Well . . . I suppose that's still a possibility," I said. But I didn't really believe it.

I knew our parents weren't just going to pop up at the office and apologize for not calling. But I hoped that maybe someone there would have some kind of logical explanation for us.

But what would be a logical explanation?

I tried not to think. I tried not to think of all the horrible things that could have happened to them. But of course there was no way to shut those thoughts out. The worst thoughts, the ugliest, most terrifying thoughts always find you, always work their way into your brain.

We found the entrance to the industrial park and followed the sign to Cranford Industries. It was an enormous three-story white building, not as modern as I'd imagined, surrounded by a beautifully manicured lawn dotted with evergreen trees. We weren't sure where to park, and there wasn't anyone around to help us. Finally, we found a large lot in the back of the building. As we pulled up to it, an armed guard stepped out from a small booth beside the drive and motioned for us to stop.

"Pass," he said, reaching out his hand to Mark.

"Huh? You're letting us pass?"

"Pass," the guard repeated, a little more insistent.

"Oh! Uh . . . we don't have a pass. We're visitors."

The guard held up a long pad and glanced down a list. "Names?"

"We're not on your list," I said. "We don't have an appointment. We came to see our parents."

"Their names?" He flicked through the pad until he came to another, longer list.

"Burroughs. Lucy and Greg Burroughs," Mark said.

"Not on my list," the guard said, eyeing us suspiciously.

"They're pretty new," I said weakly.

He leaned down and peered into the car, looking Mark and me up and down. Then he looked into the backseat. "Well . . . park in Twenty-three-B over there. Then go around to the front. They'll check you out inside."

"Thank you," Mark and I both said gratefully. I felt as if I'd passed some important test. But why should it be such a big deal to let two teenagers park so they can see their parents?

Anyway, we parked in 23-B and walked around to the front entrance, just as the guard had ordered. "Hey, wait up!" I yelled. Mark was practically running.

"Sorry." He stopped and waited for me to catch up. "This place is pretty impressive," he said.

"It's so big," I said, pushing open one of the glass doors of the front entrance. "How does anyone find anyone here?"

Another guard, this one very young, with cold blue eyes and a blond stubble under his nose that was trying to become a mustache, came up to meet us the instant we entered.

"You're the visitors?" he asked, looking us up and down the way the parking-lot guard had.

"Yes," we both managed to say.

"Burroughs," he said. The other guard had talked to him by phone or radio already. "Hold still. This won't hurt a bit."

He had a metal detector in his hand, the kind they have at airports, and he moved it over Mark and then me, checking us out from head to foot.

Mark and I looked at each other. I think we were both thinking, What kind of crazy place to work at was this!

"Okay," the guard said. "Follow me."

He led us through the large, open lobby. It appeared to go the entire length of the building. It looked very plush. There were leather couches and chairs in small clusters all around. There were large oil paintings on all the walls. A polished brass staircase wound up to the top floors from the center of the enormous lobby. Our sneakers squeaked over the marble floor as we tried to keep up with the guard, who was walking really fast.

I glanced at Mark. He looked as nervous as I felt.

Finally, after walking for what seemed like miles, we came to a young woman seated behind a long, wooden desk set diagonally near the foot of the staircase. The guard left us there without a word and returned to his post by the door. We waited for her to look up from her notebook, a logbook of some kind which she was staring into. She was very pretty, I noticed. She had her straw-blond hair pulled back tight, and she was wearing a great-looking plum-colored suit with matching tie.

Finally, she put down her notebook and flashed us an automatic smile. "Can I help you?"

"Uh . . . we came to see our parents," Mark blurted out.

"Do they work here?"

Before we could answer, the desk phone buzzed and she picked it up. She talked for three or four minutes, looking up at us from time to time. The longer we waited, the more nervous I felt. I had pains in my stomach and I was starting to feel a little light-headed.

Finally, she put down the phone. But it rang again, and again she had a three- or four-minute conversation while Mark and I stood there, trying to keep it together.

I stared at everyone who passed by. They were mostly people in business suits, heading for the staircase, their well-polished shoes clicking loudly over the marble floor. I kept thinking maybe Mom and Dad would just show up.

And then I saw them.

They were walking quickly toward us from the far end of the lobby, walking arm in arm.

"Mom! Dad!" I cried. "Hi!"

Mark and I started running toward them. They didn't seem to see us.

"Hey! Hi, you two!" I cried happily.

But as we got closer, I realized it wasn't them.

Mark and I stopped running. The man and woman looked a little like Mom and Dad, but not that much, really. I think my imagination was working overtime.

They walked right past us and headed up the stairway.

Mark and I avoided looking at each other. I guess he felt as fool-ish as I did. "Sorry," I said.

He didn't say anything. We walked back to the receptionist and waited for her to get off the phone.

"Now, who did you wish to see?" she asked after a few more end-less minutes had passed.

"Our parents," I said. "The name is Burroughs. Lucy and Greg Burroughs."

She pushed a few keys on her desk computer and then stared at the screen. "Hmmm . . . How do you spell Burroughs?"

I spelled it for her and she typed a few words on the keyboard. A list of names appeared on the green monitor screen, and she slowly ran her finger down them. After a few seconds she looked up, her finger still on the screen. "Sorry. No Burroughs listed here."

"But that's impossible," Mark said. He suddenly looked angry.

"Know what? I'll bet you're in the wrong building," the recep-tionist said.

"Wrong building?" Marked turned and looked back toward the entrance at the end of the lobby.

"This is Cranford Industries," the receptionist said. "There are a lot of buildings in this industrial park. You probably want—"

"Cranford Industries," Mark insisted. "That's right. This is where our parents work."

"They just started in September," I told her. "Maybe they aren't in the computer yet."

"Well . . ." She thought about it for a while. "The computer list-ing is updated every week. Tell me, do you know what division they work in?"

"Computers," I said. "They install mainframe computers."

"Computers?" She frowned. "Tell you what. Let me talk to Mr. Blumenthal. He's the personnel director."

"Thank you," Mark and I said at the same time.

I felt very confused. Why weren't Mom and Dad in the directory?

As I watched the receptionist phone Mr. Blumenthal, I answered my own question. It was quite simple. Mom and Dad weren't regular employees of Cranford Industries. They were special project workers. They were here to install mainframe computers. They weren't really part of any division. So of course they weren't listed in the company directory.

These thoughts made me feel a little better. But I was still terribly nervous, and the endless shuffle of people across the large lobby, the clicking shoes on the marble, the bright lights were all making me feel very uncomfortable.

She turned away as she talked to Mr. Blumenthal, and I couldn't hear what she was saying. A few seconds later, she hung up and, looking very concerned, punched another phone number. "Mr. Blumenthal told me to call. Is Mr. Marcus available?" I heard her say.

Who was Mr. Marcus?

She turned away again and I couldn't hear the rest of her conversation. Finally she put down the phone and turned back to us. "Mr. Marcus will see you in a few minutes."

"Is he in personnel?" I asked.

"He's our CEO," she said, looking at me as if I'd just barfed all over her desk. I guess I was supposed to know who Mr. Marcus was.

"CEO?" Mark asked.

"Chief executive officer," the receptionist said, frowning at Mark's ignorance. "Why don't you have a seat?" She pointed to two enormous leather chairs across from her desk. Then she took another call.

Mark and I walked over to the chairs, but we didn't sit down. We were too nervous, too eager to get this over with.

"Why is the big boss going to see us?" Mark whispered.

I shrugged. His guess was as good as mine.

A few minutes later, a young woman came down the staircase. She was carrying a stack of files. She told us she was Mr. Marcus's secretary and led us up the stairs, down several long hallways of offices and cubicles, and finally into Mr. Marcus's gigantic corner office.

Mr. Marcus smiled at us and put down the phone. He was a young man with short brown hair slicked straight back. He wore heavy black-framed glasses. "Hi. Nice to meet you. No school today?" he said, speaking quickly. He motioned for us to sit down in the two chairs in front of his desk.

"We skipped school," Mark said abruptly, looking very uncomfortable.

Mr. Marcus laughed. But he stopped when he saw the serious looks on our faces.

"We want to see our parents. We have a problem," I added.

"Well, I'll get them for you right away," he said. "I can see you kids are upset. Emergency at home?"

"No. Not really," I said. "We just need to see them."

"I'll get them for you right away. Even sooner," he said, giving us a warm smile. I liked him immediately. I could see how he got to be the big cheese at such a young age. He seemed so . . . trustworthy, so dependable. He seemed like a real person.

"Who are your parents?" he asked.

"Burroughs. Lucy and Greg Burroughs," I told him.

He took off his heavy eyeglasses and rubbed the bridge of his nose. Quickly replacing them, he punched some keys on the computer next to his desk. "Burroughs . . . Burroughs . . ."

"They just started in September," I said, my voice shaking. "They came here to install mainframe computers."

He looked away from the computer screen. "Computers?"

"Yes. They install computers. They—"

"We're not having any computers installed," he said, suddenly looking very confused. He stared first at Mark, then at me.

"You're not?"

"No. I don't have anyone here installing new computers."

"But our parents—"

He stood up. He was much taller than I'd thought. "Are you sure you kids have the right company?"

"Yes," I said. I was getting tired of that question.

"Well, I'm really sorry," Mr. Marcus said. "But I don't see how I can help you." He studied the computer screen for a moment. He pushed a few more keys and studied it some more.

"Nope," he said finally. "There's no one named Burroughs working here. There never has been."

CHAPTER 10

"I felt like I was in a dream or something," I said. "Like nothing was real. Everything was all topsy-turvy."

Cara nodded. "I know. I felt the same way. I don't think I'll ever forget the look on Marcus's face. He felt so bad for us."

"Yeah. I know. And what he said just keeps repeating in my mind. 'There's no one named Burroughs working here. There never has been.'"

Cara and I were sitting in Shadyside Park, the large park that stretches behind the high school and ends at the Conononka River on the edge of town. The park was bleak and empty. The trees were bare. Everything was gray.

I was sitting on a low tree stump. Cara was sitting with her legs crossed on the hard ground, her down jacket zipped up to her chin, her blond hair fluttering in the gusting wind.

We hadn't said anything to each other all the way back from Cranford Industries. I think we were both in total shock.

It was just a little hard to accept the fact that our parents had lied to us, that they didn't work where they said they worked. And that now we had no way to get in touch with them at all.

At first we hadn't believed Mr. Marcus. We were sure he had to be mistaken. But he checked the computer three times. And he called the personnel department to make sure there hadn't been a computer error.

But no. What he had told us was correct. *There's no one named Burroughs working here. There never has been.*

Marcus had offered to help us. He really was very sympathetic. He saw how destroyed Cara and I were. But what could he do?

We practically ran out of the building. We just wanted to get away from there. The parking-lot guard tried to stop us at the exit, but I just bombed right past him and drove away.

And now we sat in the cold park, looking up at the back of the high school, trying to figure out what to do next. Across the grass, two robins pecked at the cold, hard ground. They didn't seem to be having much luck finding lunch. Things were tough all over.

"So what are we going to do?" I asked.

Cara shook her head. "Call the police, I guess."

"I guess."

"Why did they lie to us?" Cara cried, suddenly sounding very emotional.

"I don't know. I haven't a clue. I just don't get it, Cara." I stared at the robins. I didn't want to look at her. I didn't want to get too emotional. I wanted to stay as calm as possible, but I could feel myself starting to lose it.

"Let's think," she said, uncrossing her legs. "Let's try to put together everything we know."

"What for?" I asked gloomily.

"Because maybe we'll think of something. Maybe we can figure it all out."

"Yeah. Sure." What was there to figure out? Our parents lied to us and then they left.

No. That was impossible. I told myself to stop thinking like that. "Okay. Let's put together the pieces," I said.

"What day is it?" Cara asked.

"Oh. You're in great shape," I muttered sarcastically. "It's Wednesday."

"Okay. So yesterday was Tuesday. Mom and Dad left for work in the morning."

"Only we don't know if they left for work because the car was still in the garage," I reminded her. "And we don't know where they work—or even if they *do* work!" I cried, jumping up and walking around in a circle.

"Okay, okay. Try to stay calm." She motioned for me to sit back down, but I didn't feel like it.

"Let's concentrate on what we know," Cara said, leaning back, supporting herself with her hands on the ground. "We know they didn't come home last night."

"Duh."

"Stop being so sarcastic. You always think getting angry and moody is going to solve things. But it never does."

She was right. I apologized.

"Then we found that white monkey head in their bed," she continued. "That's some kind of clue, don't you think?"

"I guess. And don't forget we caught Roger snooping around in Mom and Dad's room."

"He was at the window. What could he have been doing at the window?" she asked.

We both thought hard.

"I know. He could have been signaling to the guy in the van," I said.

Cara nodded. "Maybe. You could be right. And what do we know about the van?"

"Nothing," I said.

"Just that it was parked across from our house most of the night. And you saw Roger sneak out and get into the van."

"That guy in the van with the platinum hair said he didn't know Roger," I said.

"He had to be lying," Cara said. "And don't forget we found a gun hidden in Roger's room. That's a clue, too."

"So we have some clues. But what help are they?" I asked impatiently.

"Will you stop whining?"

"I'm not whining. Get off my case."

"We have to talk to Roger," Cara said, "before we call the police. He *is* our cousin, after all. Maybe he's in some kind of trouble."

"Okay," I agreed. "We'll talk to Roger. Then we'll call the police."

We turned toward the school and saw kids hurrying out of the building. "It must be lunchtime," I said.

"We can go in now and try to call Roger on the pay phone."

We got to the door to the school just as Cory Brooks and his pal David Metcalf were coming out.

"Hey—you guys sleep in today?" Cory asked, grinning.

"Great party last night," Metcalf said. "We gonna do it again tonight?"

"Looks like they had *too much* partying," Cory said. "Look at 'em!"

He and Metcalf laughed. "Later," Metcalf said, and they headed toward the student parking lot.

"Funny guys," I muttered.

We walked through the crowded, noisy corridors to the pay phone by the principal's office. A girl was using it and we had to wait.

"Maybe Mom and Dad are home," Cara said. "Maybe Mom will pick up the phone."

"Maybe fish can talk," I said. She shoved me. I fell into the phone booth, and the girl inside gave me a dirty look.

A few minutes later she came out and I stepped in. I dropped in my quarter and pushed our home number. The phone rang once. Twice. "It's ringing," I told Cara.

"What?" It was so noisy in the hallway, she couldn't hear me.

I didn't know whether the phones at home were fixed or not. Sometimes phones ring normally even though they're out of order. I let it ring eight times. I was about to hang up when I heard a click. Someone had picked up.

"Hello?"

I recognized the voice at once. "Roger?"

"Yeah. Mark? Where are you?"

"In school. The phones are fixed?"

"Yeah. I guess so. We're talking to each other, so they must be fixed."

"That's great. Listen, are my mom and dad home?"

His voice dropped. "No. Not yet,"

"No word from them or anything?"

"No."

"Listen, Roger, we've got to talk. I want to ask you—"

"I've got to run, Mark. I was just on my way out the door. We'll talk later, okay?"

"Okay, but—"

"You and Cara are all right?"

"Yeah, sure, we're fine. But—"

"Good. Talk to you later. Don't worry." And he hung up.

"Well, at least the phones are fixed," I told Cara.

"Let's go get lunch," she said. "I'm starving."

When we got to the lunchroom, Cara wandered off to have lunch with Lisa and Shannon. I looked for Gena, but she wasn't there. She wasn't at our usual meeting place across from the gym, either. And she wasn't in our fifth-period government class, so I figured she must have stayed home.

I hoped she wasn't sick. I really wanted to talk to her.

I daydreamed about her the rest of the afternoon. I guess I was trying to avoid thinking about Mom and Dad. I didn't stop thinking about her. I kept trying to relive last night on the couch, trying to remember how she felt, how she *tasted*. I wondered if I was in love or something. She was such a fox! There were girls I'd daydreamed about at my other schools, but not like this.

I called her as soon as I got home—well, right after checking to see if Mom and Dad were back. They weren't. And Roger wasn't home, either.

I was feeling really down. I planned to go out in the backyard and fire off a whole quiver of arrows after I talked to Gena.

The phone rang and rang. Finally, Gena answered. I could tell by the sound of her voice as she said hello that something was wrong. Her voice was shaky, as if she'd been crying.

"Hi, Gena? It's me. Where were you today? Are you okay?"

And then she started to talk and cry at the same time. She sounded very strange; upset but frightened, too. I had trouble understanding her at first. I guess I didn't *want* to understand her because of what she was saying.

"I don't *believe* this," I said, my heart pounding. I suddenly had a throbbing pain at both temples. "But, come on, Gena—you don't—you're not serious! But why? I mean—I don't *believe* you! *Why are you doing this?*"

CHAPTER 11

I got home about five o'clock. The house was dark. No one seemed to be home.

What a rotten day. It had to be the worst day of my life, and finding the house dark and empty didn't help to lift my spirits any.

If only Mom and Dad would get back. I just felt so strange not talking to them for two whole days. I let out a little cry as the thought flashed through my mind that I might never talk to them again.

Where was Mark, anyway?

I dropped my book bag on the kitchen counter and checked the refrigerator for a message. Nothing. Feeling totally worn out and miserable, I slumped into the living room.

"Hey!"

Someone was sitting in the dark on the couch.

"Only me." It was Mark. He didn't move or look up.

"You scared me to death," I said, feeling my heart pound. "Why are you sitting in the dark?"

He didn't answer.

"What's wrong? What are you doing, Mark?"

Still no reply.

My first thought was that he had gotten bad news about Mom and Dad.

I flicked the light switch. The lamp by the front window lit up. Mark turned away so I couldn't see his face.

"What *is* it?" I screamed. "Is it Mom and Dad? Are they—"

"No," he said, without turning around.

"Have you heard from them?"

"No."

I felt really relieved. I walked over to the couch and stood in front of him.

"Get out of my face," he said, looking down. "Take a walk."

"Mark, what is your problem?"

He took a deep breath and slowly let it out. He looked up at me. I think he'd been crying. I wasn't sure. I don't think I'd seen him cry since he was eight or nine. But his face looked puffy and his eyes were red.

"Are you okay?" I sat down at the other end of the couch.

"Take a walk," he muttered.

"Come on."

He shook his head. "Okay. If I tell you, will you leave me alone? Gena broke up with me."

I wasn't sure I heard right. "She *what?*"

"She broke up with me. Do you understand English? She doesn't want to see me again."

The scene on this same couch the night before flashed into my mind. I saw Gena sitting on Mark's lap. I saw them making out despite the room full of people.

I stared at Mark in disbelief and he turned away again. "Don't look at me like that."

"I'm sorry," I said. I really was. "I don't know what to say."

"Well, don't say anything." Whenever he was upset about something, Mark got angry at the nearest person. I decided if it would make him feel better to yell at me, then let him.

"When did she tell you?"

"I called right after school. She wasn't in school today."

"And she said—"

"She sounded weird. Scared, sort of. I don't know. She didn't sound like herself."

"She said she wanted to break up?"

"She said she couldn't see me anymore."

"Couldn't, or didn't want to?"

He scowled. "Give me a break."

"Well, it's an important difference," I said. "Did she give a reason?"

"No. No reason. Just said not to call her anymore or try to talk to her in school or anything."

"Weird. So what did you say?"

"I went over to her house."

"You did? Just now?"

"Yeah. Right after she told me."

"And what did she say?"

Mark got up quickly and walked to the window. He stood staring out into the graying night, his back to me. "I didn't see her. Her father answered the door."

"And?"

"He was very nice about it. He just said that Gena was very upset, so upset she stayed home from school. I told him I just wanted to talk to her. But he said she didn't want to talk to me."

"So what did you do?"

Mark spun around angrily and scowled at me. "So what *could* I do? I turned around and came home, of course. Then you arrived and started giving me the third degree."

"I did not. I just asked why you were sitting like a statue in a dark room."

"Well, now you know," he said bitterly.

I should've dropped it, but knowing when to shut up isn't one of my better talents. "But it doesn't make any sense. Gena really seemed to like you. I mean, last night—"

"Shut up about last night!" he flared.

"Sorry. I just meant that you two didn't have any kind of fight or disagreement or anything."

"No. Nothing," he agreed, pacing the length of the room. "I've only known her three weeks. We didn't have *time* to fight about anything."

"So why in heaven's name—"

"I don't know. It's a mystery."

"But you and she—"

"I don't want to talk about it anymore." He started pacing faster.

"Mark, I think we should call the police right now," I said.

He stopped pacing and turned around to face me. It was pitch-black outside the window now. Darkness came so early in November. The lamp by the window wasn't bright enough. The dim light it cast over the old furniture just made the room more gloomy. I suddenly felt chilled.

"Yeah, I guess you're right. Sorry I barked at you like that, Cara. I just felt like—like my whole life is crumbling, you know?"

"Yes, I know," I said quietly.

We walked into the kitchen to call the police. I turned on every light we passed. The house was just too creepy in the dark.

"Let me do it," Mark said, picking up the receiver. "Should we just dial nine-one-one?"

"I guess—no, wait." I suddenly remembered the policeman who had come to the door the night before and the card he had given me. Now, where had I put it? I reached into my jeans pocket and found it crumpled up in there.

"What's that?" Mark asked suspiciously.

"That policeman who was here—Captain Farraday. This card has his direct line."

"Good. Maybe you should call." Mark backed away from the phone. I wondered if I looked as worried and upset as he did.

"Are you okay?" I asked. His broad forehead was covered with little drops of perspiration.

"No," he said, frowning. "Why should I be okay?"

I held the little card in one hand and pushed the numbers with the other. He picked up after the first ring. "Police. Farraday speaking."

"Oh. Captain Farraday. Hi."

"Yes. Who's this?" he asked brusquely.

"It's Cara Burroughs. Remember me?"

"Sure, Cara. Of course I remember you. That party isn't still going on, is it?"

"No. I'm . . . uh . . . calling about my parents."

His voice turned serious. "Yes. What about them?"

"Well . . ." I suddenly felt very strange, as if this wasn't really happening. I wasn't really calling the police to report my parents missing, was I? That didn't happen in real life.

"My parents didn't come home last night and they aren't home now."

There was a long silence. "That's strange," he said finally, his voice quieter, sympathetic. "Did they call or anything?"

"No. The phone was broken for a while. But my brother and I haven't heard a word from them."

"I'm writing this down, Cara," he said. "I don't think there's anything to worry about, but I'm getting it down. Have they ever done this before? You know, not come home?"

"A couple of times. Especially when they were starting new jobs. But they always called."

"I see." There was silence while he wrote. "Did you call their office?"

"Well, that's sort of a problem," I said. I told him quickly about our trip this morning to Cranford Industries and what Mr. Marcus had told us.

"This is very strange, isn't it," Farraday said. I could tell he was taking notes. "But I'm sure we can clear it up really fast." His voice was calm and reassuring. I wished I had called him sooner.

"Let me look through some things here," Farraday said. I could hear him shuffling through papers. "I don't have any accident reports." More shuffling. "No serious crime reports, either. So you don't have to think the worst. Nothing terrible has happened to them."

"That's a relief," I said.

Mark grabbed my shoulder. "Does he know where they are?"

I waved him away and shook my head no. "They weren't in an accident or anything," I whispered to Mark.

"I know how it is," Farraday said, still rustling papers. "You start imagining the most horrible things, right?"

"Yeah, I guess," I said. "Do you think we should—"

"Tell you what," he interrupted. I could hear a police radio start to blare in the background. "I'll get some men on this right away. Maybe I'll even send one out to Cranford just to make sure there wasn't some kind of mistake."

"Oh, thank you," I said.

"Shadyside is a pretty small town," Farraday said. "I think we'll locate your parents very soon."

"Will you call me back?" I asked.

"Right. I'll either call or send a patrolman by."

"Thanks, Captain. I really feel better already."

"Well, don't get crazy worrying, you hear? When I catch up with your parents, I'm gonna give 'em a good talking to, tell them they shouldn't be neglecting such good kids."

"Okay, I—"

"But the main thing is not to worry. If something bad had happened, I would've received a report by now."

"Thanks again," I said. "'Bye."

I was about to hang up the receiver when I heard a loud click. I realized immediately what it was.

Roger was upstairs. And he'd been listening in on the attic extension.

I felt a sudden chill. Why didn't he just come downstairs if he wanted to know what was going on?

Why was Roger *spying* on us?

CHAPTER 12

"Roger was spying on us," Cara said, hanging up the phone.

"Huh?"

"You heard me. He was listening m on the upstairs extension."

"Are you sure?"

She didn't answer me. She went running to the front steps. "Hey, Roger! Roger!"

I followed her and heard Roger coming down the attic steps. "Yeah?"

"Why were you spying on us, Roger?" Cara wasn't exactly being subtle.

Roger appeared on the second-floor landing. He looked tired. The front of his sweatshirt had dark stains on it. His usually perfectly slicked-back hair was heading in all directions.

"Hi, Cara. What did you say? I just got home. I was upstairs."

"I know you were upstairs. You were upstairs listening in on my phone conversation," Cara said angrily, glaring up at him.

Roger's eyes bulged in surprise. He ran a hand back through his hair. "What? No. I went up to get changed. I spilled stuff on my sweatshirt and—"

"I heard the click, Roger." Cara wasn't going to let him off the hook. I agreed with her. Roger had been acting too suspicious ever since Mom and Dad disappeared. It was time to confront him.

"Phones click for a lot of reasons," Roger said, not making any move to come down to us. "I wasn't listening in, Cara. I'd never do that."

"Roger, there are some questions Mark and I need to ask you," Cara started.

But Roger interrupted. "Cara, who were you talking to—your mom and dad?"

"No. You know it wasn't," Cara insisted.

"I really wasn't listening in," Roger said, leaning against the banister. "You have no reason to suspect me."

"Yes, we do," I broke in. "I saw you run out last night."

"You mean real late? Right. I told you when I came in. I couldn't sleep. I went for a walk."

"But I saw the van, Roger. I saw you climb into it."

He looked surprised. "Climb into a van? Me? Are you sure, Mark? Are you sure it was me?"

"Well, of course. Who else?" He was starting to get me steamed.

"Are you sure you were fully awake? When I went out for my walk, I did see a van parked outside. But why would I climb into it?"

"That's what we want to know," Cara said angrily.

"And why do you have a gun in your room?" I added.

"Huh?" His mouth dropped open. "A gun?"

"In your bottom desk drawer."

He dropped down onto the top stair. "You searched my room?"

"Well, yes," I said. "But we—"

"You searched my room, and then you accuse *me* of spying?" He sounded really hurt and upset.

"Roger, we—" Cara started.

"Who gave you the right to go through my things?"

"Nobody," I said. "It's just that you've been acting weird lately, so we thought we'd look around."

"I haven't been acting weird. You two have," Roger said, shaking his head. "Of course I can understand why. You're upset about your parents. But sneaking into my room, making crazy accusations, and hallucinating people climbing into vans isn't going to help get your parents back."

"We didn't hallucinate the pistol," I said. "We saw it."

"Yes, I have a pistol," Roger said. "It so happens that that pistol means a lot to me."

"What do you mean?" I asked.

"It belonged to my dad. He was a policeman. He gave it to me on my eighteenth birthday. He told me I should always keep it nearby. He said he hoped I never had to use it, but he wanted me to have it anyway. A few weeks later, he was shot dead in a drug raid." Roger turned away. "That pistol is about the only thing I have left from my dad."

"Look, Roger, I'm sorry that we went in your room," I said.

"Me, too," Cara said quietly.

"No need to apologize," Roger said, climbing to his feet. "It's just that we've got to stick together now. We've got to trust each other. Know what I mean?"

"Yeah," I said.

"We can't panic and start turning on each other. We have to—"

"I called the police," Cara said, interrupting.

"Very good idea," Roger said. "We should've done it sooner." He glanced at his watch. "Oh, I'm late. I've got to run. I'll be back later and we can talk. Okay?"

Cara didn't say anything. She just turned and headed back toward the kitchen.

"Yeah. Later," I said, and gave Roger a little wave. Then I followed Cara.

"He's a very bad liar," Cara whispered after we heard him climb the attic stairs.

"How do you know he's lying?" I asked. "He seems like such a nice guy," I said.

"You think *everyone* is a nice guy," Cara cracked. "But I don't believe his story about the gun. It was just too cornball for words. Also, if he just keeps it as a memento, why was the gun loaded?"

"Cara!" She was always so cynical. I was sure Roger was telling the truth. He looked so sad, thinking about his father.

"Hey, we've got to get some dinner. Is there any food in this house?" Cara asked.

We began to search the kitchen for something to eat. I found a loaf of white bread in the bread drawer that was only a little stale. Cara found a jar of peanut butter on the top shelf of the food cabinet.

She opened the lid and looked inside. "Just enough for two sandwiches if we spread it pretty thin."

"What a feast," I said sarcastically. "At least is there some jelly?"

Cara opened the refrigerator and found a jar of grape jelly. She said something to me, but I didn't hear her. I was thinking about Gena. I kept hearing her voice again and again, hearing her words again as she told me we couldn't see each other again.

What had happened? Why did she do it?

"You didn't hear a word I said." Cara's voice broke into my thoughts.

"You're right," I said glumly.

"Poor Mark," she said. I looked up to see if she was being sarcastic, but she wasn't.

"It's like I've lost everyone at once," I said.

"Don't say that," Cara snapped. "Nobody is lost forever. Stop thinking like that. Just eat your peanut-butter sandwich. You'll feel better if you eat something."

"You sound just like Mom," I told her.

We both sort of stared at each other, then picked up our sandwiches. Peanut butter is such a bad idea when you're upset and not terribly hungry. It sticks to your mouth and teeth, and it takes so much effort to chew. Neither of us was in a mood to work so hard—for so little reward. We sat there glumly, not talking, not looking at each other.

I had only taken a couple of bites when I heard Roger run down the front stairs and then heard the door close behind him. Cara jumped up. "Let's follow him."

"What?"

"Let's follow him. I want to know where he's going."

"No," I said, trying to pull her back into her chair. "That's a bad idea."

"If you won't come, I'll go alone," she said. She pulled out of my grasp and ran toward the front hall.

"But someone has to stay here for when the police call," I said.

"What that means is you want to call Gena," she said, pulling on her down jacket "Well, that, too," I admitted. "But I really don't see the point of—"

"'Bye." And she was out the door.

"What a wild-goose chase," I said aloud to the empty room. Roger was probably going off to a friend's place to study. I figured that Roger had made some friends at college. He'd never mentioned any or brought anyone home with him. And he never talked on the phone that much. But he must have had some friends, at least some people he liked to study with.

Why did Cara decide to play detective? I guess it was better than sitting around this creepy old house waiting for the phone to ring.

Just as I had that thought, the phone rang.

"Hello," I said, expecting to hear the police captain Cara had spoken to.

"Mark? It's me. I—"

It took me a while to recognize Gena's voice. She sounded terribly frightened.

"Gena? What's going on?"

"I can't talk now. I have to tell you . . . It's very important that—
you have to—"

"Gena? Gena?"

It sounded like some kind of struggle. I thought I heard her cry
out. Then I heard a click.

"Gena? Gena? Are you still there?" I cried.

The dial tone buzzed in my ear.

CHAPTER 13

The most direct way to Gena's house was through the Fear Street woods. Sure, the kids at school had told me all these scary stories about the Fear Street woods. But I didn't care. I had to get there as fast as possible.

I put on my down jacket and pulled a flashlight off the shelf in the front closet. I knew that if I went straight through the woods behind our house, I'd eventually come out in Gena's backyard.

We had kidded around a few times about how sometime I'd sneak out some night, go through the woods, and climb the rose trellis at the back of her house up to her bedroom window. Now here I was about to do just that. But this wasn't kidding around.

Gena had sounded truly terrified. There was something she wanted to tell me. And it sounded to me like someone else didn't want her to say it.

Was she in some kind of real danger? Or was my imagination going wild? I had no choice. I had to find out.

I pushed open the screen door and stepped outside. I was surprised by how cold it was. I could see my breath, gray steam against the black sky.

I headed quickly around the side of the house to the back. The ground was crunchy beneath my sneakers. There had been a heavy dew and I guess it had frozen on the ground. It was a windless night. Everything seemed very still, so still it was almost unreal. It was silent except for my sneakers crunching over the hard, frozen ground.

Our backyard slopes steeply down for a while before it levels off. Once I got down the hill, I started jogging until I reached the woods. I knew if I just kept going straight for a while, I'd see some lights from houses on the other side of the woods, and then I could make my way to Gena's backyard.

The trick, of course, was to keep going perfectly straight. It wasn't easy in these woods. There was no path, of course, and sometimes thick clumps of trees or high weeds would block your way and force you to veer one way or the other.

It seemed to grow colder as I stepped into the woods. I had to slow down. The dead leaves that blanketed the ground were up over my ankles, wet and slick. I kept stumbling over small rocks and upraised roots hidden by the leaves.

The flashlight flickered and grew dimmer. I shook it, but it didn't help. The light had gone from white to yellow, and it was so dim, I could barely see two feet in front of me.

Something scampered past my feet. My heart skipped a beat. I saw the leaves move as if they were jumping out of the way.

"Whoa," I said aloud.

So, big deal. So there were animals running around in the woods. Big surprise. I forced my heart to stop pounding like that, pushed some tall reeds out of my way, and kept walking.

I suddenly remembered a story about the Fear Street woods a guy named Arnie Tobin had told me at school. It was about these five teenagers who went camping out in the woods, sort of on a dare. Everyone bet them they could never spend the whole night in the Fear Street woods, and they bet they could.

So that night they set up two tents and built a campfire and were about to cook supper. The next thing anyone knew, these five teenagers came running out of the woods, knocking on doors of houses, terrified out of their skulls.

They said some kind of monster had attacked the camp. None of them could really describe it. They said it looked sort of like a guinea pig or white rat—only a hundred times bigger! They said it was bigger than a full-grown horse!

They were five terrified kids, Tobin told me, but most people didn't believe them. The cops came to take them home. And *they* didn't believe them, either.

The next day, the five teenagers went back to the campsite with their parents to retrieve all their stuff. And *finally* someone believed them! Because when they got to the camp, everyone could see that one of the canvas tents had been gnawed to bits. All of the food had been eaten—even the unopened cans of beans. It seems the creature—whatever it was—had chewed right through the cans!

Whoa!

I wished I hadn't suddenly remembered that story. Now, every rustle, every crack of a twig made me spin around, expecting to see a giant rat lumbering toward me, its enormous teeth bared, ready to chew me to pieces like a tin can.

I stopped and listened. Silence.

I raised the flashlight, shook it, trying to get more light from it, and shone it through a clump of low shrubs ahead of me. Nothing moved.

The silence was too eerie. I wished a dog would bark or an owl would hoot—anything. I suddenly felt as if I were walking on the moon or on a distant, uninhabited planet.

And then I realized that I had completely lost my sense of direction.

Which way was Gena's house? Was I still heading in the right direction? Which way was my house?

I turned off the flashlight. It was no use to me now, and I decided

I'd better save the batteries. I waited for my eyes to adjust to the darkness. Then I slowly turned, peering into the distance, looking for a light, any light.

There was only darkness.

I'm lost, I thought.

But just as I thought that and a cold shudder ran down my back, the trees seemed to light up. I looked up to see that the moon had emerged from a bank of rolling clouds. I stared at it gratefully. I had been walking with the moon on my right when I entered the woods. Now if I kept it on my right, I would be going in the same direction.

I began to feel good again. Well, not good. Let's say that I got some of my confidence back. I tried the flashlight. It had completely died. I moved forward, guided only by the moon.

I was moving pretty quickly, jogging over the blanket of wet leaves. It's amazing how well you can see at night in the woods. I never realized that human eyes were so good in the dark.

That's what I was thinking about when I heard the footsteps behind me.

I knew at once that they were footsteps. And I knew at once that they weren't mine. It was so still, so airless, so silent in the woods, that I could hear every sound.

I stopped and listened, suddenly feeling very afraid. The footsteps were moving quickly, growing closer. My legs suddenly felt weak and wobbly. I tried to figure out if it was a four-legged creature or a two-legged creature running toward me. But it was impossible to tell.

I saw the giant white rat again in my mind. What kind of footsteps would that creature make as it scurried after its prey?

Prey?

Somehow I shook off my fear and started running. I made sure to keep the moon on my right so I wouldn't get completely turned around.

Even though I was running as fast as I could now, keeping my arms in front of my face to shield myself from low tree limbs, the footsteps grew closer. Whoever—or whatever—was pursuing me was closing the gap.

I thought of turning and stopping, facing whoever it was. But I quickly decided that was stupid.

I started to run again—and cried out as my feet went out from under me. Suddenly I was sliding down, down, off balance, out of control. *"Help!"* I cried as I fell.

I realized at once that I had fallen into some kind of a trap.

CHAPTER 14

Roger seemed to be walking toward town. He took long strides and never looked back. I had to hurry to keep him in sight. It was a very dark night. The streetlights on Fear Street were out, as usual, and the moon had disappeared behind a heavy cloud bank.

Wisps of fog felt wet and cold against my face as I moved silently, staying against the hedges and shrubs that lined the street. I wished he would slow down just a little. But the fact that he was in such a hurry made me even more suspicious.

He turned left on Mill Road and picked up his pace. A car went by, its headlights glaring into my eyes nearly blinding me for a few seconds. I ducked behind a low evergreen and waited for the yellow spots to disappear.

When I walked back onto the road, he had gotten even farther ahead. I started to jog. I didn't want to lose him in the darkness. The ground was hard and wet. My sneakers moved silently. The only sounds were the rush of wind from the north and the occasional low rumble of a passing car.

Roger turned onto Hawthorne Drive and looked from side to side. I dived for the ground and crawled behind a mailbox, hoping that he hadn't spotted me. When I looked up, I saw nothing but dark trees. He was gone.

I climbed to my feet quickly and crept forward. There was a

small coffee shop called Alma's on Hawthorne, where a lot of local college kids sat around studying and drinking coffee till all hours. I wondered if he was headed there.

As I drew closer, his tall, loping form came into view again. Yes, he was heading into Alma's. But why? He definitely didn't plan to study. He wasn't carrying any books.

He was probably just meeting a friend. And I was out here on this cold, wet night, walking around in the dark, wasting my time.

Well, Mark would have a good laugh at my expense. I pictured Mark, sitting at home, waiting for Captain Farraday to call. My poor brother. He was already in an emotional state because of Mom and Dad. Gena's breaking up with him had really sent him over the edge.

I probably should've stayed home with him. But it was too late now.

After Roger entered Alma's, I waited a few minutes. Then I walked up to the window and peered inside. It wasn't very crowded. Only a few booths were filled, the usual college students and a few solitary old people nursing steaming white mugs of coffee.

I couldn't see Roger. I figured he must be sitting way in the back or in one of the side booths by the counter. Should I go in?

I'd come this far. I decided what the heck, I might as well just take a peek and see what Roger was up to.

I pulled my jacket hood up to hide my face and stepped into the coffee shop. It was very warm inside and smelled of bacon and frying grease. I kept my head down inside the hood and walked slowly toward the row of booths. Ducking down behind the wall of the first booth, I poked my head around the side and looked for Roger.

He was sitting in the last booth in the back of the restaurant. He was busily talking and gesturing with his hands. I had to take a few steps closer to see whom he was talking to.

It was the man with the white-blond hair, the man from the

van. They were both talking very excitedly. Both of them looked upset. The man from the van kept slapping his hand on the table as he talked.

So Roger *was* lying, I thought. This little trip of mine hadn't been a waste of time, after all. He had lied about the van, and he must have been lying about the gun. Roger and this white-haired guy were working together to—to do what?

Whatever it was, I knew it had something to do with Mom and Dad.

I leaned against the back of the booth and watched as Roger took a piece of paper out of his pocket and started drawing something on it. He was drawing and pointing to parts of the drawing. What was it? A map?

I would've done anything to see what it was. But I knew I couldn't go any closer without being seen. I turned to see a waitress glaring at me from behind the counter. I guess I must have looked pretty suspicious.

I decided to get out of there. I had seen enough to prove that Roger was a liar and that we had to tell Captain Farraday about him as quickly as possible.

Holding my hood up, I turned and started to leave when a hand grabbed my shoulder. A voice called, "Hey, Cara!"

"Ouch!" I cried out more in surprise than pain. But the hand dug into my shoulder as if trying to pin me there in place.

I spun around to see who it was. It was Roger.

"Spying on me again?" he asked, not loosening his grip on my shoulder. His eyes burned into mine.

He's dangerous, I thought.

I never realized it. I never even seriously considered it. But he's dangerous.

"Ouch. You're hurting me, Roger," I said. My hood fell back on my shoulders. Great disguise!

He let go of my shoulder, but his expression didn't change. "Sorry. I didn't mean to."

Yes, he did. Of course he meant to.

I looked past him to his companion back in the booth, who was studying me, a tight-lipped frown on his pale, white face.

To my surprise, Roger suddenly smiled, as if he had regained control of his anger. He saw me staring at his friend. He took my elbow and led me back to the booth. "Oh . . . uh . . . Cara, this is Dr. Murdoch," Roger said, sliding back into the booth. "He's my . . . faculty advisor."

Yeah, right. Sure, Roger. And I'm the Queen of England.

"Nice to meet you," I said, not even pretending to mean it.

"Dr." Murdoch gave me a wide, phony grin.

"We were just meeting about my major," Roger added. What a rotten liar! He saw me looking at the piece of paper he'd been writing on, and folded it in half. His eyes turned cold again. "So what are you doing here?"

"I'm . . . meeting a friend here." My story wasn't any worse than his. "But it looks like she's not coming," I quickly added. "See you later."

"Nice to meet you," the so-called Dr. Murdoch called after me as I ran down the aisle and out of the restaurant.

I didn't breathe until I was out the door and outside. I bumped into two guys coming in, and they both laughed as I continued to run down the street.

It felt even colder out. A fine, misty rain was falling. I pulled my hood up, this time for warmth. My heart was pounding. I felt like such an idiot.

Oh, well. The first thing I was going to do, I decided, when I got home was to run up to Roger's room, take that pistol out of his desk, and hide it somewhere.

Roger frightened me. The idea that he had a loaded pistol right in my house was even more frightening. Anyway, I had proven that Roger was a liar. And so was his friend Murdoch. . . . He told Mark and me he didn't even know Roger!

I suddenly felt very afraid. I started to jog toward home. But I wouldn't be safe there either, I realized. My parents were gone. And Mark and I shared the house with a liar who had a gun.

Feeling chilled through and through, I started to jog faster. If only Mark and I knew somebody in town, had some relatives, had some place to go . . .

I was about two blocks from home when I realized there was a car following me.

CHAPTER 15

Okay, okay, Mark. Cool it, man.

Take a deep breath and cool it.

It was a very crude trap. Just a deep pit covered over with leaves. The hole wasn't more than six feet deep and ten or twelve feet wide.

You can handle it. You don't have to panic. You're not trapped here forever. You can pull yourself out. Just reach up with your arms and hoist yourself up. You can do it.

Go ahead. Take another deep breath. Then get back up on your feet and get moving again.

That's how I talked myself calm. That's how I got my heart to stop pounding like the drums on a Def Leppard record and got myself standing up.

But as soon as I pulled myself out of the pit and stood up, still unsteady, still a little panicked, I wished I hadn't. Because the creature that had been following me came charging at me.

It was so dark I couldn't see what it was.

I just heard it running toward me, felt its powerful forelegs hit my chest, heard a low growl, and inhaled its hot, sour breath as I fell back into the pit.

"*Help!*"

I don't know why I screamed. There was no one around.

I was flat on my back. With another low growl, the creature jumped down on top of me. It wrapped its jaws around my left wrist and started to clamp down.

Despite my terror, I began to think more clearly. I realized I was wrestling with a large dog, some sort of shepherd.

"Down, boy! *Down!* Go home!"

I didn't recognize my voice. It was the voice of a terrified child.

It was certainly high enough for dogs to hear. But this dog chose not to listen. I pulled my wrist from his grasp, spun away, and crawled from the animal to the corner of the pit.

The creature circled toward me now, keeping its head down, its growl a low, menacing rumble.

It's the biggest dog I've ever seen, I thought, backing away as it circled. What is it doing out here? Is it a wild dog?

And am I its dinner?

No. It wasn't wild. I could see that it was wearing a collar. Something was hanging from the collar under the dog's chin.

"Down, boy. Good dog. Good dog."

It lowered its head and pulled back its lips to reveal a mouthful of teeth. The teeth, long and pointed, seemed to gleam in the moonlight. And I knew I'd never forget them.

"Good dog. Good dog. Go home, boy."

I was muttering those words over and over like an idiot. This dog couldn't go home. This dog *was* home. The Fear Street woods were his home. And he was about to show me how good he was at protecting his home.

Never let a dog see that you're afraid of him. For some reason those words from my dad flashed through my mind. That may have been the dumbest thing my dad ever said to me!

How do you let the dog know you're not afraid of him when you're frozen on your knees in a pit, trembling all over, squeaking in a high-pitched voice for him to go home like a nice doggy?

I didn't have time to think about that for long. The dog uttered a loud groan and leapt at my face. I ducked. I could feel his weight as he slid over my back, yipping in surprise.

He landed hard, but was back on his feet immediately.

Again he lunged for me. I fell backward, out of his way.

I tried scrambling up the side of the hole, but fell back, landing on the dog's back. He roared out his unhappiness and tried to struggle out from under me, but I grabbed his head under the chin and started to pull up.

His fur was hot and wet. I inhaled the most powerful dog smell I'd ever smelled. It clogged my nose.

I held my breath. I thought I was going to be sick.

The dog started twisting and turning, trying to get out of my grip. But I held on with both hands, hugging the dog tighter and tighter, squeezing its middle as I pulled its head back.

Its growl turned into a howl of pain, but I didn't let go. I was losing my hold. My hands were slipping off the wet fur. I exhaled and took a deep breath, inhaling the heavy, repulsive odor.

The dog gave a hard tug. I stumbled forward, digging my knee into its back, pulling up its head, pulling, pulling with all the strength I had left.

Suddenly I heard a loud crack.

Startled, I let go and fell backward against the dirt wall of the pit.

I had broken its neck.

The dog stopped howling.

It stared at me in silence, a look of surprise, a look of pain. Then its eyes closed, and it slumped to the ground with a thud.

I stared down at it, gasping for breath. I wiped my forehead with my hand. I was covered in sweat—cold, cold sweat. I could smell the disgusting dog smell on my hand.

Then for a long time I just stood there, leaning against the side of the hole, staring at the dead dog. I kept hearing that horrifying crack again and again. And I saw the surprised look on the dog's face, that look of pain, of total defeat.

I bent down to make sure the dog was dead. Holding my breath, I rolled the big creature onto its back—and saw the object that was attached to the front of its collar.

It was a white monkey head.

I gasped in surprise.

This didn't make any sense. I grabbed the monkey head and held it in my hand to make sure I wasn't seeing things! What was the same object I had found in my parents' bedroom doing around the neck of a dog in the middle of the Fear Street woods?

Then something else caught my eye. Part of a chain leash was still attached to the collar. I followed the chain to the end and discovered a broken link. The dog had obviously broken its leash.

As I climbed out of the pit, I saw a wooden stake just a few yards away. I walked over to it and, sure enough, the other part of the chain leash was attached to the stake.

So the dog had originally been placed near the trap. It must have broken away a little while before I came on the scene. It saw me approaching its spot and chased after me.

Chased after me without barking.

It had obviously been trained to sneak up on people, to attack quietly.

Someone wanted to keep people away from this part of the woods. But why?

All of my muscles ached. I shivered. I'll never feel normal again, I thought.

Looking around, trying to clear my head, I suddenly realized I was on the edge of a large, round clearing. The moon was right overhead now, shining brightly, so brightly I could see dozens of shoe prints in the soft dirt.

It looked as if a lot of people had been here recently.

Obviously the trap and the attack dog were here to keep people out of this clearing. But why?

"I've got to get away from here," I said aloud, feeling chilled and frightened.

I knew there were houses at the edge of the woods. But, standing here I felt far away from civilization. Take a few steps into these woods and anything can happen, I thought. This is a different world, a world without any rules.

I had to do something to stop these grim thoughts.

Gena. Remember Gena. I reminded myself to think about Gena, about how upset she had sounded on the phone.

I suddenly remembered what I was doing out here. I had to get to Gena's. I had to talk with her, find out why our phone conversation had been cut off. I had to make things right with her again.

I thought about Cara, out somewhere following Roger. What a crazy idea! I wondered if she was home yet. I wondered if Mom and Dad had come home, or if the policeman had any news for us.

"I'll call her from Gena's," I said aloud.

I walked a bit, my legs unsteady at first. Eventually I began to feel stronger. I saw a light through the trees, a pale gray-green light, shimmering like a firefly between two trees.

A house. I began running toward the light, ignoring the thorns and tall, spiny weeds and upraised tree roots that tried to slow me down.

A few moments later, I was standing at the edge of Gena's backyard. It wasn't far from the mysterious clearing, I realized. Trying to catch my breath, I stared up at the dim light behind the shade of her bedroom window.

Was she up there? I couldn't tell. The lights were on in the den downstairs, and I could see the flickering glow from the TV screen. Someone walked past the window. It was Gena's dad. I moved closer, being careful to stay in the dark shadows by the side of the big garage.

Her dad was standing in front of the TV, sipping from a can. I watched him walk back to the couch and sit down. Then I looked up at Gena's room again.

Could I really do this? My eyes followed the tall, wooden rose trellis down from just under Gena's second-story window to the ground. Of course the roses were all gone, but the long, thorny vines remained.

I walked quickly over to the trellis and took hold of it. It seemed sturdy enough. It would probably hold my weight.

I grabbed its sides with my hands, careful to avoid the thick, thorny vines, and put a foot on the bottom slat. I leaned over and peered into the den window just to make sure Gena's father was still on the couch in the den. He was.

So I started to climb. One step at a time. The trellis shook a little, but it was sturdier than it looked.

I was about a third of the way up when my hand slipped, and I started to fall.

CHAPTER 16

As I continued to jog home, I heard the car approach. The head-lights lit up the street in front of me. I slowed down and waited for the car to pass me.

But it didn't pass.

Mark was right. I never should have gone out of the house tonight. I started running faster and the car started moving faster, too.

What was going on? I turned around but couldn't see beyond the bright yellow headlights.

I didn't know what to do. Why wasn't the car passing me? If it was someone I knew, why didn't they catch up to me? Or honk or something?

I decided to turn and run back the other way, past the car. In the time it would take the car to turn around, I figured, I could get away.

So I spun around and, shielding my eyes from the headlights, started to run at full speed. The car squealed to a stop.

"Cara! Hey, stop! Cara!"

It was a familiar voice.

I stopped. A man climbed out from the driver's side.

I recognized the big blue Caprice. Then I recognized Captain Farraday.

"Captain Farraday! Hi!" I cried, so relieved.

"I wasn't sure if it was you or not," he said, walking up to me quickly, his boots clicking on the pavement. "Hope I didn't frighten you. I was on my way to your house."

"Do you have any news about my parents?"

The streetlight was reflected in his deep blue eyes. He looked very tired. He shook his head. "No. Not yet. I was wondering if you heard anything."

"No," I said, sighing.

"Hey, don't look like that," he said, putting a gloved hand on the shoulder of my jacket. "We don't have any *bad* news, right?"

"Right," I muttered. "But we don't have any good news, either."

He led me toward the car. "You have to keep thinking good thoughts," he said. "My men are on the case. Your parents will turn up soon."

I didn't say anything. I couldn't hide my disappointment.

"I need to get a photo of them from you," he said. "I'll put out an APB, get a copy of it to every police department in the state. Can you think of anything else, any kind of clue or information that might be at all helpful to me?" He was so tall, he leaned his head down when he talked to me.

"Well . . . let me think . . ." I said.

"Why don't I give you a lift home and you can think about it on the way? And you can give me that photo. My men are all on the case. I also alerted the newspaper. Sometimes people phone in tips to them."

He held the front door open and I slid in. I'd never been in a police car before. I was a little disappointed to see that the Caprice wasn't a police car at all. It was just a regular car. The radio suddenly came to life and spit out a burst of static and then a brief message. It was a police radio, the only evidence that this was a police car.

As he drove me home, I told Farraday about Roger, about Roger's pistol, and Murdoch and the gray van. I expected him to say something, but he kept his eyes straight ahead on the road and didn't react at all.

"Do you think Roger might know something about my parents?" I asked finally.

"Maybe. I'll have to check out this Roger and—what did you say the other guy's name was?"

"Roger called him Dr. Murdoch."

"I'll check him out, too. Anything else, Cara? Anything else at all that might be helpful to us?"

We pulled up the drive. The house was dark. I was annoyed that Mark hadn't turned the porch light on for me.

"I can't think of anything. Nothing at all," I told Farraday. I opened the door and started to get out. "Oh, yeah. Wait. There *is* one other thing."

He turned to look at me. "Yes?"

"Mark and I found this strange thing in my parents' bedroom. It was a little monkey head; a little white monkey head with rhinestone eyes. Do you think that could be a clue?"

Again he didn't react. "Maybe," he said quietly. "It doesn't ring any bell with me, but maybe it means something. I'll ask around at the station. Do you have it? It might be a good idea to get it to the lab. They can do a check on it."

I ran into the house. I didn't see Mark. I hurried upstairs and pulled a fairly recent photo of my parents out of the album they keep in their bed table. Then I searched around for the white monkey head. I couldn't find it. I'd have to ask Mark what he did with it.

Back outside, I handed Farraday the photograph. "Thanks for the lift," I said glumly. "And for all your help."

"Get some sleep," he said. "I know it's hard, but it'll help."

"I'll try," I said.

"You'll hear from me as soon as I know anything at all. And,

Cara—you've got my number. Call me anytime, day or night. Call me for any reason, hear?"

"Thanks," I said. "That makes me feel a lot better."

"I'm glad," he said, and a smile almost broke out beneath his bushy mustache.

I hurried into the house, closed the door behind me, locked it, and called, "Mark! Mark, where are you?"

No answer.

"Mark, are you upstairs?" I shouted.

Still no answer.

I searched the living room and den and then went upstairs to see if he had gone to bed. He wasn't home.

Returning to the living room, I was overcome with a feeling of dread. First Mom and Dad disappeared. Now Mark. Was he gone, too?

Maybe he left a note. I ran into the kitchen and checked the refrigerator. No. I checked the pad by the telephone. No note.

Now Mark is missing, I thought.

No. He probably went over to Gena's. That's right. Of course he did.

I picked up the phone receiver. I was going to call Gena's house to talk to him. But then I thought better of it. Mark wouldn't want his little sister calling at Gena's to check up on him. Besides, I had no news for him about Mom and Dad, no news at all.

I decided to go into the den and watch TV until Mark got home. Maybe it would take my mind off everything.

I was crossing the living room when I saw the lights climbing up the wall—twin spotlights moving slowly. It took me a while to realize they were car headlights.

Someone had pulled into the driveway.

Was it Mark? Was it Mom and Dad?

CHAPTER 17

I knew I was going down. I grabbed frantically at the trellis but my hand caught a thorny vine. As I dropped, the big thorns cut through my left palm.

I didn't have time to cry out. I landed hard on my back. It knocked the wind out of me. I thought I was dead. There's no worse feeling in the world. You can't breathe. You know you're never going to breathe again. I must've passed out or something. I'm not sure. Everything became bright red and then yellow, blindingly bright yellow.

I don't know how long I was lying there on the ground, probably not as long as it seemed to me. The bright colors faded away. Then I realized I was breathing again.

My left hand throbbed with pain. I held it up close to my face to examine it. The thorns had cut two deep lines down the center of my palm. My hand was bleeding pretty badly, the blood seeping out in two straight lines.

I looked up to the top of the trellis. The light was still on in Gena's room. I decided I had to try the climb again. Once inside, Gena could find something I could wrap my hand in to stop the bleeding.

Gena was so close. I wanted to see her. I *had* to see her. I thought about her long, black hair, about her smile, about the way she felt sitting on my lap on the couch with her warm arms around me, and I pulled myself up the trellis, slowly at first, then more quickly as I gained confidence.

Gena's bedroom window was a foot above the trellis. It was closed. I couldn't tell whether it was locked or not. I tapped on the glass and waited for her to come to the window.

The trellis creaked under my weight. Suddenly I wasn't so sure it could hold me.

Where was Gena?

I tapped again on the window, this time a little louder. No response.

I leaned forward, reached up, and pushed the window with all my strength. It didn't budge.

I was trapped. I couldn't get into the house. And any second, the trellis was going to fall and take me down with it.

Taking a deep breath, I reached up and pushed with both hands against the window frame. This time the window slid up a few inches. What a relief! It wasn't locked.

A few seconds later, I scrambled headfirst into Gena's bedroom. It wasn't exactly a romantic entrance, but at least I'd made it—and the trellis was still standing.

"Gena?" I whispered.

I looked around the room, which was lit by a single lamp on Gena's dresser. She wasn't there. In fact, it looked as if she hadn't been there at all.

The bed was made. Her stuffed-animal collection was lined up along the wall over the bed. Her backpack was hung over the back of her desk chair. Her desk was totally neat, some papers and pencils stacked up in a corner. The carpet looked as if it had just been vacuumed that day. You know the way rugs stand up after they've been vacuumed. The only footprints I could see in the rug were mine.

I crept over to the closet door, which had hundreds of photos taped to it from top to bottom. There were snapshots of Gena and her dad; of her mother, who lived outside Detroit; snapshots of people I didn't recognize; and lots of photos of her favorite movie stars cut out of magazines. I was pleased to see that the photo I had given her, my class photo from last year, was taped up right above the doorknob, right between Dennis Quaid and Tom Cruise.

Suddenly feeling tired, I sat down on the edge of her bed, careful not to rest my bleeding hand on the white bedspread. Where was she? If she wasn't here, why was the light on?

It's pretty late. She'll probably be up soon, I told myself. I decided I'd just wait for her.

But I quickly decided that was stupid. I couldn't just sit there. For one thing, I had to do something to stop my hand from bleeding.

I got up and walked over to her dresser. I pulled open the top drawer. It was filled with underwear and socks and stuff. I pulled out a long, white wool knee sock and wrapped it around and around my hand. Gena won't mind, I thought.

But where was she?

When she'd called she sounded so upset, so completely freaked. She couldn't be sitting downstairs watching TV with her dad now.

Holding the sock tightly around my hand, I walked back over to the closet door and pulled it open. It was the neatest closet I'd ever seen. All of her clothes were hung up. Her sweaters were folded neatly on the top shelf. I had no idea she was such a neat freak.

I closed the closet and was heading back toward the bed when something caught my eye. There was something shiny down on the rug at the foot of the bed.

I kicked it out from under the bed with the toe of my sneaker, then bent down to pick it up. I carried it over to the lamp on the dresser and examined it.

I couldn't believe it. It was a carved white monkey head.

It was identical to the others. The rhinestone eyes sparkled and seemed to peer out at me. The monkey's mouth was pulled back in an eerie grin.

What was this thing? And why was it popping up everywhere I went?

Suddenly I had a chilling thought. Was this the *same* monkey head?

Had it somehow followed me?

I remembered waking up and finding the monkey head beside my bed when I had no memory of carrying it to my room. Was I holding the same monkey head now, staring into the same blank, glowing eyes?

Don't be a dork, Mark. You've been watching too many old *Twilight Zones*.

I didn't have any more time to think about it. I heard footsteps in the hall. They were approaching quickly.

I tucked the monkey head into my jeans pocket and looked around for a place to hide. But there wasn't any.

The footsteps were right outside the bedroom door.

"Gena?" I whispered happily.

And her father stepped into the room.

My eyes dropped from his startled face to the small, silver pistol in his hand.

CHAPTER 18

"Mark!" he cried. He tossed the pistol onto the bed. "I could've shot you! I—I thought you were a burglar!"

"Sorry." The word choked in my throat.

Dr. Rawlings was a big man—so big he blocked the entire doorway. He was dressed in a gray-and-white running suit. It must have been the biggest size they made! He had black hair like Gena's, only it had thinned back, giving him a high forehead above his bushy black eyebrows.

He was very muscular, too. Big biceps. He looked as if he worked out. I'd never noticed that till now, as I stared back at him, watching the look on his face change from anger to confusion.

I'm in trouble now, I thought. But how much trouble?

He took a couple of steps toward me. For an instant, I thought he was going to fight me. It's crazy the things you think when you're in total panic.

Then I realized he was staring at the white sock wrapped around my hand. Blood had soaked through in several places. It looked really gross. I lowered my hand to my side.

"Mark . . . I feel so bad," he said. "The gun. Good heavens! You should have told me you were here."

"Dr. Rawlings, I—" I just stopped. I didn't know what to say. I mean, what can you say? "I'm sorry. I didn't mean to frighten you. I wanted to talk to Gena, and—"

"What happened to your hand?" he asked. He had a very deep voice. It was usually booming. He talked very loudly and shouted a lot, not from anger but from enthusiasm. But now he was talking so softly, I could barely hear him. He was really freaked that he'd almost shot me.

I reluctantly held up my injured hand. "I cut it," I said. "Listen, I want to explain. I—"

"You came to see Gena?" Dr. Rawlings sat down heavily on her bed. The mattress was soft and sagged nearly to the floor under his weight. He picked up the pistol, then put it down again.

"Well, yeah. She called and—"

He shifted his weight on the bed. "Gena's very upset, Mark," he said, looking up at the ceiling. "I told you that when you were here earlier."

"I know. I'm upset, too," I said. That was the truth, for sure.

"Ah, young love," Dr. Rawlings sighed, and shook his head. He stood up quickly. He moved like a much lighter man. "Sorry, Mark. I don't mean to be facetious. I know this is serious for you and Gena. But even so, you shouldn't have sneaked in."

"I know. I'm really sorry. Uh . . . where is Gena, anyway?" I asked, pulling the sock tighter around my aching hand.

"She went to her cousin's. She was so upset, she thought it might be a good idea to go away."

"Her cousin's? The one upstate?"

He nodded.

"She went without her book bag?" It just happened to catch my eye. I was so confused at this point, I don't think I really knew *what* I was saying.

Dr. Rawlings chuckled. "I *told* you she was very upset. I don't think her book bag was the first thing on her mind." He walked over and put a big, beefy hand on my shoulder. "Want me to take a look at that hand? I am a doctor, after all."

I pulled the hand away. "No. No, thanks. It's not really serious. I'll bandage it up when I get home." I suddenly just wanted to get out of there, to get home and think this all through.

I looked to the window. It was still wide open. Mr. Rawlings was looking at it, too. Now he knew how I got inside. If he didn't know already.

I felt really embarrassed. I had broken into his house and he was being so nice about it.

"Come on downstairs and go out the door this time," he said, guiding me to the bedroom door with his hand on my shoulder.

"I'm really sorry," I said. "I shouldn't have—"

He squeezed my shoulder, probably a little harder than he realized. "Don't apologize. It's okay. I understand these things. I'm sorry, too. I'm sorry about you and Gena. She's very unpredictable sometimes. I hope I didn't frighten you with that gun."

"You're not going to tell my parents or anything?"

My parents. I had forgotten about them. And about Cara. What time was it? She had probably gotten back a while ago—and I hadn't left her a note!

"No. Not this time," he said, leading the way down the stairs. Then he added, "I'm looking forward to meeting your parents sometime."

I apologized again to Dr. Rawlings and stepped out into the cold. "Take care, Mark," he said softly. He reached out, took my hand, and shook it.

"Thank you," I said. I didn't know what else to say. I felt really awkward.

I turned and walked quickly down the drive. My hand throbbed. The white sock was soaked with blood. This time, I decided, I would definitely take the *front* way home!

CHAPTER 19

Who had pulled up the drive? I tore across the living room, took a deep breath, and pulled open the front door. "Oh."

"Thanks a lot, Cara. Some greeting," Lisa Blume said.

"Sorry," I said quickly, still unable to hide my disappointment.

"Who were you expecting? Tom Cruise?" Lisa asked, giving me her customary half-sneer as she stepped into the front hallway.

"No. It's just that—well . . . come in," I said. "I'm really glad to see you."

"Yeah. I can tell," she said sarcastically. "Listen, I thought maybe we could go over our history notes together. But if this is a bad time . . ."

"It's a bad time," I said, deciding to tell Lisa what was going on. "But I'm glad you're here, anyway." I led her into the den. She plopped down on the couch and tossed her backpack on the floor.

We're a strange pair of friends, I thought, watching her lean down to open her backpack and pull out a notebook. We look like two different species. I'm so blond and immature looking, and she has that great, curly black hair and that sly, knowing smile. She looks a lot like Cher, I thought. I really was glad she had stopped by. I needed the company, and she was always funny and sarcastic—just what I needed to take my mind off everything.

"What's with your brother and Gena Rawlings?" Lisa asked,

rolling her big, dark eyes. "I couldn't believe them in your living room last night. They didn't even take a *breath!*"

"Well, you're not going to believe *this*, either," I said. "She broke up with him tonight."

Lisa's mouth froze in an O of surprise. "Huh?" she finally managed to say. "Run that by me again, Cara."

"You heard me. She broke up with him."

"But . . . why?"

I shrugged my shoulders. "Mark is in bad shape," I said. "Don't tell him I told you. He went running over there. At least, that's where I think he is."

Lisa pulled at one of her long, black curls. "Weird. Just plain weird."

"Yeah, I know. Mark didn't have a clue."

"Weird," Lisa repeated. She sat there for a while, staring at me thoughtfully. Then she said, "Was Mark chewing gum that night?"

"You mean at the party?"

"Yeah."

"Well, how would I know? What on earth are you talking about, Lisa?"

"Well, I was just thinking about this girl I used to know. Her name was Shana and she went with a guy named Rick for a short time. And I don't know what made me think of it, but I just remembered that Shana told me about this time she was making out with Rick, and Rick was chewing gum, only Shana didn't know it, and somehow the gum ended up in Shana's mouth."

"Yuck."

"Yeah. That's what Shana thought. So she broke up with him and never said another word to him."

"Great story, Lisa," I said, picking up her sarcasm the way anyone did after being around her for a few minutes.

"Well, that's why I was wondering if Mark was chewing gum," Lisa said.

"I've got bigger problems than Mark's love life," I said, sighing.

"Yeah. You've got your *own* love life!" Lisa cracked.

"No, I'm serious," I said.

"So am I."

"My parents are missing," I blurted out.

Lisa didn't react at all. "Go ahead. Next tell me you're growing a second head," she said, staring at me. "I'll believe that, too."

"No. Really, Lisa."

I think she saw by the look on my face that I wasn't kidding. She propped her head up with one hand and stared at me. "They're missing? You mean they didn't come home tonight?"

"Or last night."

"They didn't call?"

I shook my head.

Suddenly all of the humor left Lisa's face. It was as if a mask had been pulled away and her serious, real face was revealed for the first time. "Did you call the police?"

"Yes. Captain Farraday."

"But he hasn't found them?"

I shook my head. I suddenly felt sick. I had thought that telling Lisa what was happening would make me feel better, but instead, saying it all aloud was making me feel more afraid.

"Do you want to come stay at my place?" Lisa asked. She looked really upset, too.

"No, thanks," I told her. "Mark is—"

"He could come, too. There's plenty of room. Really."

This was so nice of her. I'd only known Lisa for a short while, after all. It wasn't like we were lifelong buddies or anything.

I thanked her again and told her I thought Mark and I would be more comfortable waiting here. Where *was* Mark, anyway? I looked at my watch. It was getting late. I wondered if he'd made up with Gena. If so, he might not be home for quite a while.

I heard a car outside and started to get up. But it drove past without slowing down. Chill out, Cara, I scolded myself. You can't start jumping out of your chair every time a car drives by.

Lisa was looking more upset than me. "They've done this before," I told her, trying to get the grim look off her face.

"Really? They've left for two days without calling?"

"No, not without calling." I stood up. "I'll get my history notes. Let's try to study."

She looked very uncomfortable. "You sure?"

"Yeah. Be good to take my mind off things. Stop me from staring at the clock all night."

She followed me into the living room, where I'd left my backpack. "You know, I think Gary Brandt likes you," she said.

"Huh?"

"Yeah. That's what I heard."

"From who?" I asked. I found my notebook and pulled it out of the bag. Papers fell all over the rug, but I didn't bother to stuff them back in.

"He told a friend of mine that he'd like to go out with you. He's a fox, don't you think?"

"Gary?"

"Yeah. Gary."

"He's okay." For some reason I didn't want to reveal how pleased I was by this news. Gary was a pretty neat guy. "Maybe if my parents don't come back, we'll have another party," I cracked.

Lisa laughed, but it was a halfhearted laugh.

"Not funny, huh?" I squeezed past her and headed back to the den. "Just trying to keep it light."

"If—if my parents just disappeared, I'd *freak*!" Lisa said.

"I'll probably freak after they come back," I told her, plopping down on the leather couch. *If they come back*, I added to myself, and shuddered.

What if I'm an orphan? I thought. What if I'm already an orphan and just don't know it yet?

Who would Mark and I go to live with? Aunt Dorothy? No. She was much too old. Grandma Edna? No. She was too old, too. And she couldn't stand us.

Do teenagers have to go live in an orphanage? I wondered.

"What are you thinking?" Lisa asked.

"Just stupid thoughts," I replied, forcing a smile.

We tried going over our history notes for a while, but I was too distracted to think clearly. I kept looking up at the clock, wondering why Mark wasn't back, and jumping up from the couch every time a car drove past.

Finally, we decided that studying just wasn't in the cards. We talked a little more about kids at school. Then Lisa left, telling me again that Mark and I could come stay at her house, and asking me to call as soon as I heard any news.

I felt pretty good for a while after she'd left. I'd made a real friend.

I looked at the clock. It was past eleven. Where was Mark?

I sat down in the living room. What a drab, disgusting room. I got up and started to pace. I walked into the den and gathered up my history notes. I shoved them into my notebook. I started to the kitchen to get another soda—and stopped halfway across the living room.

Roger's gun.

How could I have forgotten my plan? I was going to go upstairs and take it out of his desk and hide it somewhere. I wanted Roger out of our house. But I knew that might take some doing. In the meantime, I didn't want him to have a loaded pistol.

I ran up the stairs and stopped at the landing under the attic. "Roger—are you up there?"

He's always so quiet, he could've come in while Lisa and I were talking. There was no reply. I called again, and again no reply.

So I climbed the narrow stairs and let myself into his room.

I fumbled around until I found the switch on his desk lamp, and clicked it on. The room was empty. Roger had tossed a shirt and a pair of chinos on the cot. Everything else looked the same.

I bent down quickly and pulled out the bottom desk drawer.

A creak.

Was that a footstep? Was that Roger returning?

I stopped and listened. Another creak. It was just this stupid old house making noises.

Still listening for any sounds outside the tiny room, I lifted out the underwear from the bottom drawer. Then I reached for the small pistol.

My hand couldn't find it, so I leaned over and looked into the drawer.

Then I let out a little gasp as I realized the pistol was gone.

CHAPTER 20

Thursday went by in a blur. Mark and I were too tired and too lost in our own thoughts to say hardly anything over breakfast. Somehow we got ourselves to school. My body was there, but my mind was in a million other places.

After school, we drove home together. Mark glumly told me about what had happened to him in the woods, about the trap near the clearing and the dog that had been trained to attack silently.

"I—I killed it, I think," Mark said. I could see that he was still badly shaken. Then he told me about Gena's dad, how he had almost shot Mark.

As we drove, I told Mark about Roger and Murdoch at the coffee shop, and about the gun being missing from Roger's drawer.

"We've got to tell Farraday about Roger," Mark said, pulling up the drive. "After last night, Roger knows that we're suspicious of him. That could make him even more dangerous."

"I already told Farraday," I said.

We pulled into the drive. "Call Farraday again," Mark said, sounding a little desperate. "See if he's done anything."

I ran into the house to call Farraday. I saw Mark heading out to the backyard. I knew what he was going to do—shoot arrows into the target until his arm was tired.

I threw down my books and crept to the front stairs. I went

halfway up, listening for any sounds that might reveal that Roger was home. Finally, I decided to take a more direct approach. "Roger—are you up there?" I shouted.

No reply. Feeling relieved, I went to the kitchen phone to call Captain Farraday.

I slammed the phone down in disgust when I realized that it was dead again. "Mark, the stupid phone is out again!" I shouted through the kitchen window.

He didn't hear me. Or at least he pretended not to hear me. He fired off another arrow, then another, staring intently, never taking his eyes from the target.

A few minutes later, I went out back. Mark was just firing off the last arrow in the quiver. "Feel better?" I asked.

"No," he replied, frowning.

We drove to the mall and shared a pizza for dinner. Neither of us felt much like talking. Afterward, we glumly stepped out into the cold, blustery night. The air was heavy and wet. It felt as if it might snow.

We were halfway home when I remembered something that changed *everything*.

"Wally," I said.

Mark, driving with one hand, kept his eyes on the road. "Huh? What did you say?"

"Wally."

He looked annoyed. "That's what I thought you said. Is there more to that sentence?"

"I don't know his last name," I said, my mind desperately searching for it. I was excited. I knew I had just remembered something very important. Now, if I could just calm down enough to think clearly and remember . . .

"Wally who? You mean on *Leave It to Beaver*?" Mark turned onto Fear Street, and it suddenly became much darker. The streetlights were still out.

"No. I mean Mom and Dad's friend. Wally Wilburn!"

Even in the pitch black I could see Mark's mouth drop open. "From work! That guy who called a lot and invited them to go bowling. You're right, Cara! Wally Wilburn. That's his name."

He roared up the drive and stopped with a loud squeal. "We'll get their phone book. I'll bet they wrote his phone number in their phone book."

We both slammed car doors and went running into the house. "This guy Wally—he can *prove* they worked at Cranford Industries," I said. "And once we've proven that, we can . . ." I stopped. I didn't know *what* the next step would be.

"Let's just talk to Wally," Mark said.

We ran into the kitchen, and Mark grabbed the little phone book. "Let's see. . . ." Mark squinted up his face. His finger moved down the ruled pages of the little phone book. "Here it is. Wally Wilburn."

"Where does he live?"

Mark's face fell. "Just a phone number. No address."

I picked up the phone. Still dead. "No problem," I said. "Let's find the area phone book. His address is bound to be in there."

"Unless he has an unlisted number," Mark said dejectedly.

"Mr. Pessimist. You sure give up easily," I said, pulling the big phone directory off the shelf and turning to the back. It only took me a few seconds to find the listing for W. Wilburn. "He lives at Two Thirty-one Plum Ridge."

"Where's that? Never heard of it."

I had to laugh. "Mark, you'd make a lousy detective."

"I never said I wanted to be a detective," he grumbled.

I found the area map in the front of the book. Plum Ridge Road was in the next town, about halfway between our house and Cranford Industries. "Come on. Let's go." I pulled him to the back door. "I know how to find it."

"Wally Wilburn," he muttered, shaking his head. "Maybe Wally will help clear up this whole mystery."

It was about a twenty-minute drive to Waynesbridge, the next town. When we reached the outskirts, endless, depressing housing developments of identical, boxlike houses stretching over low hills, I turned off the car radio and began to read street signs.

"What are we going to say to this guy?" Mark asked, suddenly sounding worried.

"Well, I don't think we should come right out and tell him our parents have been missing for three days," I said. "We should let him tell us what he knows first. If we come on too strong, we might scare him or something."

"Yeah. That's smart," Mark agreed.

"Let me do the talking," I said.

He nodded.

"Plum Ridge," I said, reading the sign. "That was easy. Turn right."

"Can you read the numbers?" Mark asked, slowing down nearly to a stop.

"Yeah. They're above the front doors. Keep going. It should be in the next block."

Sure enough, the Wilburn house was on the next corner. There was a Ford Mustang in the drive, so we parked on the street and walked up the narrow concrete walk. The air smelled of fresh dirt and fertilizer.

I could hear voices and music from a TV as we stepped onto the front stoop. I knocked loudly, then found the doorbell and rang it. The TV voices stopped abruptly and I heard footsteps, and then the front door was pulled open by a middle-aged man.

"What are you selling?" he asked. He had a pleasant voice and a very friendly smile beneath a bushy black mustache. He was nearly bald, I saw, except for a thick fringe of black hair around his ears.

"Mr. Wilburn?" I asked, suddenly wondering just what I was going to say.

"You've come to the right place. That just happens to be me. But most folks call me Wally. And who might you be? I haven't seen you around the neighborhood."

"No. We live in Shadyside," Mark said, sounding nervous.

I thought we'd agreed that I would do the talking. I hoped Mark wasn't going to blow it now.

"Well, you've come pretty far to sell raffle tickets." Wally chuckled. He seemed to find himself very amusing.

"No. We're not selling anything. I'm Cara Burroughs, and this is my brother, Mark."

"Burroughs?" He recognized the name immediately. He pushed open the storm door. "Are you Greg and Lucy's kids?"

Mark and I both nodded.

"Well, how are your parents? Where are they? I haven't seen them at work this week."

"You haven't?" Mark blurted out.

"No. They needed me in the C division, so I've been down in the subbasement all week. Haven't picked my head up once. Do your parents miss me?"

Mark and I didn't know how to answer. So I plunged ahead and changed the subject. "We were visiting a friend near here," I said, trying to make it sound believable, "and we stopped here to use your phone, if we could. We forgot to call Mom and Dad. I think they're still at work."

"At this hour?" Wally looked at his watch. "Fanatics." He chuckled. "Good people. But fanatics."

A very thin woman with wavy blond hair walked into the room, surprised to see visitors. She wore faded jeans and a black-and-red Grateful Dead T-shirt. "Hi, hon. These are Greg and Lucy's kids," Wally said. "This is my better half, Margie."

"Nice to meet you," Mark and I said in unison. We both looked at each other uneasily.

"Well, hi," Margie said, giving us a warm smile. "Did you bring your parents?"

"No. They just stopped by to call them," Wally told her.

"Do you have their direct line?" I asked him. "Mark and I haven't memorized it yet."

"No problem." Wally bounced over to a side table and pawed quickly through a stack of magazines and papers. "I work at home sometimes, so I brought a company directory home. Here you go."

He pulled out a stapled directory with a bright yellow cover. I looked quickly at the front. It read: CRANFORD INDUSTRIES PHONE DIRECTORY.

I hoped the Wilburns didn't notice how my hands were trembling as I found the Bs and then searched for my parents' names. There they were, followed by their phone extension.

So. The guy at Cranford, Mr. Marcus, had lied to us. Our parents *did* work at Cranford, just as they had told us. The proof was in our hands. Now we could go to Captain Farraday and tell him to get the truth out of the Marcus character.

I held the book up and showed the listing to Mark, who was standing beside me with his mouth hanging open. I debated whether or not to ask Wally to let us borrow the directory. But I decided that might arouse his suspicions. Besides, we had seen it. And the book was always here if Farraday needed to see it, too.

"Well, thank you very much," I said, handing the directory back and then heading to the door.

"Yeah, thanks," Mark repeated. We were both eager to get out of there.

"Uh . . . aren't you forgetting something?" Wally asked, looking very amused. We both looked at him blankly. "The phone call. You were going to make a phone call."

"Oh. Right!" How embarrassing.

We went through the motions. I dialed my parents' direct line and let it ring several times. "No answer. They must be on their way home," I told Wally.

It took us a few more minutes of thank-yous and nice-to-meet-yous to get out the door. "He must think we're pretty weird," Mark said, sliding behind the steering wheel.

"I don't care," I said. "We just proved that our parents didn't lie to us. They did work at Cranford."

"Did that receptionist at Cranford lie to us?"

"No," I said. "Mom and Dad's names definitely weren't on her computer screen. It only takes a second to delete a name from a computer file. But that big shot Marcus *did* lie."

"Why would he do that?" Mark asked, pulling away from the curb.

"I don't know. But the police will help us find out," I said, feeling very excited about our detective work. "Let's go find Captain Farraday. We've got a lot to tell him!"

The twenty-minute drive back to Shadyside seemed to take forever. Back on the Mill Road, Mark suddenly turned down Fear Street. "Let's go home just for a second," he said. "Maybe Farraday left a message on the answering machine or something."

"Sure. Good idea," I agreed.

"Oh, no. Cara, look—"

I followed Mark's eyes. The gray van was parked a block from our house.

"It's back," Mark said, speeding past it. I couldn't see if Murdoch was inside it or not.

We pulled up the drive. "That's strange," I said. "Some of the upstairs lights are on. I didn't turn those on."

"Neither did I," Mark said warily. "Let's see what's going on. Maybe it's Roger."

We crept in through the back door. I closed it quietly behind us. Then we walked to the front steps. "Hey, Roger? You home?" I called.

We climbed the stairs. The lights up to the attic had been turned on. "Hey, Roger! You up there?"

Silence.

"Did he turn on all the lights and then leave?" Mark asked.

"He's never done that before," I said. "Let's go upstairs and check out his room."

I led the way. The stairs groaned and squeaked loudly beneath us. "Roger? Roger?"

The light was on in his room. The door was half-open. It was about twenty degrees warmer up here. I pushed the door open wider and walked in. Since I was the first one in the room, I was the first one to see Roger.

I wanted to scream, but no sound came out of my mouth.

I thought I was going to faint. Everything went white for a second or two. Then the colors returned.

And there was Roger sitting at his desk, slumped forward, his head facedown, his arms hanging at his sides, hands down on the floor. An arrow was stuck in his back just below his neck. His shirt was soaked with dark red blood.

I took a step to the side so that Mark could get into the small room. My sneakers squished on the carpet. I looked down to see why. Roger's blood had soaked the rug. I was standing in it.

"Oh, no! I don't believe it!" Mark cried. He put an arm around my shoulder, more to hold himself up than to comfort me. My legs were trembling. My heart was pounding like crazy.

There were arrows scattered across the blood-soaked rug.

"He—he's dead," Mark cried. "But why?"

Suddenly, the door to the room swung in, bumping Mark and me hard. Farraday stepped in front of us. He had been hiding behind the door the whole time.

"Oh!" I cried out.

Farraday was holding Mark's bow. He blocked the doorway and glared at Mark accusingly. "This your weapon, son?" he growled. "Why'd you kill him?"

CHAPTER 21

I stared at Cara and my mind just went blank. At first I thought maybe Farraday was kidding.

But when he didn't take his eyes off my face, just stared at me, holding up my bow like that, I realized he was serious. He was accusing me of killing Roger!

"Now, wait a minute—" I started. My knees felt weak. The tiny room was tilting, first one way then the other. I looked down. My sneakers were soaked with Roger's blood.

Farraday put a hand on my shoulder. "Don't say anything, son. First I have to read you your rights."

I saw his lips moving, but I couldn't hear a word he said. I guess I was in some kind of shock.

"Mark didn't kill Roger!" Cara's angry voice burst into my thoughts. "That's crazy!"

"She's right!" I cried, finally finding my voice. "I didn't kill him. No way! Why would I kill him?"

Farraday kept his hand on my shoulder. He tossed down the bow. "Easy now. Take it easy," he said softly. He started to guide me out of the room. "Let's all just stay calm. A murder has been committed here." He stared at Cara as if trying to read some answers in her eyes. "A murder has been committed with Mark's weapon, and—"

"It's not a weapon!" I cried. I didn't recognize my own voice. It sounded so frightened, so strained.

"Let's go downstairs. We'll sit down and discuss this calmly," Farraday said. He kept his hand on my shoulder as if guiding me, and followed us down the stairs.

I can't describe what I was thinking as I entered the living room. My thoughts were just a wild jumble. Nothing made any sense. Was Roger really dead? Was he killed by my bow and arrow? Who would have done it? Were they trying to make it look as if I did it?

Cara and I were about to sit down on the couch when we saw the living-room door swing open. Murdoch burst in, a pistol in his hand.

He stared in surprise at Farraday. "Who the hell are you?" he cried. "Everybody against the wall! Move!" He was waving his pistol.

"That's him!" Cara screamed. "That's the one who was meeting with Roger!"

Farraday drew a pistol and fired three shots. All three of them hit Murdoch in the chest. His eyes rolled up, he uttered a voiceless cry, and his knees buckled. He fell face forward onto the hallway tiles.

"Oh no, oh no, oh no!" Cara covered her face with her hands.

Farraday moved forward quickly and put a comforting arm around her shoulder. "It's okay now," he said softly. "It's okay now."

I was feeling pretty weird. The floor seemed to tilt and roll. Two dead men. Two. Right in our house. Two people killed. The blood . . . so much blood . . .

Before I realized it, Farraday had an arm around me, too. He was leading Cara and me back to the living-room couch. "It's okay now," he kept repeating softly.

Cara and I sat on opposite ends of the couch. Cara still covered her face. I looked up at Farraday. The room was still tilting crazily. I kept hearing the gunshots again and again, kept seeing Murdoch let out that silent cry and tumble down to the floor.

"You two sit still and get yourselves together," Farraday said softly. He scratched the side of his face, then replaced the pistol in his holster.

He walked back over to Murdoch, rolled him over onto his back, squatted down low beside the body, and stared into his face. "So you saw this guy with Roger?" he asked.

"Yes," Cara said, looking down at the floor. "I saw them together."

"Now maybe we can start to piece this all together and find out what they did to your parents," Farraday said. He groaned loudly as he climbed to his feet.

He picked up the phone on the desk. "I'm just going to call for backups," he said. "My guys'll be here before you know it. They'll clean everything up. Don't move. Just take deep breaths and try to get calm. I didn't figure you for a killer, son."

He walked over to the phone on the desk and dialed the police station. "Yeah, Schmidt. It's me. I'm on Fear Street. Right. Burroughs. Need some help here. I've got two down. Too late for the ambulance. Yeah. Yeah. Bring 'em. And tell 'em to step on it, okay? Right."

He replaced the receiver and walked back over to us. He looked eight feet tall standing right above us. Cara was sitting with her hands tightly knotted in her lap. I was just trying to keep the room steady.

"You kids have been through a bad time," Farraday said, looking down at us. "But the worst is over. I think we're going to get to the bottom of things now. How are you feeling?"

"Pretty bad," Cara said. "I've never seen anyone . . . dead before."

I got up unsteadily, holding on to the side of the couch.

"Where are you going, Mark?" Farraday asked, helping me up.

"Just into the kitchen. My mouth is so dry. I just want to get a drink of water."

"Yeah. Bring me one, too," Cara said.

"Okay, go ahead," Farraday said. "But get back here. I still have a lot of questions to ask you two."

As I headed to the kitchen, I saw Farraday go over to the front window and look out. "What's keeping my guys?" I heard him ask.

I walked into the kitchen and was crossing to the sink when I noticed something that sent an icy chill down my back. I stopped. I stared at it. I blinked, trying to change it. But it wouldn't change.

My eyes *weren't* playing tricks on me. The wall phone receiver— it was off the hook.

I picked it up and held it to my ear. Silence. I replaced it, then picked it up again.

Silence.

The phone was dead. Still dead.

Farraday had only pretended to call the police station.

CHAPTER 22

So Farraday was a fake, probably not even a policeman at all.

He hadn't called for backups. He had us all alone here now.

He had killed Murdoch right before our eyes. Had he killed Roger, too? Did he plan to do the same to us?

What did he want? Who *was* he?

What was going on?

My head was spinning with all of these questions.

I replaced the receiver and stood there staring at the phone. Dead, dead, dead.

I had to find a way to warn Cara. I had to let her know that Farraday wasn't who he said he was. He was a fake. A very dangerous fake.

"Hey, Mark, where are you?" Farraday called.

I thought of running out the back door, going for help.

But before I could make a move, Farraday appeared in the kitchen. "Did you get your drink?"

"No. I . . . uh . . ."

I poured a glass of water, took a few sips, then carried the rest for Cara. Farraday guided me gently back to the couch.

Cara took the glass gratefully. I stared at her, rolled my eyes toward Farraday. I had to find a way to tell her, had to find a way to make her understand the danger we were in.

"Uh . . . could Cara and I talk together for a moment in the kitchen?" I asked, trying to sound innocent.

Farraday's nostrils flared slightly, as if he were sensing danger. "No, I don't think that will be necessary," he said calmly, smiling at us. He sat down on a low hassock across from us. "We have so much to talk about."

Cara gave me a funny look. I stared back at her. But she didn't understand.

"Let me just ask you both a few questions," Farraday said softly. He gave Cara a reassuring smile. "I'm sure we can prove that Mark had nothing to do with the young man's death upstairs. As soon as we can get some IDs on this man"—he looked back at Murdoch—"and the one upstairs, I think we'll be able to get on the trail of the real killer."

I tried to get Cara's attention, but she was staring at Farraday. "Who are they?" she asked. "Do you think they know where Mom and Dad are?"

Farraday shrugged. "We'll find out."

"What were *you* doing here?" I asked. I wanted to show Cara that I was suspicious of Farraday. I *had* to let her know that he was a phony. But how?

"I came to talk to you two," Farraday said, scratching his cheek. "I saw lights on upstairs. It looked suspicious, so I went up to investigate. I found the young man—Roger—with the arrow in his back. Then I heard voices approaching, so I hid behind the door."

He seemed so calm, so professional, so nice. I rolled my eyes at Cara. I made a face at her. She didn't see me.

"Now, you've both been through a terrible shock. Do you think you can answer just a few quick questions for me?"

"Yes, I think so," Cara said softly, clasping her hands tightly in her lap.

How could I get her attention? How could I let her know what I'd discovered?

"Where were you two just before you came home?" Farraday asked, looking to the window as if wondering where his men were, the men he had never really called.

"We went to see a man who knew our parents," Cara told him.

"Cara—no!" I shouted. *"Don't tell him anything!"*

Suddenly I realized I had no choice. I had gone too far. I had to take some kind of action. I took a deep breath and lunged at Farraday. I pushed him hard and he fell over backward off the hassock. "Hey!" he cried out angrily.

"Mark! What are you *doing*?" I heard Cara scream.

I leapt on Farraday and reached for his gun, but he twisted out from under me. He shoved me away and jumped to his feet.

The gun was in his hand. "Smooth move, ace," he said, pointing the gun at me. "But not smooth enough. Get back on that couch."

"Mark! What on *earth*!" Cara cried, looking at me as if I were crazy.

All of the friendliness had dropped from Farraday's face. He stared down at us coldly, pointing the gun at us. "So you *do* know things you haven't told me. I think it's time for you to start talking."

Cara's mouth dropped open in shock. "What?"

"I think you heard me," Farraday snapped. "Let's start with the big question. Where are your parents? Tell me now and we will avoid a lot of trouble."

"But we don't know where they are!" Cara screamed. I put a hand on her shoulder to calm her.

"I'm through playing games with you two," Farraday said, and sighed. "Can't you see that I mean business? I've killed two people in your house tonight. Do you really think I wouldn't kill two more?"

"You—you're not a policeman?" Cara stammered.

"Sure I'm a cop," Farraday said bitterly. He stood up. "At least, I *was* a cop. I *was* a cop for sixteen years. But your parents—"

"What about our parents?" I demanded.

"That's my question," he said impatiently. "I've traveled a long way to find your parents. I've waited a long time to pay them a visit." He stood right above us now. "Where are they?"

"We don't know," I said.

"Why did you kill Roger?" Cara demanded.

"He was snooping around too much. I figured I had you fooled, but I wasn't sure about him. So I sneaked in and let him have it." He stared down at Mark. "Nice of you to leave me a weapon right nearby. A weapon that could never be traced to me. He never turned around, never knew what hit him." Farraday shrugged. "No big deal."

He pulled his pistol. "I've fooled around with you two long enough. Who's going to tell me where your parents are?"

"Mark is telling the truth. We don't know," Cara cried.

"I don't believe you. Sorry." Farraday pointed the pistol at Cara's head. "Know something? I'll bet if I shoot one of you, the other one will suddenly remember where your parents are. Shall we try it?"

"No!" Cara screamed.

Farraday moved the gun toward me. "One of you is going to tell me."

"But our parents are missing!" I cried. "We don't know where they are!"

"Which one of you should I shoot?" Farraday asked. "It's too bad, but you're leaving me no choice. I have to shoot one of you."

He moved the pistol back and forth, first pointing it at Cara, then at me.

"I think I'll shoot Mark," he said.

"No!" Cara shouted. "We don't know! Really!"

"Good-bye, Mark." He lowered the pistol toward my head.

I closed my eyes and waited.

One second. Two seconds. Three seconds.

How much would it hurt? Would I really feel it? Would I know when I was hit?

Four seconds. Five seconds. Six seconds.

He didn't shoot. I opened my eyes.

He slowly lowered his pistol.

I felt so dizzy. I was gasping for breath. I looked up, trying to focus.

Farraday was no longer looking at me. He was looking behind me. He looked very unhappy.

"Drop the pistol," a voice called behind us.

I spun around to see who it was.

"Gena!"

Her black hair was all disheveled. There were stains on her blue sweatshirt. Her cheeks were red and puffy, and her eyes looked swollen, as if she'd been crying.

She had an enormous hunting rifle propped against her shoulder. It was aimed at Farraday.

"Who are you? What are you doing here?" Farraday cried, lowering his gun but not dropping it.

Gena ignored him. "Come on, Mark, Cara. We've got to hurry. The meeting is starting. There's no time to waste."

"Meeting?"

"Stay where you are!" Farraday screamed. He started to raise his pistol.

Gena fired the rifle. The blast blew a hole in the wall behind Farraday. He cried out and dropped his gun. He suddenly looked very pale.

"I'll shoot you. I don't care," Gena warned him. The rifle looked as big as she was. She steadied it on her shoulder. "Don't look so shocked," she told me. "My dad took me hunting for the first time when I was four."

"Gena! Where were you?" I asked.

"There's no time to talk," Gena said. She gestured with the rifle. "What are we going to do with him? We've got to hurry!"

"Why don't we lock him in the garage?" Cara suggested, jumping up. "The garage door has a really good lock on it."

It seemed like a good idea. Gena kept the hunting rifle in Farraday's back as we pushed him outside and then into the garage.

I was surprised to see that it had been snowing. The ground was already covered with white, and it was still coming down, soft, wet flakes.

"You'll regret this," Farraday said. I pulled the door shut and then locked him inside.

"Come on, get your coats! We may already be too late!" Gena cried, lowering the rifle.

A few seconds later, we were hurrying across our backyard, slipping over the powdery snow. "We'll head through the woods," Gena said. She started running, ignoring the slipperiness of the ground.

Cara and I had to run to catch up. "Where've you been? What happened?" I asked.

"At my cousin's," she replied, her breath coming out in small, white puffs of steam. We were in the woods now, and the wind was howling, making the trees bend and crack. "My dad wanted me out of the way. But I hitchhiked back."

"Hitchhiked?" Cara cried.

"I really can't explain. Let's just run. I hope . . . I hope we can talk later."

"But . . . where are we going? I have to know!"

"It's your parents!" she cried. "We have to get there because . . ." I couldn't hear the rest of it. She had picked up her pace and her words were lost in the wind. I looked back at Cara, who was having trouble keeping up.

The wind was so cold. My face felt raw and frozen already. I remembered running through these woods last night on my way to Gena's. Was it last night? I flashed back on the trap I had fallen in, on the huge dog that attacked me near the clearing, the desperate fight. I remembered the sound of its neck cracking, the confused look it gave me as it slumped silently to the ground.

Now, the soft snow didn't make these woods any less terrifying. I knew there could be more attack dogs here, ready to pounce. And worse evils; much worse evils.

What kind of evil were we heading to? What was the meeting Gena was in such a hurry to get to?

I ran until I thought my lungs would burst. Then we walked quickly, pushing the low tree limbs and tall, snow-covered weeds out of our way. "I—I'm too tired," Cara cried. "I don't think I—"

"*Sshhh*," Gena whispered. "We're almost there."

Up ahead I suddenly saw small yellow lights, moving in and out through the trees. At first I thought they were fireflies, but of course there are no fireflies in winter. "Candles!" I exclaimed out loud.

Again, Gena signaled for quiet. "Don't let them hear you," she whispered.

"But where are we?" Cara asked.

I recognized it. We were near the round clearing, the clearing where I had seen all those footprints. And now it was filled with people carrying candles.

"The meeting hasn't started yet. We're in time," Gena whispered.

"What meeting?" I insisted. Again she ignored me.

"Follow me. My house is just beyond those trees. I know where my dad keeps some robes."

Robes?

Candles and robes?

"Whoa," I said, and held her back by the arm. "I'm not going another step until you tell me what's going on."

She put her hand over mine. Despite the cold, her hand was burning hot. "Mark, please . . . Don't you want to get your parents back?"

CHAPTER 23

I could feel the danger like shock waves in the air. I guess having it so nearby renewed my energy. Running through the woods, so wet, so cold, I told Mark and Gena I didn't think I could make it. I was just too exhausted—and too frightened, I'll admit.

But seeing the dots of yellow light through the trees, then seeing the hooded figures carrying the candles made me forget how awful I felt.

We were careful not to get too close. But I could see them clearly through the trees. They were milling about in the clearing, about two dozen people. They were all wearing dark monk's robes, their faces hidden in the shadows of their hoods. They each carried a long, black candle.

Were my mom and dad there?

Gena motioned for us to stay silent.

We kept low, walking around the circular clearing, following her, our wet sneakers making no sound on the soft, powdery snow. I could hear soft music. It sounded like a flute, maybe a recorder.

"When the music stops, the meeting will begin," Gena whispered.

She led us into a neighbor's backyard. We ducked down low behind a fence and walked quickly past the house to the front yard.

"The robes are down in my basement," Gena whispered, even

though no one was near. "We were stupid. We should've brought that man's pistol. We left it in your living room."

Gena led us toward the side of her house. We pressed against the dark side of the house, then slipped into a side door and down to the basement. I could hear voices upstairs, laughter. And I could hear the recorder music, much fainter now, but still playing.

The basement was fully finished. There was a large rec room and several smaller rooms. One of the smaller rooms seemed to be filled to the ceiling with stacks of rifles. Gena led us to a corner closet and pulled us inside before turning on the light. It was empty except for a pile of brown robes against the wall.

Suddenly she grabbed Mark's arm and looked up at him, her face filled with pain, with fear. "I knew my dad was in the Brotherhood," she said. "But I never knew they killed people."

Brotherhood?

Killed people?

"When I found out what the Brotherhood planned to do, Dad made me call you and break up with you," Gena told Mark. "Then he forced me to go to my cousin's, upstate. He didn't want me to interfere. He doesn't believe in killing. But he's too afraid to stop it."

"But I don't understand," I whispered. "What about our parents? Are they—"

"*Shhh.*" We heard footsteps on the basement stairs. "We've got to get out of here." Gena grabbed up three robes from the pile. "Quick. Put this on."

We scrambled into the robes. They were heavier than they looked. They smelled of mothballs and sweat.

"Keep your face hidden under the hood," Gena said, pulling the hood over her head and tightening the belt robe. "Just try to follow what they're doing."

"The rifle—" I said, pointing.

"I—I don't see how I can sneak it out," Gena said. She buried it under the pile of robes. "They'll see it and then it'll all be over. We'll have to think of something else. Come on!"

Now what? I thought. Why are we sneaking into this meeting? What are we going to do?

We walked quickly out of the closet, just as two men stepped down into the basement. I was careful to keep my face away from them as we passed.

"Evening," one of them said pleasantly.

We didn't reply.

We walked quickly across Gena's backyard, and then through the woods to the clearing. The snow had stopped. It was clear and cold. There was no light except for the small dots of candlelight.

I stayed close to Mark. I didn't want to lose sight of him. It would be so easy to get confused since everyone looked alike. Everyone seemed to be milling around, being social. I didn't get close enough to anyone to hear what they were talking about.

I was terribly frightened. My legs didn't want to cooperate, but I forced myself to keep walking, to keep moving along the edge of the group.

Suddenly Gena thrust a lighted candle in my hand. The candle was narrow and black. I tried to hold it steady, but my hand was trembling. I hoped no one would notice.

Suddenly, the music stopped. I still couldn't see where it was coming from.

The hooded figures became silent. They began walking into the woods. The Fear Street woods.

How long had these Brotherhood meetings taken place in these woods? How many stories of terror had been created by these Brotherhood members? What did they plan to do tonight?

I tried to force myself to stop asking all these questions, but it was impossible.

The wind blew my hood back. I quickly reached up and pulled it down over my forehead.

"Line up," Gena whispered.

I grabbed Mark's hand. It was ice-cold. I didn't want to get separated. The hooded figures seemed to be forming two lines as they moved toward the edge of the clearing. When everyone was in line, they stopped moving. Now everyone turned in and began to form a circle.

The candles bobbed and flickered. Now they formed a perfect circle of light.

Two hooded figures stepped into the center of the circle. They were holding their candles up close to their faces, and I gasped as I realized they were wearing masks.

White monkey masks—grinning white monkey masks.

They looked just like the tiny white monkey head that Mark and I had found in Mom and Dad's bed.

A third figure, his face hidden in the darkness of his hood, stepped forward.

All was silent. The wind had stopped. No one murmured or said a word.

The man stepped up to the two masked figures. He placed a hand on each mask. And then with one sudden movement, ripped off the white monkey masks.

In the flickering candlelight, I recognized my mom and dad at once.

I looked at Mark. He saw them, too. And I knew that he realized at the same time I did that Mom and Dad must be the leaders of the Brotherhood!

CHAPTER 24

It had to be a dream, just a bad dream. The snow. The dark woods. The people in their brown robes and hoods. The black candles. The circle of tiny lights. And then my mom and dad in the middle of the circle, wearing white monkey masks.

I looked at Cara. Her face had no expression on it at all. It was too much to register. It was too impossible, too weird, too unreal.

Is this why Mom and Dad had abandoned us? To come to the woods and lead this weird cult?

When they said they had club meetings on Thursday nights, were they actually out here in their robes and masks doing—doing what?

What did they do? Were they *witches*, or something?

I thought of all the moving we'd done; a new place, a new house every year or so. My parents must have been moving to start new cult chapters. They weren't computer installers. That was just a cover-up for their real jobs—cult leaders!

I thought I was going to be sick. Our lives had all been a lie. Our parents had lied to us about everything. And then they had left us without a word, abandoned us for the Brotherhood!

I looked back at Cara. She was staring straight ahead; so much fear in her eyes, so much horror.

What was going to happen to us? Why had Gena brought us here?

What were we supposed to *do*?

Suddenly the circle of hooded figures moved in closer. So Gena, Cara, and I moved closer, too.

I realized there was a large, flat tree stump near the center of the circle. The hooded figure who had ripped the masks off my parents led them to the tree stump.

A gust of cold wind came up and blew his hood off. I saw his short, dark hair and heavy, black glasses. I recognized him immediately. It was Mr. Marcus, the big cheese at Cranford.

So this is why he lied to us, I thought. Mom and Dad probably *told* him to lie to us, to tell us they weren't there. Mom and Dad didn't want to see us anymore. They were too busy leading these robed weirdos!

"Now we are ready!" Marcus shouted, not bothering to pull his hood back on. "We of the White Monkey are ready to take back the America that is ours! For too long we have stood by while others determined our nation's fate. No longer! No longer! Soon we shall rise up . . . and take back *by force* what is ours!"

He kept his arms raised high as he talked. "The government of this nation has given in to criminals, but we are going to change that! Our revenge will be swift and our justice will reign. No criminal will be safe once our army has proven its capabilities. We will take back our community—and our nation from the criminal element—by force!"

The robed figures, except for my parents, cheered behind their hoods.

"No to the courts! No to the weak-kneed police! *Yes* to the Brotherhood!" Marcus screamed, and another cheer echoed through the woods.

As the cheer died down, Marcus lowered his arms and looked down at my parents. "And they who have betrayed us shall be the first to feel the vengeance!" he shouted.

Betrayed us? What did he mean?

He raised his hands again. Now I saw a long-bladed knife in his hand.

"The Brotherhood of the White Monkey is always merciless to traitors!" Marcus shouted. The crowd cheered.

"The vengeance is always swift!" Marcus shouted, and everyone cheered again.

The wind came up and almost blew back my hood. I grabbed it and held it with both hands. I hoped no one had seen my face.

When I looked back to the center of the circle, a hooded man stepped forward and forced my dad down onto his knees. He was pushing his head down onto the flat tree stump.

"We've got to do something—now," Gena whispered to me.

Marcus raised his knife above my dad's head. "The sacrifice will be done!" he shouted. "This is the way *our* army will administer justice!"

Ohh! I uttered a silent gasp. My head throbbed. I felt a shock of fear run down my spine.

Why had it taken me so long to realize—my parents weren't the leaders of the Brotherhood. My parents were about to be *murdered* by them! And they couldn't run or fight—because the hooded man had a gun on them.

Marcus pressed his knee down onto my dad's back. He raised his knife above his head again. "Will you confess that you are a traitor to the White Monkey?" he bellowed.

"Confess!" someone in the crowd shouted.

The wind swirled. Again, I grabbed my hood. Cara squeezed my hand. "Mark," she whispered, "what are we going to do?"

"He will not confess!" Marcus cried. "The vengeance will be ours!"

He lowered the knife over my dad's head.

"No! NO! Don't kill him!" my mom screamed. She grabbed Marcus and tried to pull back the hand with the knife.

He pushed my mom away and the hooded man grabbed her from behind. Then Marcus turned back to my dad, whose head was still down against the tree stump.

"The vengeance will not be slowed!" he cried.

I knew I had to act now if I was ever going to do anything. But what could I do without a weapon of any kind? If I tried to run up and leap on Marcus, I'd only be stopped by someone in the cult, or I'd be shot.

"Mark . . ." Cara said. Her eyes were brimming with tears.

She brushed against me, and I felt something in my jeans pocket. Quickly I reached under the robe, and I pulled it out of my pocket.

It was the little white monkey head, hard and cold. The little white monkey head I had picked up off the floor in Gena's room.

I didn't think. I didn't aim. I just heaved it at Marcus, as hard as I could.

I wanted to hit him right between the eyes. If I stunned him, it might give my parents a chance to get away.

He turned in my direction just as I heaved the tiny white monkey head. His hood was back on his shoulders. His face was revealed, vulnerable.

Perfect, I thought. Perfect.

The white monkey head sailed through the darkness.

It sailed right over his shoulder.

I missed.

I missed by several inches.

"Who threw that?" Marcus bellowed.

He was staring right at me.

CHAPTER 25

I saw Mark throw something. And then I saw Marcus spin around and come toward Mark.

I guessed that Mark had missed. I couldn't really see in the darkness.

"Who threw that?" Marcus shouted,

He took two or three steps toward Mark.

Mark started to back up.

This was all the distraction my parents needed.

Suddenly my mom pulled away from the hooded man, knocking his gun to the ground. My dad leapt up and shoved Marcus hard from behind.

Marcus cried out in surprise as he fell facedown in the snow and the knife bounced out of his hand.

All of the rest of the hooded cult members seemed totally confused and surprised. Some started to run away. But most of them just froze there in the circle.

My dad dived for the gun and came up with it quickly. He kicked the knife out of Marcus's hand as my mother scrambled to his side.

Dad pressed the gun against Marcus's neck. "Don't anybody move, or I'll blow his head off!" he screamed. "You're all under arrest. FBI!"

Ignoring Dad's threat, the hooded Brotherhood members began to scatter, fleeing into the woods.

Mark and I threw back our hoods and went running up to our parents. Mom saw us first. "You—you're here!" she cried, and she rushed forward and gathered us both up in a hug. "Oh, I don't believe it! I don't believe it! You're here! You're okay!"

"Get to the house. Call for some assistance. We're a little out-numbered here," Dad shouted, keeping his gun pressed tightly against Marcus's throat.

"Dad, everyone else is getting away," I cried.

"I know who they are. They can't run far," Dad said.

Mom grabbed up the knife, then hurried toward the house.

Dad turned to Mark. "Where'd you ever learn to throw?"

"Sorry," Mark started, then he saw the smile on Dad's face.

"You saved our lives, Mark."

"Actually, Gena did," Mark said. He put his arm around her shoulder.

A big man in a robe walked up slowly, his hands raised above his head in surrender. "I tried to stop them, Greg," he said. It was Dr. Rawlings, Gena's dad. "I did the best I could. But I was afraid—afraid of them, afraid for Gena, afraid for me. At least I persuaded them not to go after your kids."

"I'll remember that," Dad told him, his hard expression not chang-ing. "But now I'm afraid I have to put you under arrest. How'd you ever get involved in the Brotherhood in the first place, Rawlings?"

Gena's dad uttered a weary sigh. "I believed in what Marcus and the others were saying—at first. I believed that we had to do some-thing about crime, that we had to make this country safe again. But I didn't know they were going to stockpile weapons, to take the law into their own hands . . . to kill people. I wanted to get out, Greg. But I was scared, scared they'd come after *me*."

Marcus scowled and spit into the snow. "You're a coward, Rawlings.

You'll die for your cowardice. The vengeance of the White Monkey will be swift," he muttered, and looked away.

Dad ignored him and turned to Gena. "I think I owe you an apology, for trying to keep you and Mark apart," he said. He shoved Marcus toward the house. "Come on. Move. I want to get out of this robe. I never did like going outside in a bathrobe."

We started walking toward the house. "I'm so sorry. I'll bet you two have been worried sick," Dad said.

"That's a bit of an understatement," I told him. I could hear police sirens in the distance. Mom must have made her call.

"Where's Roger?" Dad asked. "Isn't he here, too?"

"Uh . . . Roger is dead," I said.

Dad stopped walking. His eyes narrowed. He shook his head. "No. Oh, no. Roger was one of our best agents. After the Brotherhood found out your mom and I were agents, I was worried they'd come after Roger—and you."

"A man named Murdoch was killed, too," I told him.

Another look of shock and sadness crossed Dad's face. "Murdoch was our field director here. The Brotherhood killed him, too?"

"Not the Brotherhood," I said. "A man named Farraday."

"Who? Farraday?" Dad's face filled with shock and disbelief. He stared past me, thinking hard. "Farraday? He's here? He's out of prison? What's he doing here?"

"Who is he, Dad?" I asked.

"He was a cop, Mark. A bent cop. Your mother and I were responsible for his getting sent up on racketeering charges. He killed Roger and Murdoch?"

"We thought he was a real cop," Cara said. "He had a police radio and everything."

"Anyone can buy a radio that gets the police band," Dad explained.

"Farraday was looking for you," I said. "We locked him in the garage."

Tears formed in the corners of Dad's eyes, the first tears I had ever seen him shed. "I'm so sorry," he said. "I never meant for you two to be involved in any of this."

"It's over now," I said. I hoped against hope that I was right.

We followed Dad to the Rawlingses' house, feeling very relieved but still terribly confused.

CHAPTER 26

"We were in a terrible fix," Mom said to Cara and me. "We didn't want to lie to you, but we didn't want you involved. We just thought you'd worry about us all the time if you knew we were FBI agents."

We were home, all four of us together. The police had come to collect Farraday and remove poor Roger's body. And so it was just us four. We were so happy. Dad made hot chocolate and we sat around the kitchen table and talked.

"So you never were computer experts?" Cara asked. She looked very confused.

"Yes, sure we are. We know a lot about computers," Dad said. "But we know a lot more about subversive groups."

Mom sighed. "It isn't pleasant work. I guess you saw that tonight."

"And that's why we move so much?" I asked.

Mom nodded. "We tried to give you normal childhoods, as normal as possible. That's why we didn't tell you the truth."

"Up till now, we've been lucky," Dad said.

"We're still lucky," Mom interrupted. "Lucky to be alive."

"But this was the first time our cover was blown," Dad said, twirling the cup around between his hands. "These White Monkey followers really were going to kill us."

"But why, Dad?" I asked. "Why did all these people do what Marcus told them to?"

"He was a forceful, charismatic leader," Dad said. "And he told them what they wanted to hear. He made them believe that he could lead them to a better way of life."

"Where were you all this time?" I asked.

"Marcus kept us prisoner in the basement at Cranford for three days," Mom said. "He had to wait till the meeting night to execute us."

"Did you really work at Cranford?" I asked.

"Yes, we did," Mom said. "That's how we infiltrated the Brotherhood. Marcus and his crew planned a complete takeover of Cranford. That would have given them access to a lot of top-secret government weapons."

"I think they really would've used those weapons," Dad said, shaking his head. "If they'd gotten half a chance."

"But it was the Burroughs family to the rescue!" Mom cried, and we all cheered.

"Mark, I hope you understand why we tried to warn you about Gena," Dad explained, putting his hand on my arm. "There we were, trying to get enough evidence to arrest the Brotherhood members, and we knew that her dad was one of them. I tried to warn you away, but of course I couldn't tell you the reason."

"I guess Gena surprised everyone," I said. I wondered what she was doing now.

"She's a very brave girl," Dad said.

"And what about Roger? He wasn't really our cousin? He was working for you?" Cara asked.

"Yes. He was one of our agents."

"He acted so weird after you disappeared," Cara said. "We didn't know what to think."

"He must have been frantically trying to find us," Dad said. "He and Murdoch. They were probably searching everywhere." He looked at Mom, who looked away sadly.

We drank our hot chocolate. There wasn't much else to say. All of the questions had been answered. Well, almost all.

"What happens next?" I asked.

"We move on to the next case," Mom said. "Only this time it will be different. Our cover has been blown with our own family."

By Saturday, Mom and Dad were already packing cartons, preparing for our next move. The doorbell rang just after breakfast. It was Gena. Behind her, I saw a taxi in the drive.

"Hi. Come in," I said.

"I can't. I'm on my way to the airport."

"Where are you going?"

"Detroit. My mother is there. I'm going to live with her . . . while my dad . . . you know."

I took her hand. "Are you okay?"

"Yeah. I guess. It's going to take a long time for everything that happened to sink in. And I—I'm going to miss you."

"I'm—I mean we're leaving, too, I don't know where," I said, "but I'll write to you."

"Good. I'll write, too." The taxi driver blew his horn. He was anxious to leave. Gena reached up on tiptoes and kissed me. Her face was cold, but her mouth was warm. It was a long, wonderful kiss. I knew I'd never forget it.

Then she slipped a small package into my hand, turned, and ran to the taxi without looking back.

I stepped out onto the front porch and watched her leave. She waved, and then the taxi was gone.

I looked at the package. It was a little box, the kind jewelry comes in. I pulled it open. Inside was a little white monkey head with rhinestone eyes.

Why on earth did she give me this? I thought.

I pulled it out of the box. Something was stuck inside the

grinning mouth. It took me a while to get it out. It was a narrow strip of paper. I unrolled the strip of paper. Gena had written her Detroit address and a message on it: *Can you keep a secret? I love you. Gena.*

I rolled up the slip of paper and stuffed it back into the monkey's mouth. I held the white monkey in my hand. For the first time, it didn't feel cold. It felt very warm. I tossed it up into the air, caught it, and stuffed it into my jeans pocket.

I wouldn't need it to remember Gena and my stay on Fear Street, but I planned on keeping it a long time anyway.

ABOUT THE AUTHOR

R.L. STINE invented the teen horror genre with Fear Street, the bestselling teen horror series of all time. He also changed the face of children's publishing with the mega-successful Goosebumps series, which went on to become a worldwide multimedia phenomenon. Guinness World Records cites Stine as the most prolific author of children's horror fiction novels. He lives in New York City.

RIVETED

BY *simon* teen ♥

BELIEVE IN YOUR SHELF

Visit RivetedLit.com & connect with us on social to:

DISCOVER NEW YA READS

READ BOOKS FOR FREE

DISCUSS YOUR FAVORITES

SHARE YOUR IDEAS

ENTER SWEEPSTAKES FOR THE CHANCE TO WIN BOOKS

Follow @SimonTeen on

to stay up to date with all things Riveted!